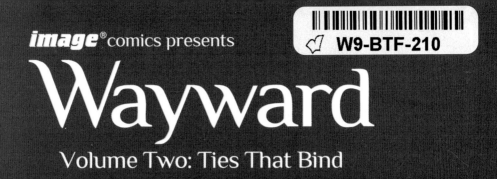

image® comics presents

Wayward

Volume Two: Ties That Bind

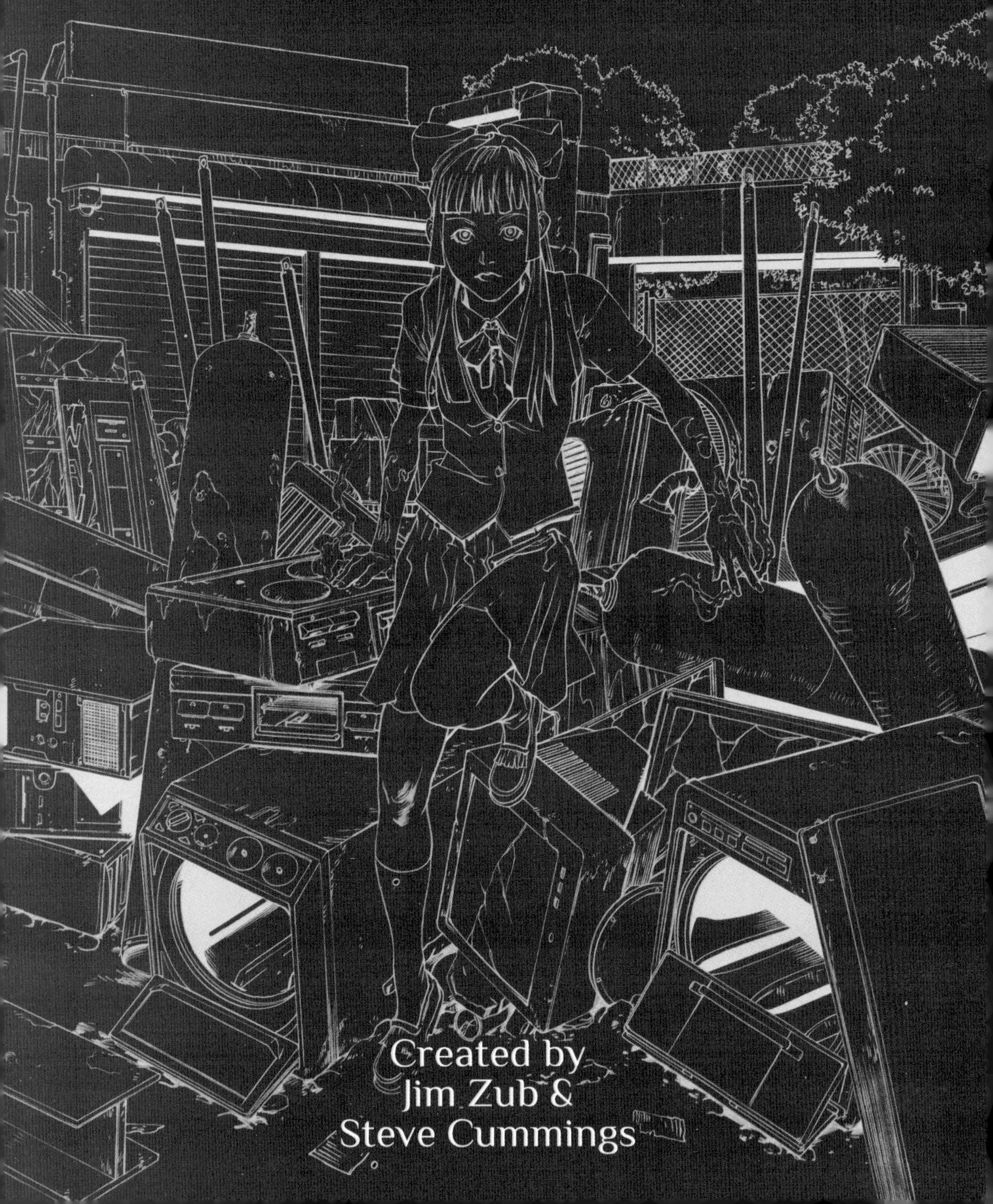

Created by
Jim Zub &
Steve Cummings

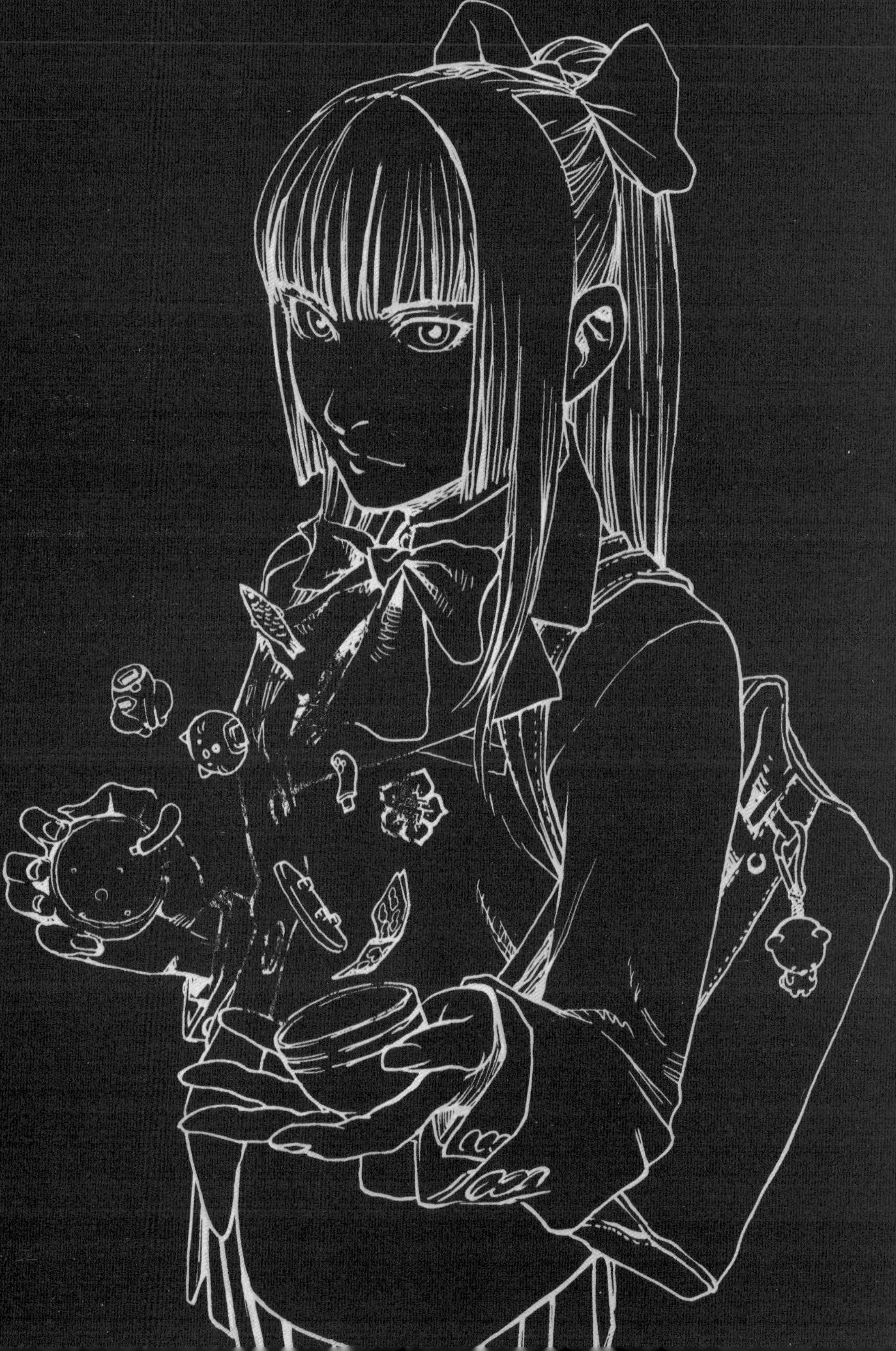

Previously

Rori Lane moves to Tokyo to be with her mother after a painful divorce split up their family. Adjusting to life and the stresses of high school in a new country is tough, but that's nothing compared to the strange experiences to come.

Rori begins having visions, seeing threads and patterns shimmering around her. Some of them pull her towards people or places while others unlock unexpected supernatural powers. She's drawn to a group of Japanese teenagers with abilities of their own - **Shirai**, a young man who feeds on the energy of spirits to sustain and empower him, **Ayane**, a capricious and feral girl with cat-like talents, and **Nikaido**, a detached young boy who absorbs and supresses emotions. These abilities have made the teens a target for **Yokai**, mythical Japanese creatures and spirits. The Yokai are focused on hunting and destroying these newcomers, for reasons as yet unknown.

A major confrontation with a group of Yokai ends in disaster as Rori's mother is slain and their apartment building is leveled to the ground, with Rori and Shirai presumed dead. Ayane and Nikaido are on their own, unsure of where to turn. Three months have passed and the story continues...

story
Jim Zub

line art
Steve Cummings

color art
Tamra Bonvillain

color flats
Ludwig Olimba

letters
Marshall Dillon

back matter
Zack Davisson

special thanks
Steve Anderson
Jonathan Chan
Jim Demonakos
Addison Duke
Kandrix Foong
Nishi Makoto
Takeshi Miyazawa
Trish Rabbitt
Lindsay Thomas
Meredith Wallace

IMAGE COMICS, INC.
Robert Kirkman – Chief Operating Officer
Erik Larsen – Chief Financial Officer
Todd McFarlane – President
Marc Silvestri – Chief Executive Officer
Jim Valentino – Vice-President

Eric Stephenson – Publisher
Corey Murphy – Director of Sales
Jeremy Sullivan – Director of Digital Sales
Kat Salazar – Director of PR & Marketing
Emily Miller – Director of Operations
Branwyn Bigglestone – Senior Accounts Manager
Sarah Mello – Accounts Manager
Drew Gill – Art Director
Jonathan Chan – Production Manager
Meredith Wallace – Print Manager
Randy Okamura – Marketing Production Designer
David Brothers – Branding Manager
Ally Power – Content Manager
Addison Duke – Production Artist
Vincent Kukua – Production Artist
Sasha Head – Production Artist
Tricia Ramos – Production Artist
Emilio Bautista – Sales Assistant
Chloe Ramos-Peterson – Administrative Assistant
IMAGECOMICS.COM

From Pitch to Print

I've known Jim Zub for a long time. He's the writer of the series collected in its second volume in the book you're currently holding (or the tablet, or the laptop, or the holo-reader, if you're checking it out in the far-flung future after it's become a classic work of literature that moved generations.) We each had our first big break in the comics industry at around the same time, with series for Image Comics. His was the amazing, hilarious swords-and-sorcery book *Skullkickers*, and mine was a book called *27*.

Comics is a complex world, and the learning curve starts steep and never really levels out. Peaks and valleys galore - one day you think you've made it, and the next you realize how much you still need to learn. Jim and I went through all that somewhat simultaneously, and in a shared-foxhole sort of way, we became pretty tight. We still are - he's one of my closest friends in the biz.

One of the many perks of having talented pals is that they tell you what they're working on way before it ever hits shelves. You get to see ideas in their nascent state - in their rawest form. I love it. And so, to tie this back to the book you're reading, let's flash back to a sunny October morning several years ago. Jim and I were sharing a cab from Brooklyn to the Javits Centre in Manhattan, on our way to New York Comicon.

Jim told me about something new he was working on - a fantasy story, set in present-day Japan. He didn't have a ton at that point, as I recall, just some amazing character designs from Steve Cummings and the outlines of a story. The cab ride in from Brooklyn is a good 40 minutes, and so we had a bunch of time to hash it out. As he went through the outline, I became increasingly convinced of one thing:

This thing was *solid gold*.

Completely fresh but just familiar enough, set in a world that was simultaneously relatable and bizarre, with a phenomenal hook for a lead character's arc that would carry a story through as many issues as he and his team felt like doing. And wow, was it ever pretty.

That was what became *Wayward*, and I am so glad that it made the sometimes perilous journey from taxi pitch to finished project.

You never know if a book will live up to that original enthusiasm, before the realities of production conspire to gnaw away at the ambitions of the creative team - but that didn't seem to hit *Wayward* at all, as you will shortly see.

Jim and Steve (and Tamra Bonvillain, who does an equally wonderful job on the colors) have made something special here. I often table next to Jim at shows, and we've heard each other pitch our books to potential readers literally hundreds of times. So, I know that his quick pitch for *Wayward* is "Buffy in Japan," and while that's not inaccurate, it's also not the full story. Buffy used American monster myths, primarily (or American versions of old monsters). *Wayward* takes Japanese folklore and carefully builds it out into a new story - the yokai and kappa and all those crazy beasts appear, reinvented for readers who may or may not have encountered them before.

It's a superhero book that stays away from the tropes - it can be dark as hell, for one thing, but that's a good thing. Life has its dark corners, after all, and fiction shouldn't be afraid to look into them - even if, occasionally, something looks back.

I don't want to take any more time away from the experience you're about to have - the second arc of *Wayward* takes the story presented in Volume 1, expands it and flips it on its head, the way any good second arc should.

I loved it, and I think you will too.

- Charles Soule
July 2015

Charles Soule is a New York-based writer, known for creator-owned titles *Letter 44* and *Strange Attractors* as well as work for Marvel and DC, including *Death of Wolverine*, *She-Hulk* and *Swamp Thing*.

Chapter Six

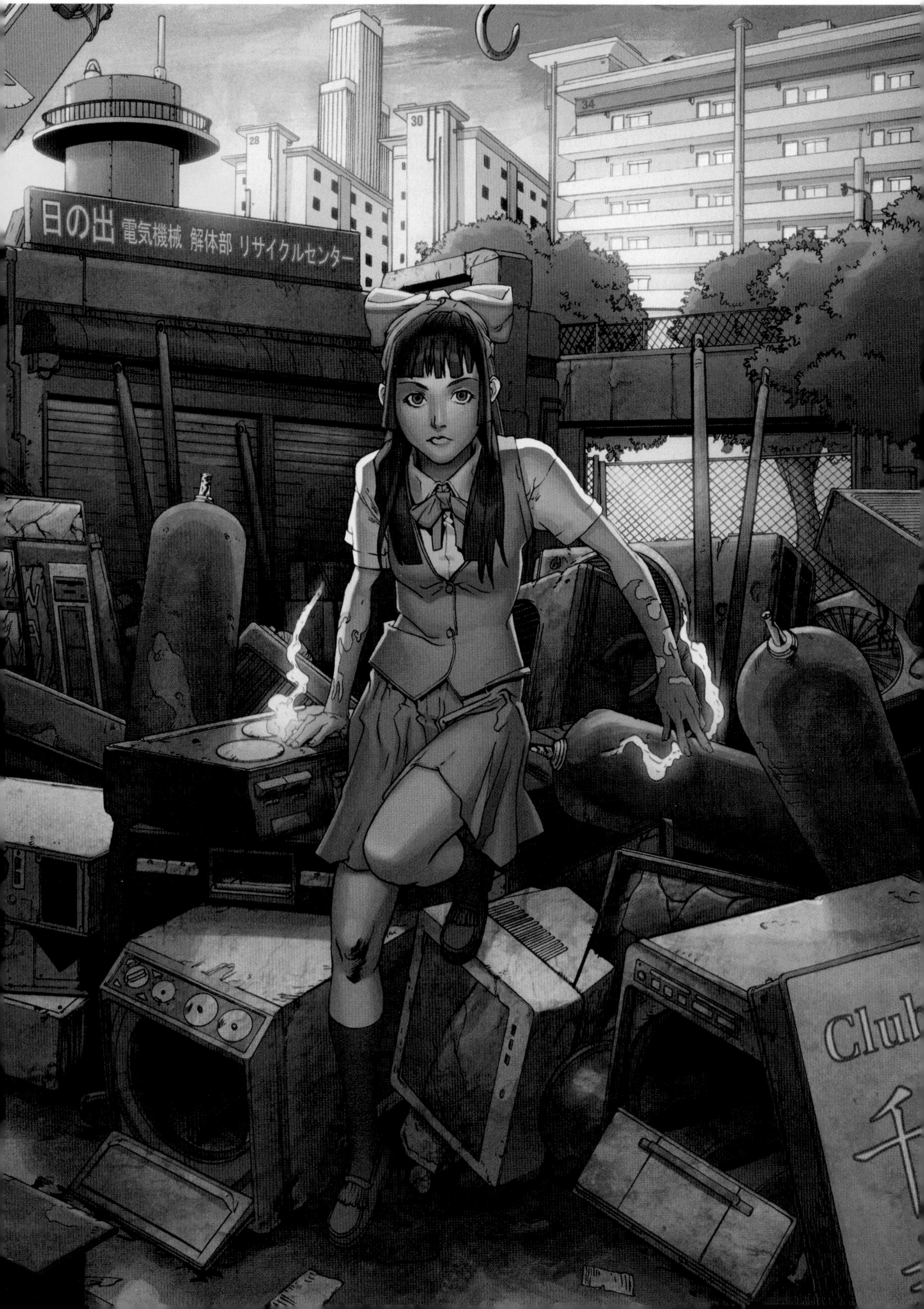
日の出 電気機械 解体部 リサイクルセンター
Club

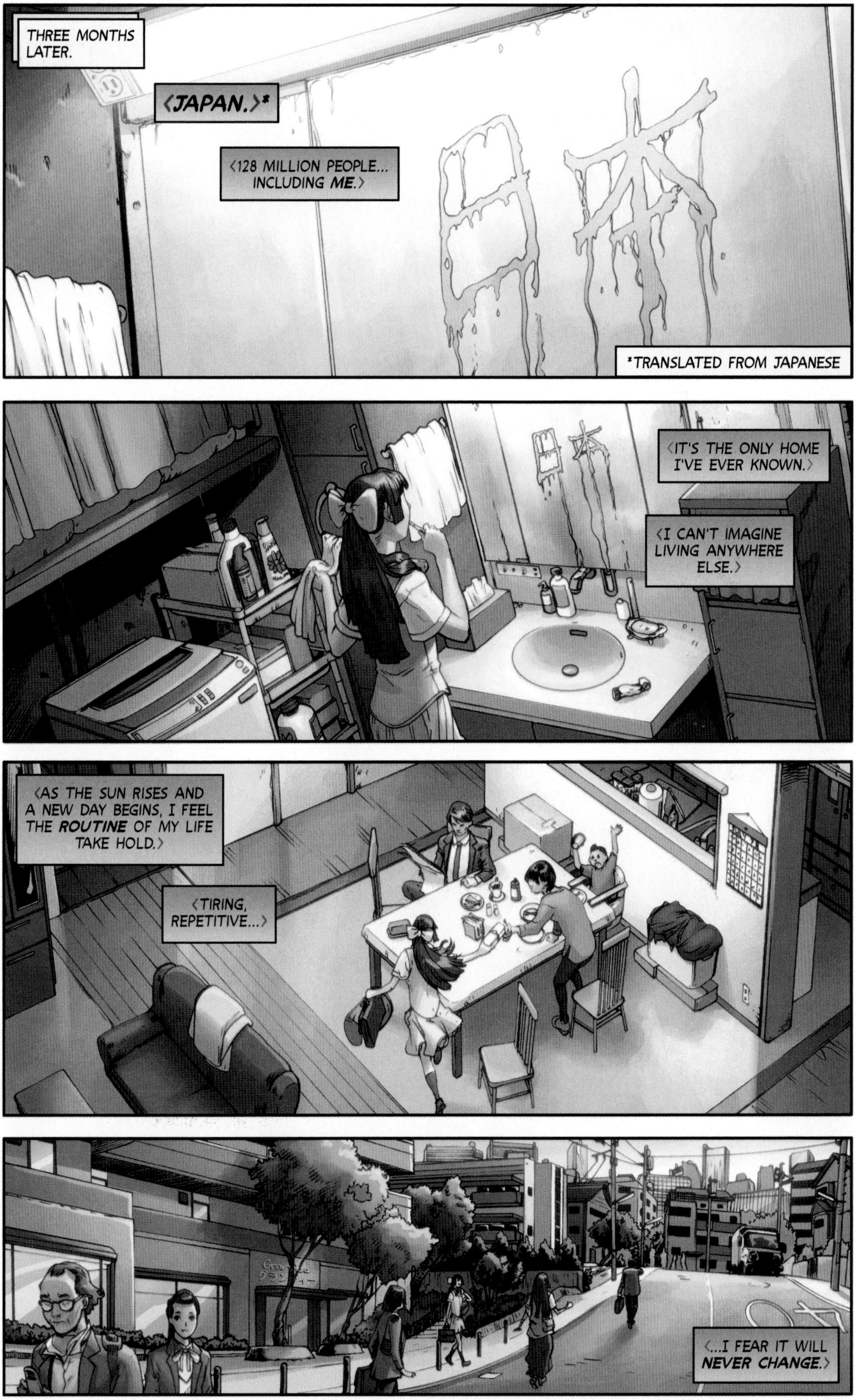
THREE MONTHS LATER.
〈JAPAN.〉*
〈128 MILLION PEOPLE... INCLUDING ME.〉
日本
*TRANSLATED FROM JAPANESE
〈IT'S THE ONLY HOME I'VE EVER KNOWN.〉
〈I CAN'T IMAGINE LIVING ANYWHERE ELSE.〉
〈AS THE SUN RISES AND A NEW DAY BEGINS, I FEEL THE ROUTINE OF MY LIFE TAKE HOLD.〉
〈TIRING, REPETITIVE...〉
〈...I FEAR IT WILL NEVER CHANGE.〉

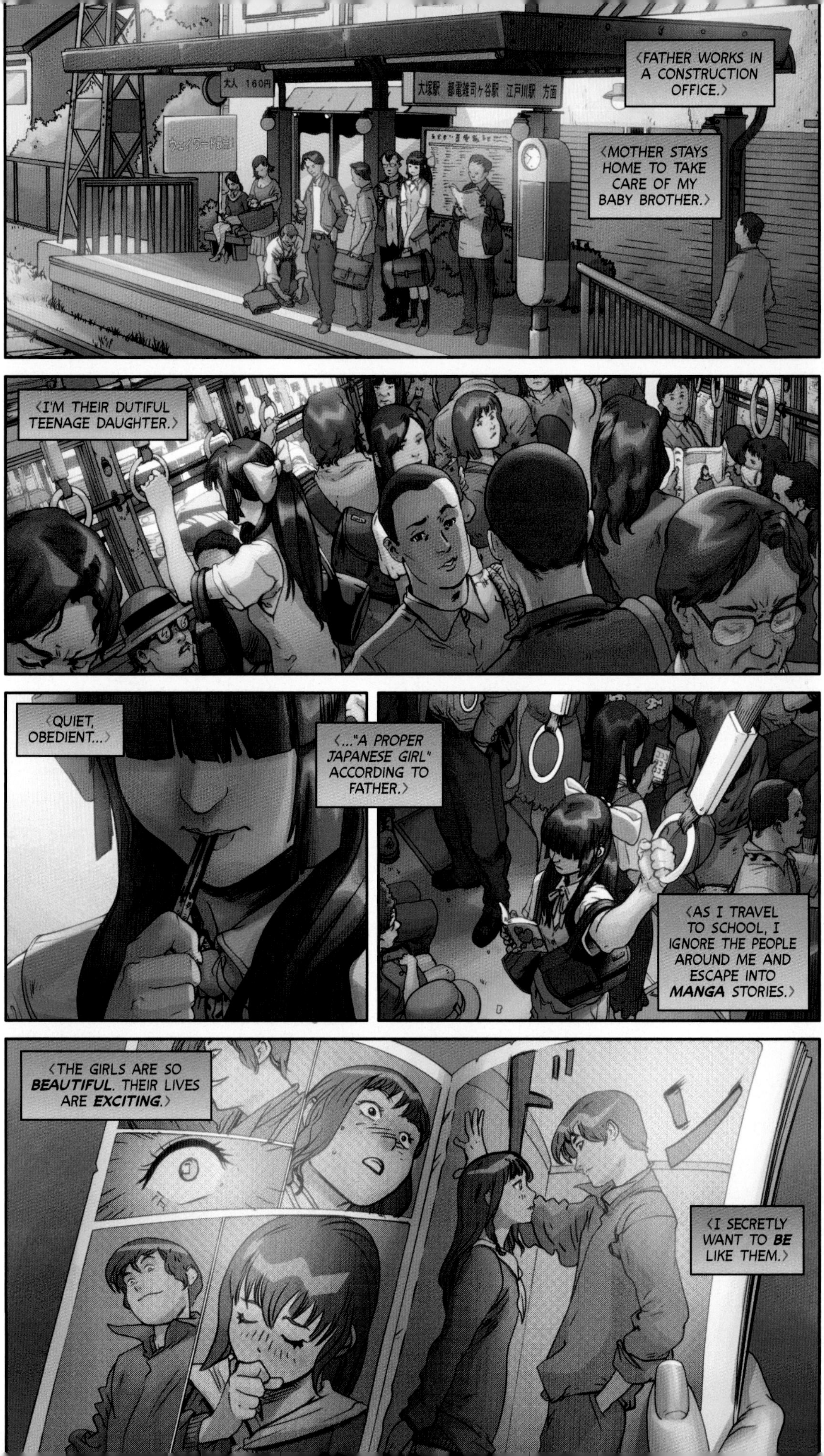

大人 160円
大塚駅 都電雑司ヶ谷駅 江戸川駅 方面
‹FATHER WORKS IN A CONSTRUCTION OFFICE.›
‹MOTHER STAYS HOME TO TAKE CARE OF MY BABY BROTHER.›
‹I'M THEIR DUTIFUL TEENAGE DAUGHTER.›
‹QUIET, OBEDIENT...›
‹..."A PROPER JAPANESE GIRL" ACCORDING TO FATHER.›
‹AS I TRAVEL TO SCHOOL, I IGNORE THE PEOPLE AROUND ME AND ESCAPE INTO MANGA STORIES.›
‹THE GIRLS ARE SO BEAUTIFUL. THEIR LIVES ARE EXCITING.›
‹I SECRETLY WANT TO BE LIKE THEM.›

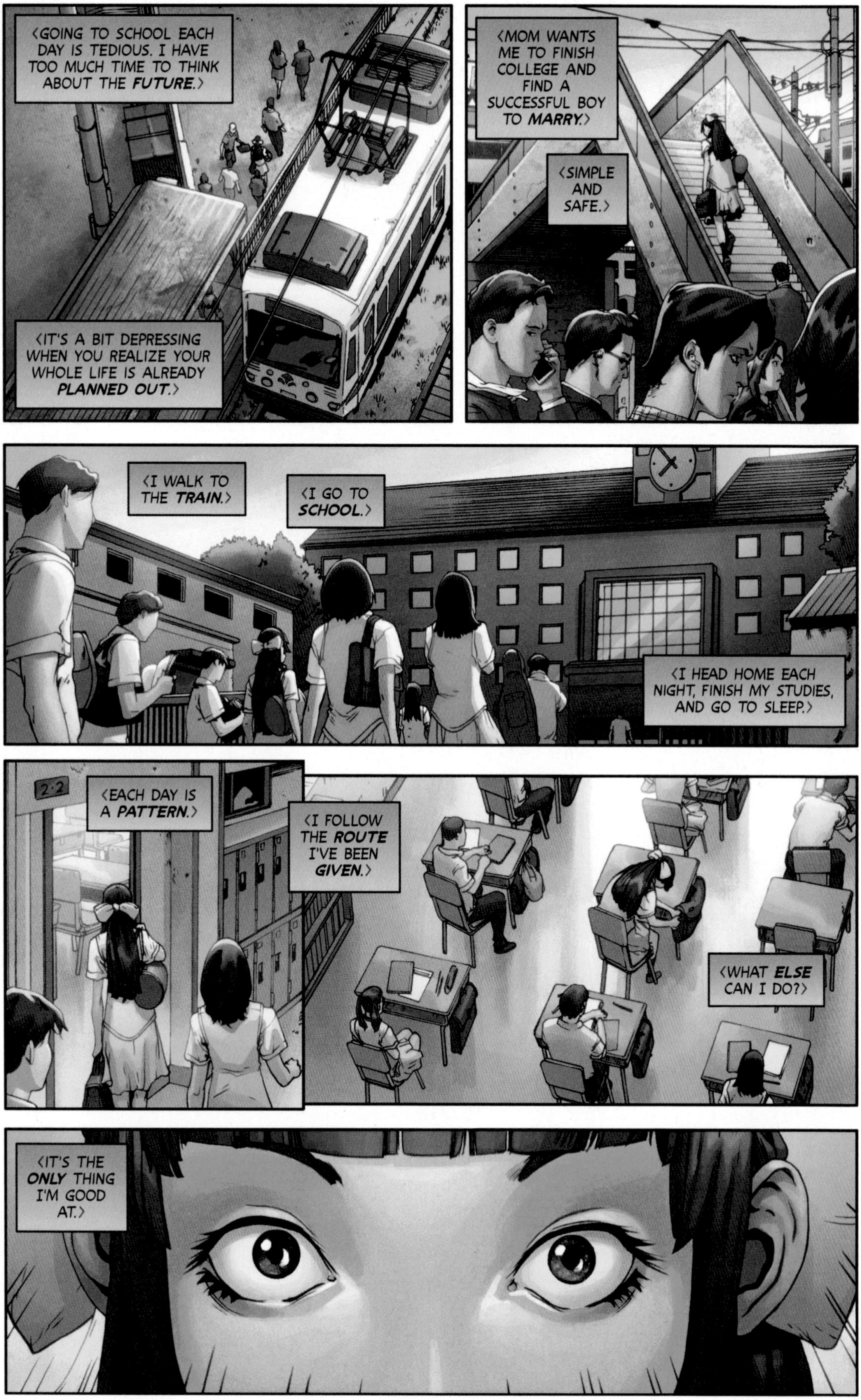
<GOING TO SCHOOL EACH DAY IS TEDIOUS. I HAVE TOO MUCH TIME TO THINK ABOUT THE FUTURE.>
<IT'S A BIT DEPRESSING WHEN YOU REALIZE YOUR WHOLE LIFE IS ALREADY PLANNED OUT.>
<MOM WANTS ME TO FINISH COLLEGE AND FIND A SUCCESSFUL BOY TO MARRY.>
<SIMPLE AND SAFE.>
<I WALK TO THE TRAIN.>
<I GO TO SCHOOL.>
<I HEAD HOME EACH NIGHT, FINISH MY STUDIES, AND GO TO SLEEP.>
2-2
<EACH DAY IS A PATTERN.>
<I FOLLOW THE ROUTE I'VE BEEN GIVEN.>
<WHAT ELSE CAN I DO?>
<IT'S THE ONLY THING I'M GOOD AT.>

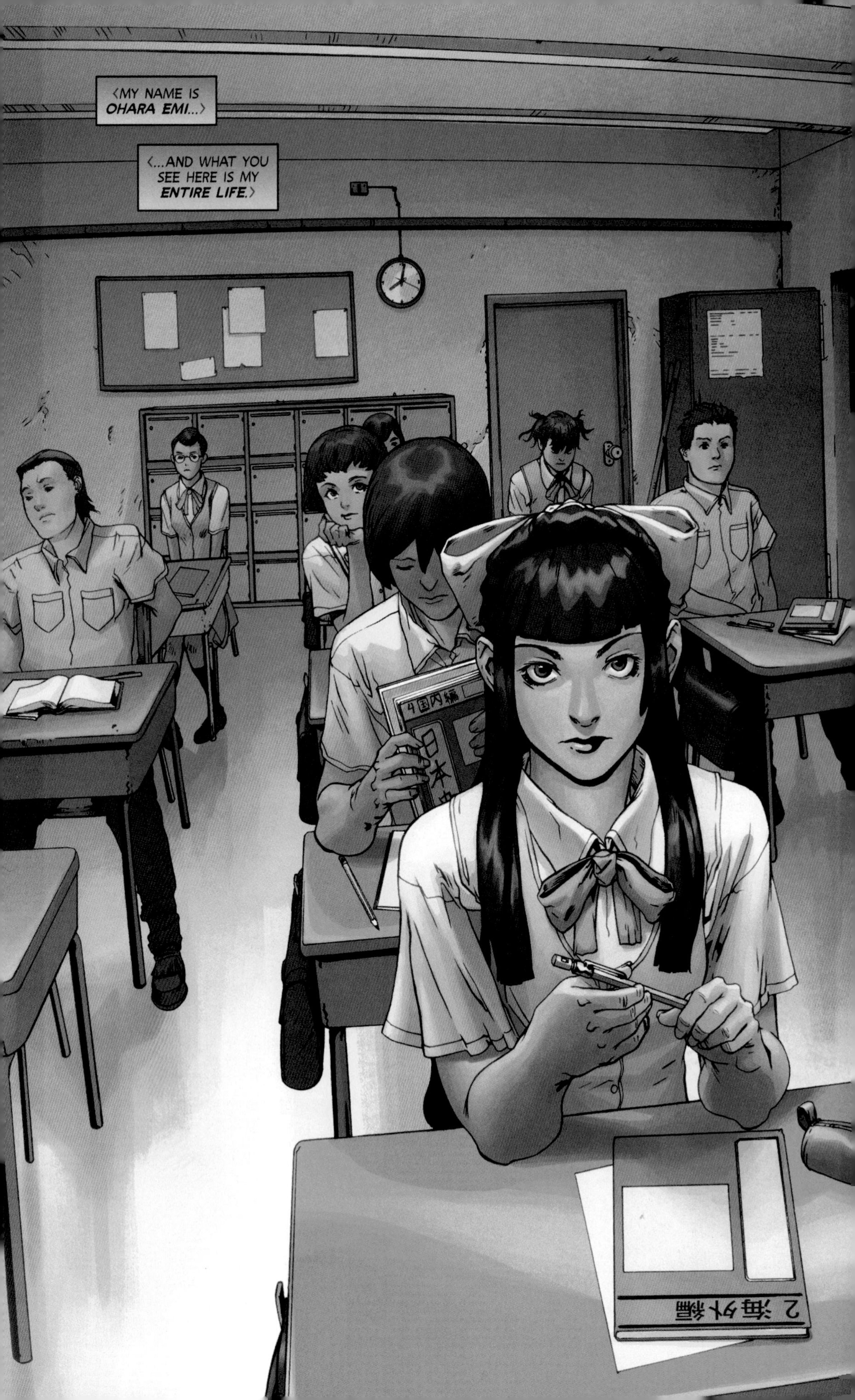
‹MY NAME IS OHARA EMI...›
‹...AND WHAT YOU SEE HERE IS MY ENTIRE LIFE.›
2 海外編

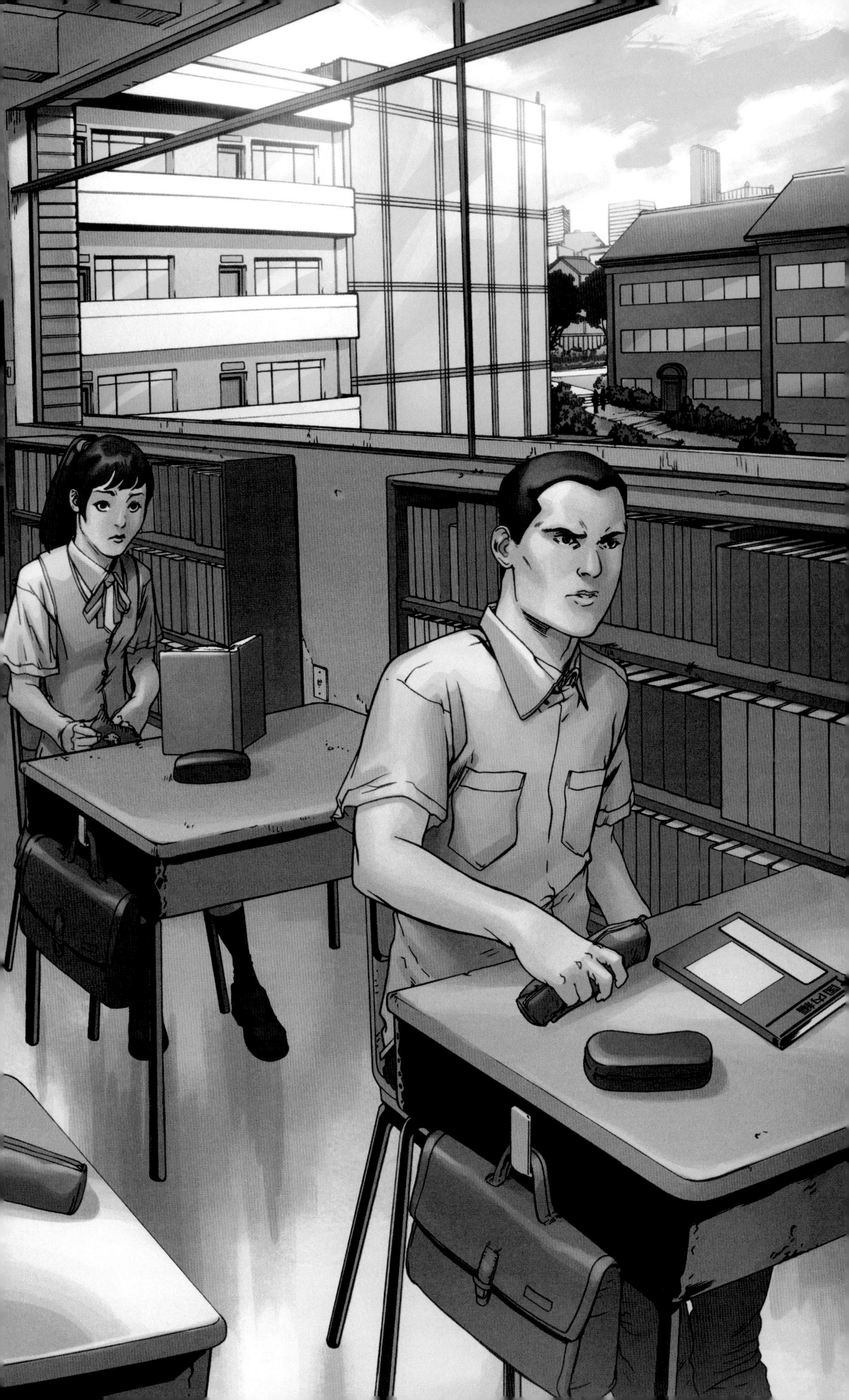

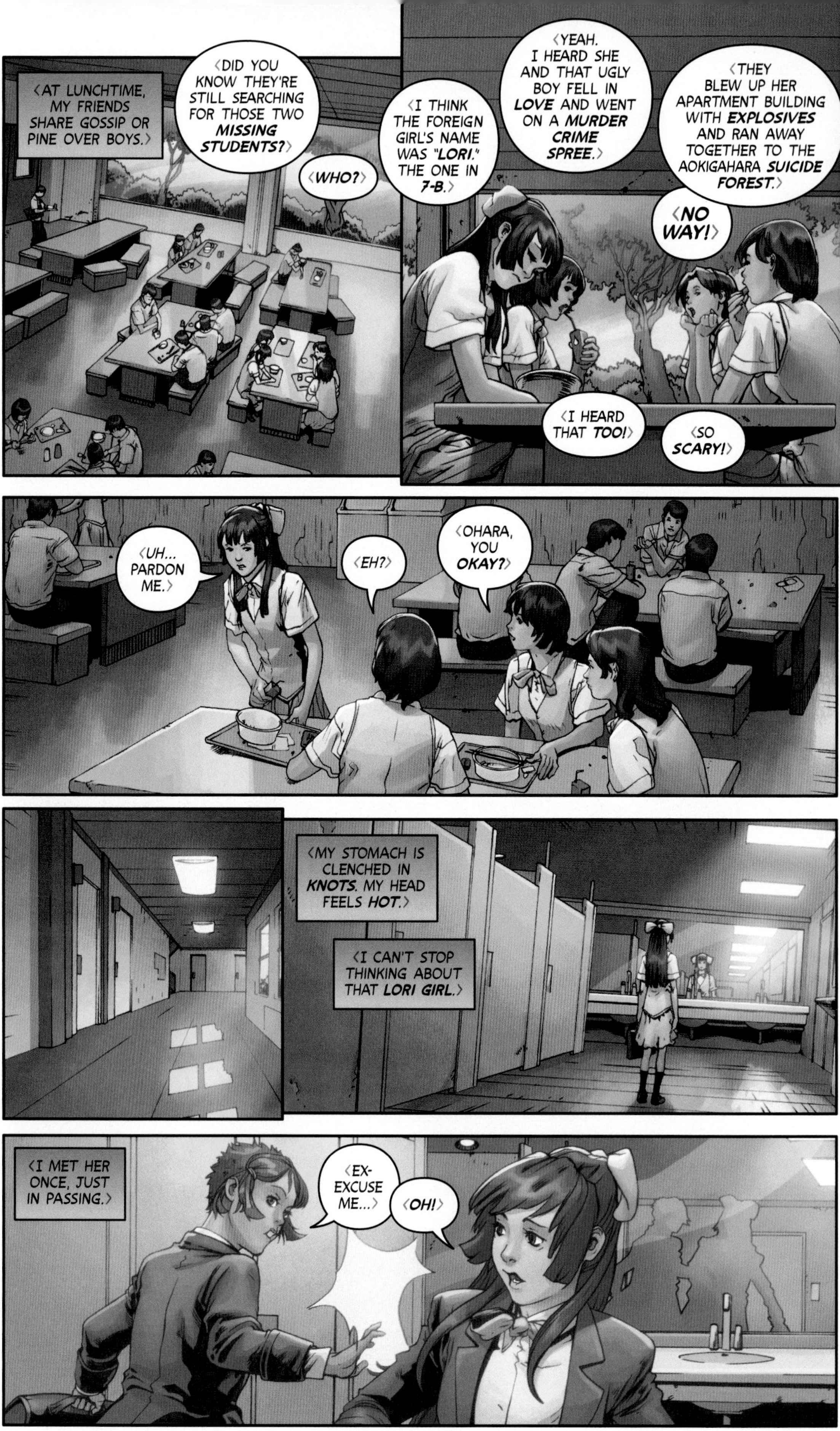

〈AT LUNCHTIME, MY FRIENDS SHARE GOSSIP OR PINE OVER BOYS.〉
〈DID YOU KNOW THEY'RE STILL SEARCHING FOR THOSE TWO MISSING STUDENTS?〉
〈WHO?〉
〈I THINK THE FOREIGN GIRL'S NAME WAS "LORI." THE ONE IN 7-B.〉
〈YEAH. I HEARD SHE AND THAT UGLY BOY FELL IN LOVE AND WENT ON A MURDER CRIME SPREE.〉
〈THEY BLEW UP HER APARTMENT BUILDING WITH EXPLOSIVES AND RAN AWAY TOGETHER TO THE AOKIGAHARA SUICIDE FOREST.〉
〈NO WAY!〉
〈I HEARD THAT TOO!〉
〈SO SCARY!〉
〈UH... PARDON ME.〉
〈EH?〉
〈OHARA, YOU OKAY?〉
〈MY STOMACH IS CLENCHED IN KNOTS. MY HEAD FEELS HOT.〉
〈I CAN'T STOP THINKING ABOUT THAT LORI GIRL.〉
〈I MET HER ONCE, JUST IN PASSING.〉
〈EX- EXCUSE ME...〉
〈OH!〉

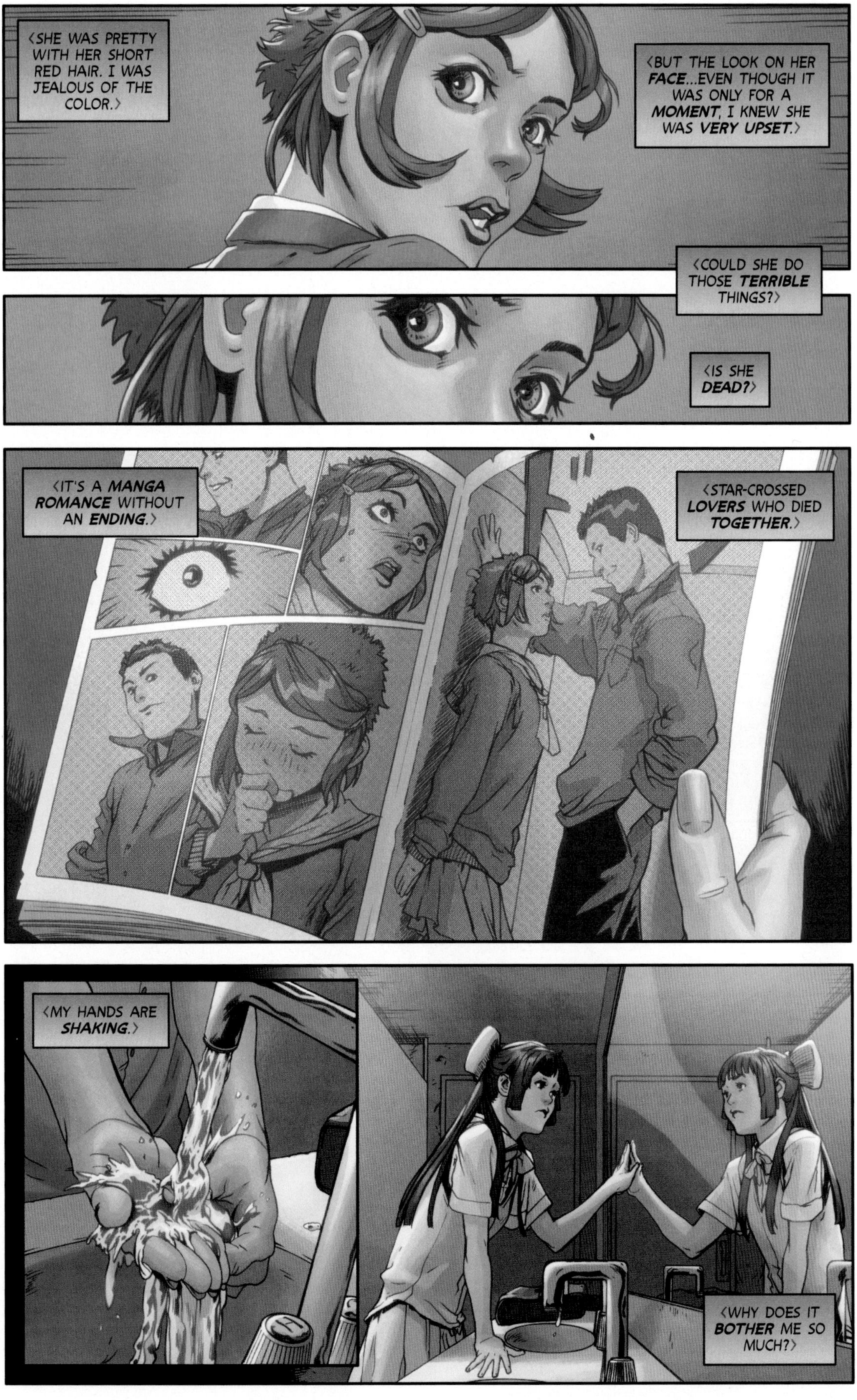
<SHE WAS PRETTY WITH HER SHORT RED HAIR. I WAS JEALOUS OF THE COLOR.>
<BUT THE LOOK ON HER FACE...EVEN THOUGH IT WAS ONLY FOR A MOMENT, I KNEW SHE WAS VERY UPSET.>
<COULD SHE DO THOSE TERRIBLE THINGS?>
<IS SHE DEAD?>
<IT'S A MANGA ROMANCE WITHOUT AN ENDING.>
<STAR-CROSSED LOVERS WHO DIED TOGETHER.>
<MY HANDS ARE SHAKING.>
<WHY DOES IT BOTHER ME SO MUCH?>

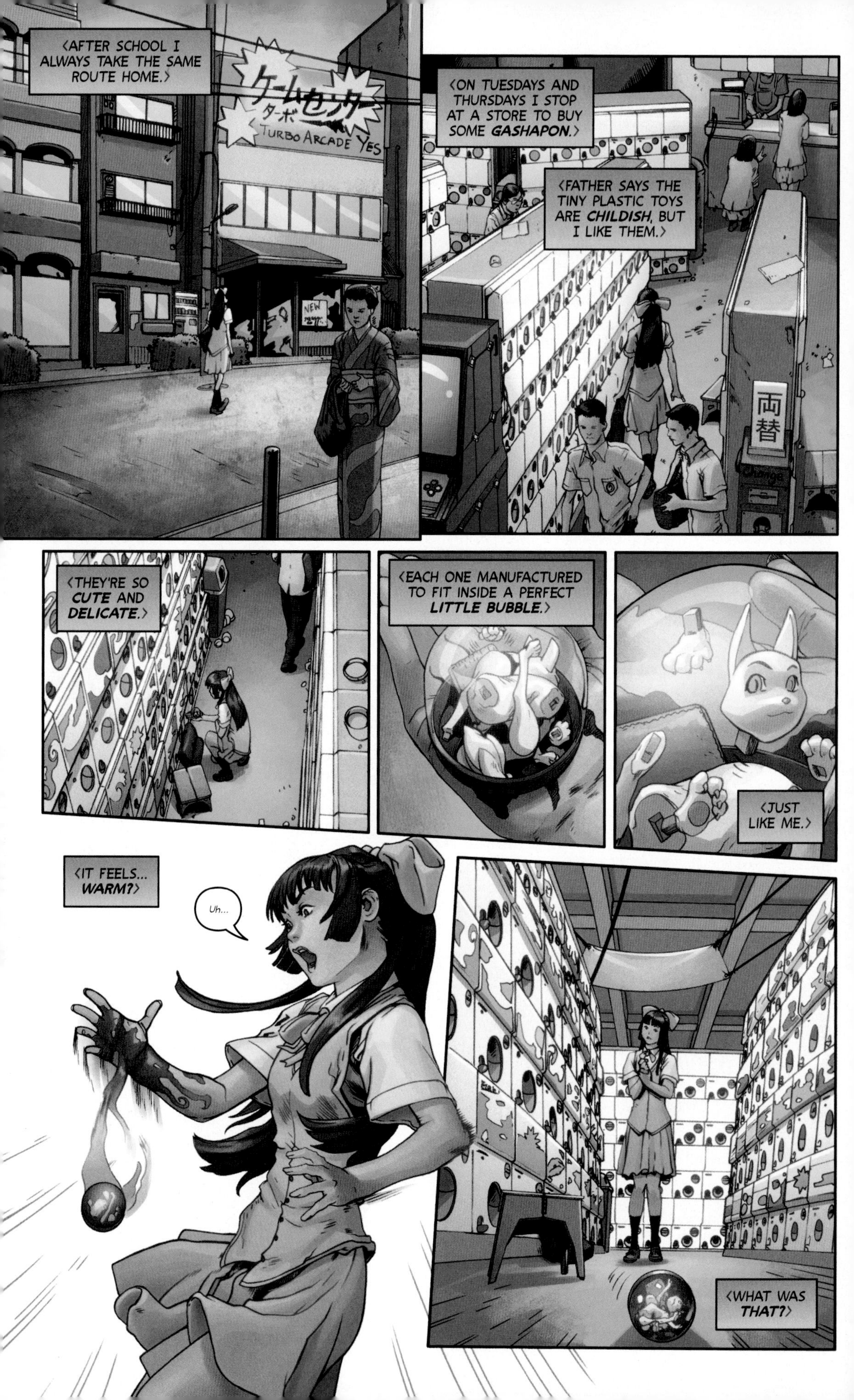
‹AFTER SCHOOL I ALWAYS TAKE THE SAME ROUTE HOME.›
ターボ
TURBO ARCADE
YES
NEW
‹ON TUESDAYS AND THURSDAYS I STOP AT A STORE TO BUY SOME *GASHAPON*.›
‹FATHER SAYS THE TINY PLASTIC TOYS ARE *CHILDISH*, BUT I LIKE THEM.›
両替
‹THEY'RE SO *CUTE* AND *DELICATE*.›
‹EACH ONE MANUFACTURED TO FIT INSIDE A PERFECT *LITTLE BUBBLE*.›
‹JUST LIKE ME.›
‹IT FEELS... *WARM?*›
Uh...
‹WHAT WAS *THAT?*›

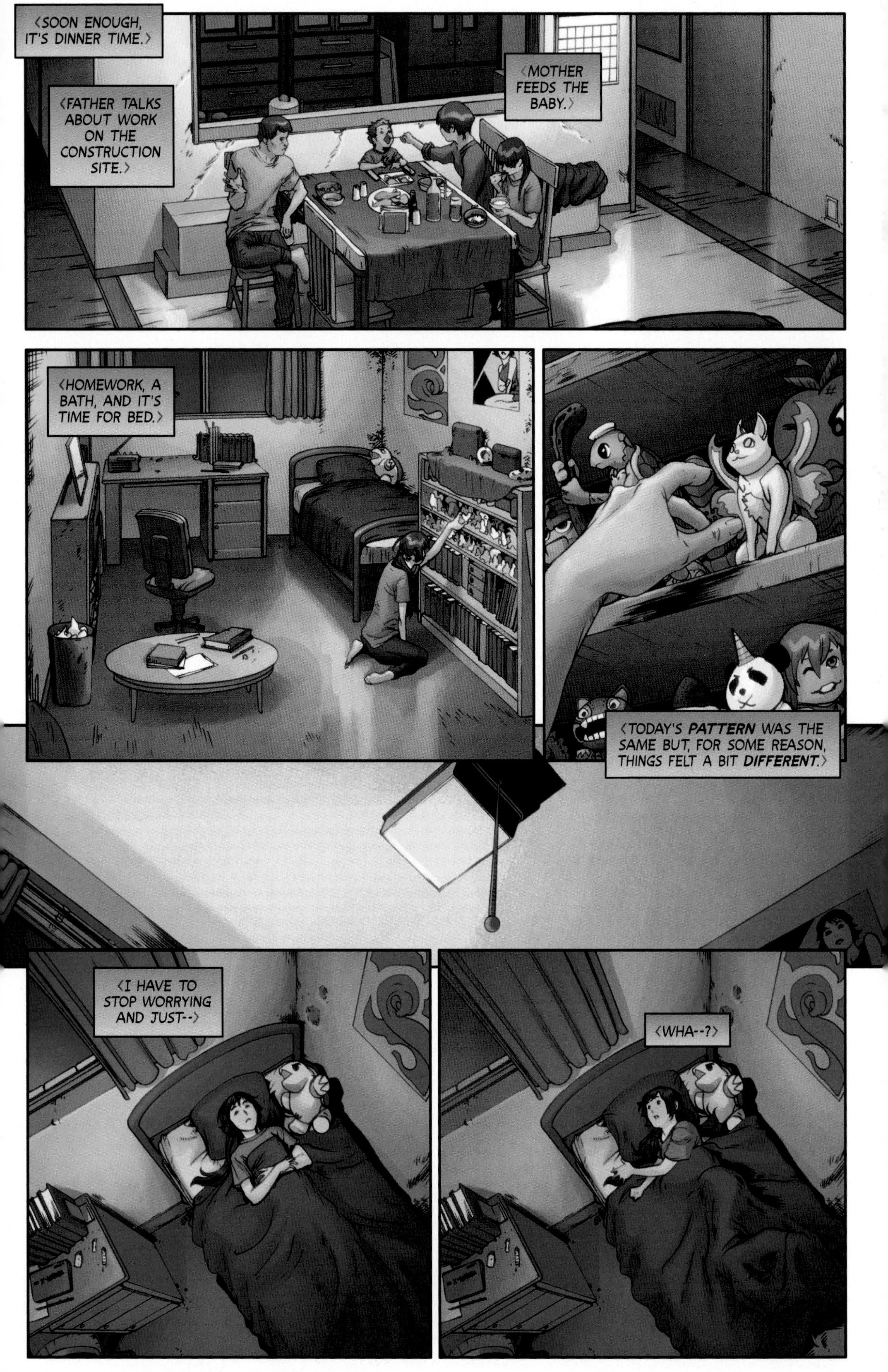

⟨SOON ENOUGH, IT'S DINNER TIME.⟩
⟨FATHER TALKS ABOUT WORK ON THE CONSTRUCTION SITE.⟩
⟨MOTHER FEEDS THE BABY.⟩
⟨HOMEWORK, A BATH, AND IT'S TIME FOR BED.⟩
⟨TODAY'S **PATTERN** WAS THE SAME BUT, FOR SOME REASON, THINGS FELT A BIT **DIFFERENT**.⟩
⟨I HAVE TO STOP WORRYING AND JUST--⟩
⟨WHA--?⟩

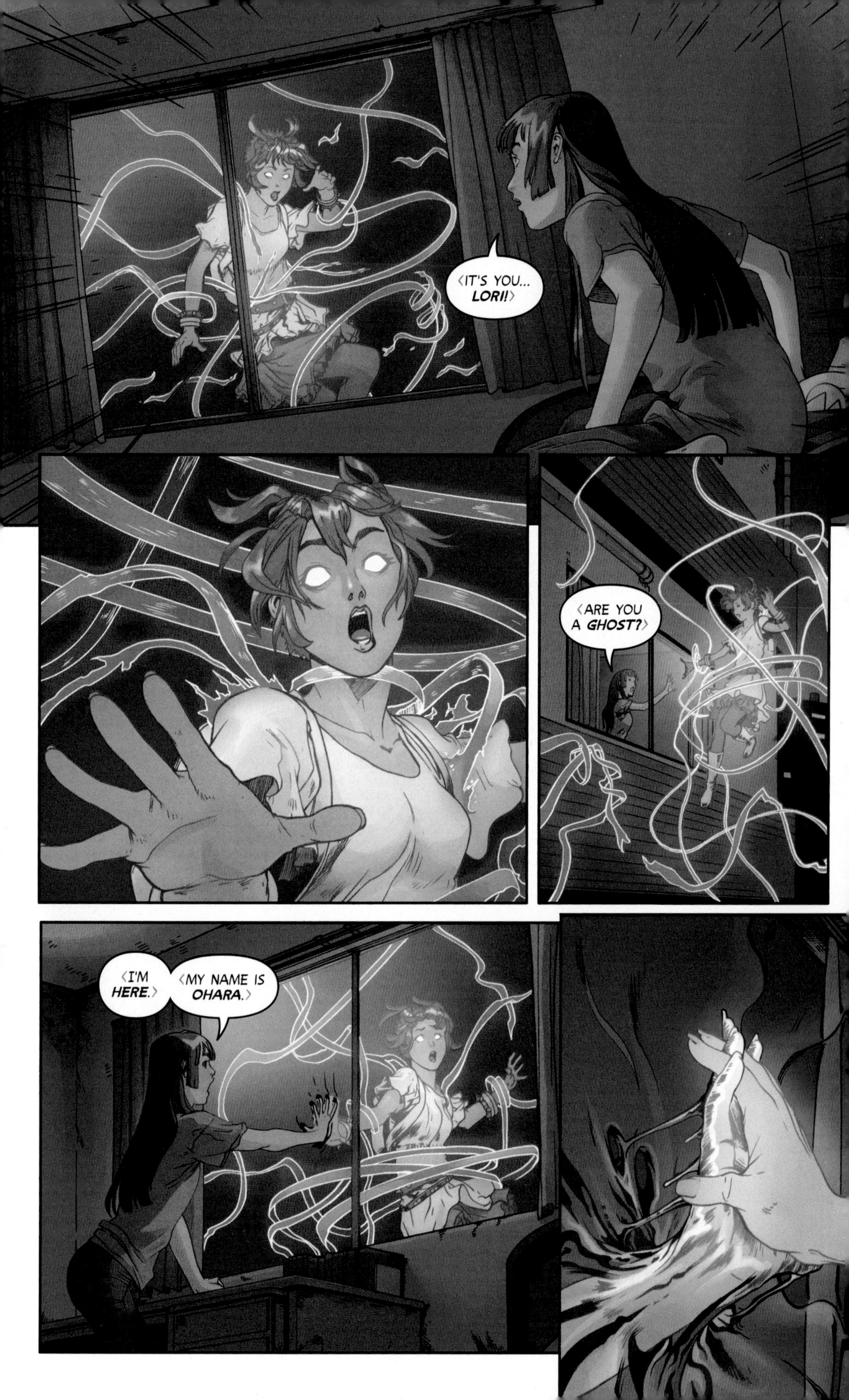
⟨IT'S YOU... LORI!⟩
⟨ARE YOU A GHOST?⟩
⟨I'M HERE.⟩
⟨MY NAME IS OHARA.⟩

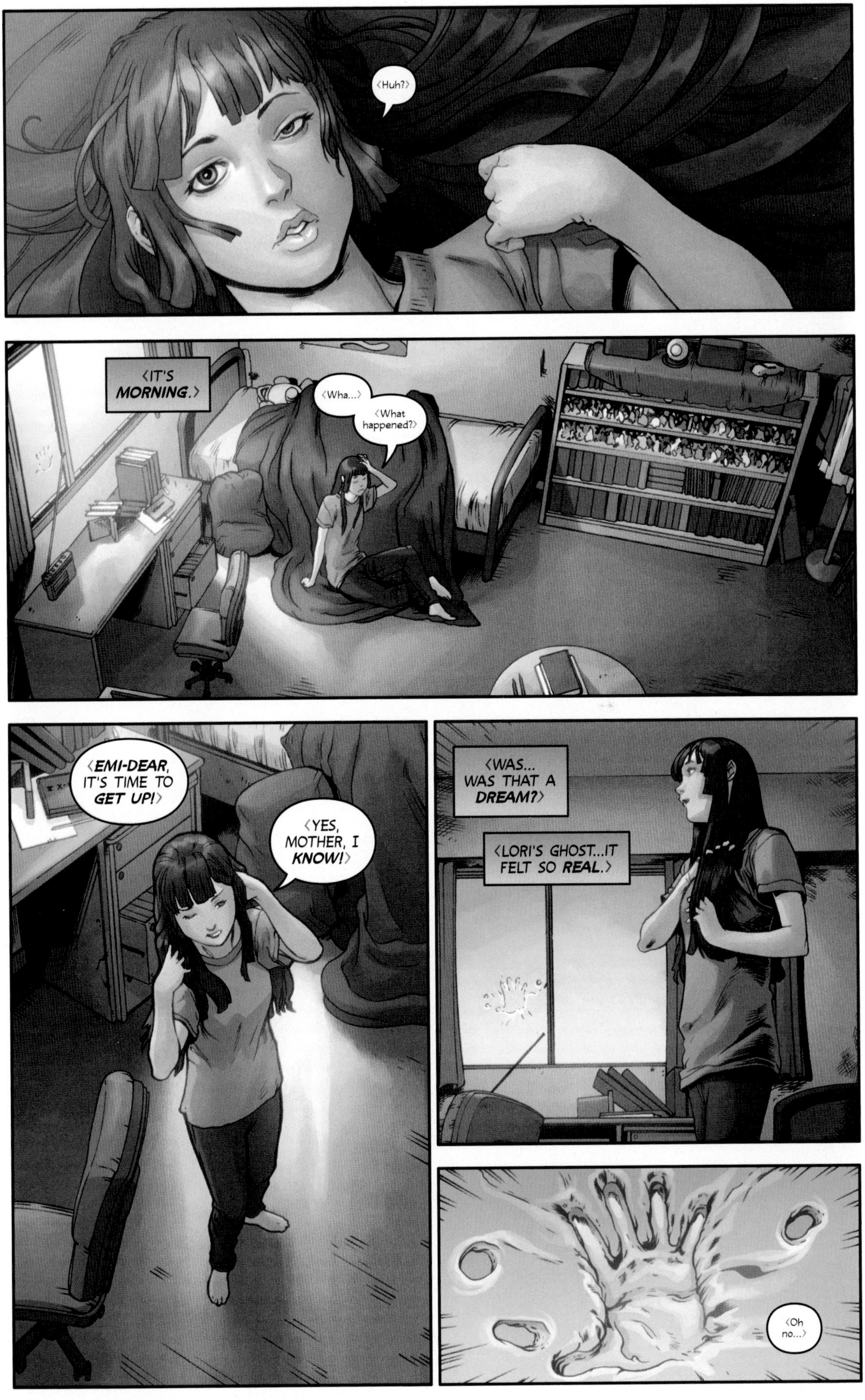

<Huh?>
<IT'S MORNING.>
<Wha...>
<What happened?>
<EMI-DEAR, IT'S TIME TO GET UP!>
<YES, MOTHER, I KNOW!>
<WAS... WAS THAT A DREAM?>
<LORI'S GHOST...IT FELT SO REAL.>
<Oh no...>

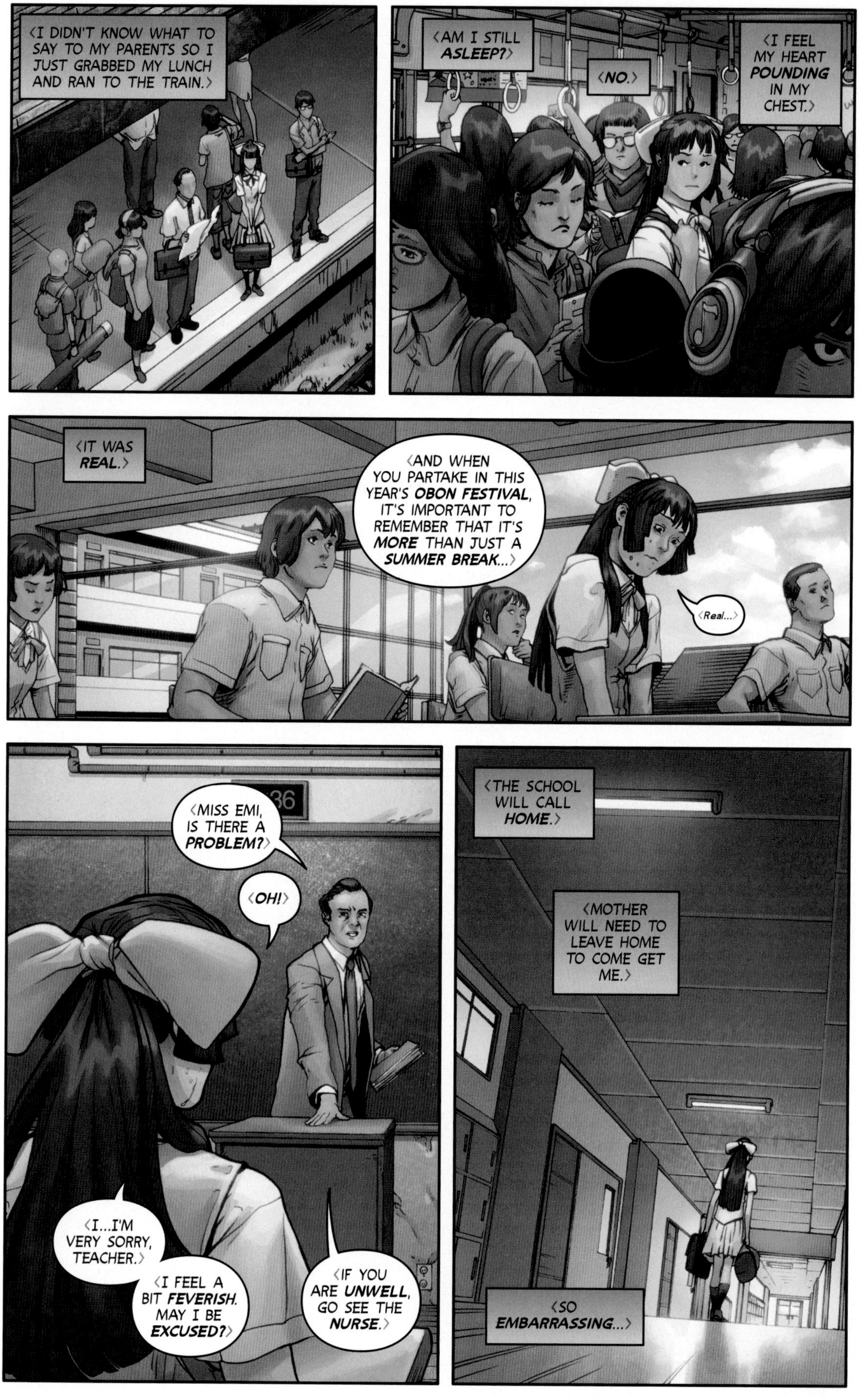

⟨I DIDN'T KNOW WHAT TO SAY TO MY PARENTS SO I JUST GRABBED MY LUNCH AND RAN TO THE TRAIN.⟩
⟨AM I STILL ASLEEP?⟩
⟨NO.⟩
⟨I FEEL MY HEART POUNDING IN MY CHEST.⟩
⟨IT WAS REAL.⟩
⟨AND WHEN YOU PARTAKE IN THIS YEAR'S OBON FESTIVAL, IT'S IMPORTANT TO REMEMBER THAT IT'S MORE THAN JUST A SUMMER BREAK...⟩
⟨Real...⟩
36
⟨MISS EMI, IS THERE A PROBLEM?⟩
⟨OH!⟩
⟨I...I'M VERY SORRY, TEACHER.⟩
⟨I FEEL A BIT FEVERISH. MAY I BE EXCUSED?⟩
⟨IF YOU ARE UNWELL, GO SEE THE NURSE.⟩
⟨THE SCHOOL WILL CALL HOME.⟩
⟨MOTHER WILL NEED TO LEAVE HOME TO COME GET ME.⟩
⟨SO EMBARRASSING...⟩

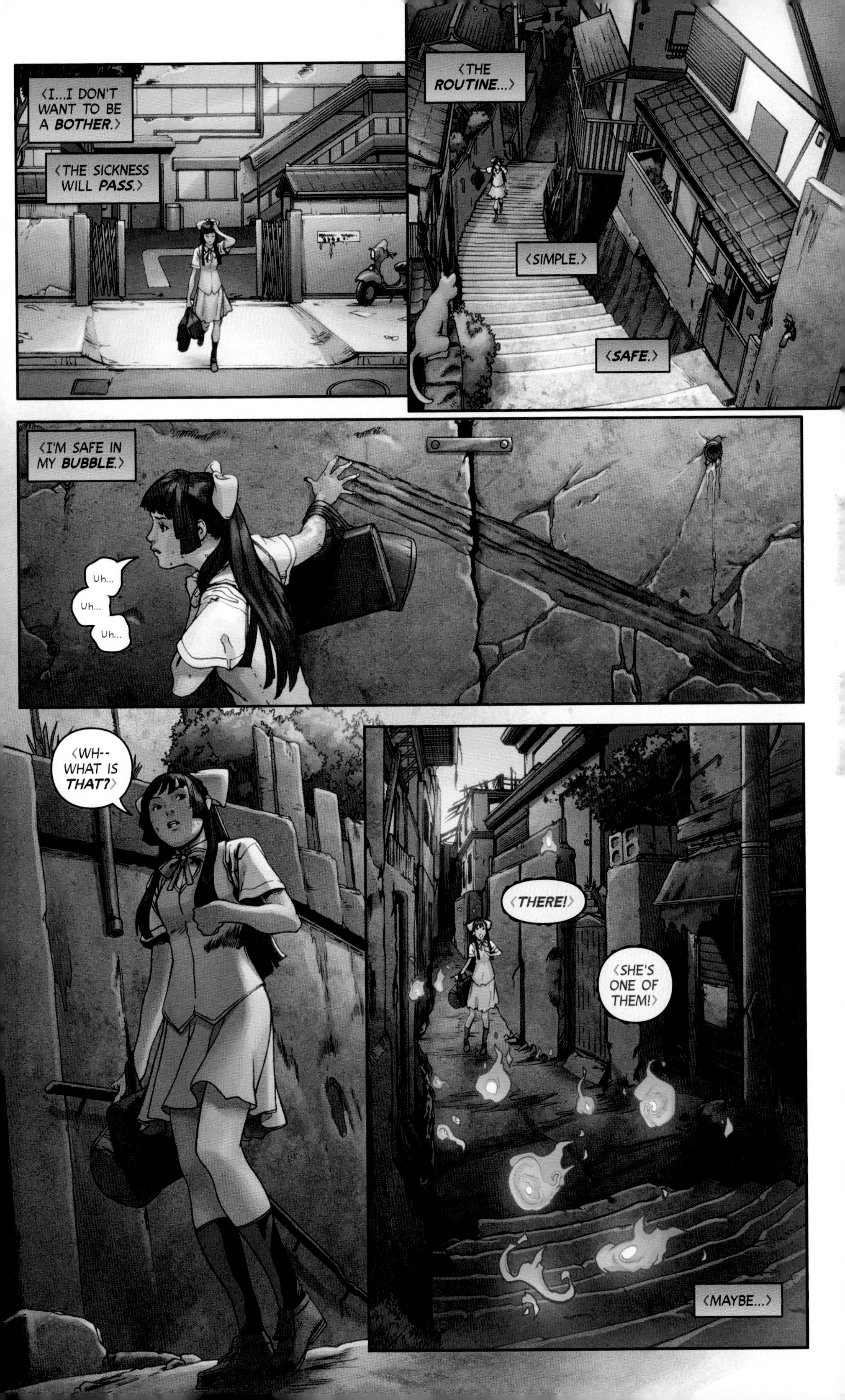

‹I...I DON'T WANT TO BE A BOTHER.›
‹THE SICKNESS WILL PASS.›
‹THE ROUTINE...›
‹SIMPLE.›
‹SAFE.›
‹I'M SAFE IN MY BUBBLE.›
Uh...
Uh...
Uh...
‹WH-- WHAT IS THAT?›
‹THERE!›
‹SHE'S ONE OF THEM!›
‹MAYBE...›

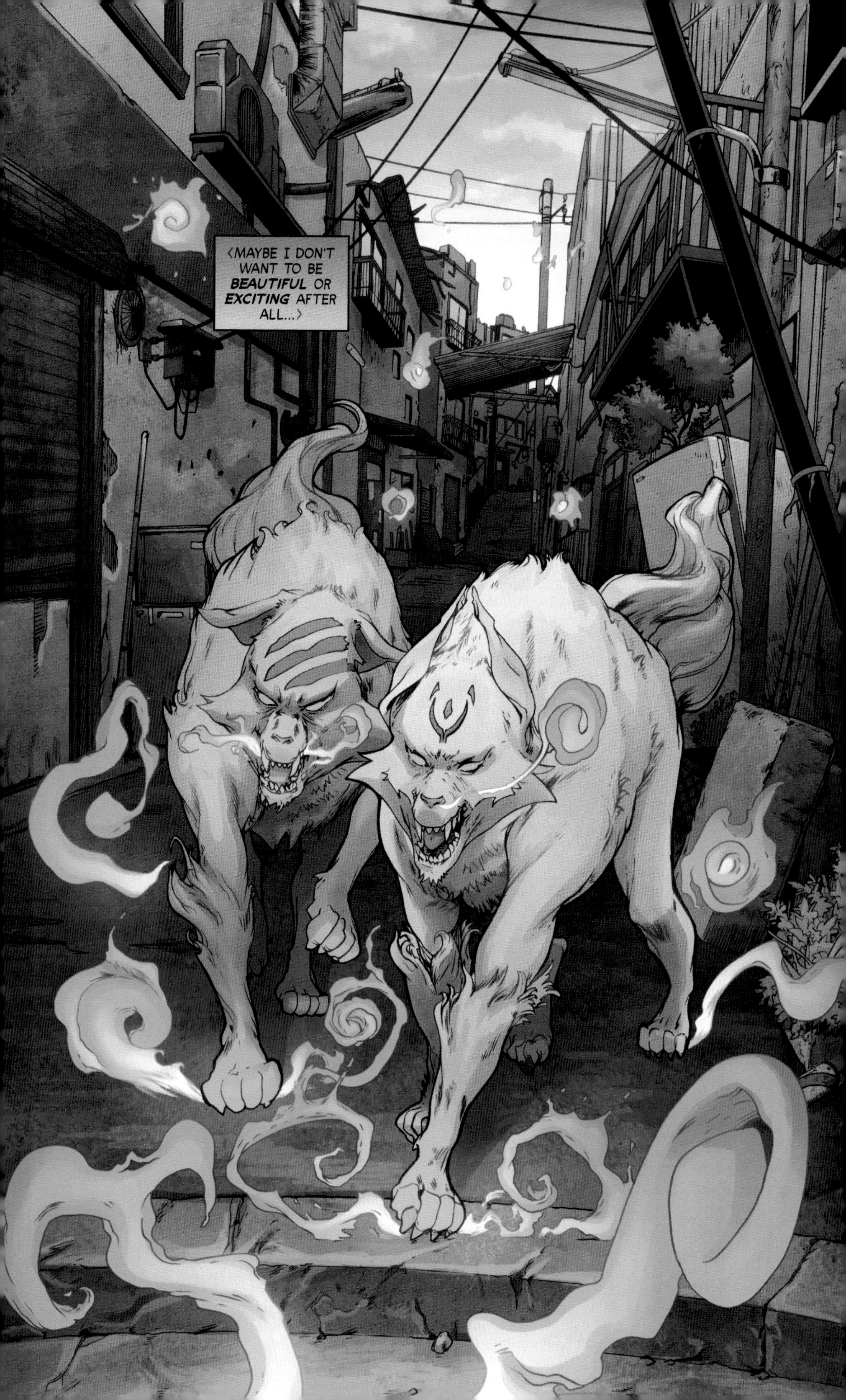

⟨MAYBE I DON'T WANT TO BE **BEAUTIFUL** OR **EXCITING** AFTER ALL...⟩

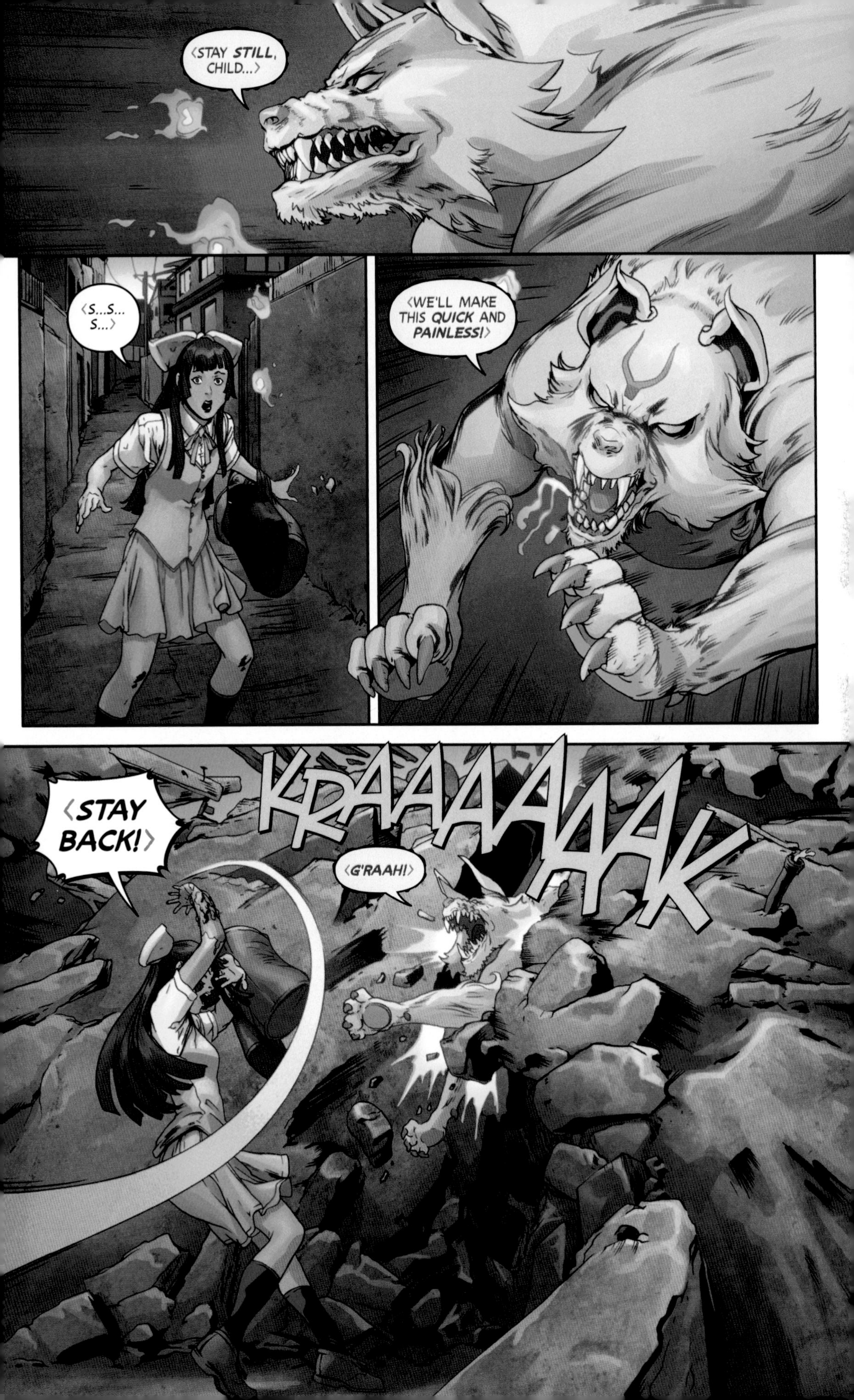

<STAY **STILL**, CHILD...>
<S...S... S...>
<WE'LL MAKE THIS ***QUICK*** AND ***PAINLESS!***>
<**STAY BACK!**>
KRAAAAAAAK
<G'RAAH!>

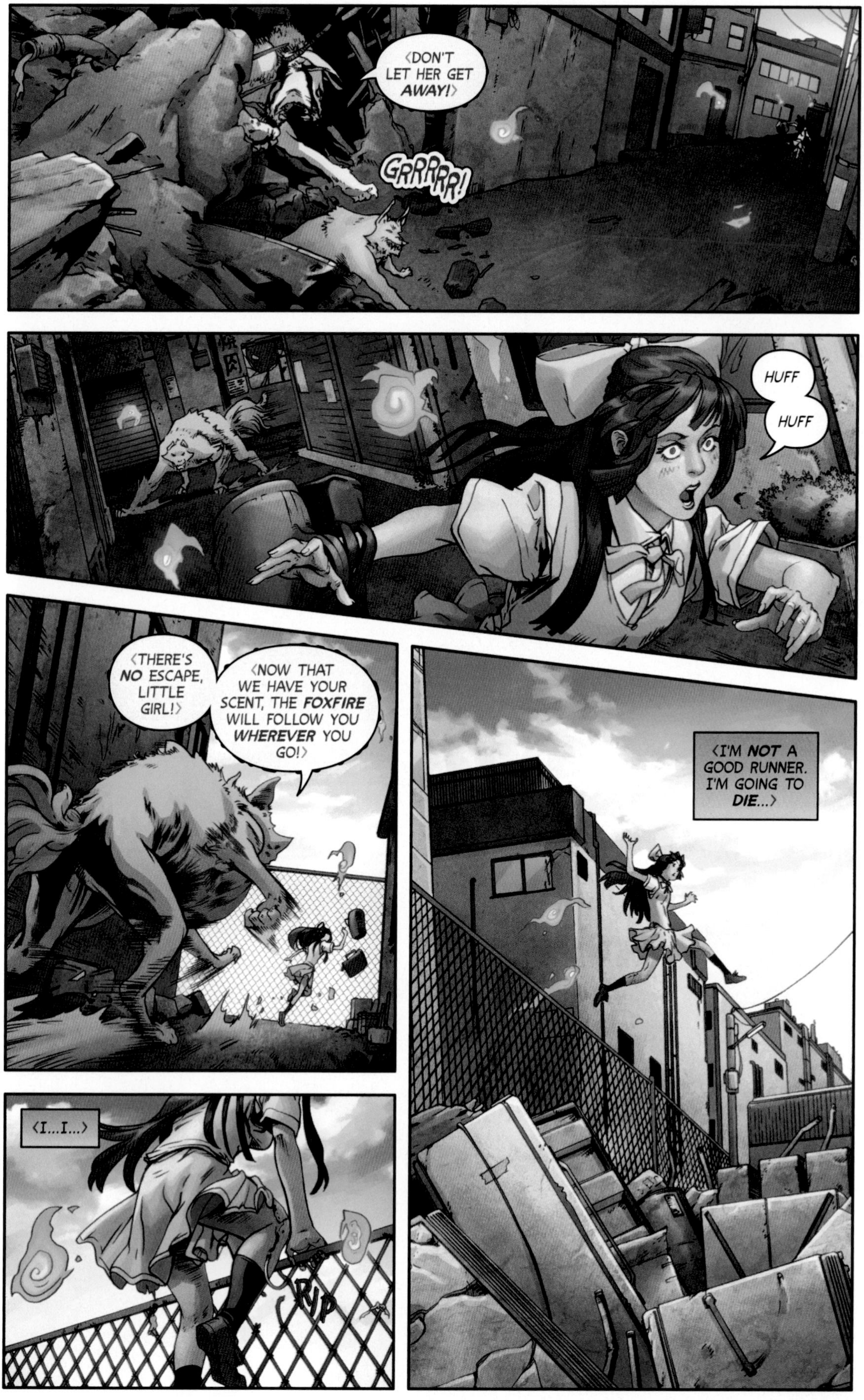

‹DON'T LET HER GET *AWAY!*›
GRRRRRR!
HUFF
HUFF
‹THERE'S *NO* ESCAPE, LITTLE GIRL!›
‹NOW THAT WE HAVE YOUR SCENT, THE *FOXFIRE* WILL FOLLOW YOU *WHEREVER* YOU GO!›
‹I'M *NOT* A GOOD RUNNER. I'M GOING TO *DIE*...›
‹I...I...›
RIP

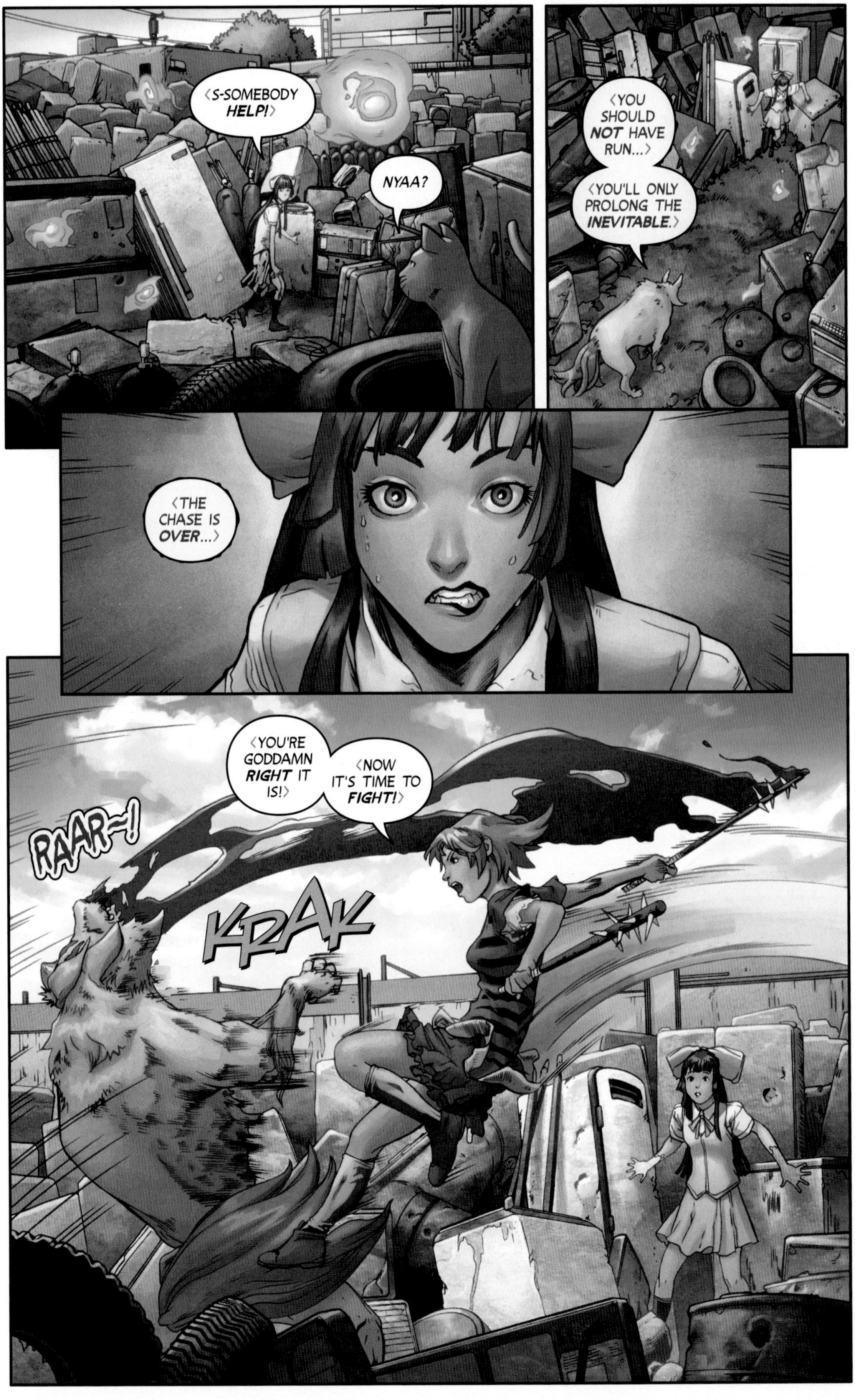

⟨S-SOMEBODY HELP!⟩
NYAA?
⟨YOU SHOULD NOT HAVE RUN...⟩
⟨YOU'LL ONLY PROLONG THE INEVITABLE.⟩
⟨THE CHASE IS OVER...⟩
⟨YOU'RE GODDAMN RIGHT IT IS!⟩
⟨NOW IT'S TIME TO FIGHT!⟩
RAAR~!
KRAK

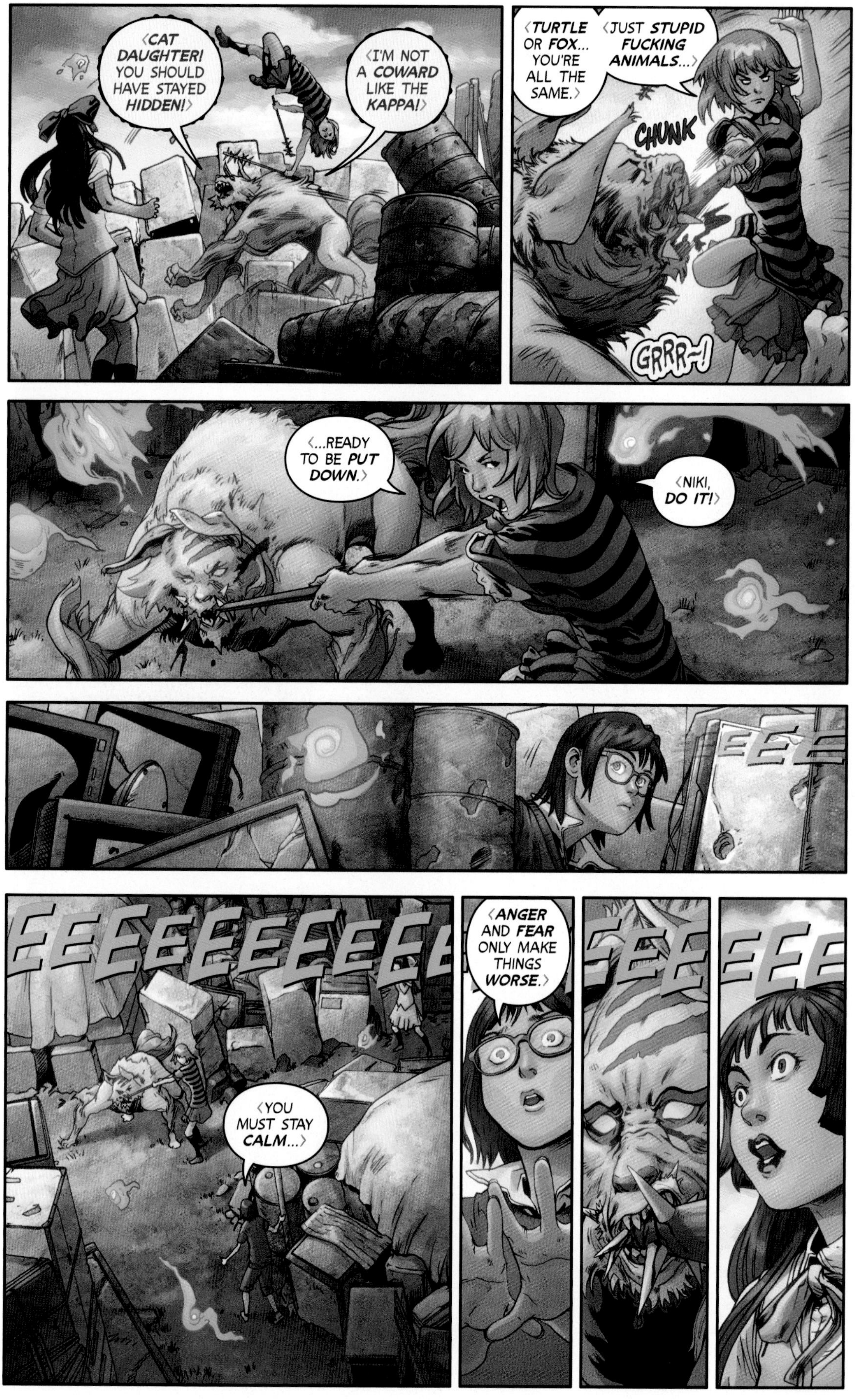
‹CAT DAUGHTER! YOU SHOULD HAVE STAYED HIDDEN!›
‹I'M NOT A COWARD LIKE THE KAPPA!›
‹TURTLE OR FOX... YOU'RE ALL THE SAME.›
‹JUST STUPID FUCKING ANIMALS...›
CHUNK
GRRR~!
‹...READY TO BE PUT DOWN.›
‹NIKI, DO IT!›
EEE
EEEEEEEEEE
‹YOU MUST STAY CALM...›
‹ANGER AND FEAR ONLY MAKE THINGS WORSE.›
EEE
EEEE

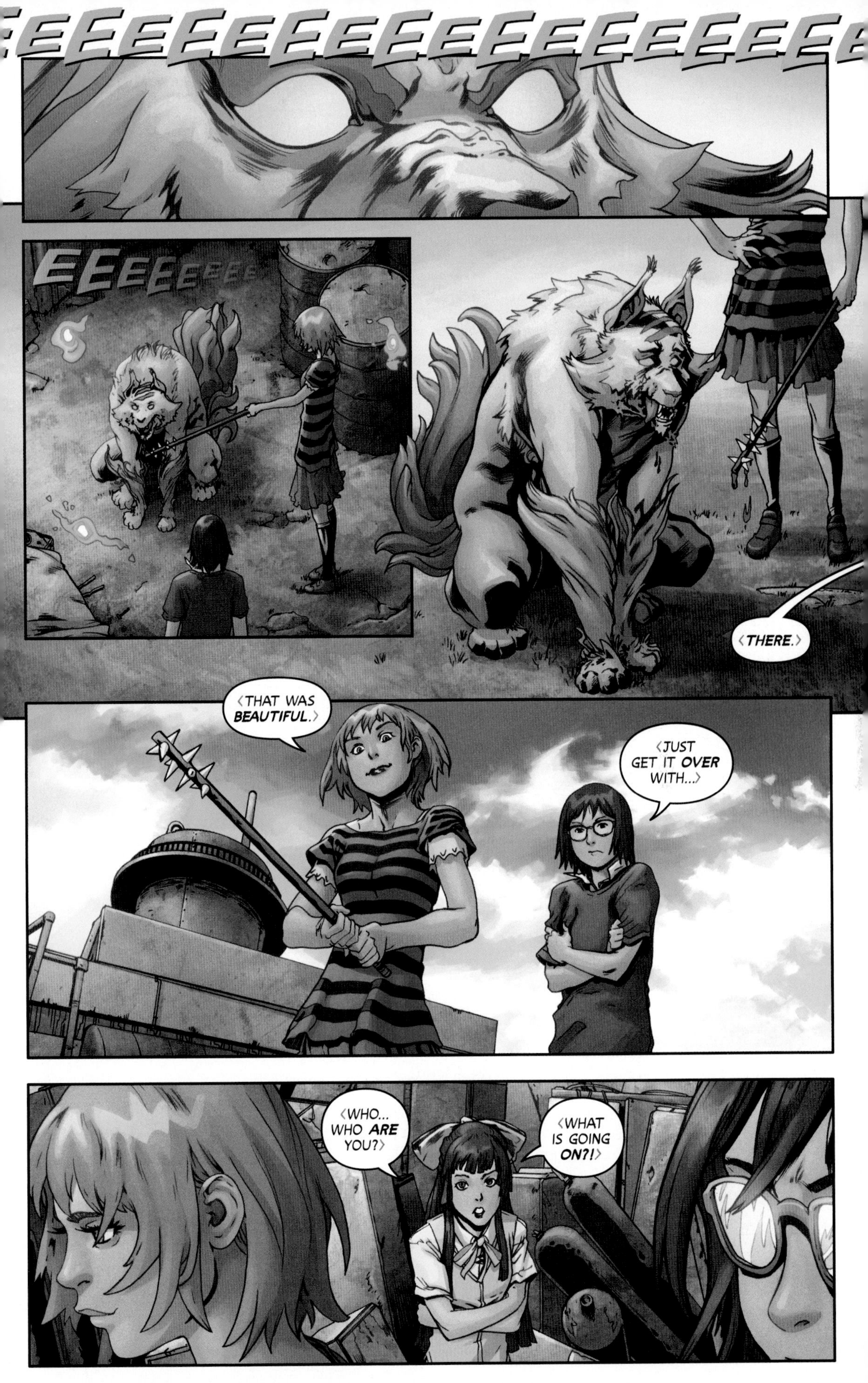
EEEEEEEEEEEEEEEEEEE
EEEEEEEEE
‹THERE.›
‹THAT WAS BEAUTIFUL.›
‹JUST GET IT OVER WITH...›
‹WHO... WHO ARE YOU?›
‹WHAT IS GOING ON?!›

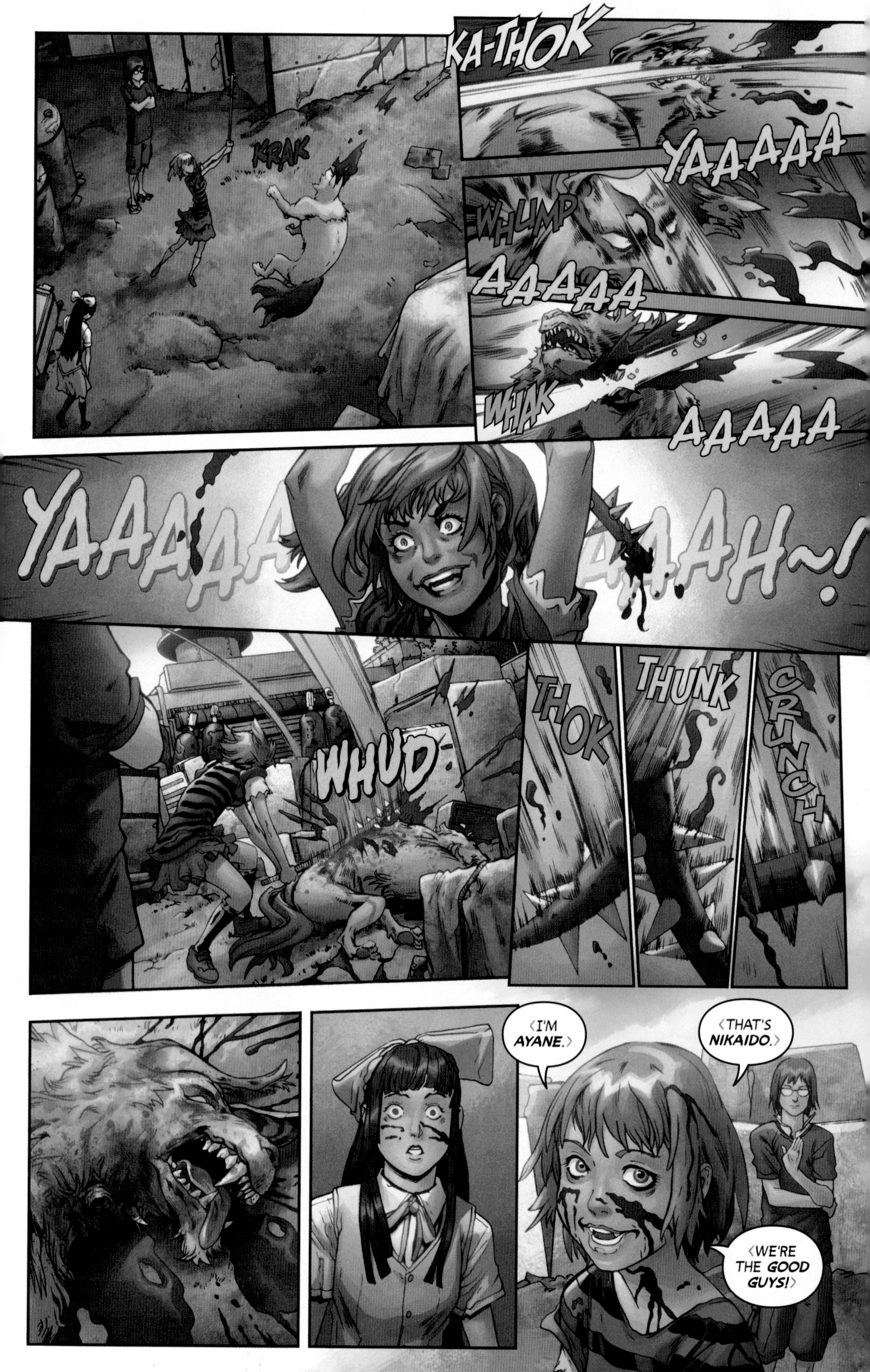
KRAK
KA-THOK
YAAAAA
WHUMP
AAAAA
WHAK
AAAAA
YAAAAA AAAH~!
WHUD
THOK
THUNK
CRUNCH
〈I'M AYANE.〉
〈THAT'S NIKAIDO.〉
〈WE'RE THE GOOD GUYS!〉

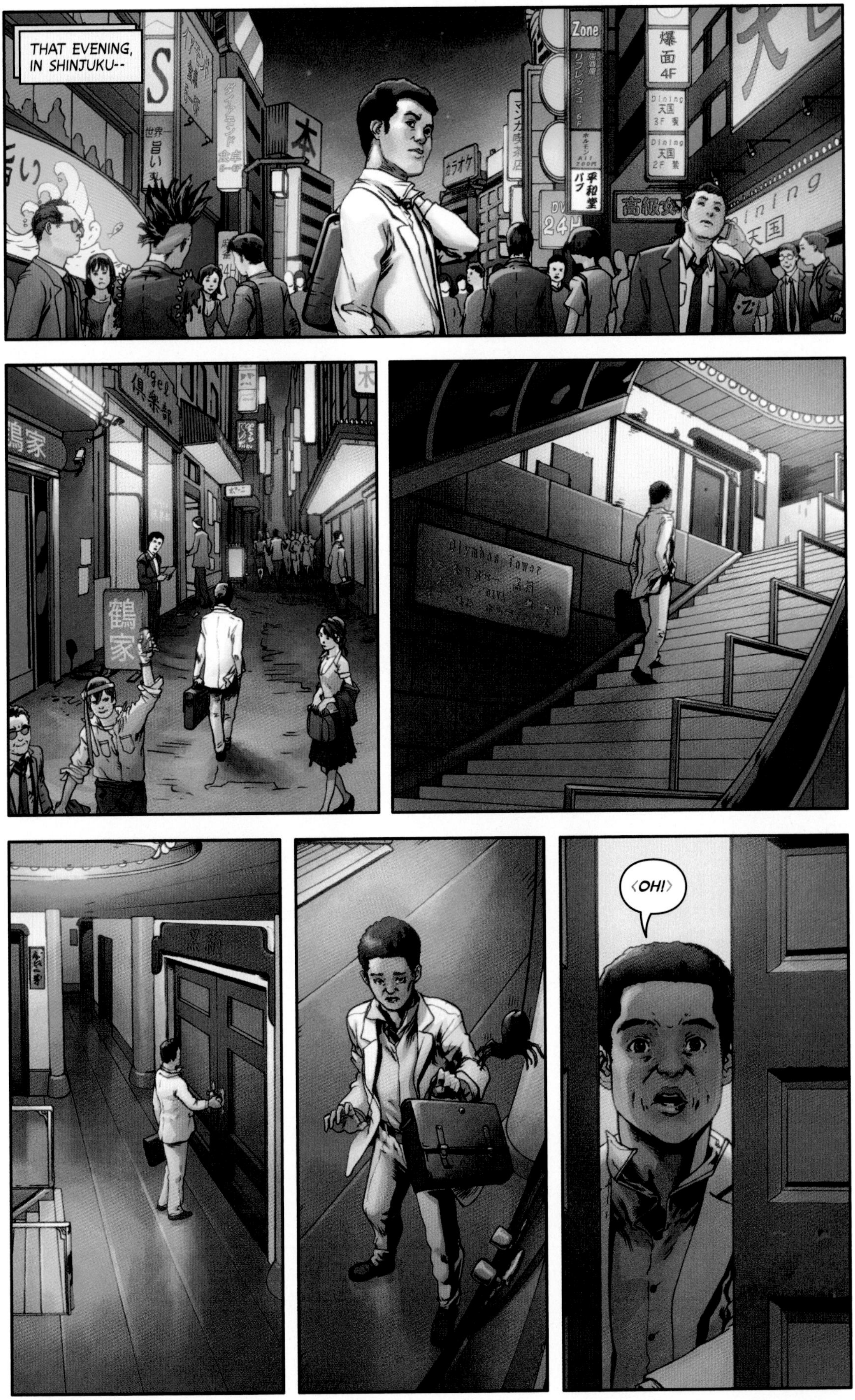
THAT EVENING, IN SHINJUKU--
〈OH!〉

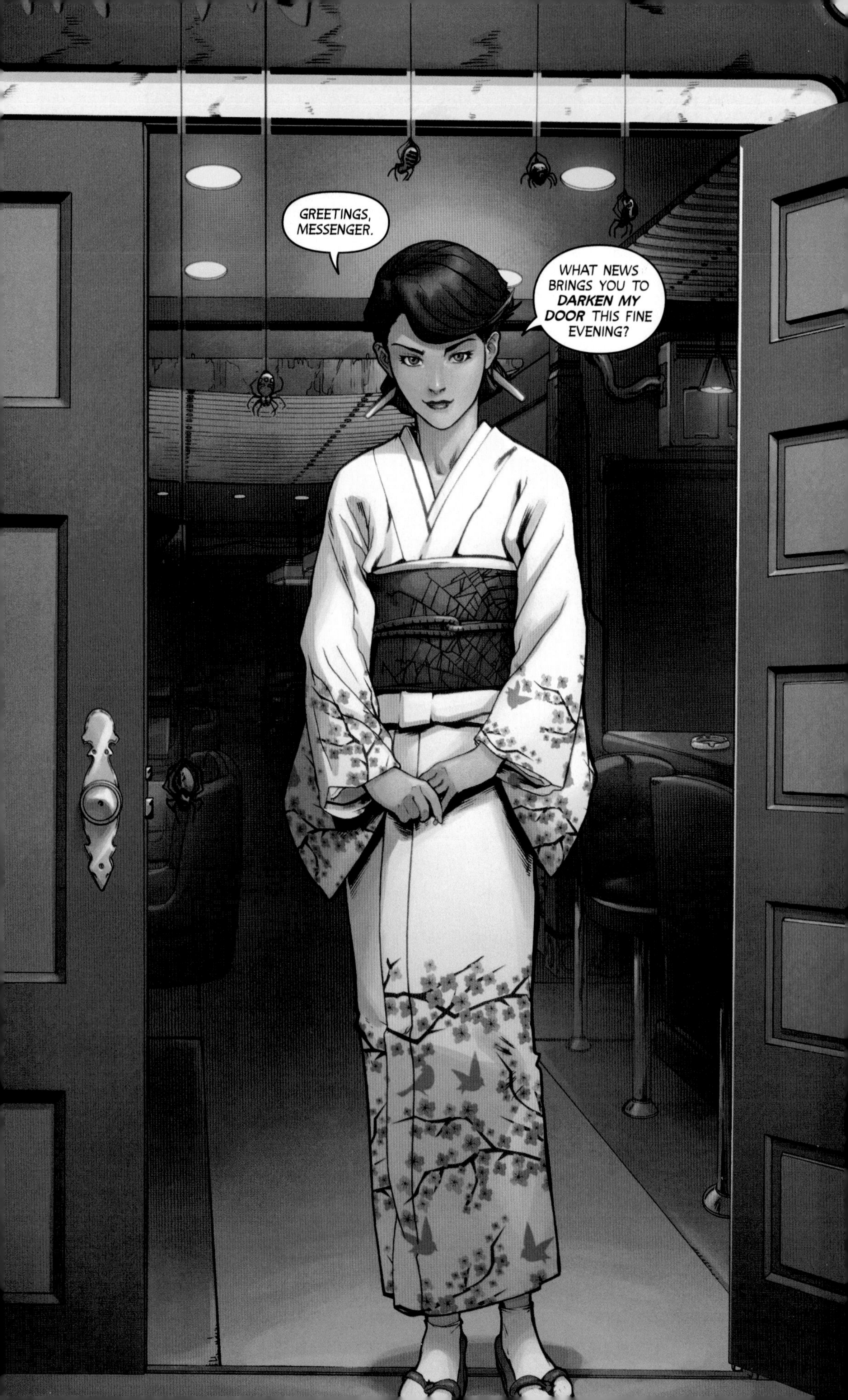
GREETINGS, MESSENGER.
WHAT NEWS BRINGS YOU TO DARKEN MY DOOR THIS FINE EVENING?

Chapter Seven

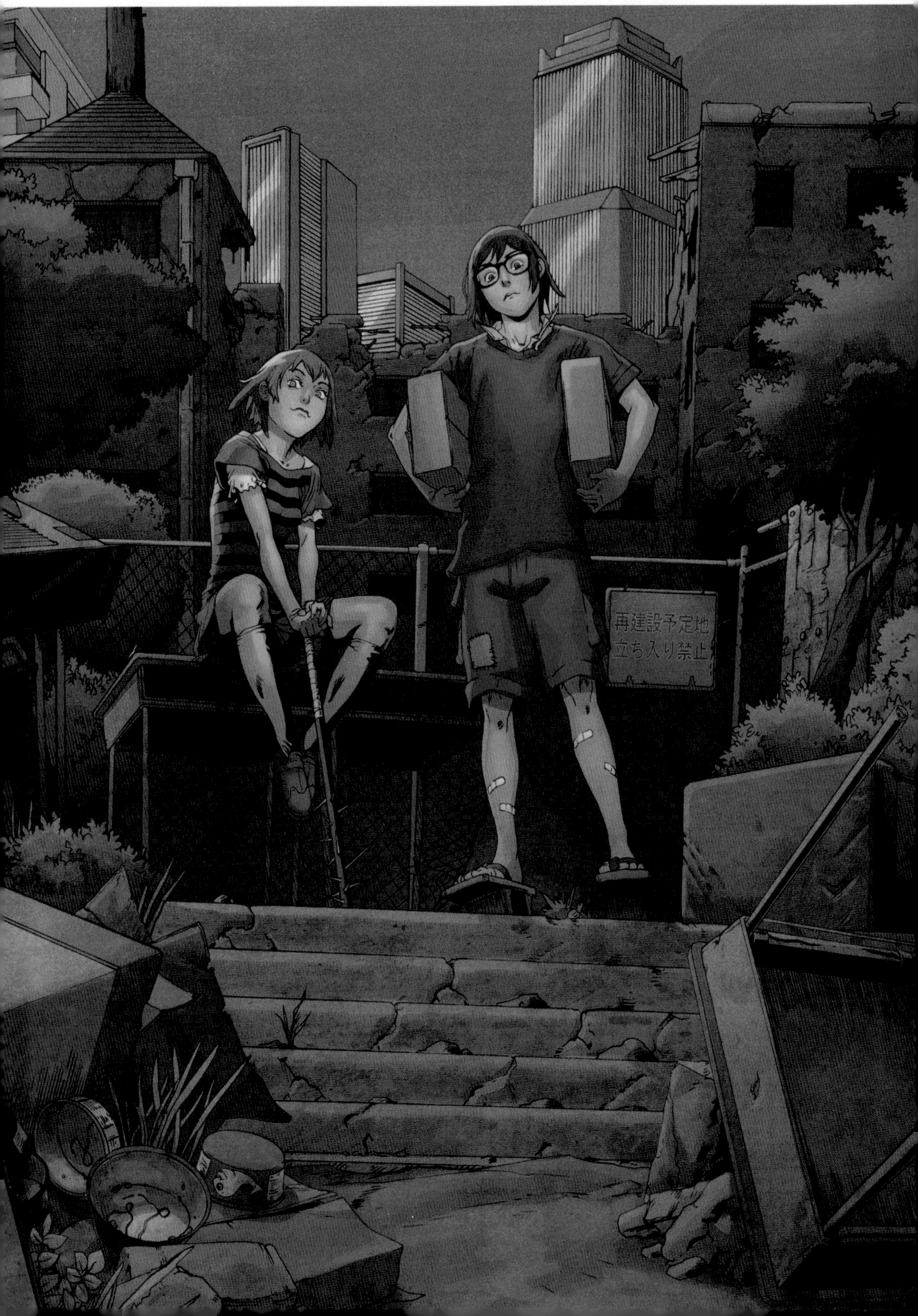

再建設予定地
立ち入り禁止

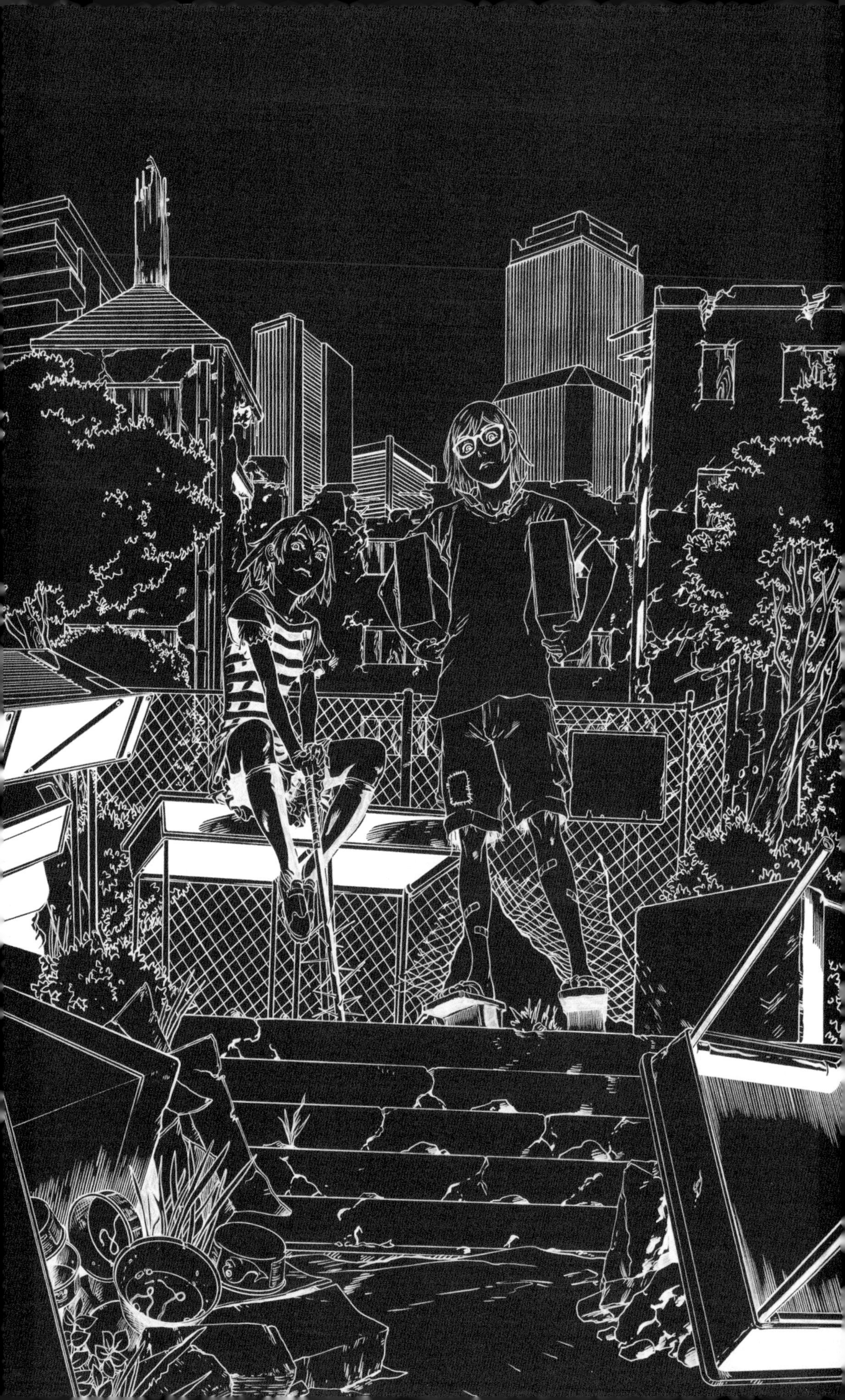

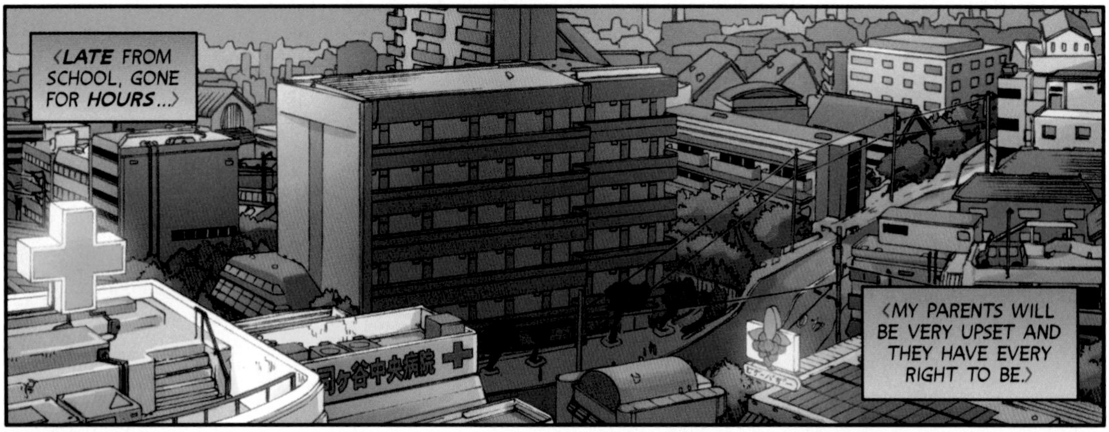
⟨LATE FROM SCHOOL, GONE FOR HOURS...⟩
⟨MY PARENTS WILL BE VERY UPSET AND THEY HAVE EVERY RIGHT TO BE.⟩

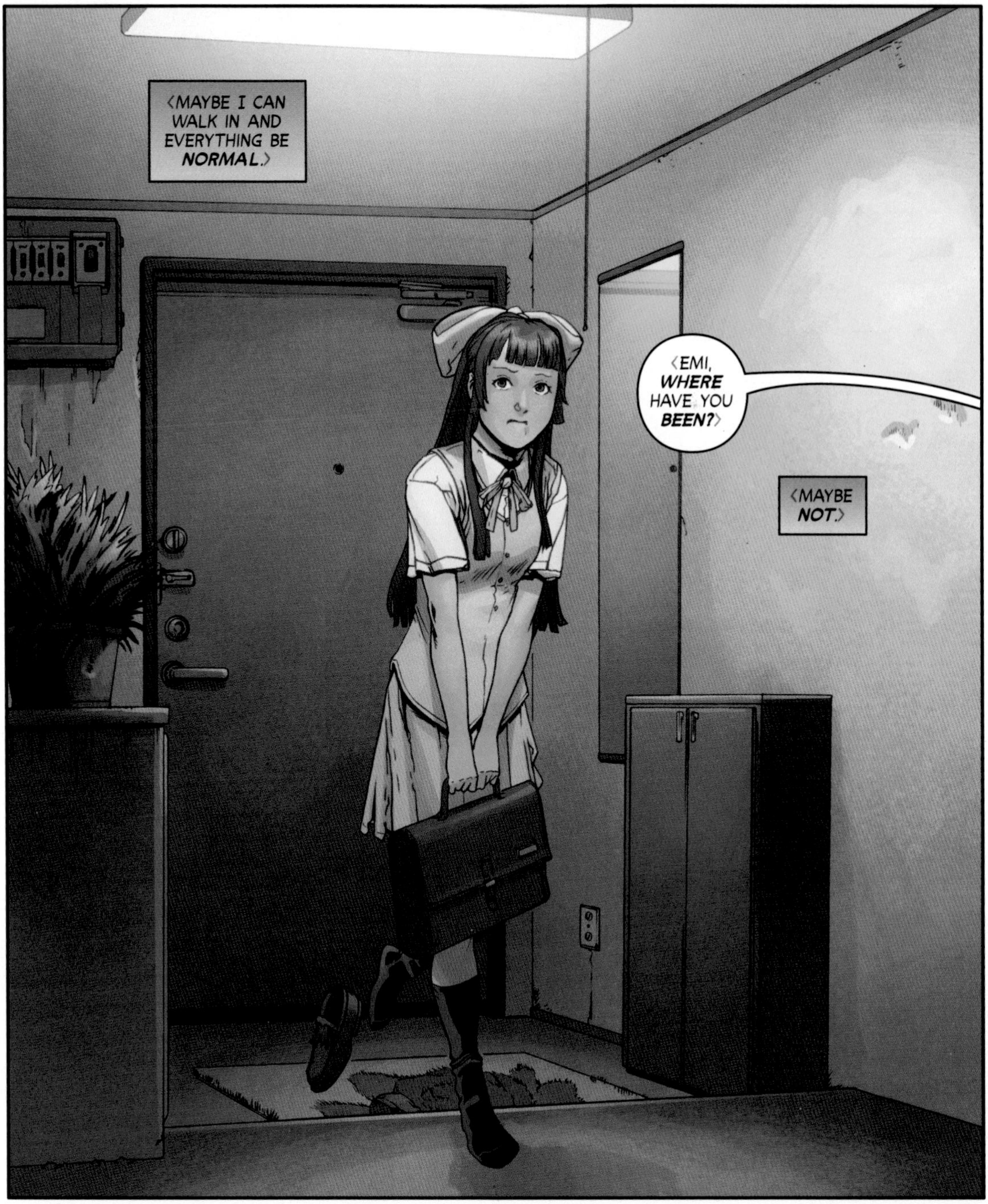
⟨MAYBE I CAN WALK IN AND EVERYTHING BE NORMAL.⟩
⟨EMI, WHERE HAVE YOU BEEN?⟩
⟨MAYBE NOT.⟩

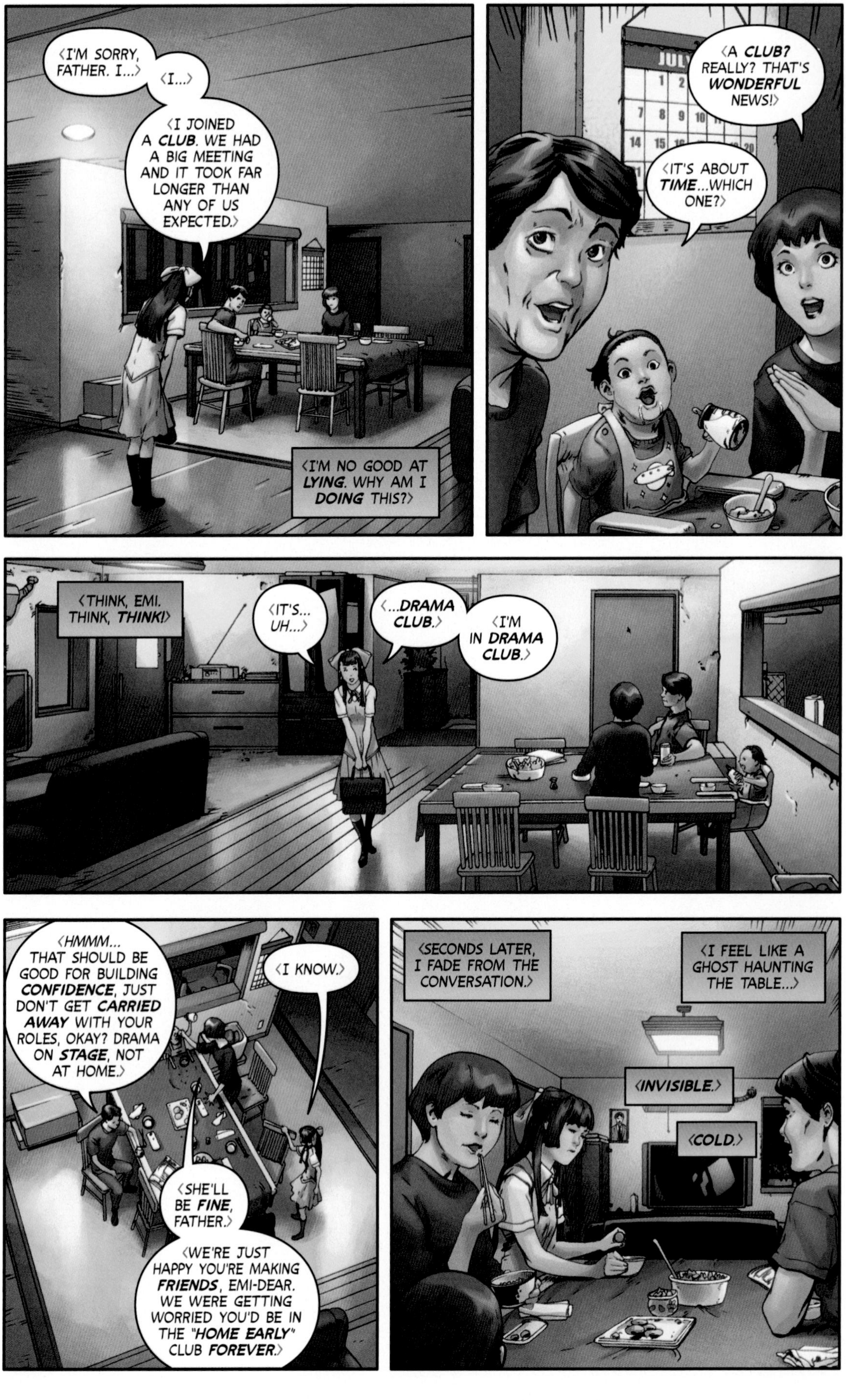

‹I'M SORRY, FATHER. I...›
‹I...›
‹I JOINED A CLUB. WE HAD A BIG MEETING AND IT TOOK FAR LONGER THAN ANY OF US EXPECTED.›
‹I'M NO GOOD AT LYING. WHY AM I DOING THIS?›
JULY
‹A CLUB? REALLY? THAT'S WONDERFUL NEWS!›
‹IT'S ABOUT TIME...WHICH ONE?›
‹THINK, EMI. THINK, THINK!›
‹IT'S... UH...›
‹...DRAMA CLUB.›
‹I'M IN DRAMA CLUB.›
‹HMMM... THAT SHOULD BE GOOD FOR BUILDING CONFIDENCE, JUST DON'T GET CARRIED AWAY WITH YOUR ROLES, OKAY? DRAMA ON STAGE, NOT AT HOME.›
‹I KNOW.›
‹SHE'LL BE FINE, FATHER.›
‹WE'RE JUST HAPPY YOU'RE MAKING FRIENDS, EMI-DEAR. WE WERE GETTING WORRIED YOU'D BE IN THE "HOME EARLY" CLUB FOREVER.›
‹SECONDS LATER, I FADE FROM THE CONVERSATION.›
‹I FEEL LIKE A GHOST HAUNTING THE TABLE...›
‹INVISIBLE.›
‹COLD.›

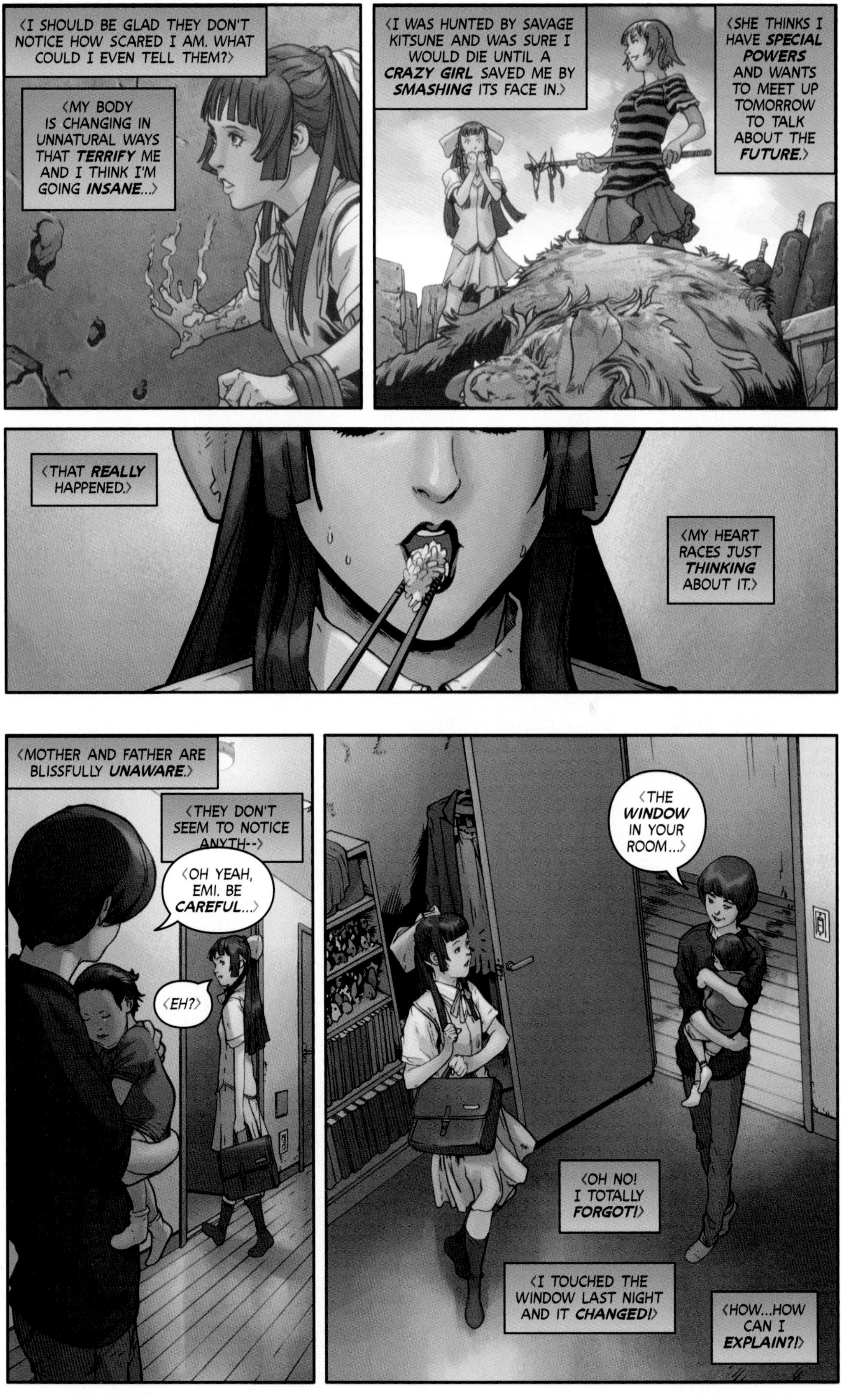

<I SHOULD BE GLAD THEY DON'T NOTICE HOW SCARED I AM. WHAT COULD I EVEN TELL THEM?>
<MY BODY IS CHANGING IN UNNATURAL WAYS THAT TERRIFY ME AND I THINK I'M GOING INSANE...>
<I WAS HUNTED BY SAVAGE KITSUNE AND WAS SURE I WOULD DIE UNTIL A CRAZY GIRL SAVED ME BY SMASHING ITS FACE IN.>
<SHE THINKS I HAVE SPECIAL POWERS AND WANTS TO MEET UP TOMORROW TO TALK ABOUT THE FUTURE.>
<THAT REALLY HAPPENED.>
<MY HEART RACES JUST THINKING ABOUT IT.>
<MOTHER AND FATHER ARE BLISSFULLY UNAWARE.>
<THEY DON'T SEEM TO NOTICE ANYTH-->
<OH YEAH, EMI. BE CAREFUL...>
<EH?>
<THE WINDOW IN YOUR ROOM...>
<OH NO! I TOTALLY FORGOT!>
<I TOUCHED THE WINDOW LAST NIGHT AND IT CHANGED!>
<HOW...HOW CAN I EXPLAIN?!>

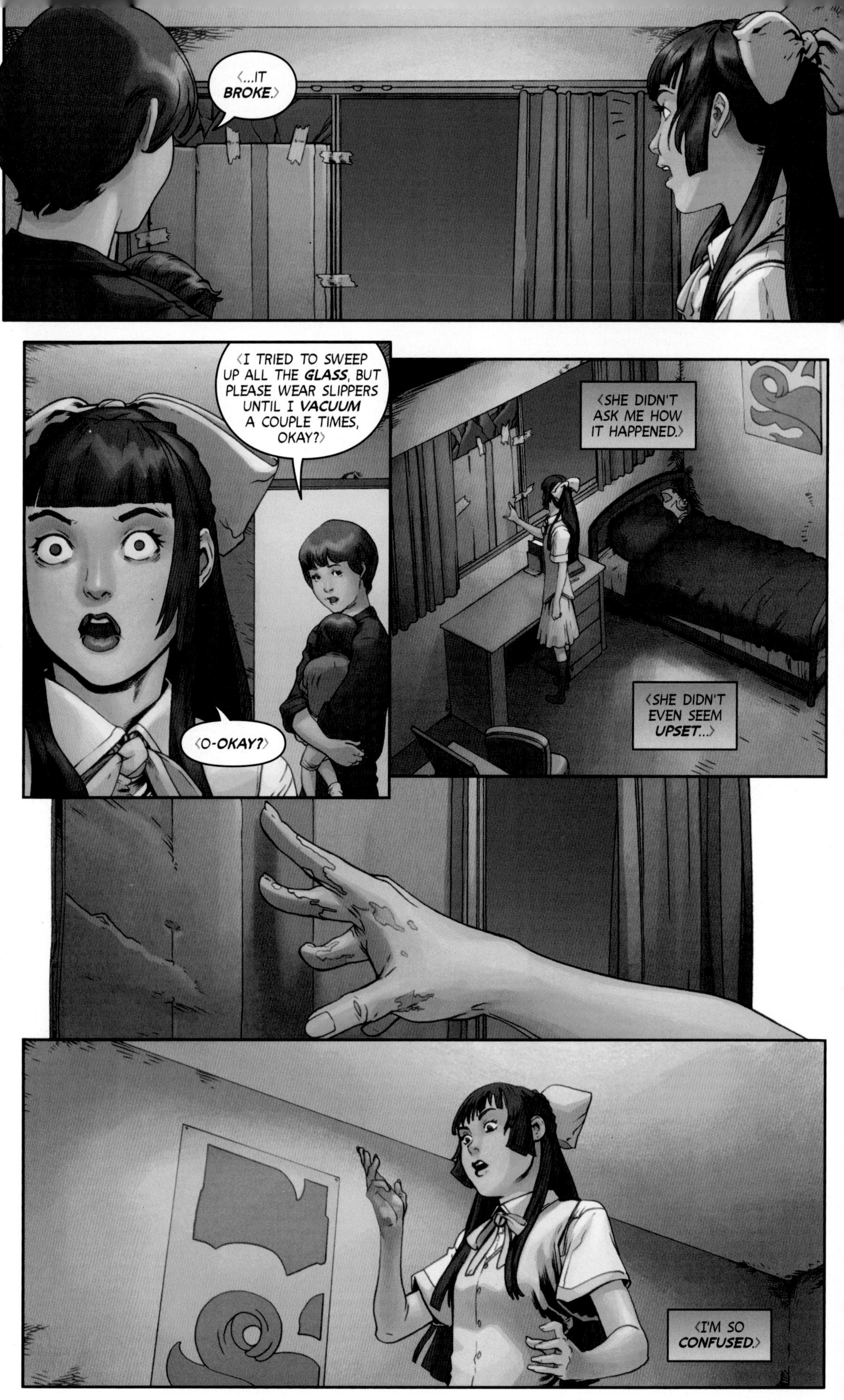
‹...IT BROKE.›
‹I TRIED TO SWEEP UP ALL THE GLASS, BUT PLEASE WEAR SLIPPERS UNTIL I VACUUM A COUPLE TIMES, OKAY?›
‹O-OKAY?›
‹SHE DIDN'T ASK ME HOW IT HAPPENED.›
‹SHE DIDN'T EVEN SEEM UPSET...›
‹I'M SO CONFUSED.›

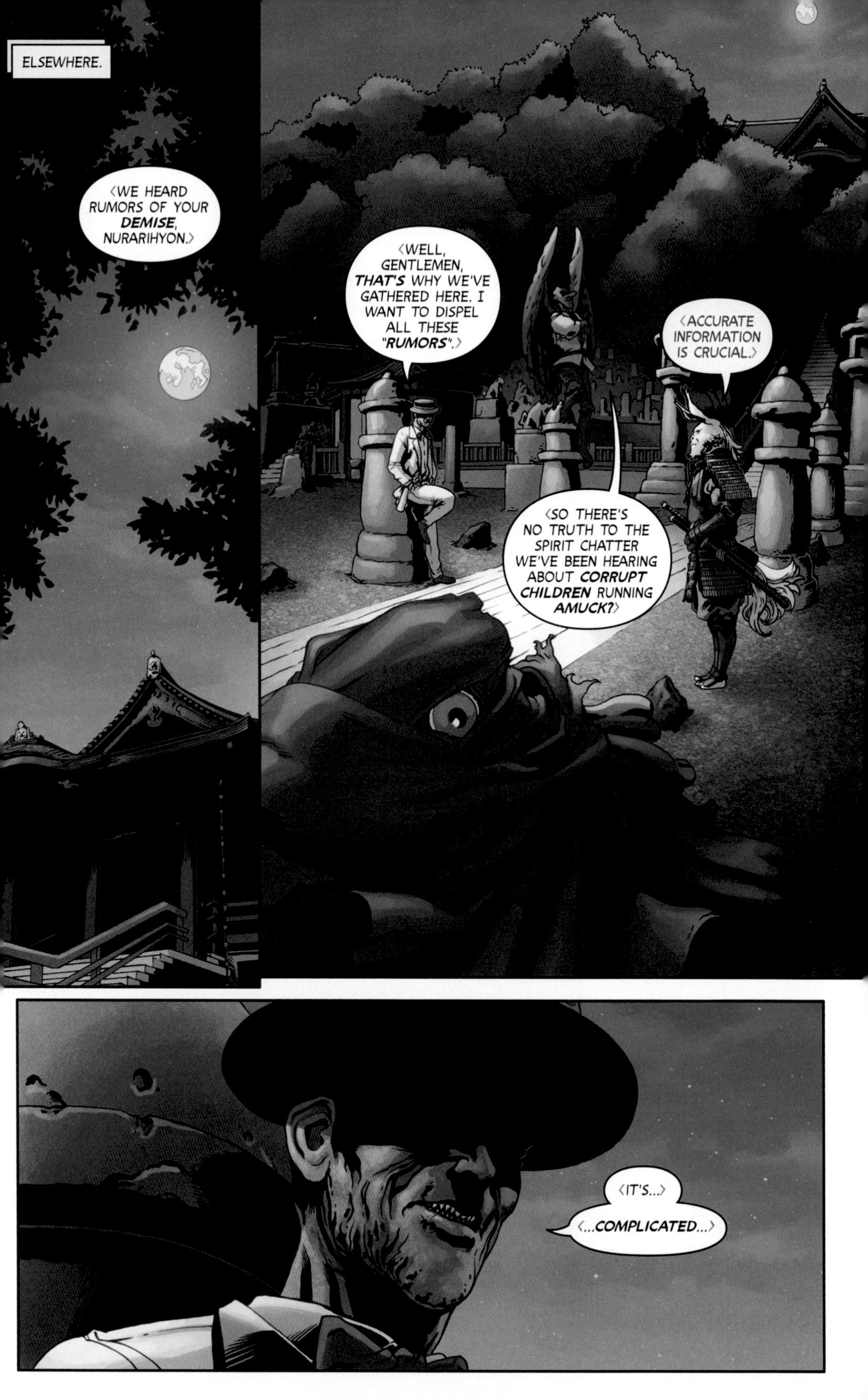
ELSEWHERE.
⟨WE HEARD RUMORS OF YOUR DEMISE, NURARIHYON.⟩
⟨WELL, GENTLEMEN, THAT'S WHY WE'VE GATHERED HERE. I WANT TO DISPEL ALL THESE "RUMORS".⟩
⟨ACCURATE INFORMATION IS CRUCIAL.⟩
⟨SO THERE'S NO TRUTH TO THE SPIRIT CHATTER WE'VE BEEN HEARING ABOUT CORRUPT CHILDREN RUNNING AMUCK?⟩
⟨IT'S...⟩
⟨...COMPLICATED...⟩

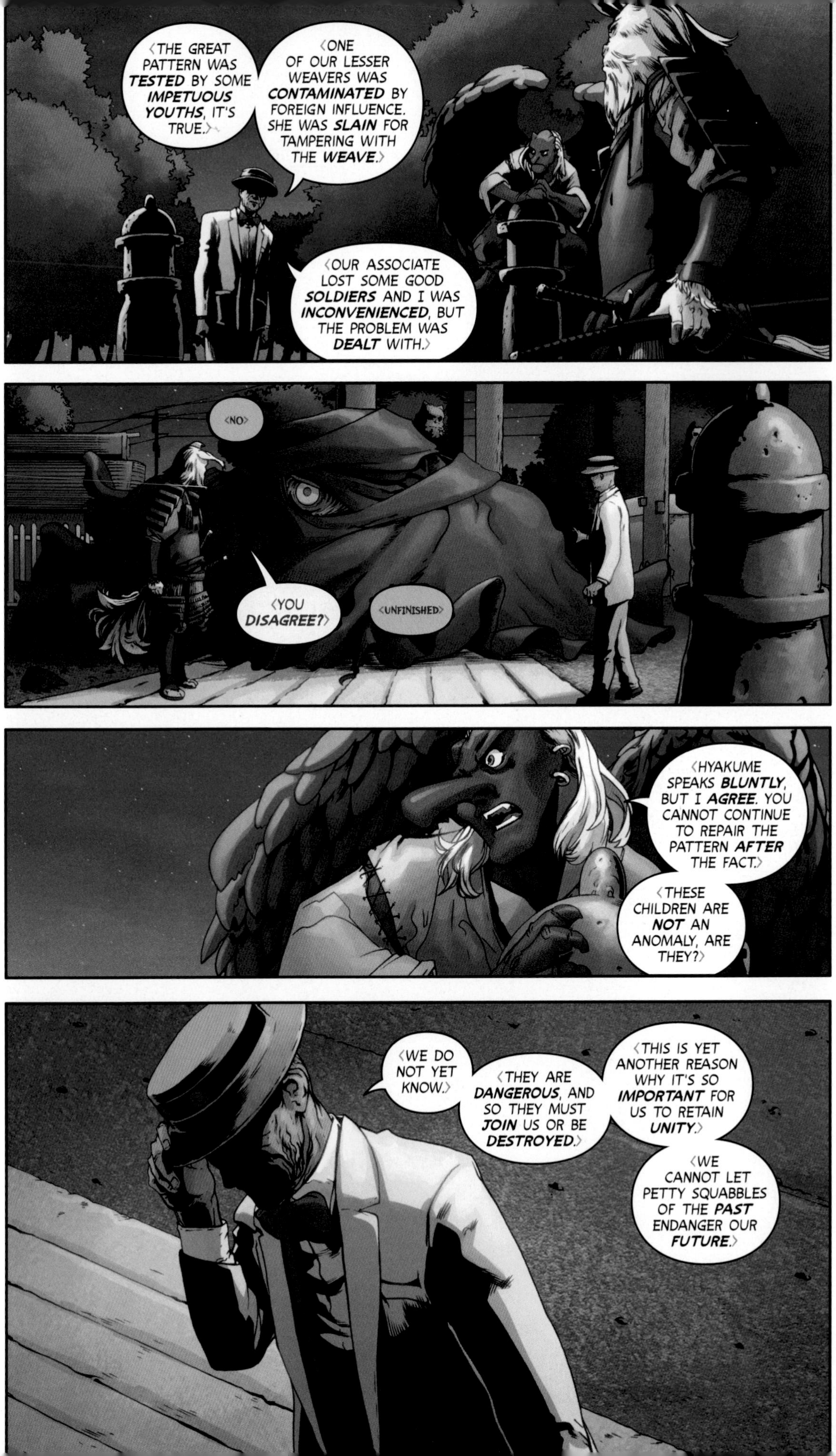
⟨THE GREAT PATTERN WAS TESTED BY SOME IMPETUOUS YOUTHS, IT'S TRUE.⟩
⟨ONE OF OUR LESSER WEAVERS WAS CONTAMINATED BY FOREIGN INFLUENCE. SHE WAS SLAIN FOR TAMPERING WITH THE WEAVE.⟩
⟨OUR ASSOCIATE LOST SOME GOOD SOLDIERS AND I WAS INCONVENIENCED, BUT THE PROBLEM WAS DEALT WITH.⟩
⟨NO⟩
⟨YOU DISAGREE?⟩
⟨UNFINISHED⟩
⟨HYAKUME SPEAKS BLUNTLY, BUT I AGREE. YOU CANNOT CONTINUE TO REPAIR THE PATTERN AFTER THE FACT.⟩
⟨THESE CHILDREN ARE NOT AN ANOMALY, ARE THEY?⟩
⟨WE DO NOT YET KNOW.⟩
⟨THEY ARE DANGEROUS, AND SO THEY MUST JOIN US OR BE DESTROYED.⟩
⟨THIS IS YET ANOTHER REASON WHY IT'S SO IMPORTANT FOR US TO RETAIN UNITY.⟩
⟨WE CANNOT LET PETTY SQUABBLES OF THE PAST ENDANGER OUR FUTURE.⟩

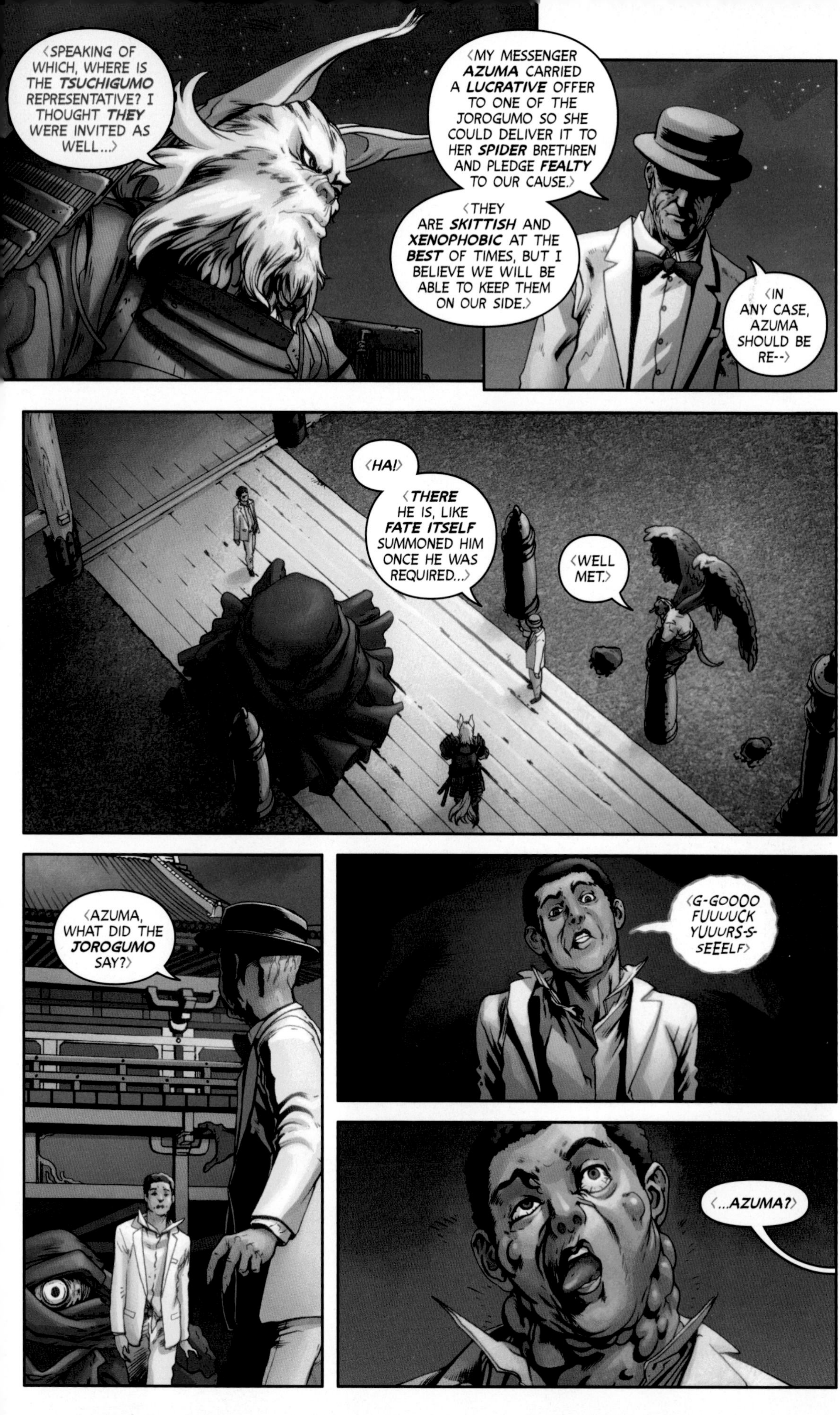

<SPEAKING OF WHICH, WHERE IS THE TSUCHIGUMO REPRESENTATIVE? I THOUGHT THEY WERE INVITED AS WELL...>
<MY MESSENGER AZUMA CARRIED A LUCRATIVE OFFER TO ONE OF THE JOROGUMO SO SHE COULD DELIVER IT TO HER SPIDER BRETHREN AND PLEDGE FEALTY TO OUR CAUSE.>
<THEY ARE SKITTISH AND XENOPHOBIC AT THE BEST OF TIMES, BUT I BELIEVE WE WILL BE ABLE TO KEEP THEM ON OUR SIDE.>
<IN ANY CASE, AZUMA SHOULD BE RE-->
<HA!>
<THERE HE IS, LIKE FATE ITSELF SUMMONED HIM ONCE HE WAS REQUIRED...>
<WELL MET.>
<AZUMA, WHAT DID THE JOROGUMO SAY?>
<G-GOOOO FUUUUCK YUUURS-S-SEEELF>
<...AZUMA?>

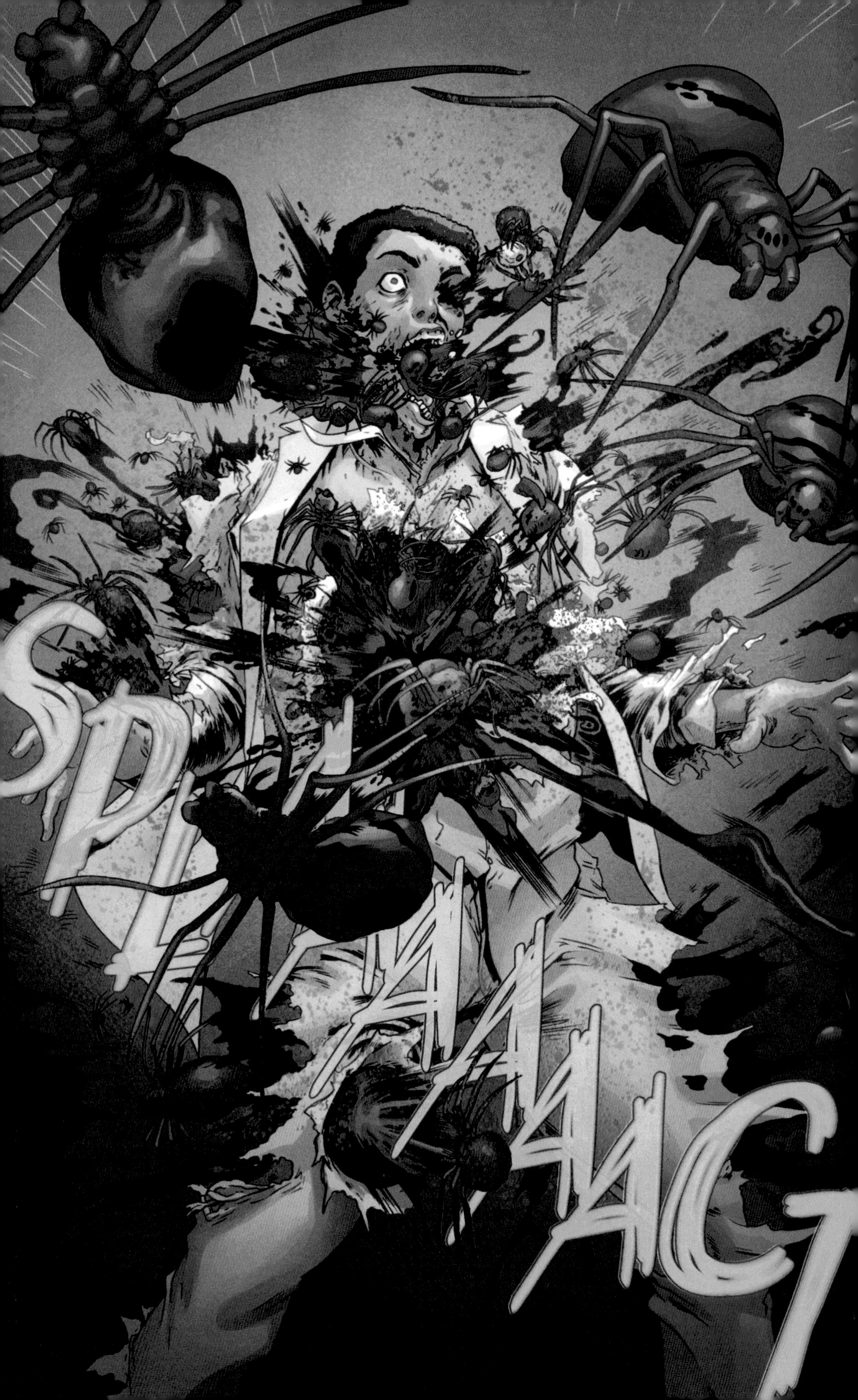

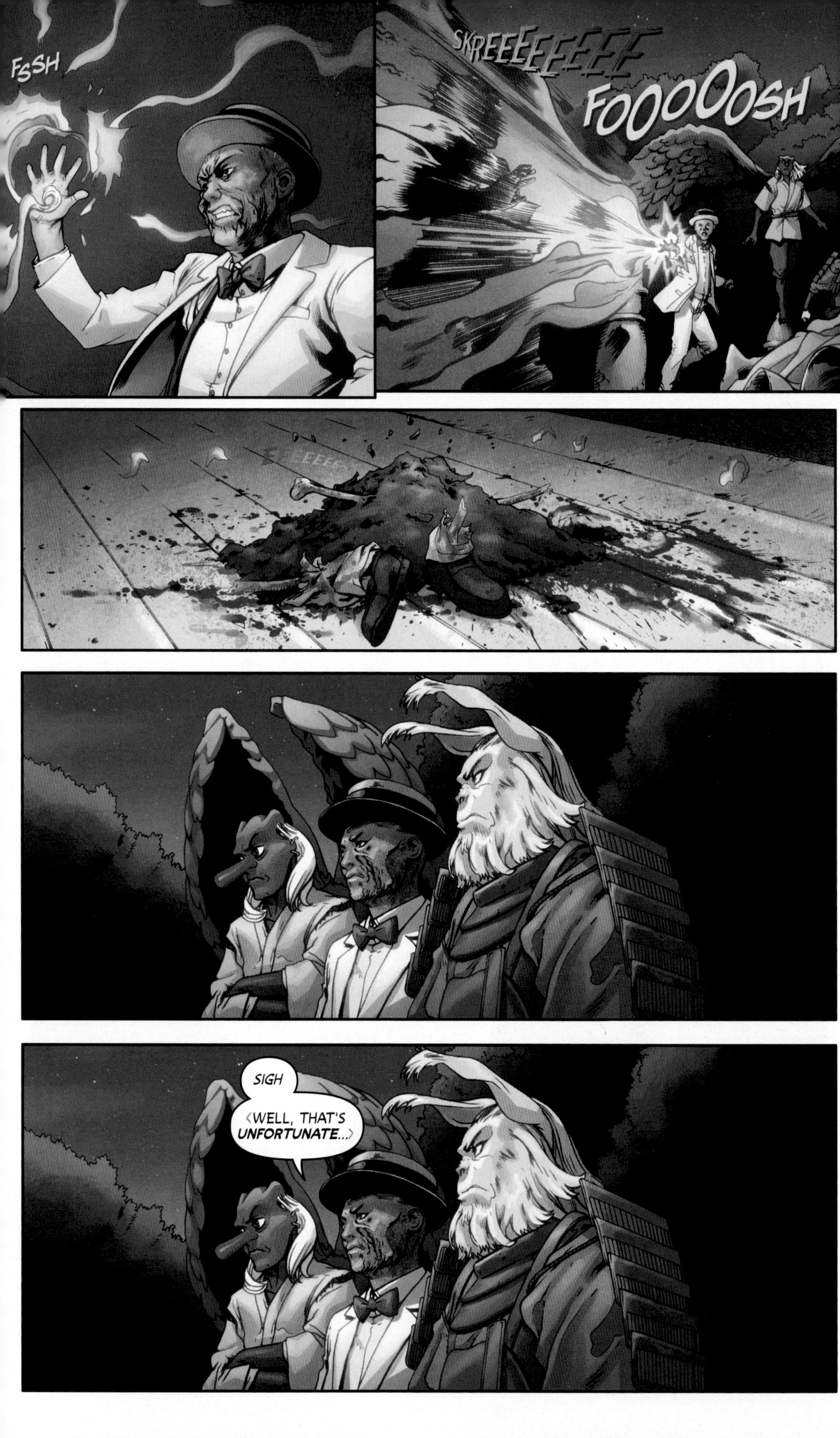
FSSH
SKREEEEEEEEE
FOOOOOSH
SIGH
<WELL, THAT'S UNFORTUNATE...>

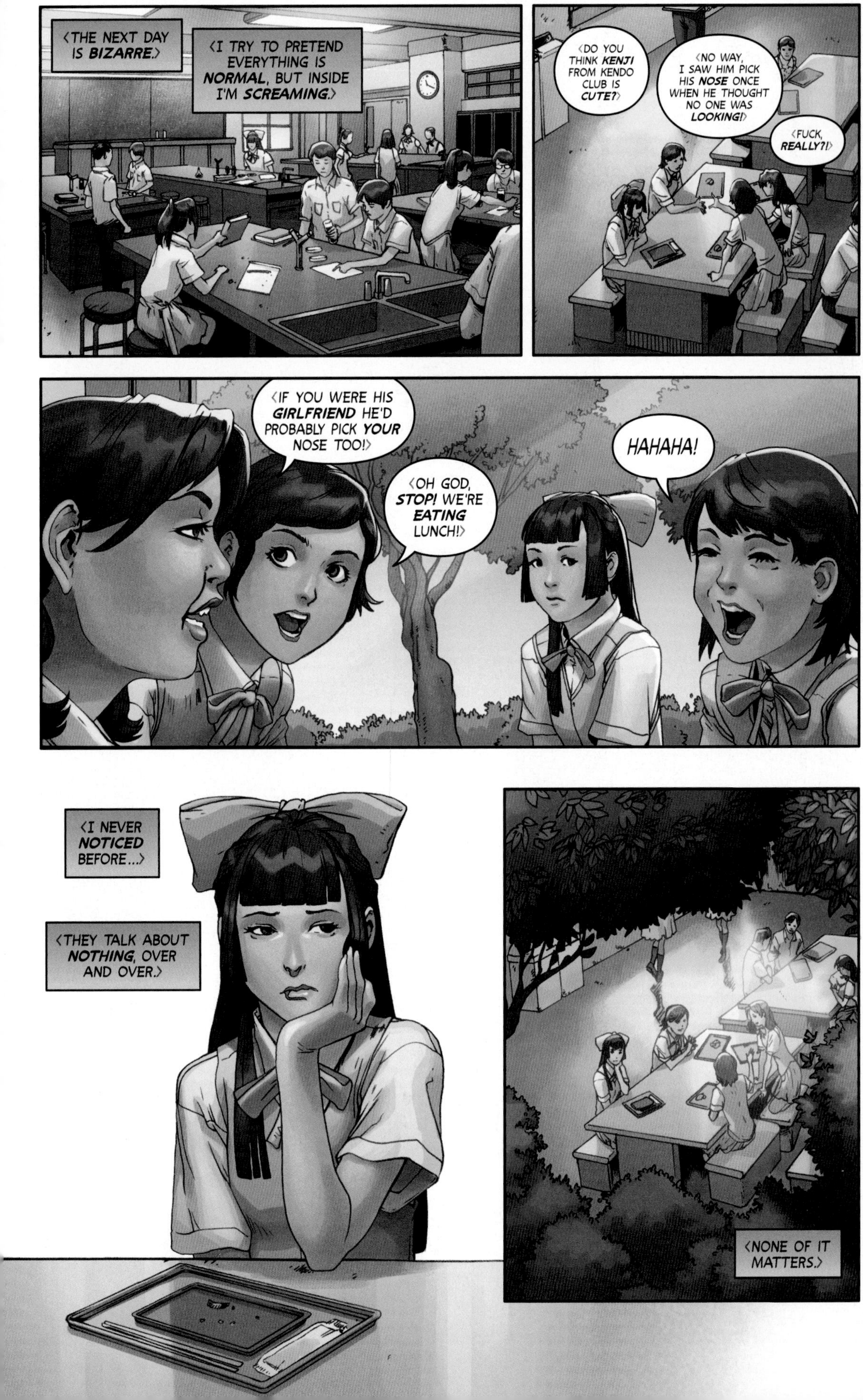

〈THE NEXT DAY IS BIZARRE.〉
〈I TRY TO PRETEND EVERYTHING IS NORMAL, BUT INSIDE I'M SCREAMING.〉
〈DO YOU THINK KENJI FROM KENDO CLUB IS CUTE?〉
〈NO WAY, I SAW HIM PICK HIS NOSE ONCE WHEN HE THOUGHT NO ONE WAS LOOKING!〉
〈FUCK, REALLY?!〉
〈IF YOU WERE HIS GIRLFRIEND HE'D PROBABLY PICK YOUR NOSE TOO!〉
〈OH GOD, STOP! WE'RE EATING LUNCH!〉
HAHAHA!
〈I NEVER NOTICED BEFORE...〉
〈THEY TALK ABOUT NOTHING, OVER AND OVER.〉
〈NONE OF IT MATTERS.〉

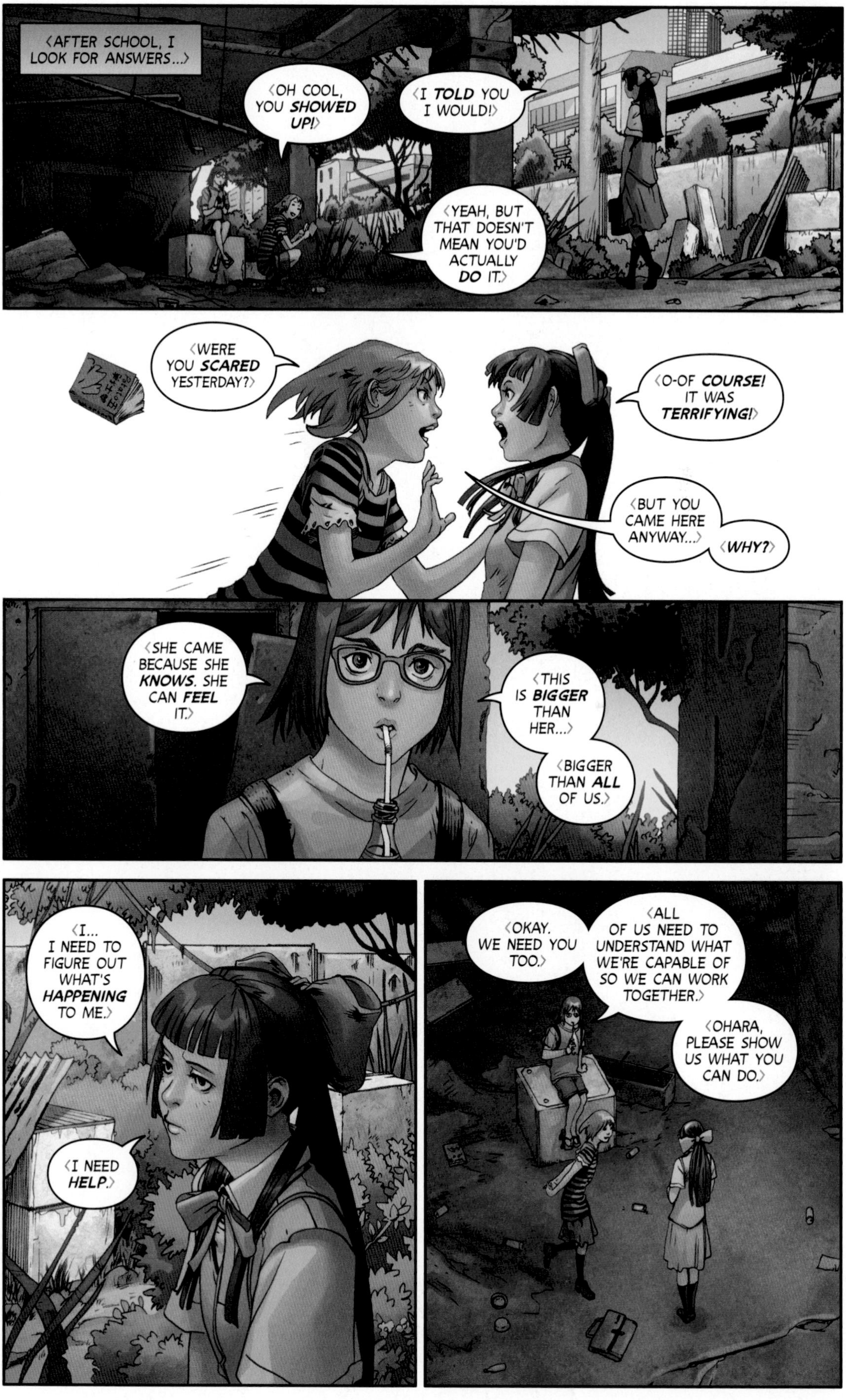
‹AFTER SCHOOL, I LOOK FOR ANSWERS...›
‹OH COOL, YOU **SHOWED** UP!›
‹I **TOLD** YOU I WOULD!›
‹YEAH, BUT THAT DOESN'T MEAN YOU'D ACTUALLY **DO** IT.›
‹WERE YOU **SCARED** YESTERDAY?›
‹O-OF **COURSE!** IT WAS **TERRIFYING!**›
‹BUT YOU CAME HERE ANYWAY...›
‹**WHY?**›
‹SHE CAME BECAUSE SHE **KNOWS**. SHE CAN **FEEL** IT.›
‹THIS IS **BIGGER** THAN HER...›
‹BIGGER THAN **ALL** OF US.›
‹I... I NEED TO FIGURE OUT WHAT'S **HAPPENING** TO ME.›
‹I NEED **HELP**.›
‹OKAY. WE NEED YOU TOO.›
‹ALL OF US NEED TO UNDERSTAND WHAT WE'RE CAPABLE OF SO WE CAN WORK TOGETHER.›
‹OHARA, PLEASE SHOW US WHAT YOU CAN DO.›

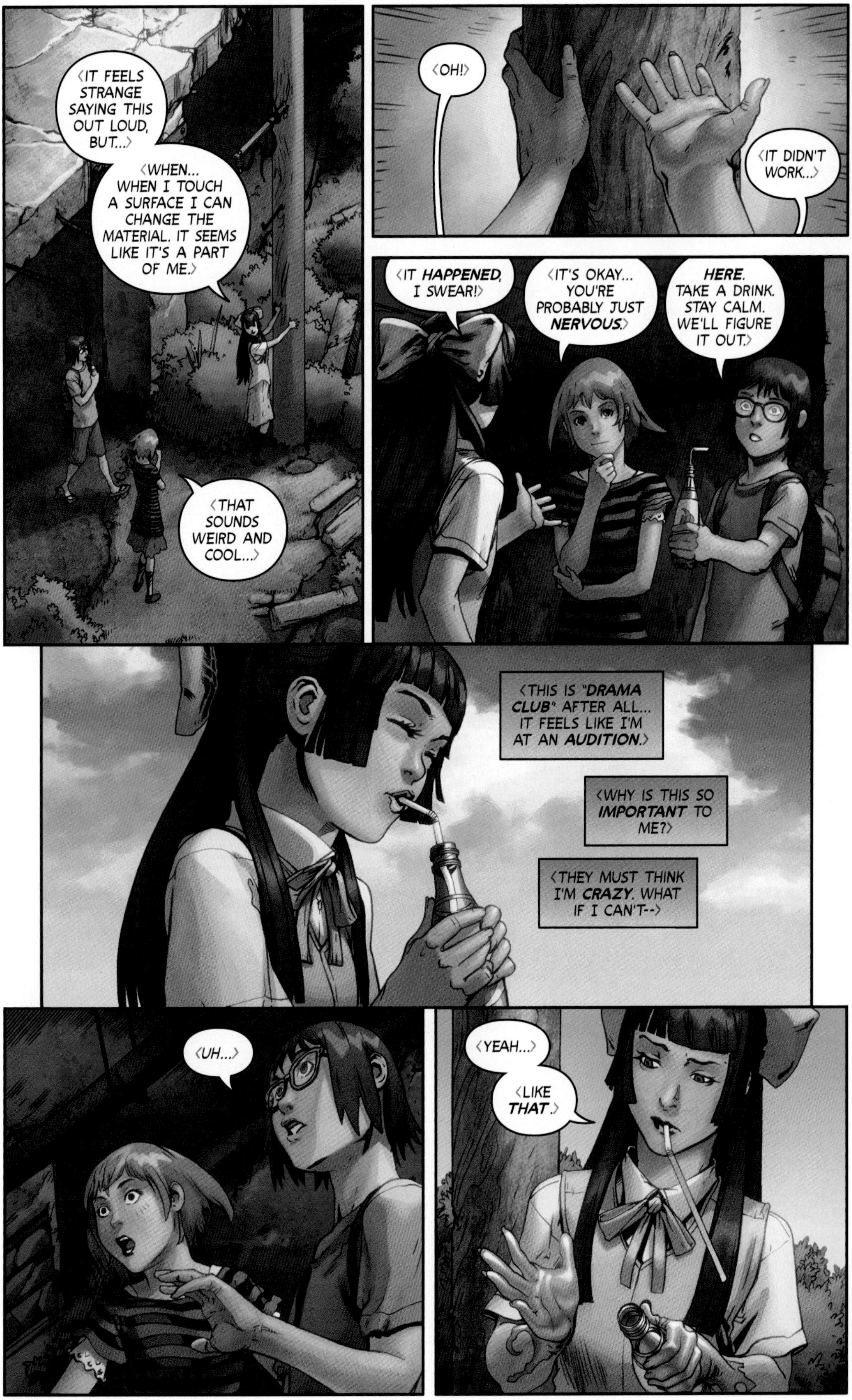

‹IT FEELS STRANGE SAYING THIS OUT LOUD, BUT...›
‹WHEN... WHEN I TOUCH A SURFACE I CAN CHANGE THE MATERIAL. IT SEEMS LIKE IT'S A PART OF ME.›
‹THAT SOUNDS WEIRD AND COOL...›
‹OH!›
‹IT DIDN'T WORK...›
‹IT *HAPPENED*, I SWEAR!›
‹IT'S OKAY... YOU'RE PROBABLY JUST *NERVOUS*.›
HERE. TAKE A DRINK. STAY CALM. WE'LL FIGURE IT OUT.›
‹THIS IS "*DRAMA CLUB*" AFTER ALL... IT FEELS LIKE I'M AT AN *AUDITION*.›
‹WHY IS THIS SO *IMPORTANT* TO ME?›
‹THEY MUST THINK I'M *CRAZY*. WHAT IF I CAN'T--›
‹UH...›
‹YEAH...›
‹LIKE *THAT*.›

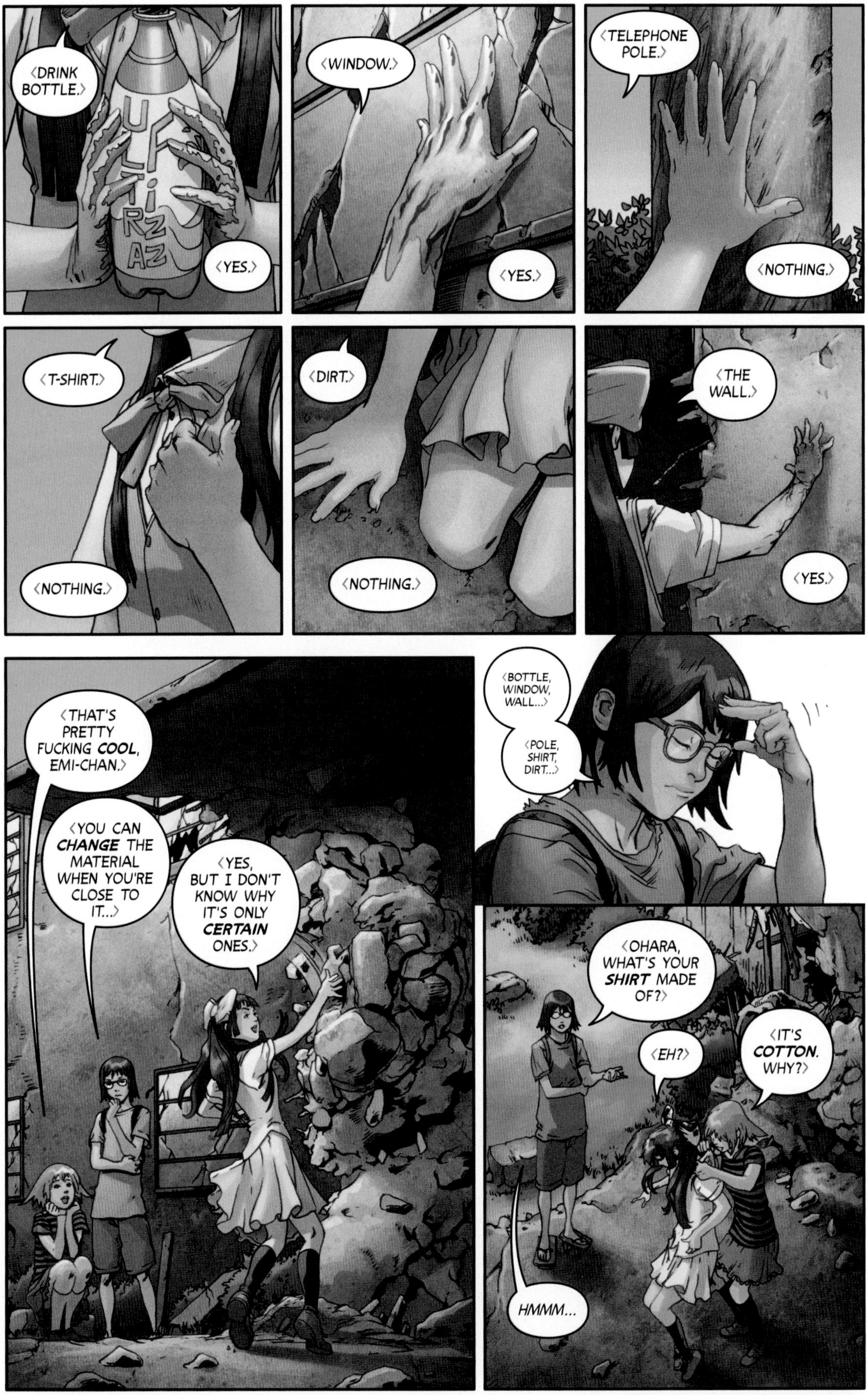
⟨DRINK BOTTLE.⟩
⟨YES.⟩
⟨WINDOW.⟩
⟨YES.⟩
⟨TELEPHONE POLE.⟩
⟨NOTHING.⟩
⟨T-SHIRT.⟩
⟨NOTHING.⟩
⟨DIRT.⟩
⟨NOTHING.⟩
⟨THE WALL.⟩
⟨YES.⟩
⟨THAT'S PRETTY FUCKING **COOL**, EMI-CHAN.⟩
⟨YOU CAN **CHANGE** THE MATERIAL WHEN YOU'RE CLOSE TO IT...⟩
⟨YES, BUT I DON'T KNOW WHY IT'S ONLY **CERTAIN** ONES.⟩
⟨BOTTLE, WINDOW, WALL...⟩
⟨POLE, SHIRT, DIRT...⟩
⟨OHARA, WHAT'S YOUR **SHIRT** MADE OF?⟩
⟨EH?⟩
⟨IT'S **COTTON**. WHY?⟩
HMMM...

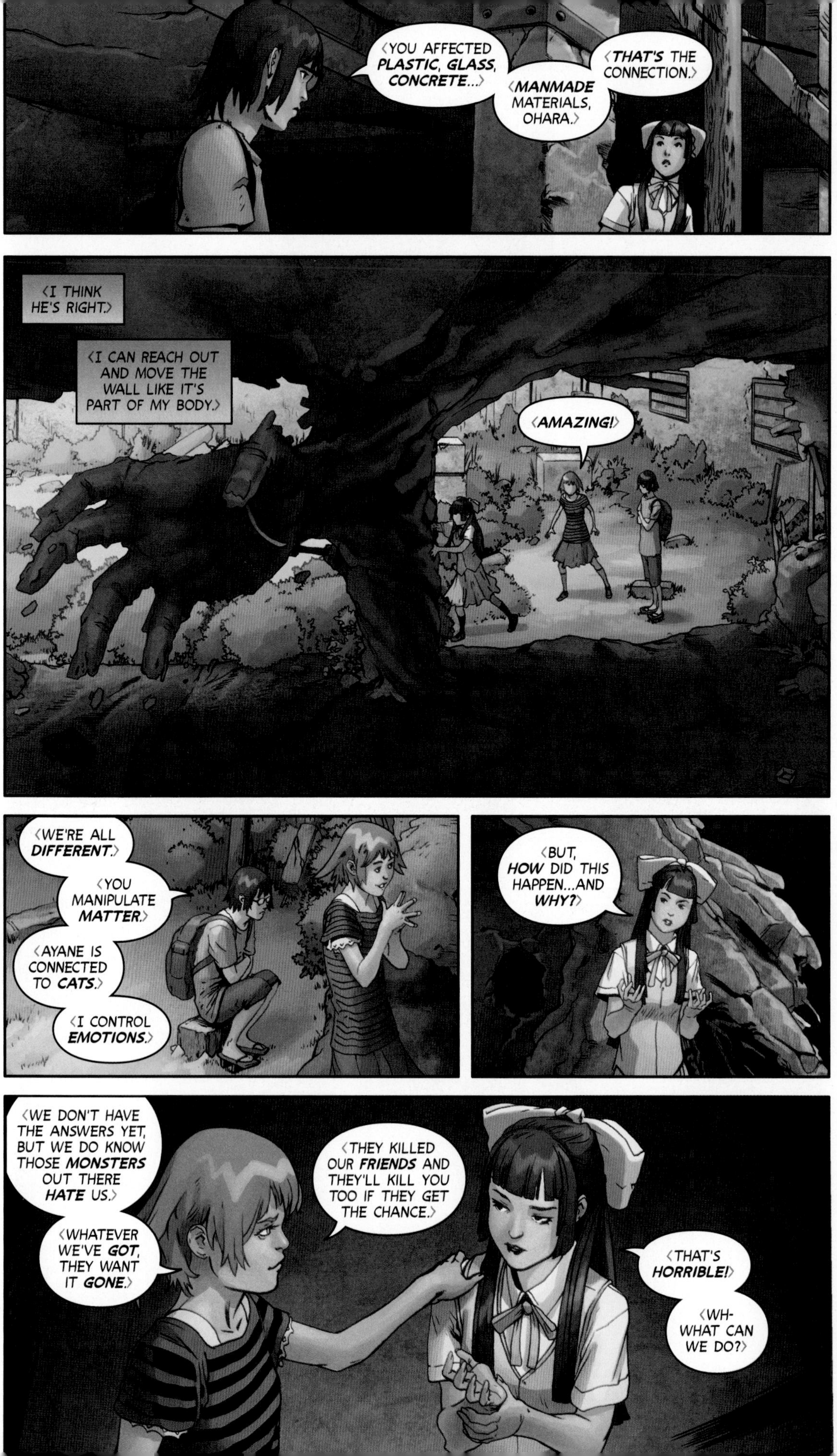

⟨YOU AFFECTED PLASTIC, GLASS, CONCRETE...⟩
⟨MANMADE MATERIALS, OHARA.⟩
⟨THAT'S THE CONNECTION.⟩
⟨I THINK HE'S RIGHT.⟩
⟨I CAN REACH OUT AND MOVE THE WALL LIKE IT'S PART OF MY BODY.⟩
⟨AMAZING!⟩
⟨WE'RE ALL DIFFERENT.⟩
⟨YOU MANIPULATE MATTER.⟩
⟨AYANE IS CONNECTED TO CATS.⟩
⟨I CONTROL EMOTIONS.⟩
⟨BUT, HOW DID THIS HAPPEN...AND WHY?⟩
⟨WE DON'T HAVE THE ANSWERS YET, BUT WE DO KNOW THOSE MONSTERS OUT THERE HATE US.⟩
⟨WHATEVER WE'VE GOT, THEY WANT IT GONE.⟩
⟨THEY KILLED OUR FRIENDS AND THEY'LL KILL YOU TOO IF THEY GET THE CHANCE.⟩
⟨THAT'S HORRIBLE!⟩
⟨WH- WHAT CAN WE DO?⟩

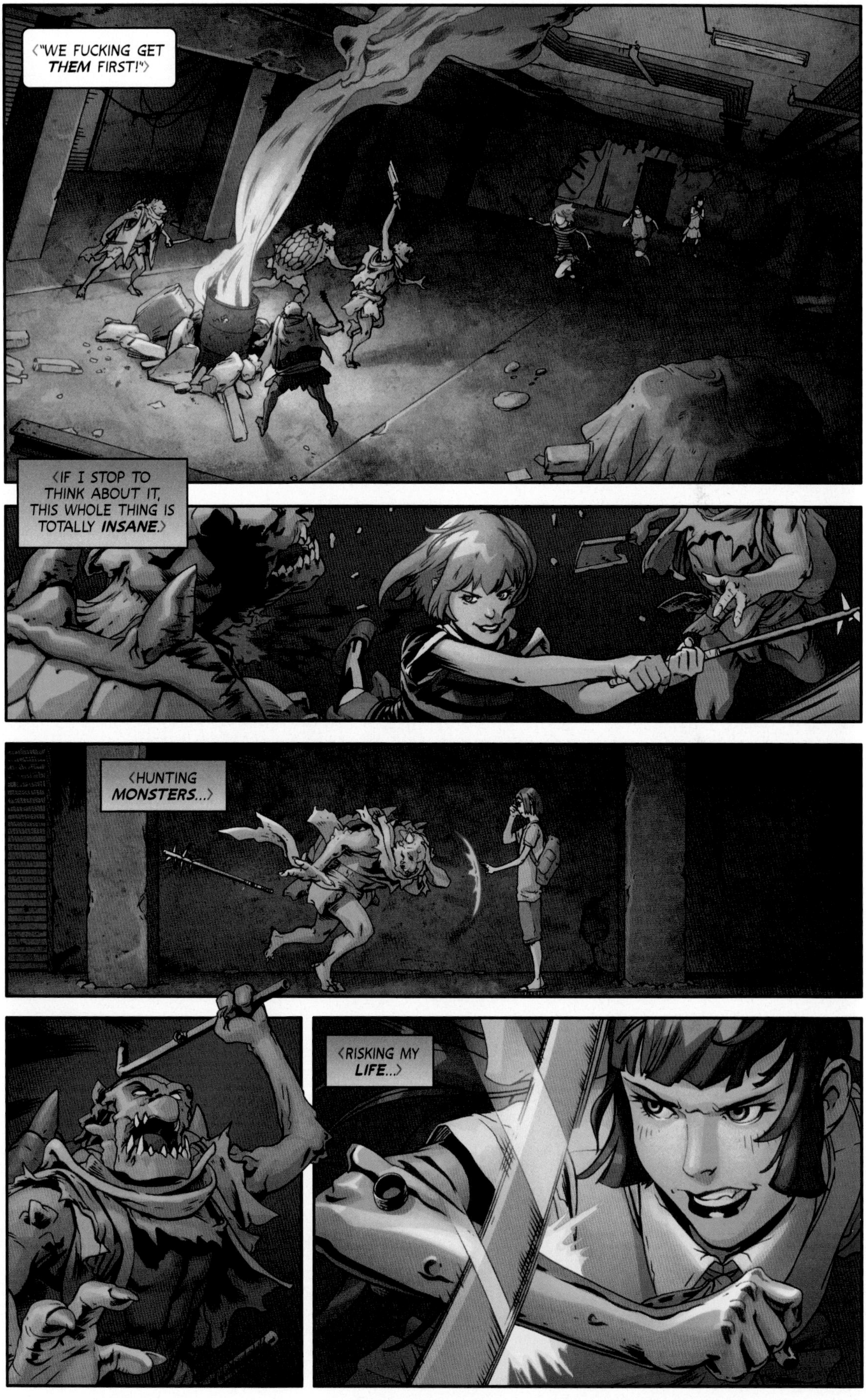
⟨"WE FUCKING GET THEM FIRST!"⟩
⟨IF I STOP TO THINK ABOUT IT, THIS WHOLE THING IS TOTALLY INSANE.⟩
⟨HUNTING MONSTERS...⟩
⟨RISKING MY LIFE...⟩

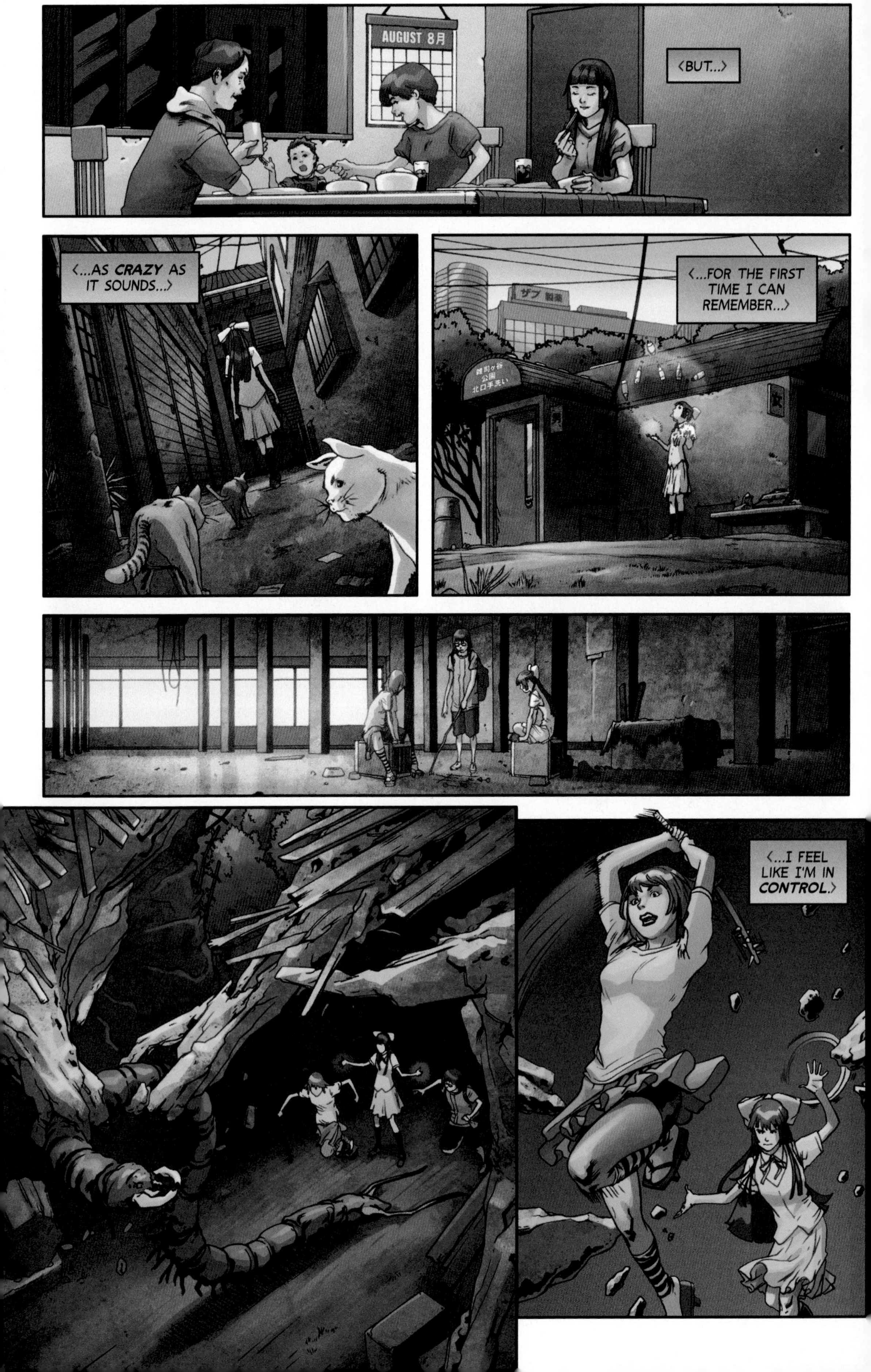
AUGUST 8月
‹BUT...›
‹...AS CRAZY AS IT SOUNDS...›
‹...FOR THE FIRST TIME I CAN REMEMBER...›
雑司ヶ谷
公園
北口手洗い
‹...I FEEL LIKE I'M IN CONTROL.›

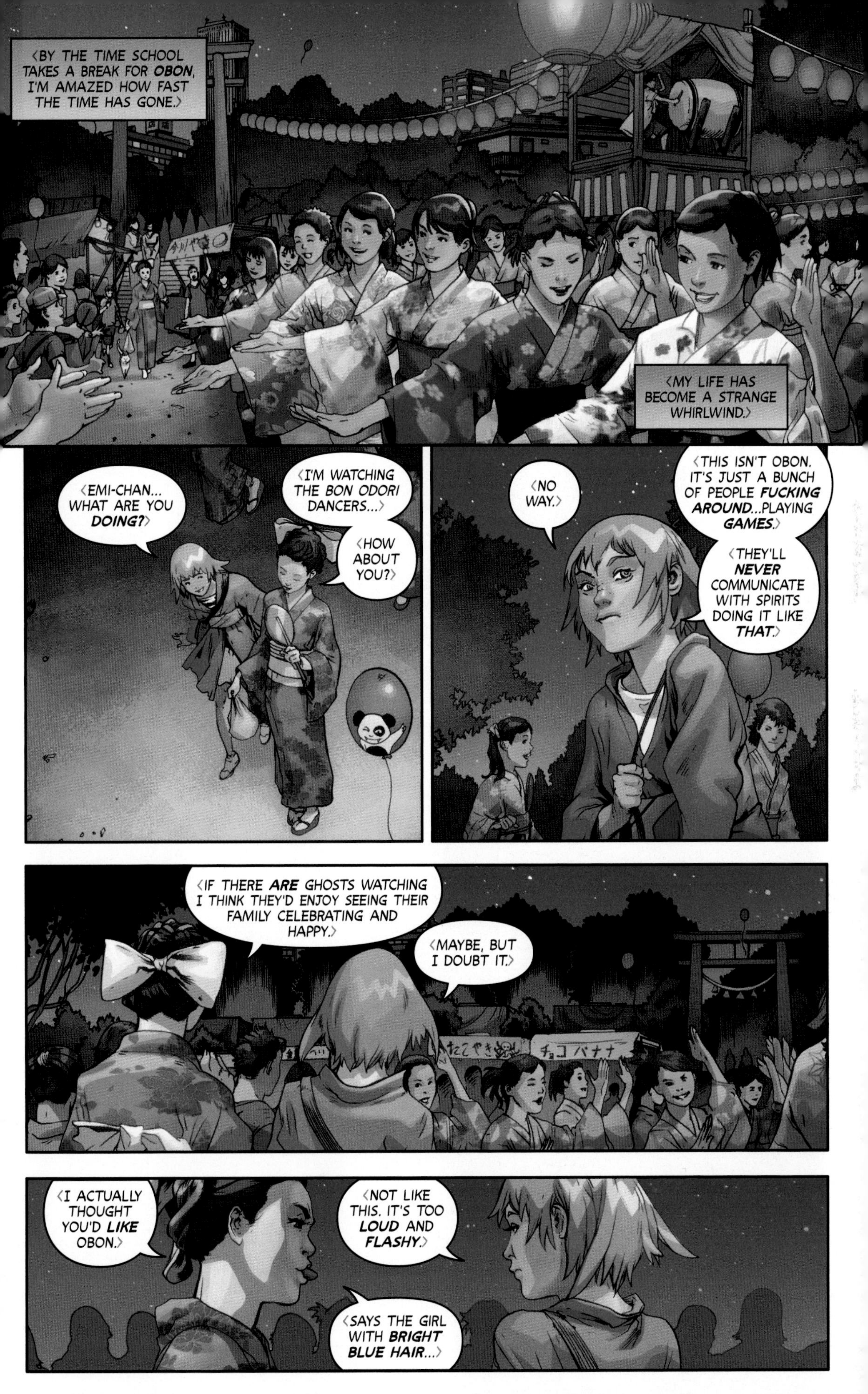
‹BY THE TIME SCHOOL TAKES A BREAK FOR OBON, I'M AMAZED HOW FAST THE TIME HAS GONE.›
‹MY LIFE HAS BECOME A STRANGE WHIRLWIND.›
‹EMI-CHAN... WHAT ARE YOU DOING?›
‹I'M WATCHING THE BON ODORI DANCERS...›
‹HOW ABOUT YOU?›
‹NO WAY.›
‹THIS ISN'T OBON. IT'S JUST A BUNCH OF PEOPLE FUCKING AROUND...PLAYING GAMES.›
‹THEY'LL NEVER COMMUNICATE WITH SPIRITS DOING IT LIKE THAT.›
‹IF THERE ARE GHOSTS WATCHING I THINK THEY'D ENJOY SEEING THEIR FAMILY CELEBRATING AND HAPPY.›
‹MAYBE, BUT I DOUBT IT.›
たこやき
チョコ バナナ
‹I ACTUALLY THOUGHT YOU'D LIKE OBON.›
‹NOT LIKE THIS. IT'S TOO LOUD AND FLASHY.›
‹SAYS THE GIRL WITH BRIGHT BLUE HAIR...›

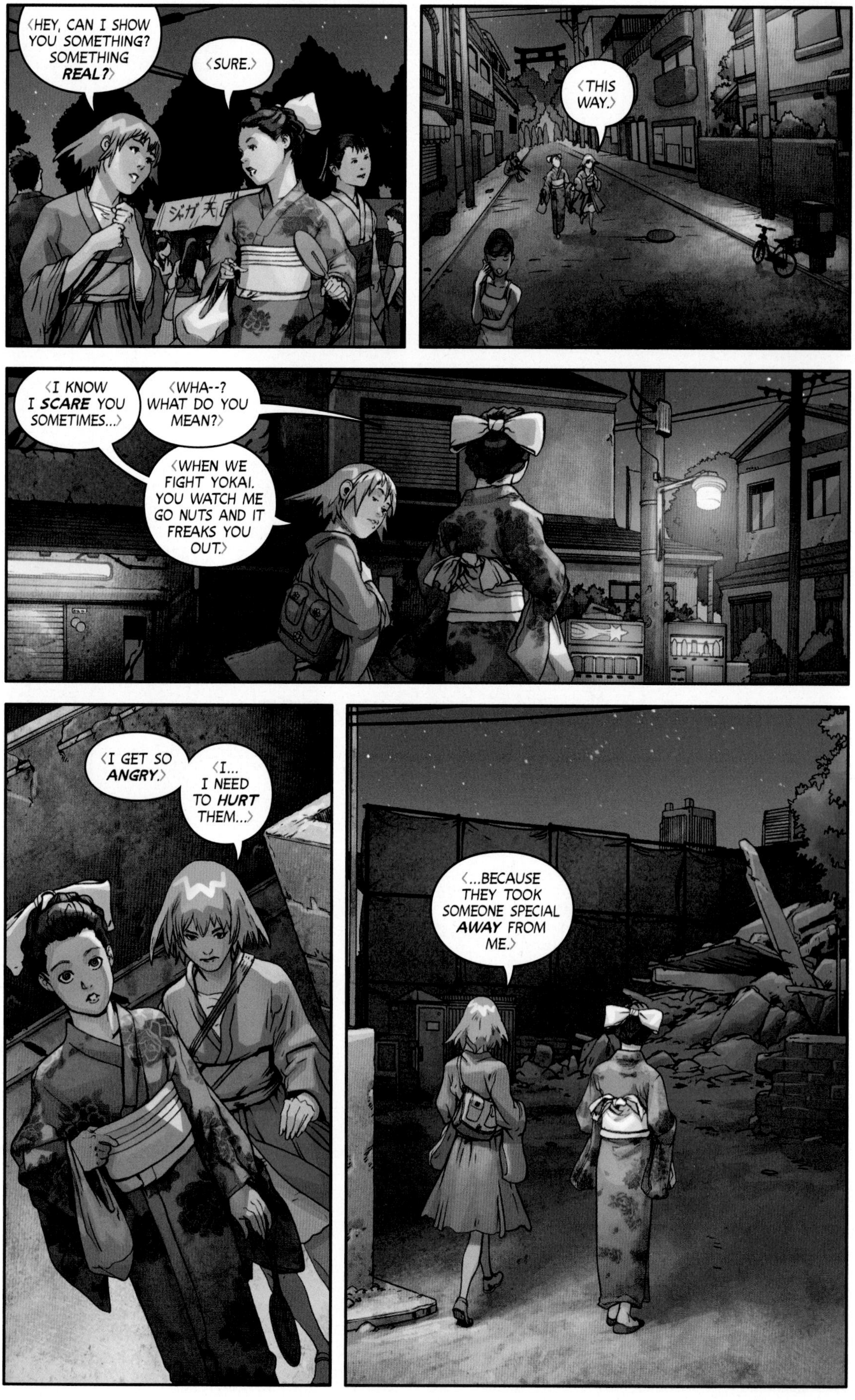
‹HEY, CAN I SHOW YOU SOMETHING? SOMETHING **REAL?**›
‹SURE.›
‹THIS WAY.›
‹I KNOW I **SCARE** YOU SOMETIMES...›
‹WHA--? WHAT DO YOU MEAN?›
‹WHEN WE FIGHT YOKAI. YOU WATCH ME GO NUTS AND IT FREAKS YOU OUT.›
‹I GET SO **ANGRY**.›
‹I... I NEED TO **HURT** THEM...›
‹...BECAUSE THEY TOOK SOMEONE SPECIAL **AWAY** FROM ME.›

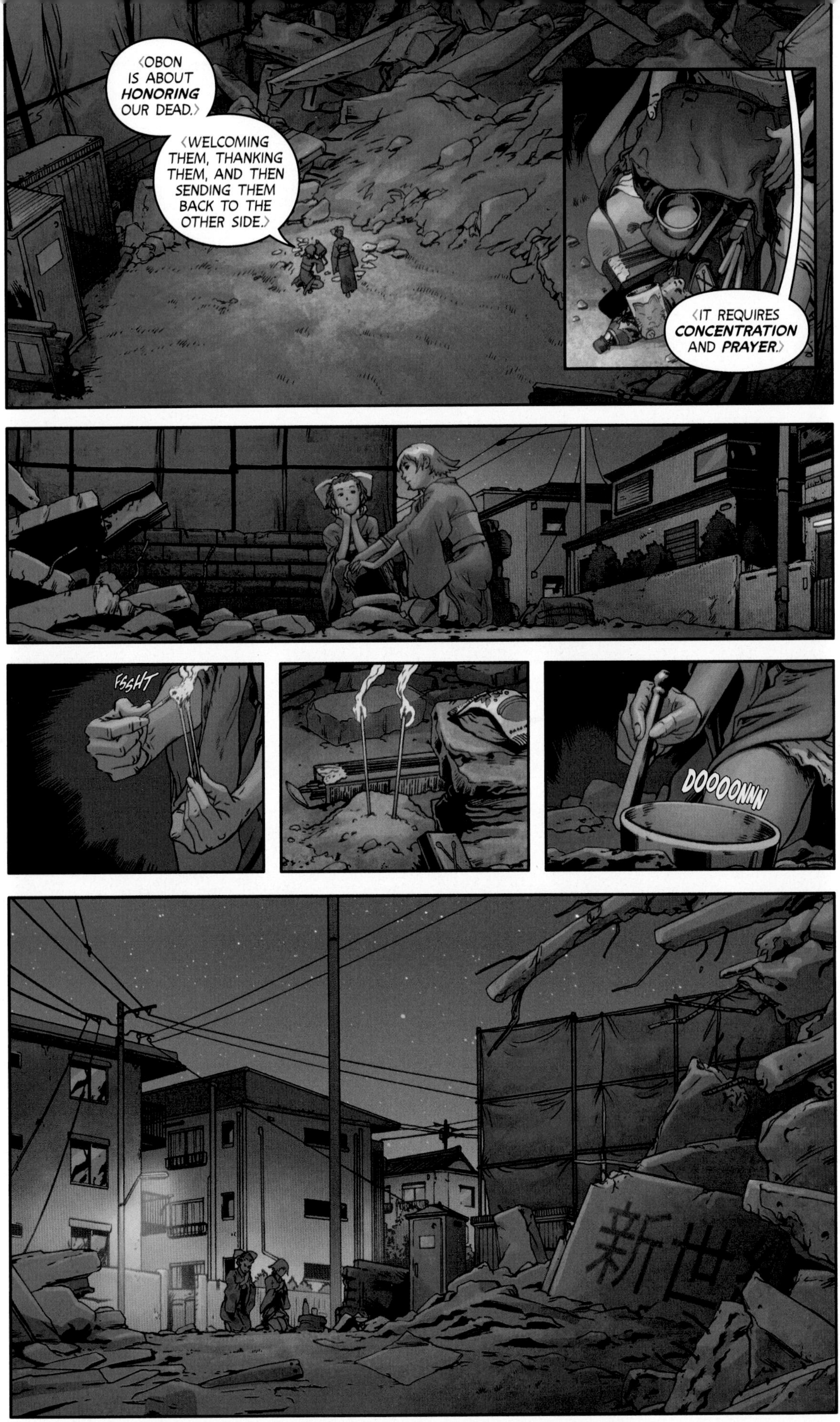
<OBON IS ABOUT HONORING OUR DEAD.>
<WELCOMING THEM, THANKING THEM, AND THEN SENDING THEM BACK TO THE OTHER SIDE.>
<IT REQUIRES CONCENTRATION AND PRAYER.>
FSSHT
DOOOONNN
新世

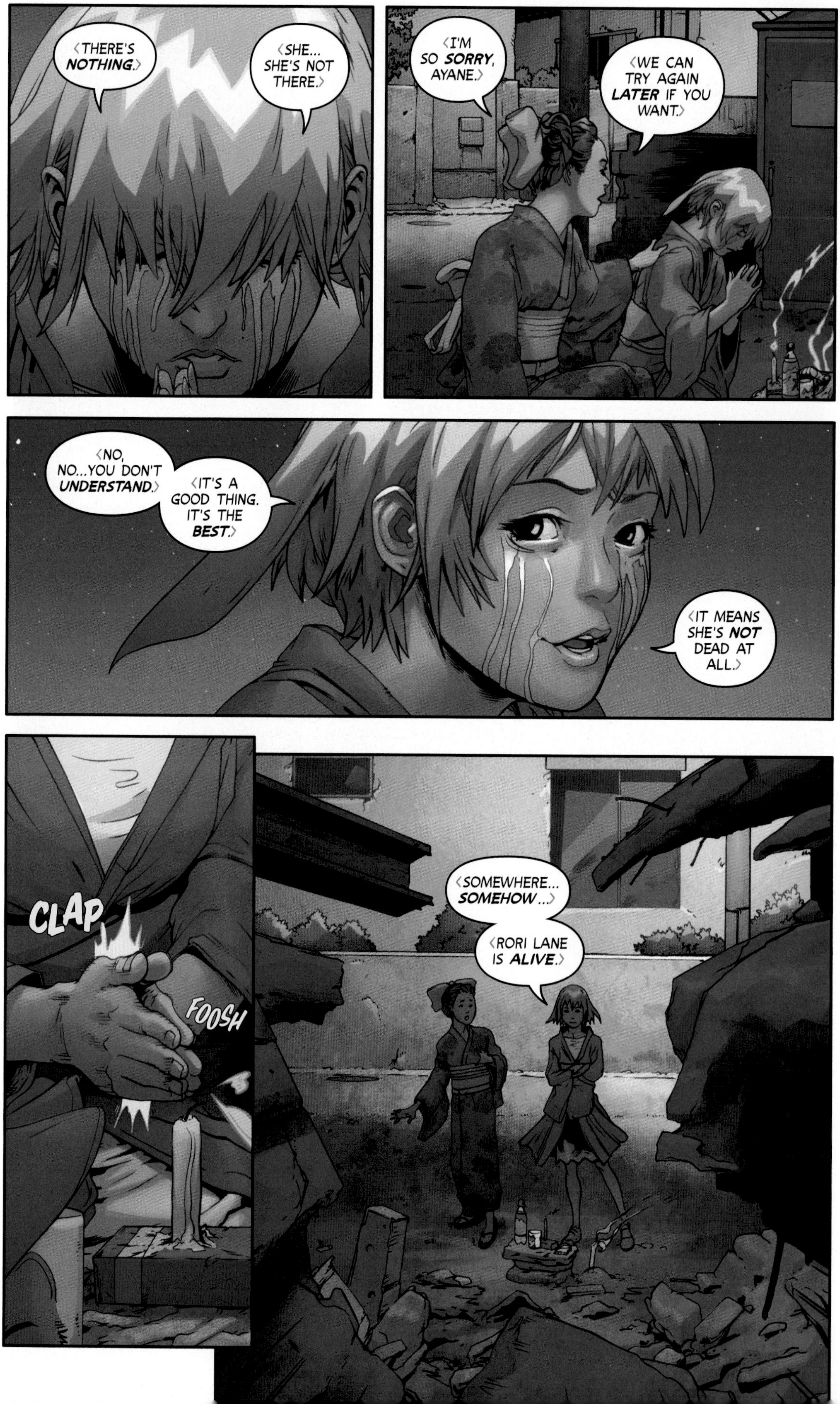

⟨THERE'S NOTHING.⟩
⟨SHE... SHE'S NOT THERE.⟩
⟨I'M SO SORRY, AYANE.⟩
⟨WE CAN TRY AGAIN LATER IF YOU WANT.⟩
⟨NO, NO...YOU DON'T UNDERSTAND.⟩
⟨IT'S A GOOD THING. IT'S THE BEST.⟩
⟨IT MEANS SHE'S NOT DEAD AT ALL.⟩
CLAP
FOOSH
⟨SOMEWHERE... SOMEHOW...⟩
⟨RORI LANE IS ALIVE.⟩

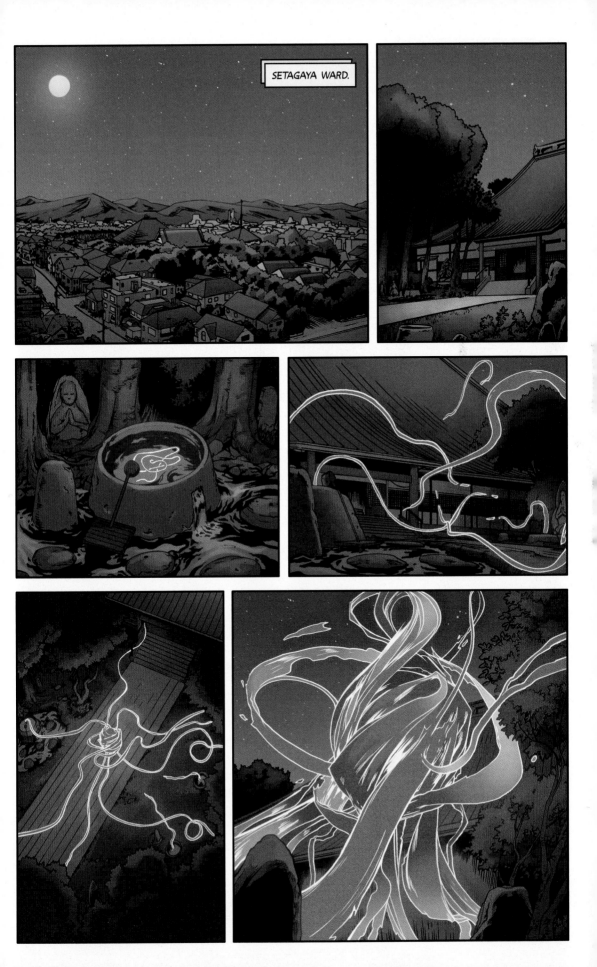

SETAGAYA WARD.

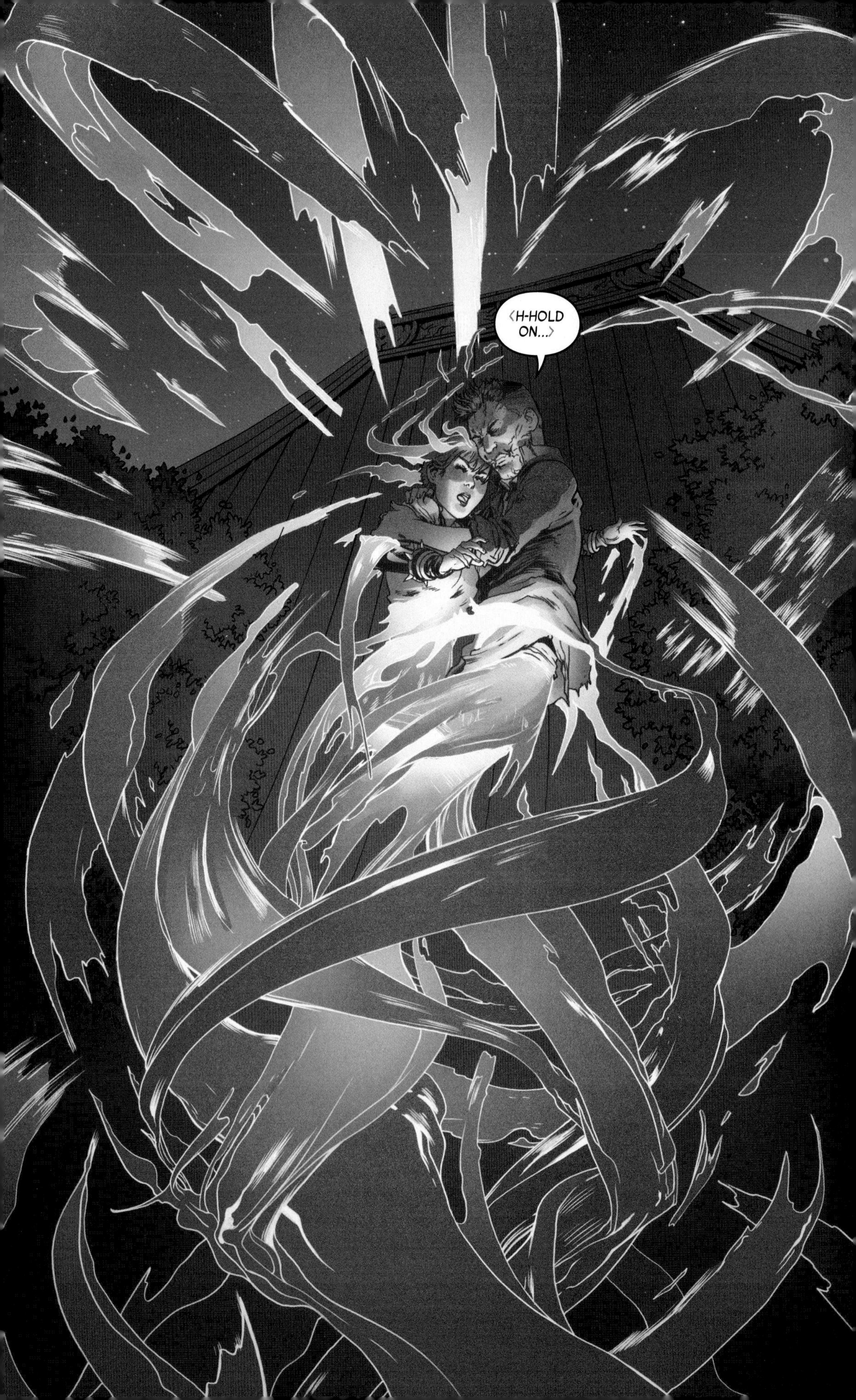
‹H-HOLD ON...›

Chapter Eight

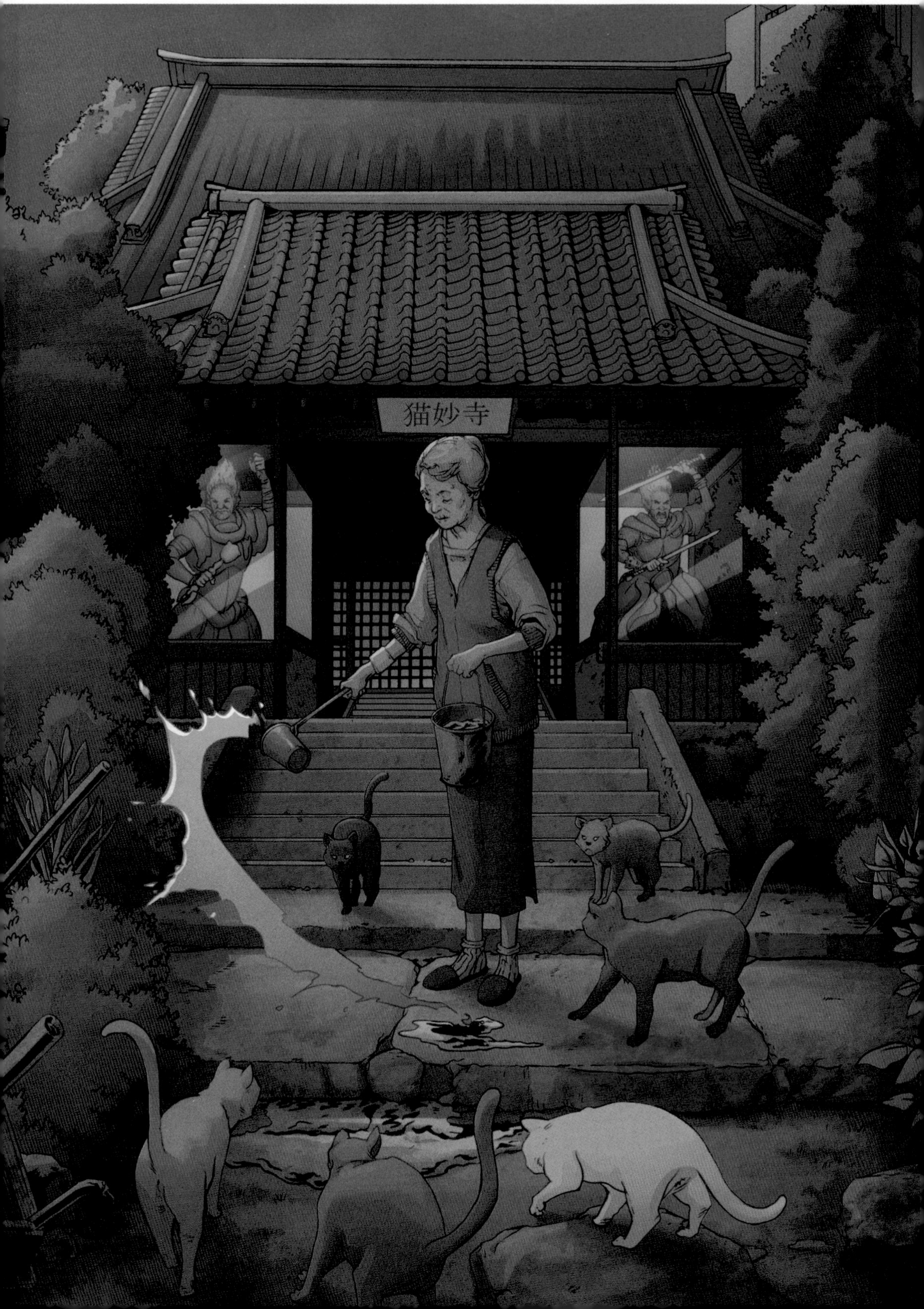
猫妙寺

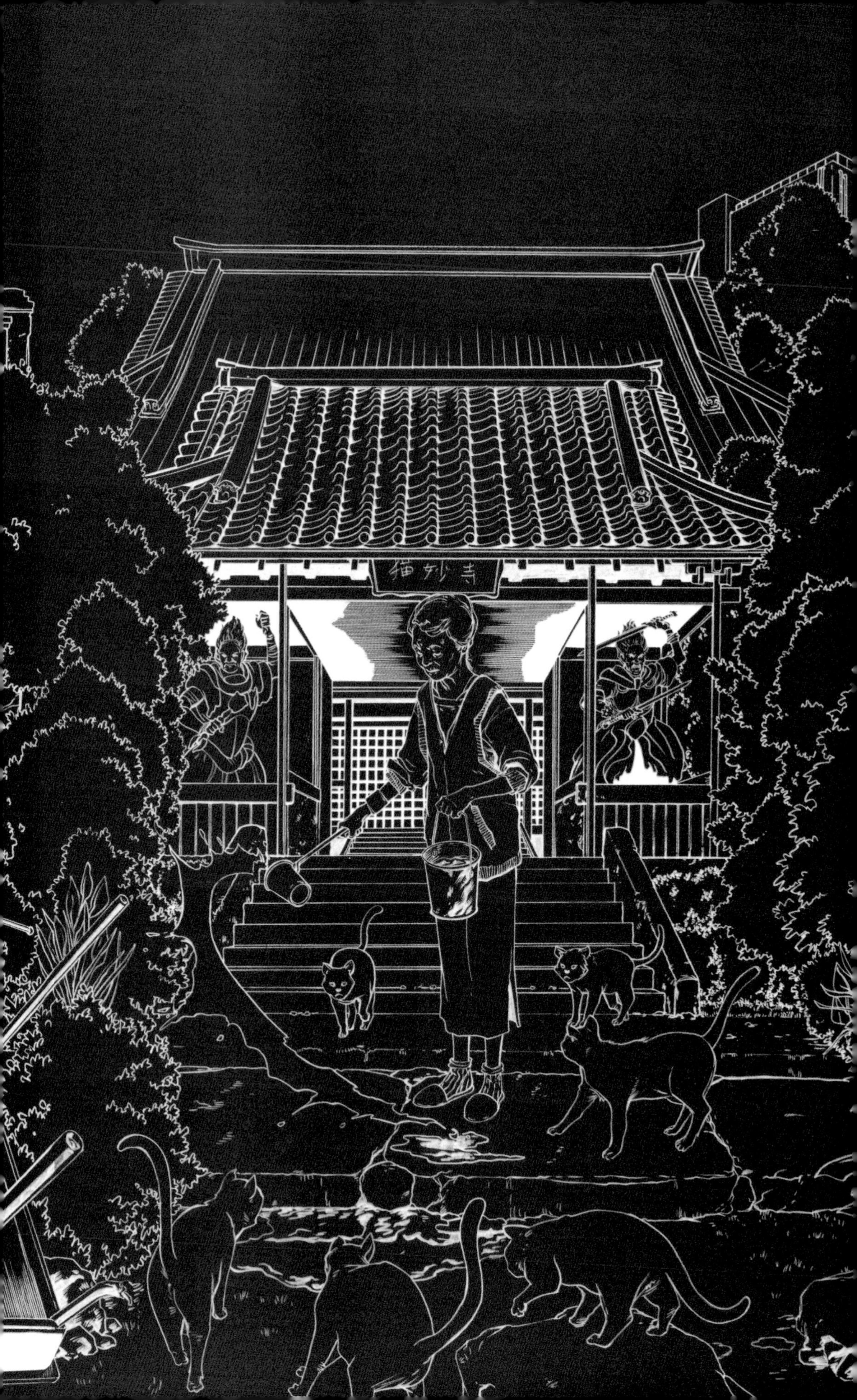
猫妙寺

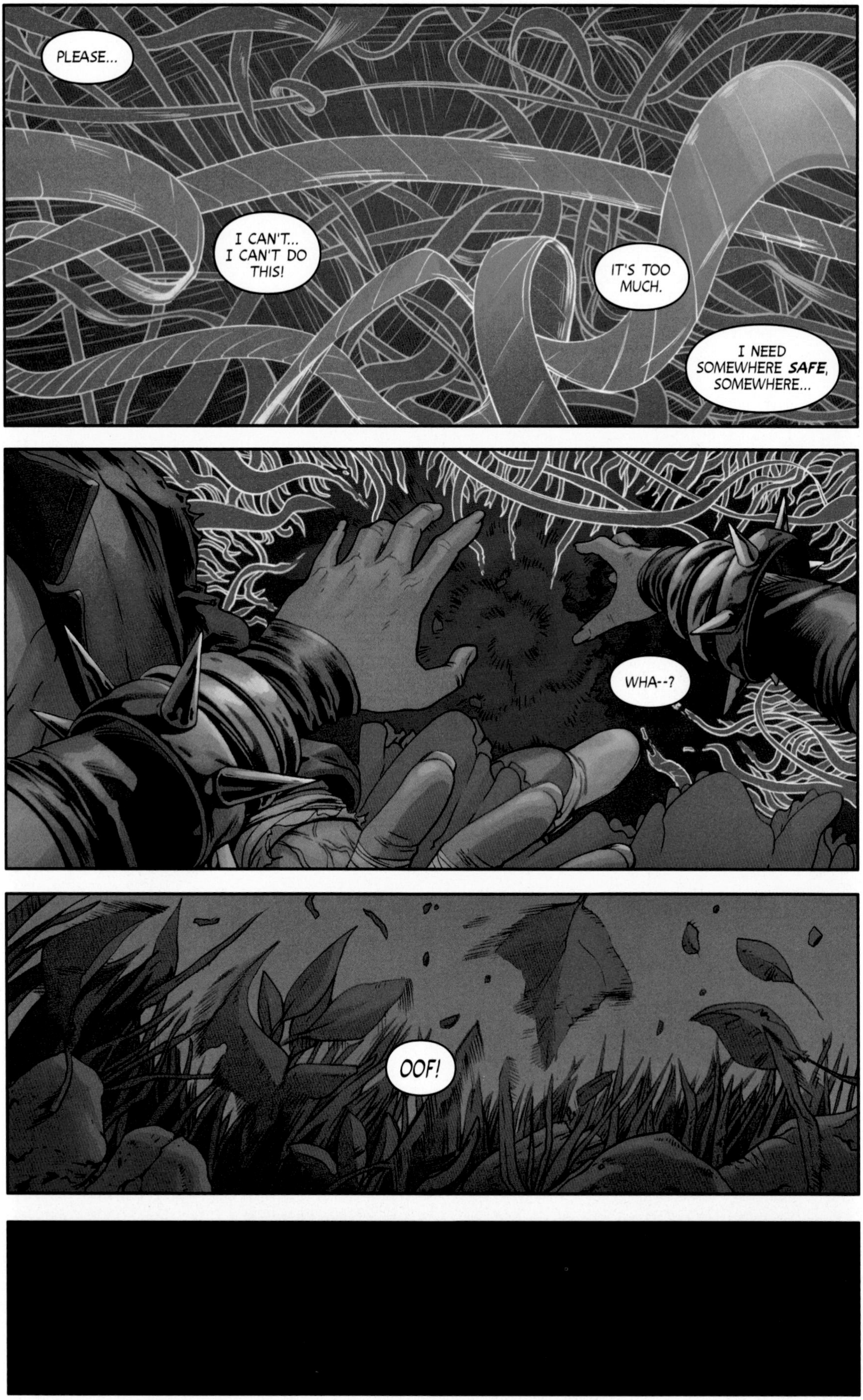
PLEASE...
I CAN'T... I CAN'T DO THIS!
IT'S TOO MUCH.
I NEED SOMEWHERE **SAFE**, SOMEWHERE...
WHA--?
OOF!

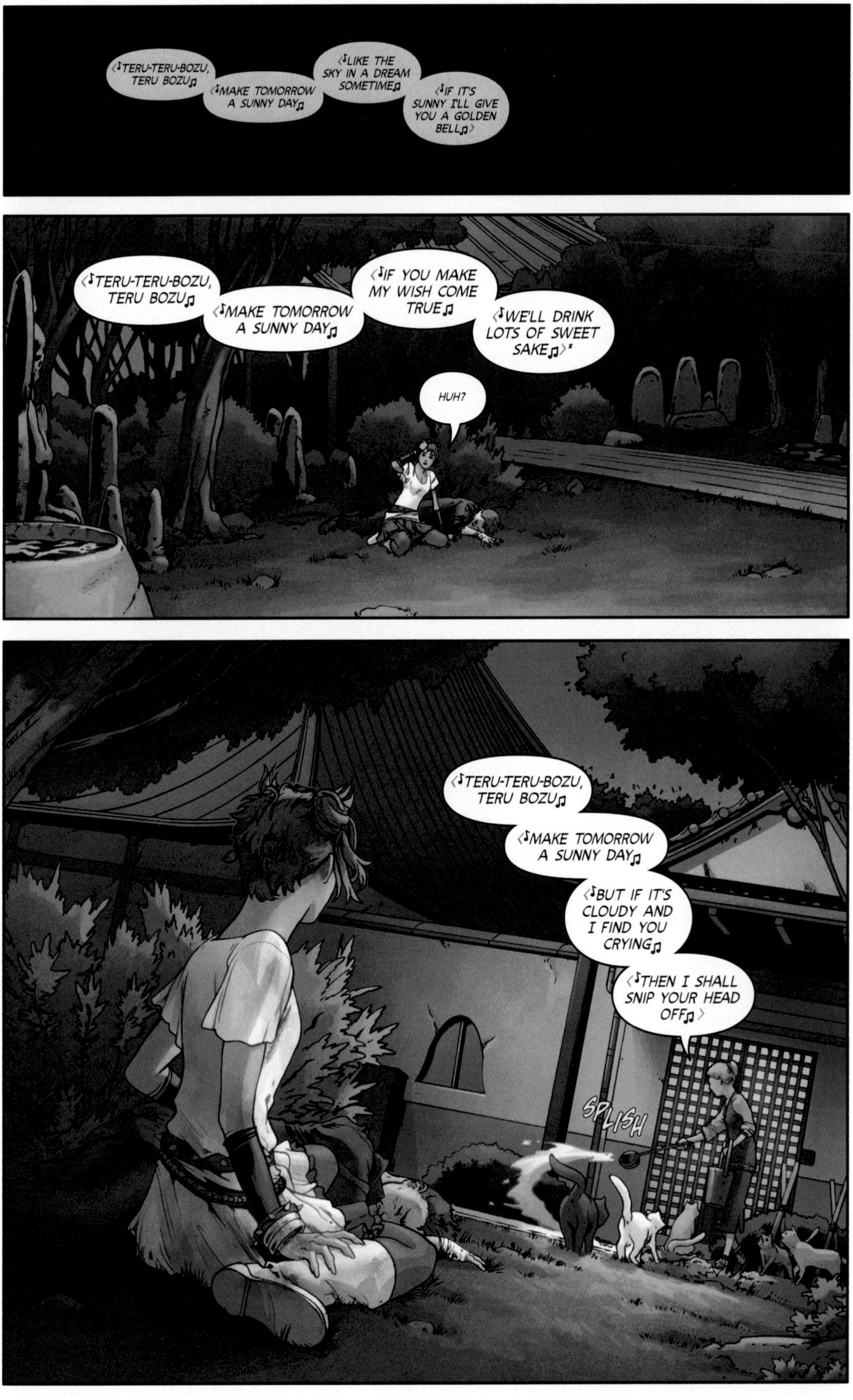
<♪TERU-TERU-BOZU, TERU BOZU♫
♪MAKE TOMORROW A SUNNY DAY♫
♪LIKE THE SKY IN A DREAM SOMETIME♫
♪IF IT'S SUNNY I'LL GIVE YOU A GOLDEN BELL♫>
<♪TERU-TERU-BOZU, TERU BOZU♫
♪MAKE TOMORROW A SUNNY DAY♫
♪IF YOU MAKE MY WISH COME TRUE♫
♪WE'LL DRINK LOTS OF SWEET SAKE♫>*
HUH?
<♪TERU-TERU-BOZU, TERU BOZU♫
♪MAKE TOMORROW A SUNNY DAY♫
♪BUT IF IT'S CLOUDY AND I FIND YOU CRYING♫
♪THEN I SHALL SNIP YOUR HEAD OFF♫>
SPLISH

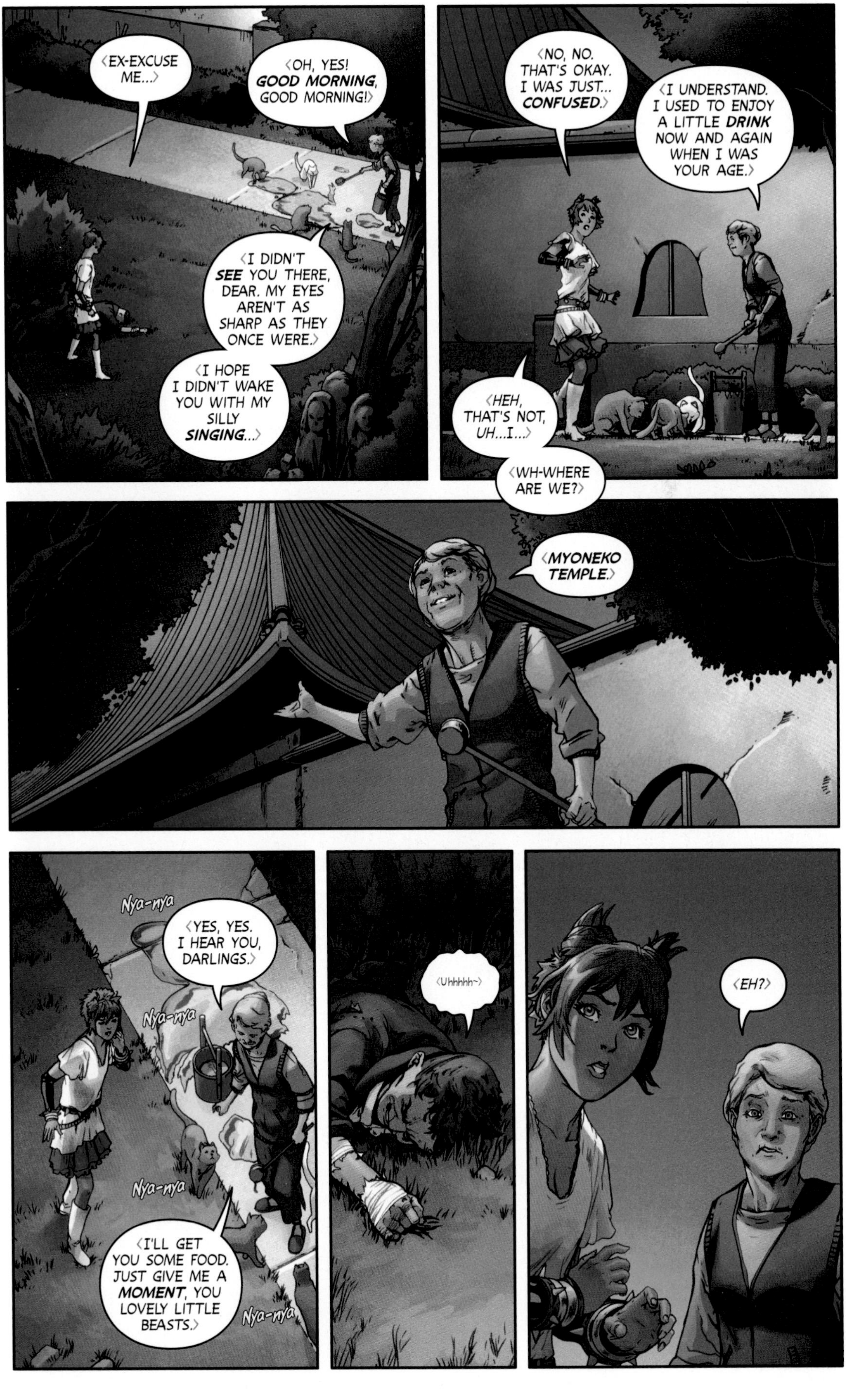
⟨EX-EXCUSE ME...⟩
⟨OH, YES! GOOD MORNING, GOOD MORNING!⟩
⟨I DIDN'T SEE YOU THERE, DEAR. MY EYES AREN'T AS SHARP AS THEY ONCE WERE.⟩
⟨I HOPE I DIDN'T WAKE YOU WITH MY SILLY SINGING...⟩
⟨NO, NO. THAT'S OKAY. I WAS JUST... CONFUSED.⟩
⟨I UNDERSTAND. I USED TO ENJOY A LITTLE DRINK NOW AND AGAIN WHEN I WAS YOUR AGE.⟩
⟨HEH, THAT'S NOT, UH...I...⟩
⟨WH-WHERE ARE WE?⟩
⟨MYONEKO TEMPLE.⟩
Nya-nya
⟨YES, YES. I HEAR YOU, DARLINGS.⟩
Nya-nya
Nya-nya
⟨I'LL GET YOU SOME FOOD. JUST GIVE ME A MOMENT, YOU LOVELY LITTLE BEASTS.⟩
Nya-nya
⟨Uhhhhh~⟩
⟨EH?⟩

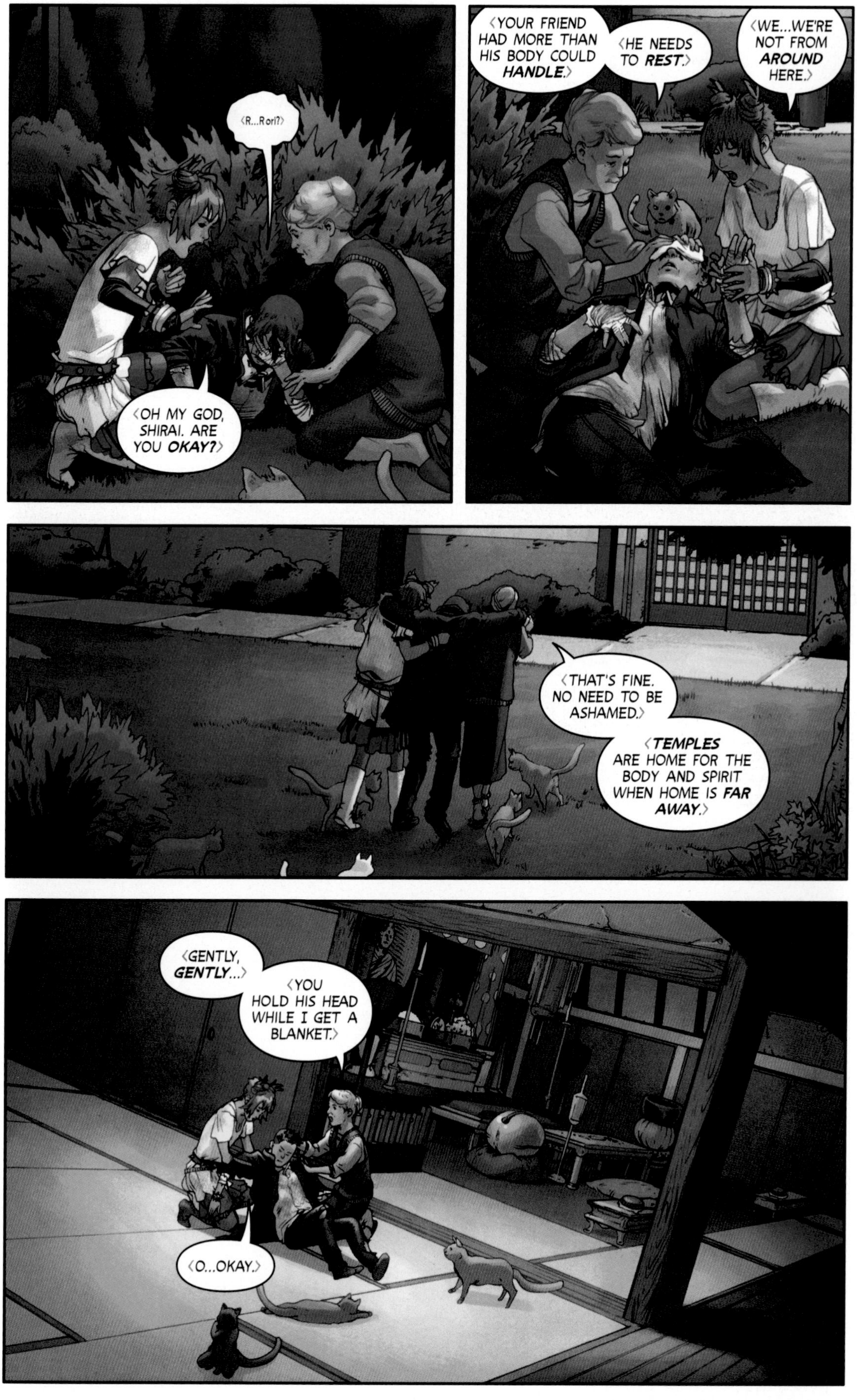
〈R...Rori?〉
〈OH MY GOD, SHIRAI. ARE YOU OKAY?〉
〈YOUR FRIEND HAD MORE THAN HIS BODY COULD HANDLE.〉
〈HE NEEDS TO REST.〉
〈WE...WE'RE NOT FROM AROUND HERE.〉
〈THAT'S FINE. NO NEED TO BE ASHAMED.〉
〈TEMPLES ARE HOME FOR THE BODY AND SPIRIT WHEN HOME IS FAR AWAY.〉
〈GENTLY, GENTLY...〉
〈YOU HOLD HIS HEAD WHILE I GET A BLANKET.〉
〈O...OKAY.〉

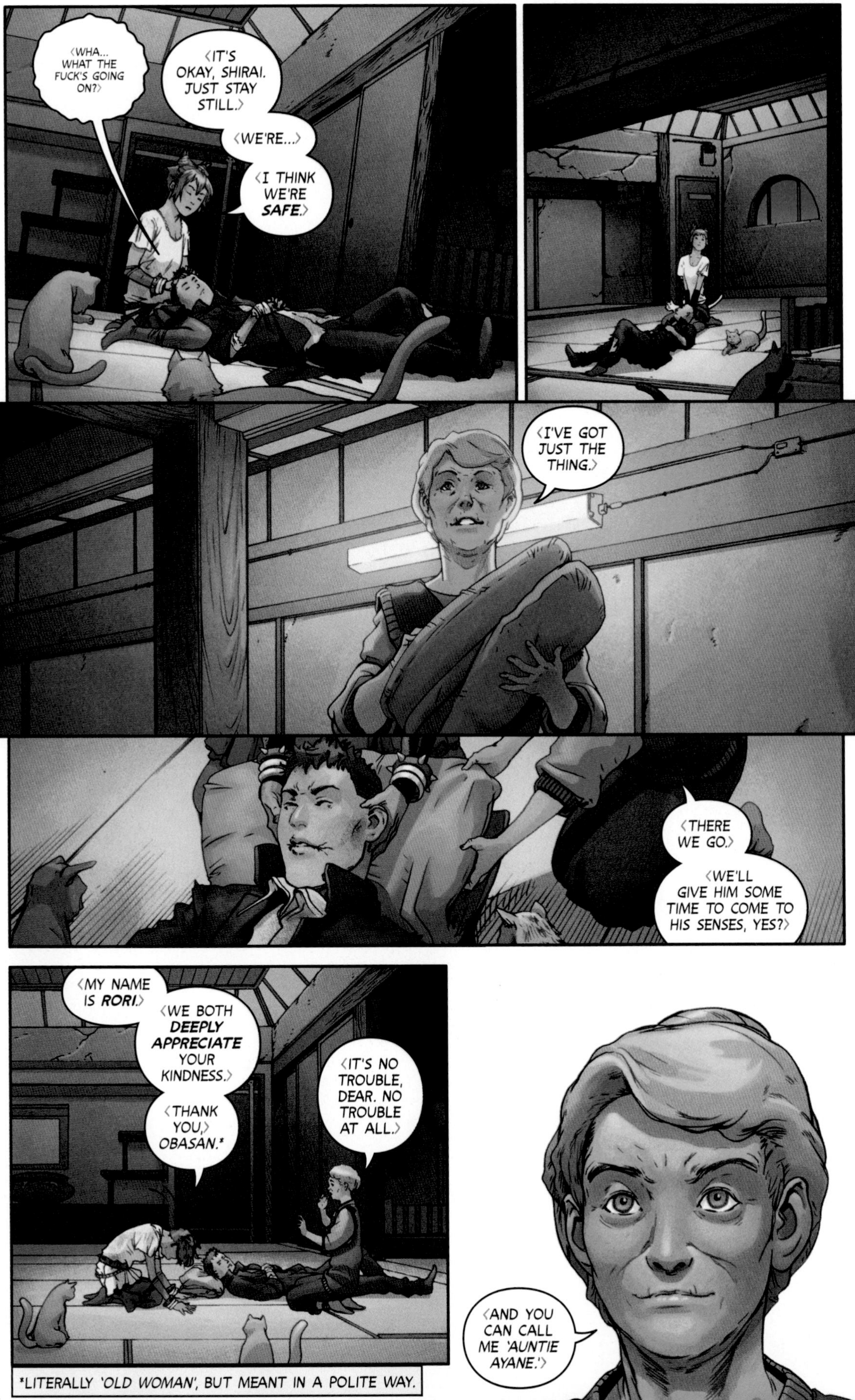
‹WHA... WHAT THE FUCK'S GOING ON?›
‹IT'S OKAY, SHIRAI. JUST STAY STILL.›
‹WE'RE...›
‹I THINK WE'RE *SAFE*.›
‹I'VE GOT JUST THE THING.›
‹THERE WE GO.›
‹WE'LL GIVE HIM SOME TIME TO COME TO HIS SENSES, YES?›
‹MY NAME IS **RORI**.›
‹WE BOTH **DEEPLY APPRECIATE** YOUR KINDNESS.›
‹THANK YOU, *OBASAN*.*›
‹IT'S NO TROUBLE, DEAR. NO TROUBLE AT ALL.›
*LITERALLY *'OLD WOMAN'*, BUT MEANT IN A POLITE WAY.
‹AND YOU CAN CALL ME *'AUNTIE AYANE.'*›

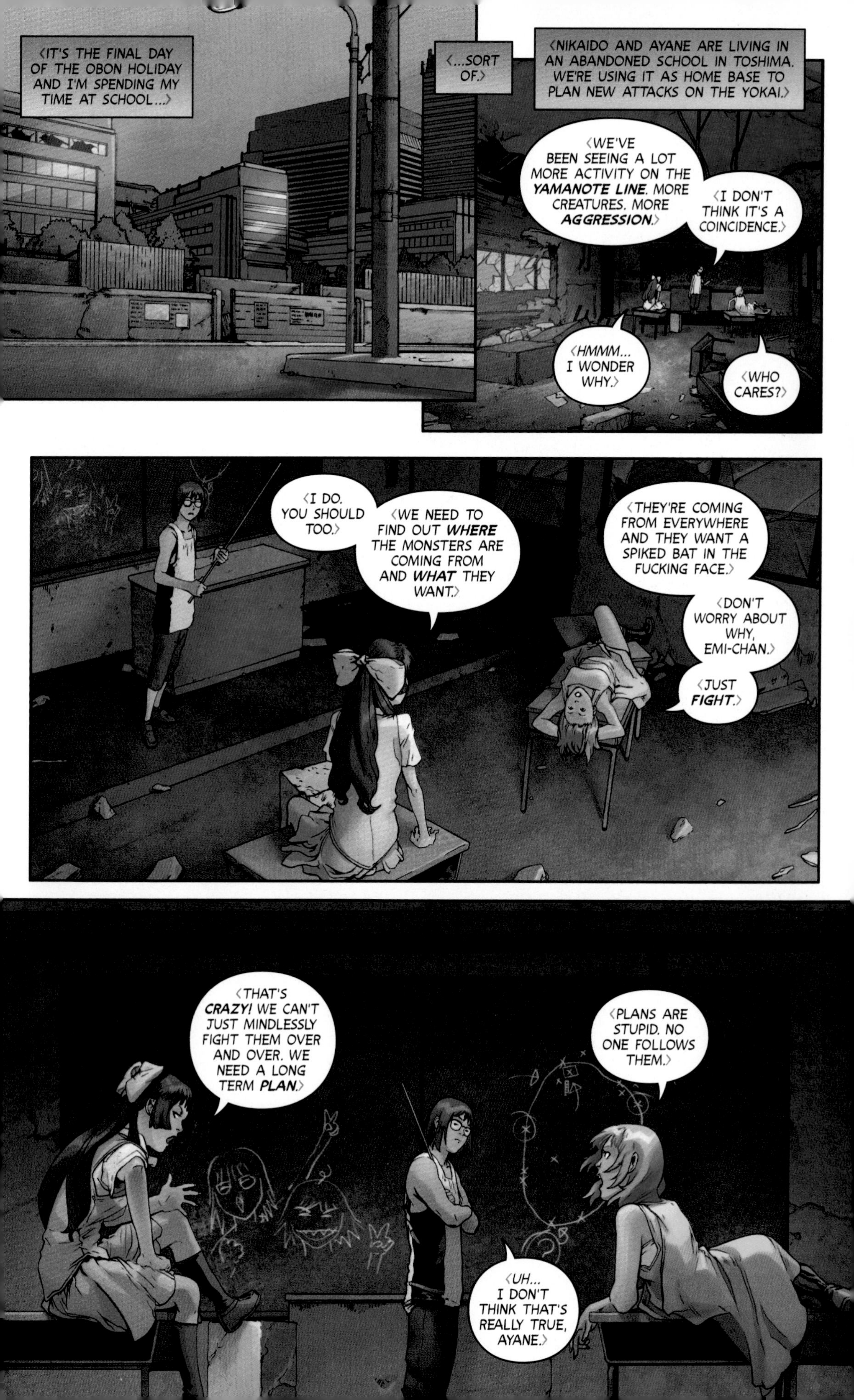
<IT'S THE FINAL DAY OF THE OBON HOLIDAY AND I'M SPENDING MY TIME AT SCHOOL...>
<...SORT OF.>
<NIKAIDO AND AYANE ARE LIVING IN AN ABANDONED SCHOOL IN TOSHIMA. WE'RE USING IT AS HOME BASE TO PLAN NEW ATTACKS ON THE YOKAI.>
<WE'VE BEEN SEEING A LOT MORE ACTIVITY ON THE YAMANOTE LINE. MORE CREATURES. MORE AGGRESSION.>
<I DON'T THINK IT'S A COINCIDENCE.>
<HMMM... I WONDER WHY.>
<WHO CARES?>
<I DO. YOU SHOULD TOO.>
<WE NEED TO FIND OUT WHERE THE MONSTERS ARE COMING FROM AND WHAT THEY WANT.>
<THEY'RE COMING FROM EVERYWHERE AND THEY WANT A SPIKED BAT IN THE FUCKING FACE.>
<DON'T WORRY ABOUT WHY, EMI-CHAN.>
<JUST FIGHT.>
<THAT'S CRAZY! WE CAN'T JUST MINDLESSLY FIGHT THEM OVER AND OVER. WE NEED A LONG TERM PLAN.>
<PLANS ARE STUPID. NO ONE FOLLOWS THEM.>
<UH... I DON'T THINK THAT'S REALLY TRUE, AYANE.>

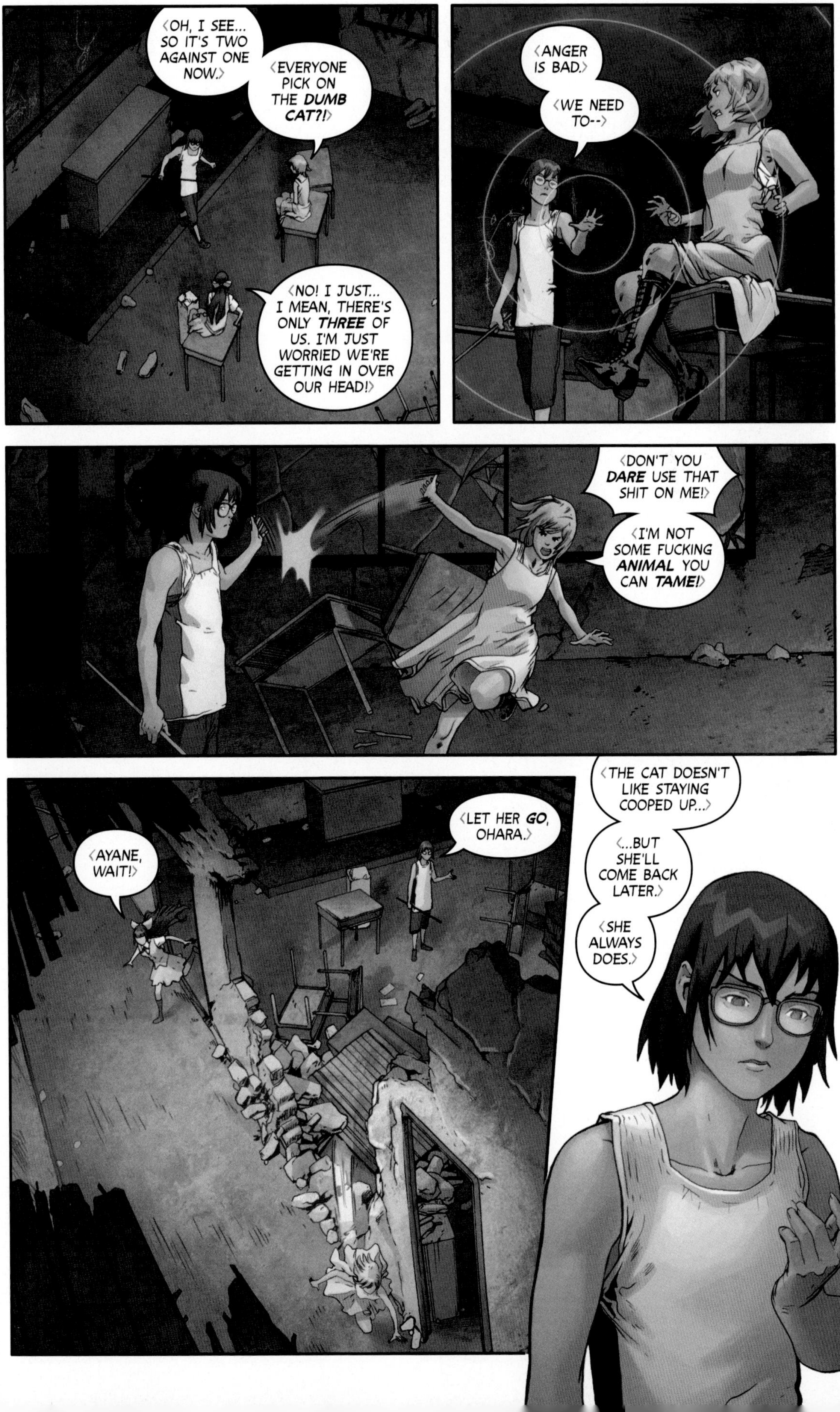

‹OH, I SEE... SO IT'S TWO AGAINST ONE NOW.›
‹EVERYONE PICK ON THE DUMB CAT?!›
‹NO! I JUST... I MEAN, THERE'S ONLY THREE OF US. I'M JUST WORRIED WE'RE GETTING IN OVER OUR HEAD!›
‹ANGER IS BAD.›
‹WE NEED TO--›
‹DON'T YOU DARE USE THAT SHIT ON ME!›
‹I'M NOT SOME FUCKING ANIMAL YOU CAN TAME!›
‹AYANE, WAIT!›
‹LET HER GO, OHARA.›
‹THE CAT DOESN'T LIKE STAYING COOPED UP...›
‹...BUT SHE'LL COME BACK LATER.›
‹SHE ALWAYS DOES.›

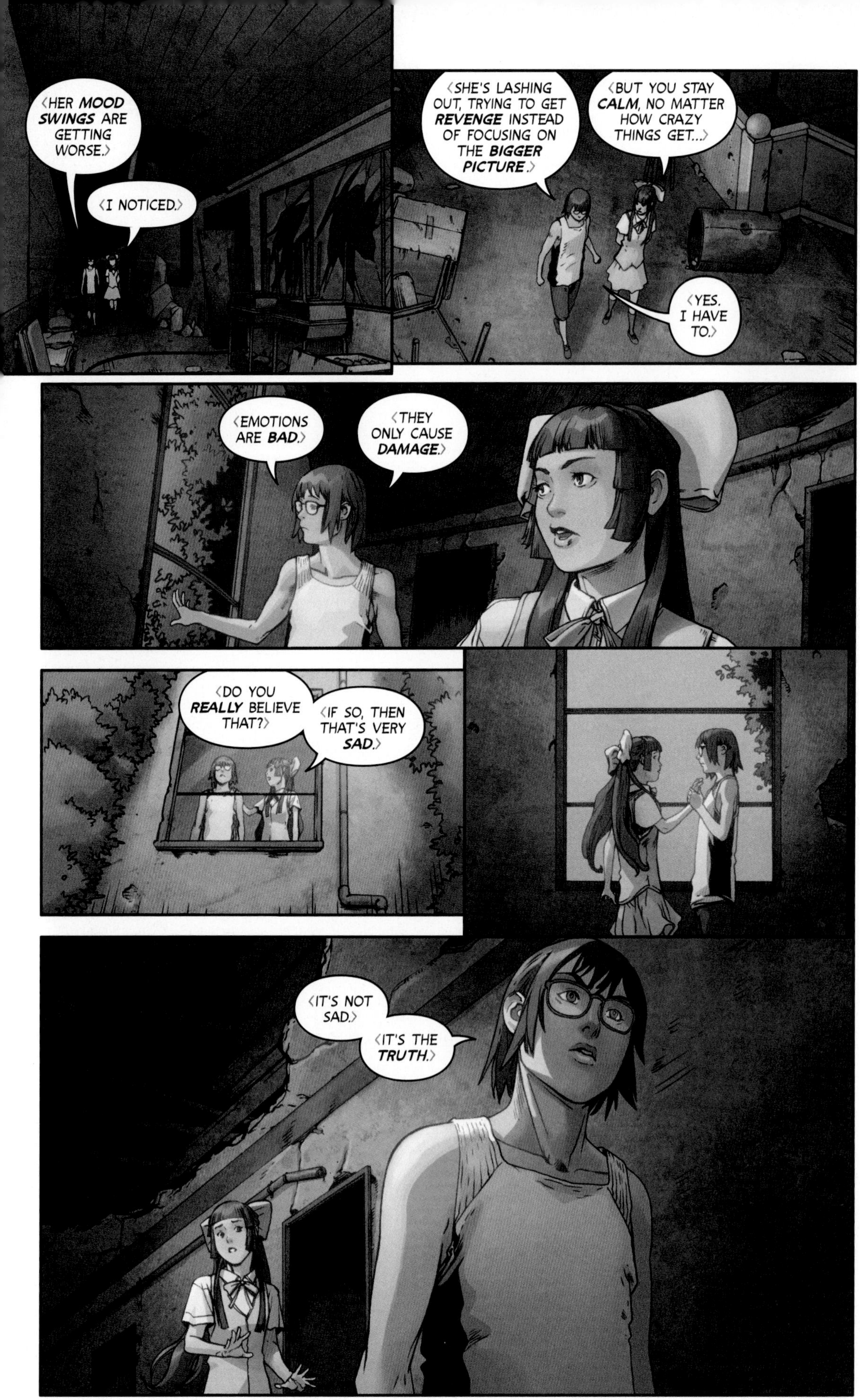

‹HER MOOD SWINGS ARE GETTING WORSE.›
‹I NOTICED.›
‹SHE'S LASHING OUT, TRYING TO GET REVENGE INSTEAD OF FOCUSING ON THE BIGGER PICTURE.›
‹BUT YOU STAY CALM, NO MATTER HOW CRAZY THINGS GET...›
‹YES. I HAVE TO.›
‹EMOTIONS ARE BAD.›
‹THEY ONLY CAUSE DAMAGE.›
‹DO YOU REALLY BELIEVE THAT?›
‹IF SO, THEN THAT'S VERY SAD.›
‹IT'S NOT SAD.›
‹IT'S THE TRUTH.›

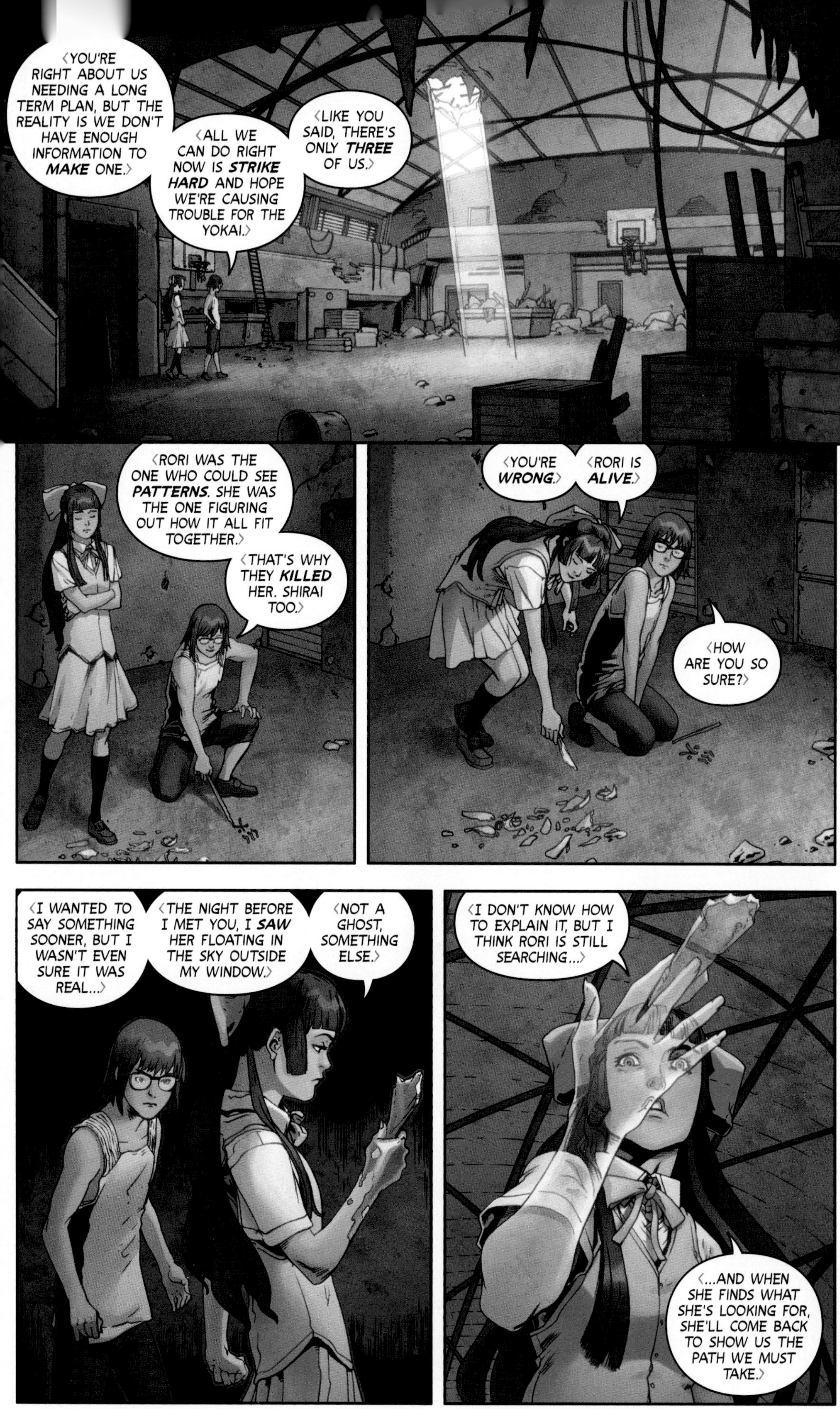
<YOU'RE RIGHT ABOUT US NEEDING A LONG TERM PLAN, BUT THE REALITY IS WE DON'T HAVE ENOUGH INFORMATION TO MAKE ONE.>
<ALL WE CAN DO RIGHT NOW IS STRIKE HARD AND HOPE WE'RE CAUSING TROUBLE FOR THE YOKAI.>
<LIKE YOU SAID, THERE'S ONLY THREE OF US.>
<RORI WAS THE ONE WHO COULD SEE PATTERNS. SHE WAS THE ONE FIGURING OUT HOW IT ALL FIT TOGETHER.>
<THAT'S WHY THEY KILLED HER. SHIRAI TOO.>
<YOU'RE WRONG.>
<RORI IS ALIVE.>
<HOW ARE YOU SO SURE?>
<I WANTED TO SAY SOMETHING SOONER, BUT I WASN'T EVEN SURE IT WAS REAL...>
<THE NIGHT BEFORE I MET YOU, I SAW HER FLOATING IN THE SKY OUTSIDE MY WINDOW.>
<NOT A GHOST, SOMETHING ELSE.>
<I DON'T KNOW HOW TO EXPLAIN IT, BUT I THINK RORI IS STILL SEARCHING...>
<...AND WHEN SHE FINDS WHAT SHE'S LOOKING FOR, SHE'LL COME BACK TO SHOW US THE PATH WE MUST TAKE.>

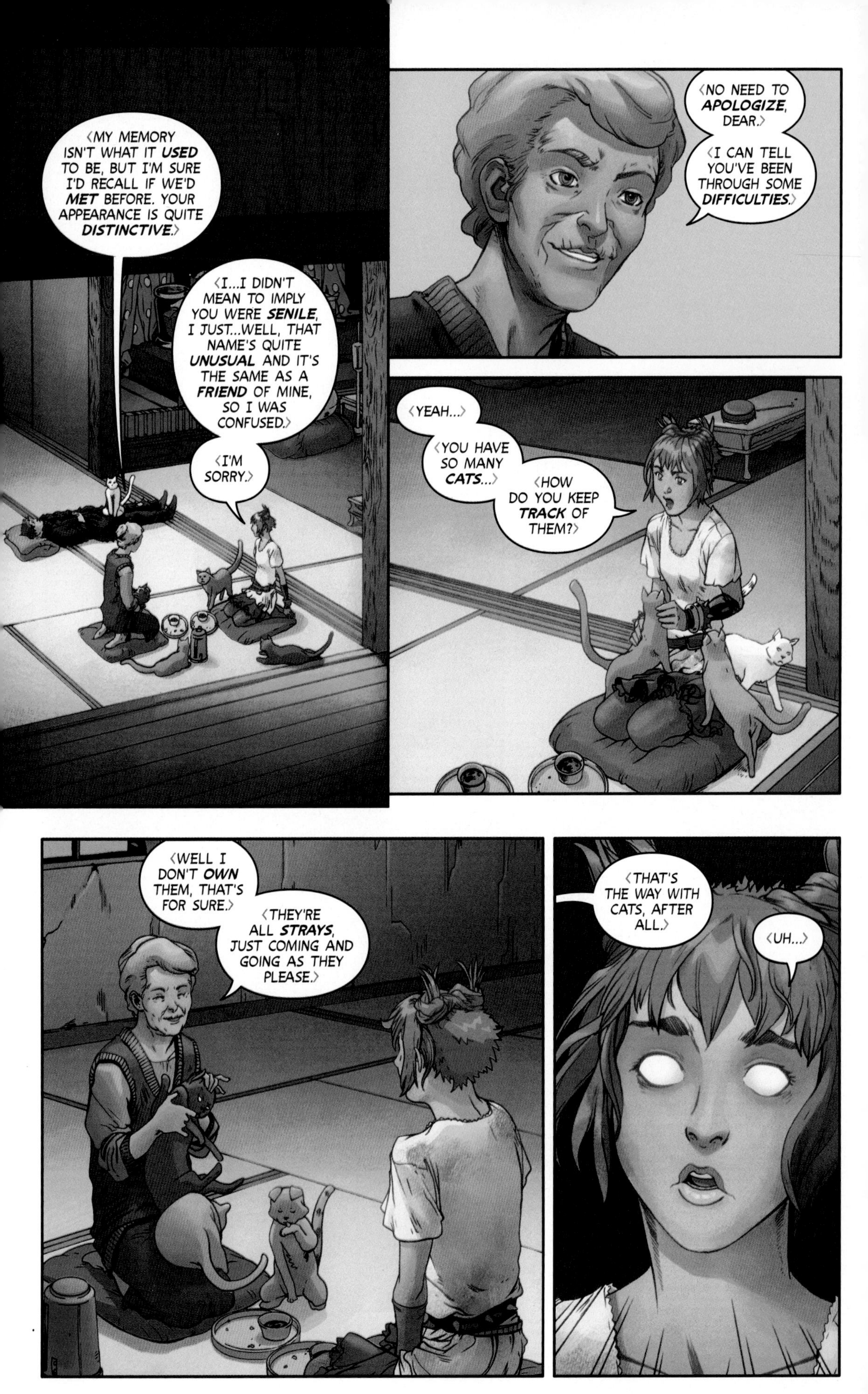

〈MY MEMORY ISN'T WHAT IT **USED** TO BE, BUT I'M SURE I'D RECALL IF WE'D **MET** BEFORE. YOUR APPEARANCE IS QUITE **DISTINCTIVE**.〉
〈I...I DIDN'T MEAN TO IMPLY YOU WERE **SENILE**, I JUST...WELL, THAT NAME'S QUITE **UNUSUAL** AND IT'S THE SAME AS A **FRIEND** OF MINE, SO I WAS CONFUSED.〉
〈I'M SORRY.〉
〈NO NEED TO **APOLOGIZE**, DEAR.〉
〈I CAN TELL YOU'VE BEEN THROUGH SOME **DIFFICULTIES**.〉
〈YEAH...〉
〈YOU HAVE SO MANY **CATS**...〉
〈HOW DO YOU KEEP **TRACK** OF THEM?〉
〈WELL I DON'T **OWN** THEM, THAT'S FOR SURE.〉
〈THEY'RE ALL **STRAYS**, JUST COMING AND GOING AS THEY PLEASE.〉
〈THAT'S THE WAY WITH CATS, AFTER ALL.〉
〈UH...〉

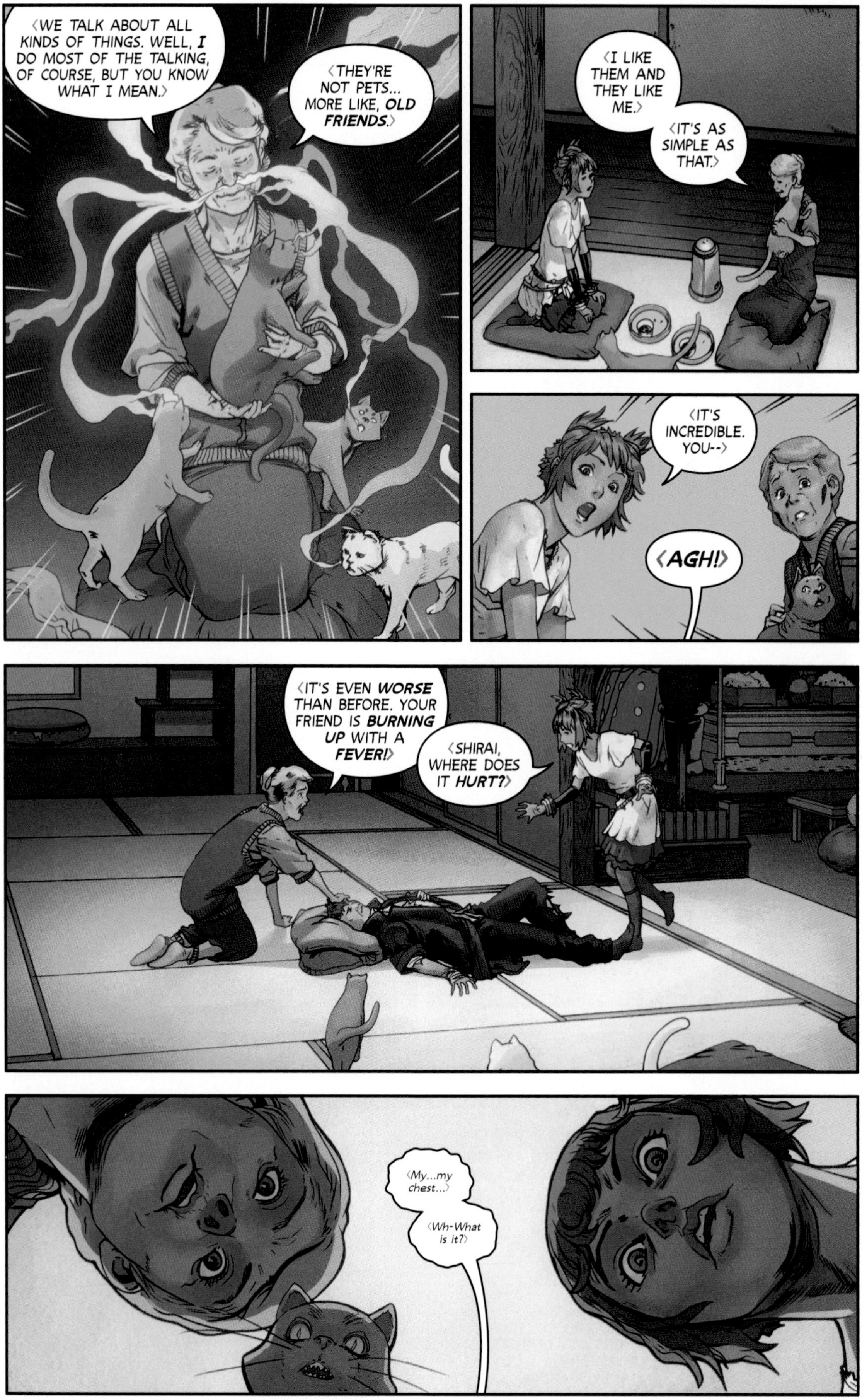

〈WE TALK ABOUT ALL KINDS OF THINGS. WELL, **I** DO MOST OF THE TALKING, OF COURSE, BUT YOU KNOW WHAT I MEAN.〉
〈THEY'RE NOT PETS... MORE LIKE, **OLD FRIENDS**.〉
〈I LIKE THEM AND THEY LIKE ME.〉
〈IT'S AS SIMPLE AS THAT.〉
〈IT'S INCREDIBLE. YOU--〉
〈**AGH!**〉
〈IT'S EVEN **WORSE** THAN BEFORE. YOUR FRIEND IS **BURNING UP** WITH A **FEVER!**〉
〈SHIRAI, WHERE DOES IT **HURT?**〉
〈*My...my chest...*〉
〈*Wh-What is it?*〉

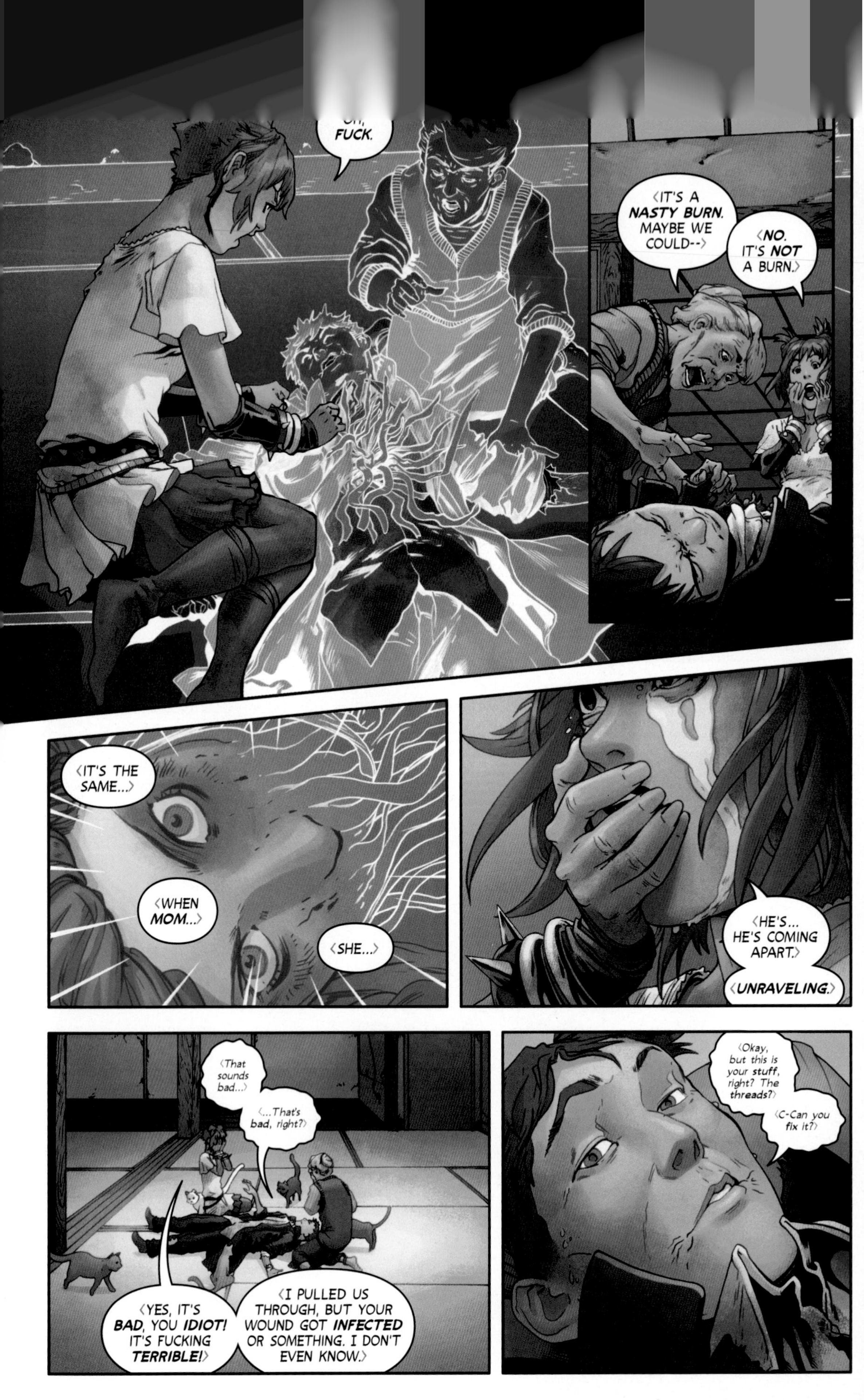

FUCK.
⟨IT'S A NASTY BURN. MAYBE WE COULD--⟩
⟨NO. IT'S NOT A BURN.⟩
⟨IT'S THE SAME...⟩
⟨WHEN MOM...⟩
⟨SHE...⟩
⟨HE'S... HE'S COMING APART.⟩
⟨UNRAVELING.⟩
⟨That sounds bad...⟩
⟨...That's bad, right?⟩
⟨YES, IT'S BAD, YOU IDIOT! IT'S FUCKING TERRIBLE!⟩
⟨I PULLED US THROUGH, BUT YOUR WOUND GOT INFECTED OR SOMETHING. I DON'T EVEN KNOW.⟩
⟨Okay, but this is your stuff, right? The threads?⟩
⟨C-Can you fix it?⟩

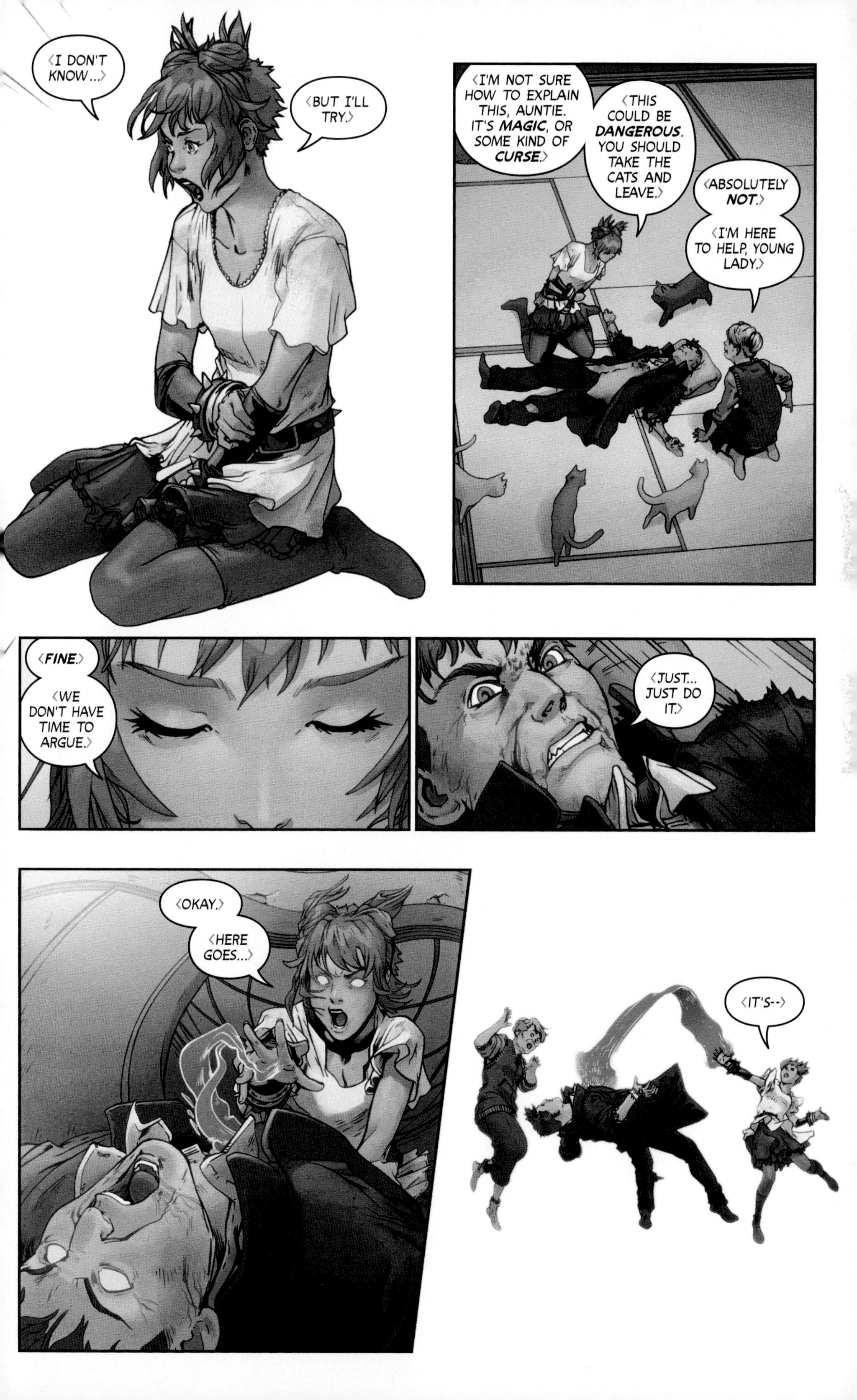
‹I DON'T KNOW...›
‹BUT I'LL TRY.›
‹I'M NOT SURE HOW TO EXPLAIN THIS, AUNTIE. IT'S MAGIC, OR SOME KIND OF CURSE.›
‹THIS COULD BE DANGEROUS. YOU SHOULD TAKE THE CATS AND LEAVE.›
‹ABSOLUTELY NOT.›
‹I'M HERE TO HELP, YOUNG LADY.›
‹FINE.›
‹WE DON'T HAVE TIME TO ARGUE.›
‹JUST... JUST DO IT.›
‹OKAY.›
‹HERE GOES...›
‹IT'S--›

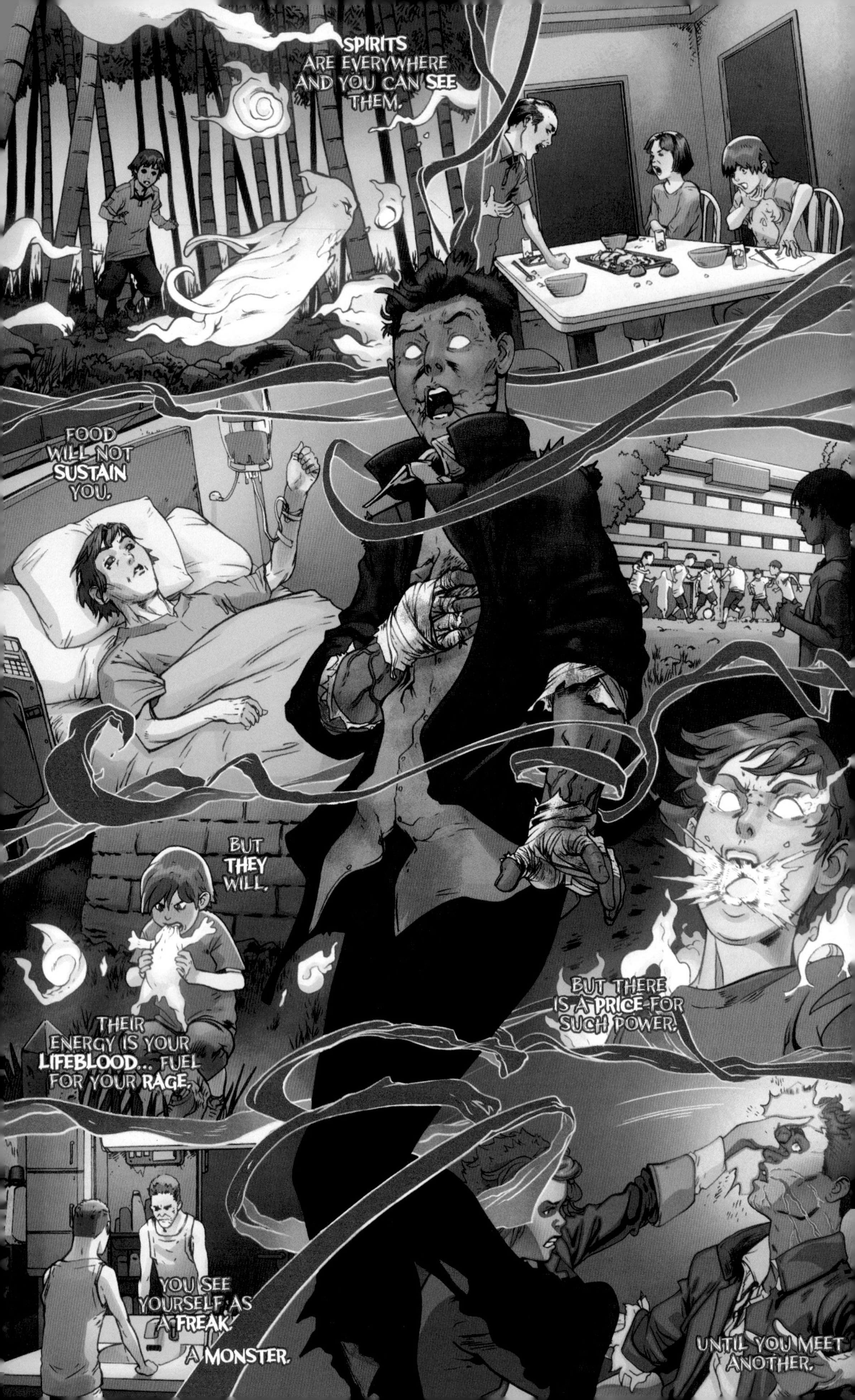
SPIRITS ARE EVERYWHERE AND YOU CAN SEE THEM.
FOOD WILL NOT SUSTAIN YOU.
BUT THEY WILL.
THEIR ENERGY IS YOUR LIFEBLOOD... FUEL FOR YOUR RAGE.
BUT THERE IS A PRICE FOR SUCH POWER.
YOU SEE YOURSELF AS A FREAK.
A MONSTER.
UNTIL YOU MEET ANOTHER.

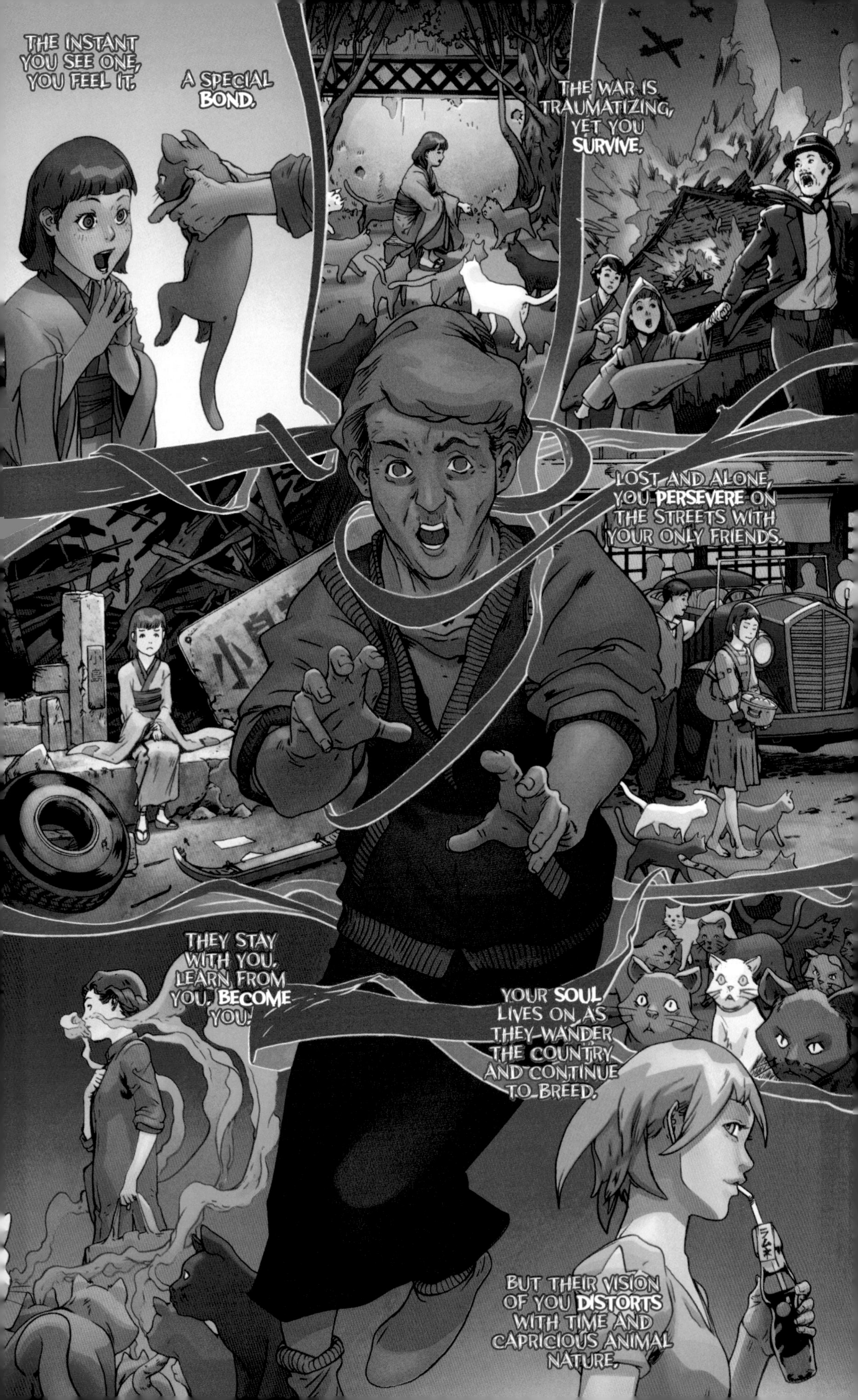
THE INSTANT YOU SEE ONE, YOU FEEL IT.
A SPECIAL BOND.
THE WAR IS TRAUMATIZING, YET YOU SURVIVE.
LOST AND ALONE, YOU PERSEVERE ON THE STREETS WITH YOUR ONLY FRIENDS.
THEY STAY WITH YOU, LEARN FROM YOU, BECOME YOU.
YOUR SOUL LIVES ON AS THEY WANDER THE COUNTRY AND CONTINUE TO BREED.
BUT THEIR VISION OF YOU DISTORTS WITH TIME AND CAPRICIOUS ANIMAL NATURE.

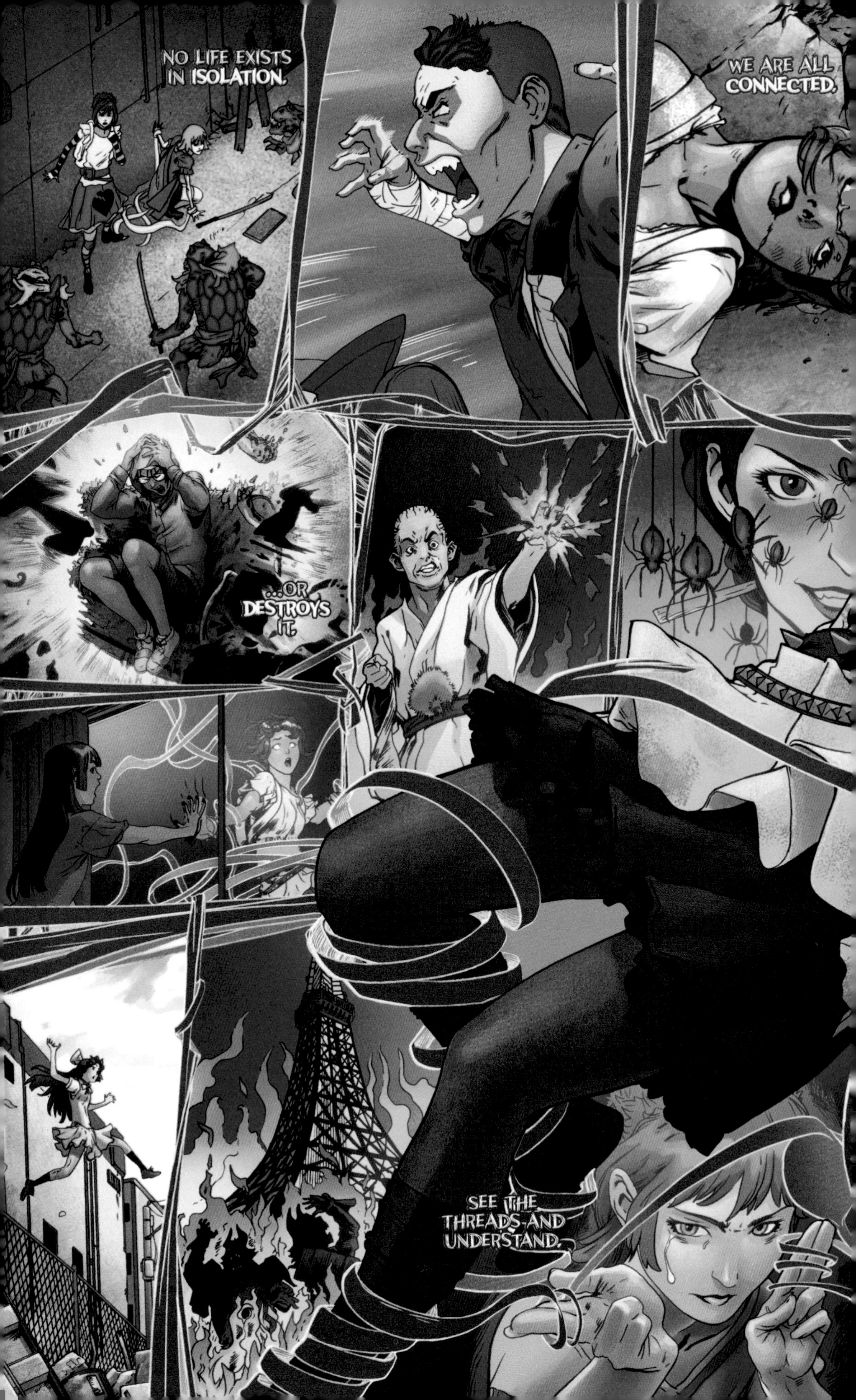
NO LIFE EXISTS IN ISOLATION.
WE ARE ALL CONNECTED.
...OR DESTROYS IT.
SEE THE THREADS AND UNDERSTAND.

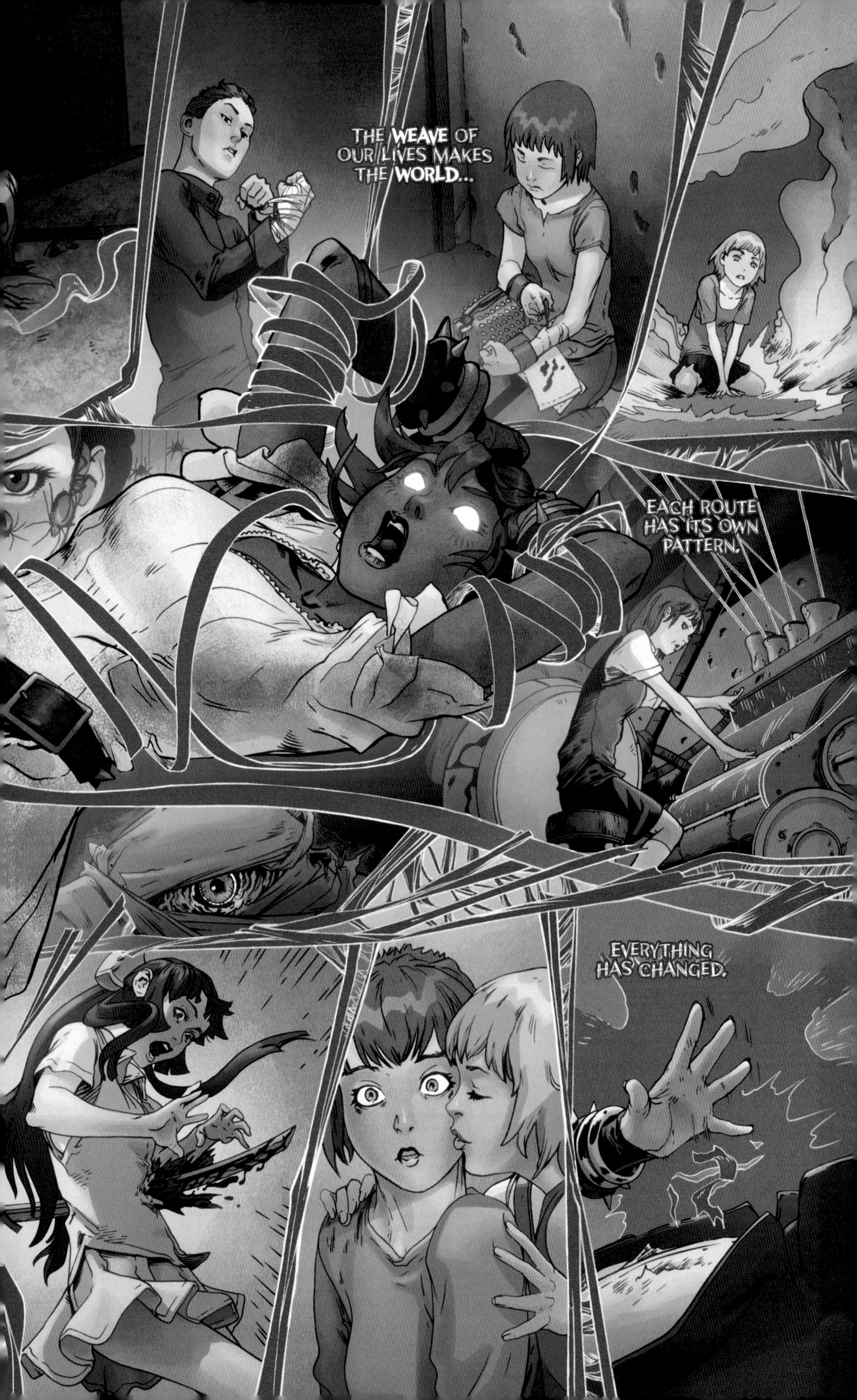
THE WEAVE OF OUR LIVES MAKES THE WORLD...
EACH ROUTE HAS ITS OWN PATTERN.
EVERYTHING HAS CHANGED.

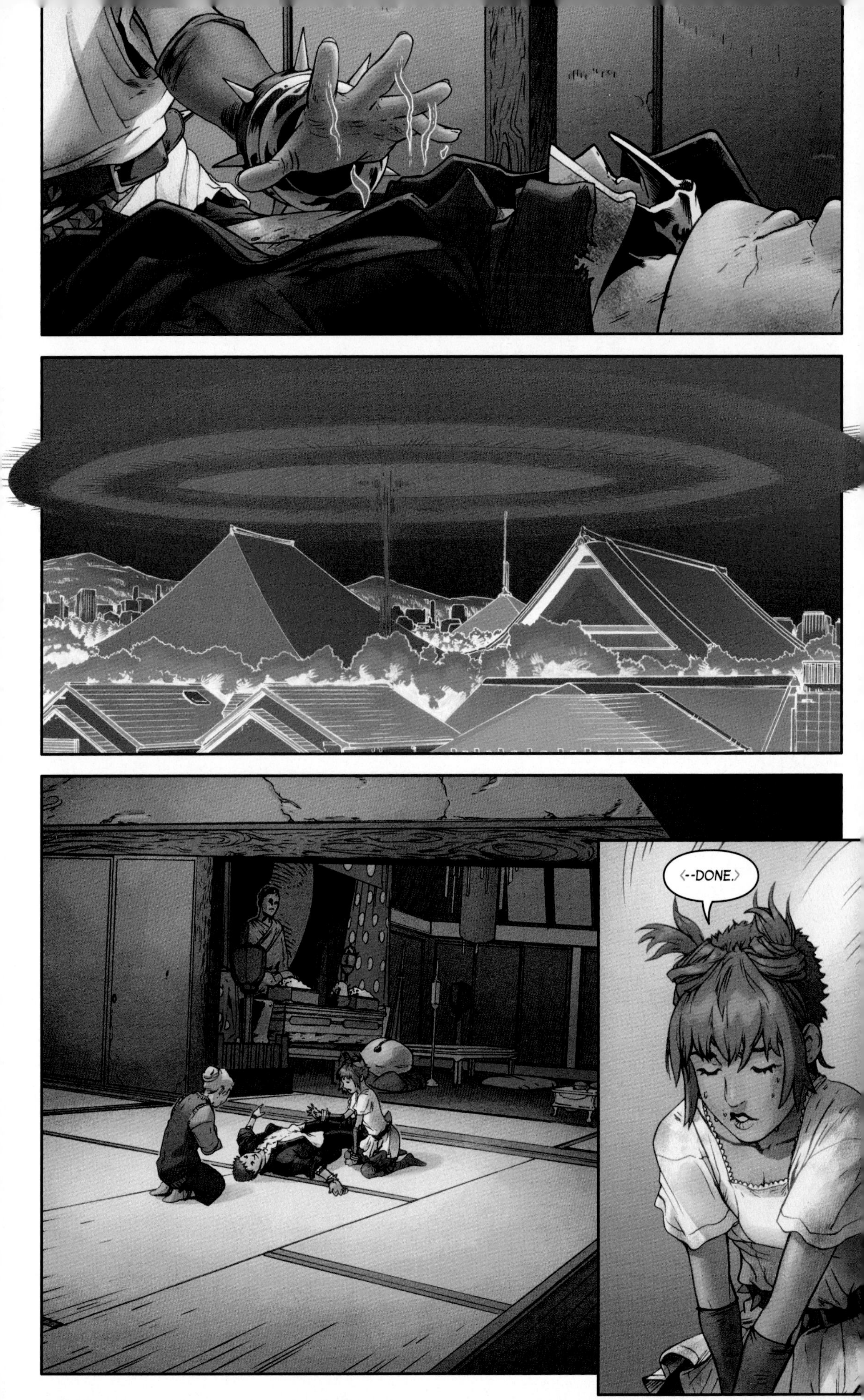
⟨--DONE.⟩

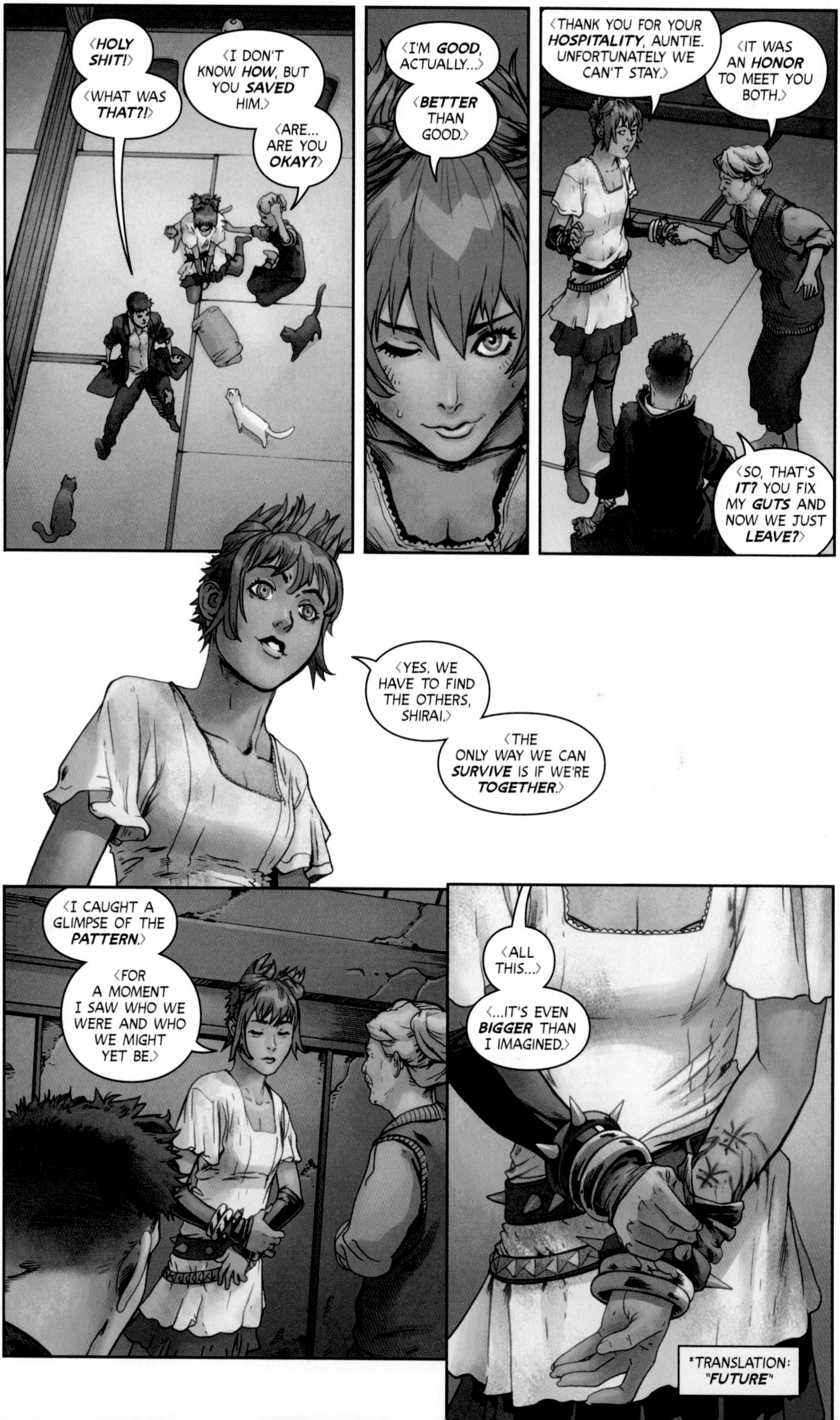
‹HOLY SHIT!›
‹WHAT WAS THAT?!›
‹I DON'T KNOW HOW, BUT YOU SAVED HIM.›
‹ARE... ARE YOU OKAY?›
‹I'M GOOD, ACTUALLY...›
‹BETTER THAN GOOD.›
‹THANK YOU FOR YOUR HOSPITALITY, AUNTIE. UNFORTUNATELY WE CAN'T STAY.›
‹IT WAS AN HONOR TO MEET YOU BOTH.›
‹SO, THAT'S IT? YOU FIX MY GUTS AND NOW WE JUST LEAVE?›
‹YES. WE HAVE TO FIND THE OTHERS, SHIRAI.›
‹THE ONLY WAY WE CAN SURVIVE IS IF WE'RE TOGETHER.›
‹I CAUGHT A GLIMPSE OF THE PATTERN.›
‹FOR A MOMENT I SAW WHO WE WERE AND WHO WE MIGHT YET BE.›
‹ALL THIS...›
‹...IT'S EVEN BIGGER THAN I IMAGINED.›
*TRANSLATION: "FUTURE"

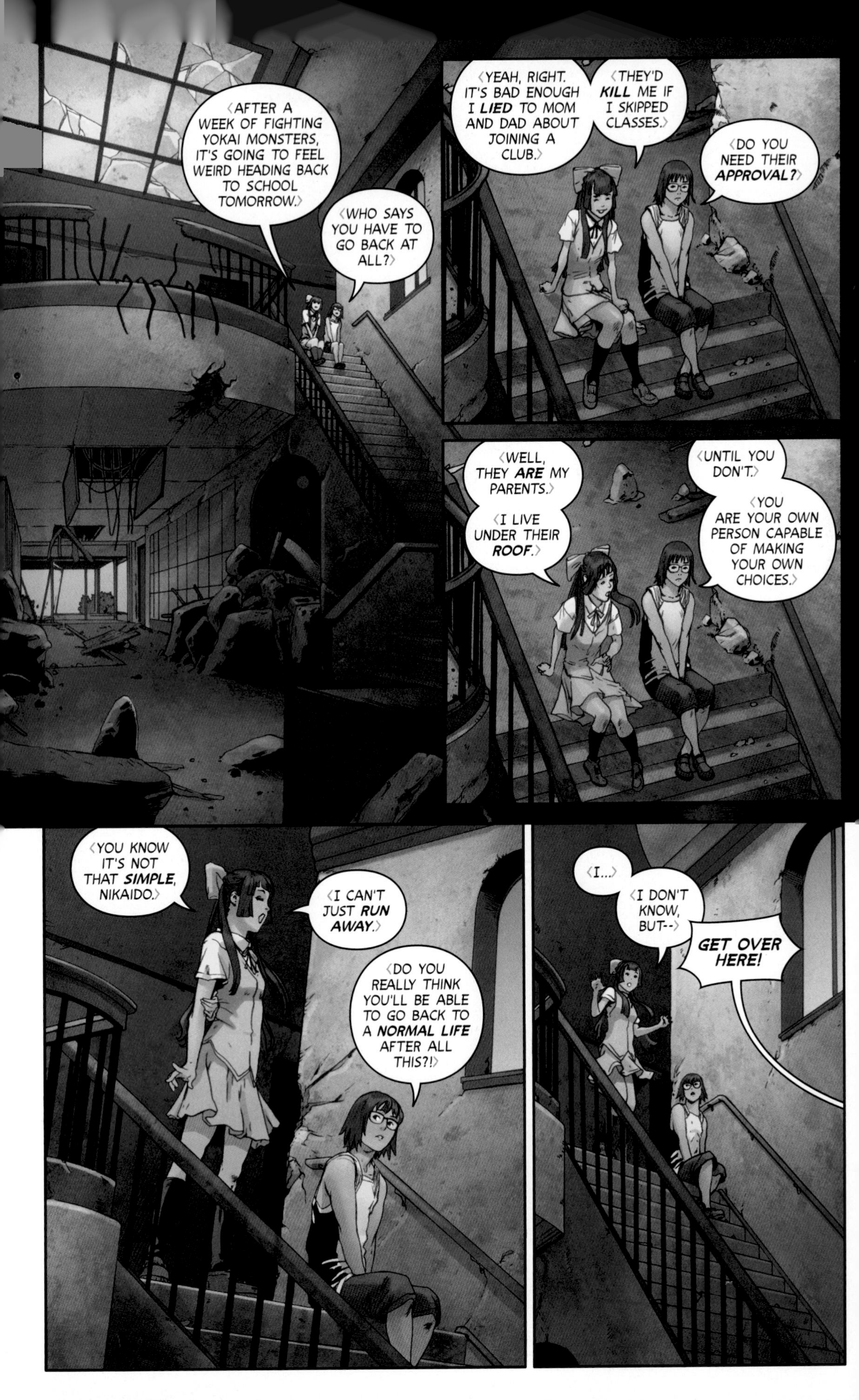
〈AFTER A WEEK OF FIGHTING YOKAI MONSTERS, IT'S GOING TO FEEL WEIRD HEADING BACK TO SCHOOL TOMORROW.〉
〈WHO SAYS YOU HAVE TO GO BACK AT ALL?〉
〈YEAH, RIGHT. IT'S BAD ENOUGH I **LIED** TO MOM AND DAD ABOUT JOINING A CLUB.〉
〈THEY'D **KILL** ME IF I SKIPPED CLASSES.〉
〈DO YOU NEED THEIR **APPROVAL?**〉
〈WELL, THEY **ARE** MY PARENTS.〉
〈I LIVE UNDER THEIR **ROOF**.〉
〈UNTIL YOU DON'T.〉
〈YOU ARE YOUR OWN PERSON CAPABLE OF MAKING YOUR OWN CHOICES.〉
〈YOU KNOW IT'S NOT THAT **SIMPLE**, NIKAIDO.〉
〈I CAN'T JUST **RUN AWAY**.〉
〈DO YOU REALLY THINK YOU'LL BE ABLE TO GO BACK TO A **NORMAL LIFE** AFTER ALL THIS?!〉
〈I...〉
〈I DON'T KNOW, BUT--〉
GET OVER HERE!

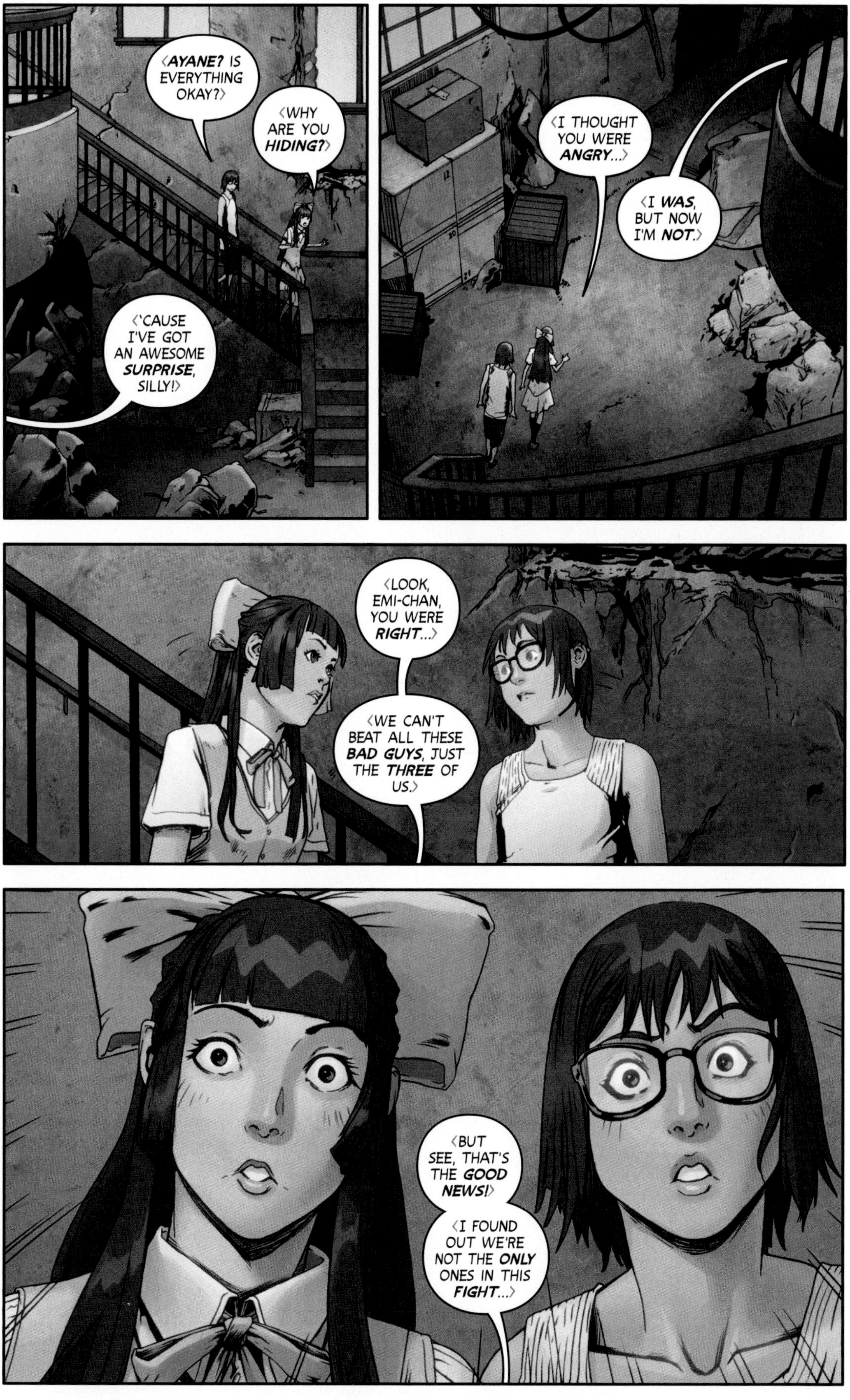

〈AYANE? IS EVERYTHING OKAY?〉
〈WHY ARE YOU HIDING?〉
〈'CAUSE I'VE GOT AN AWESOME SURPRISE, SILLY!〉
〈I THOUGHT YOU WERE ANGRY...〉
〈I WAS, BUT NOW I'M NOT.〉
〈LOOK, EMI-CHAN, YOU WERE RIGHT...〉
〈WE CAN'T BEAT ALL THESE BAD GUYS, JUST THE THREE OF US.〉
〈BUT SEE, THAT'S THE GOOD NEWS!〉
〈I FOUND OUT WE'RE NOT THE ONLY ONES IN THIS FIGHT...〉

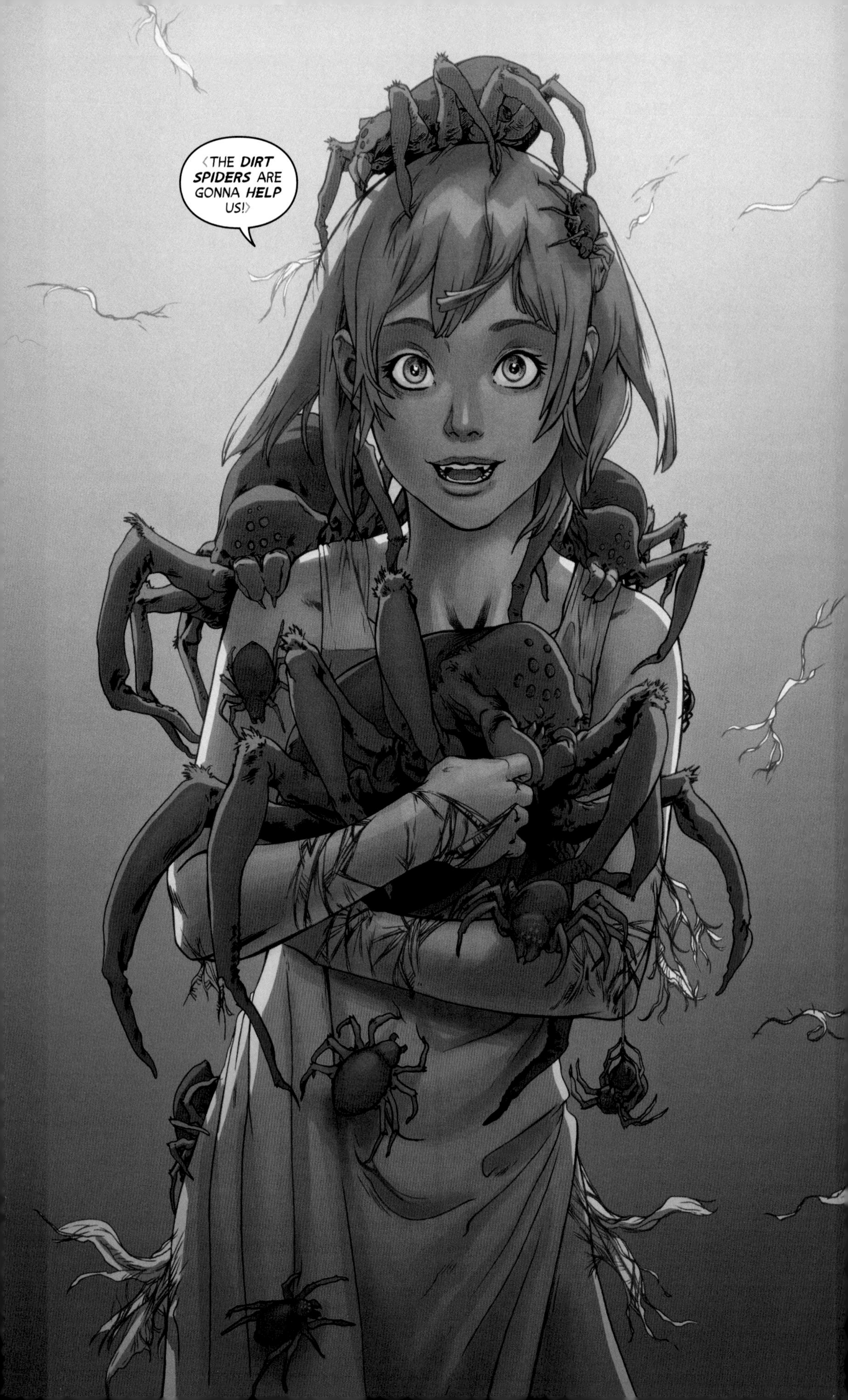
<THE DIRT SPIDERS ARE GONNA HELP US!>

Chapter Nine

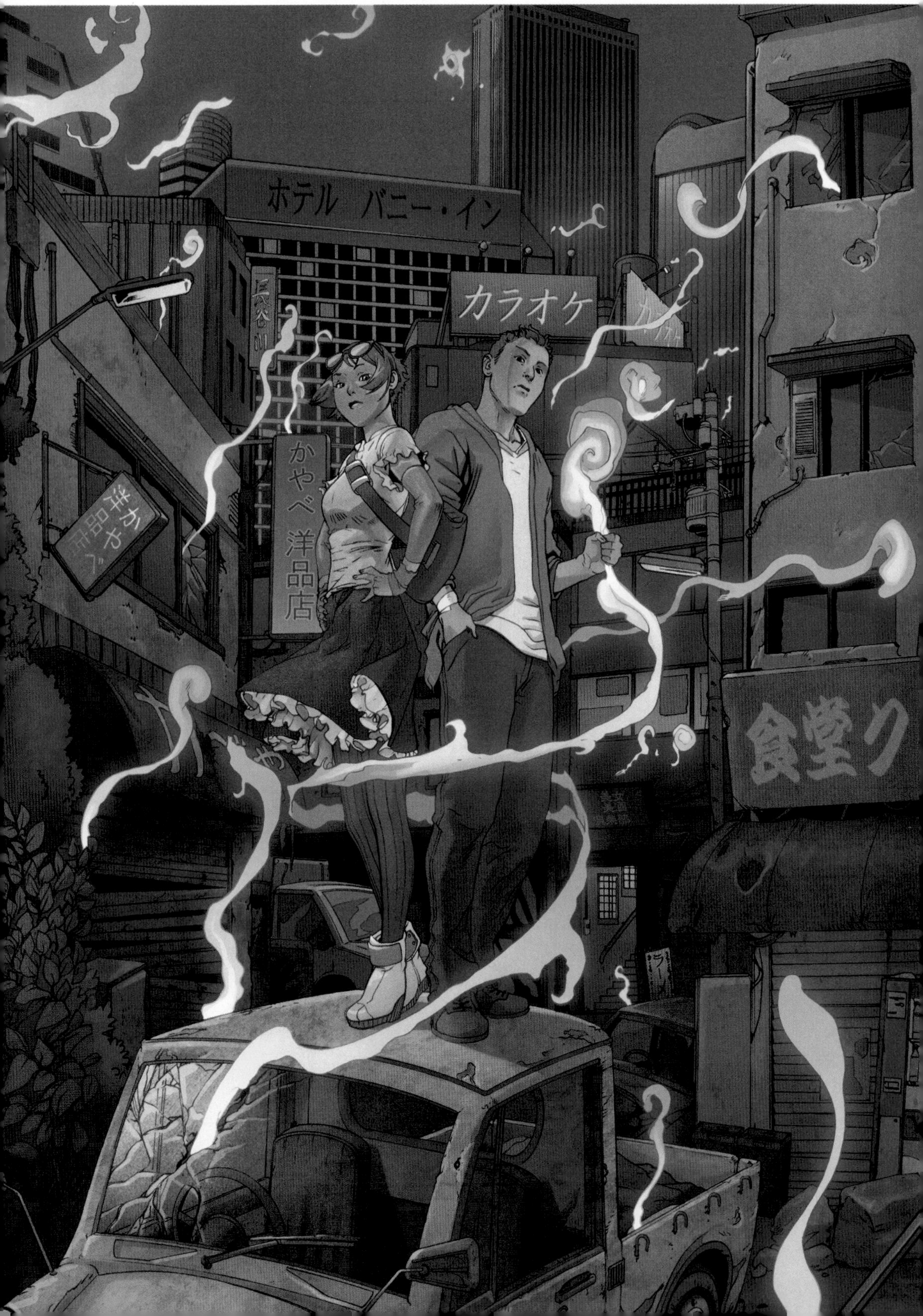
ホテル バニー・イン
カラオケ
かやべ 洋品店

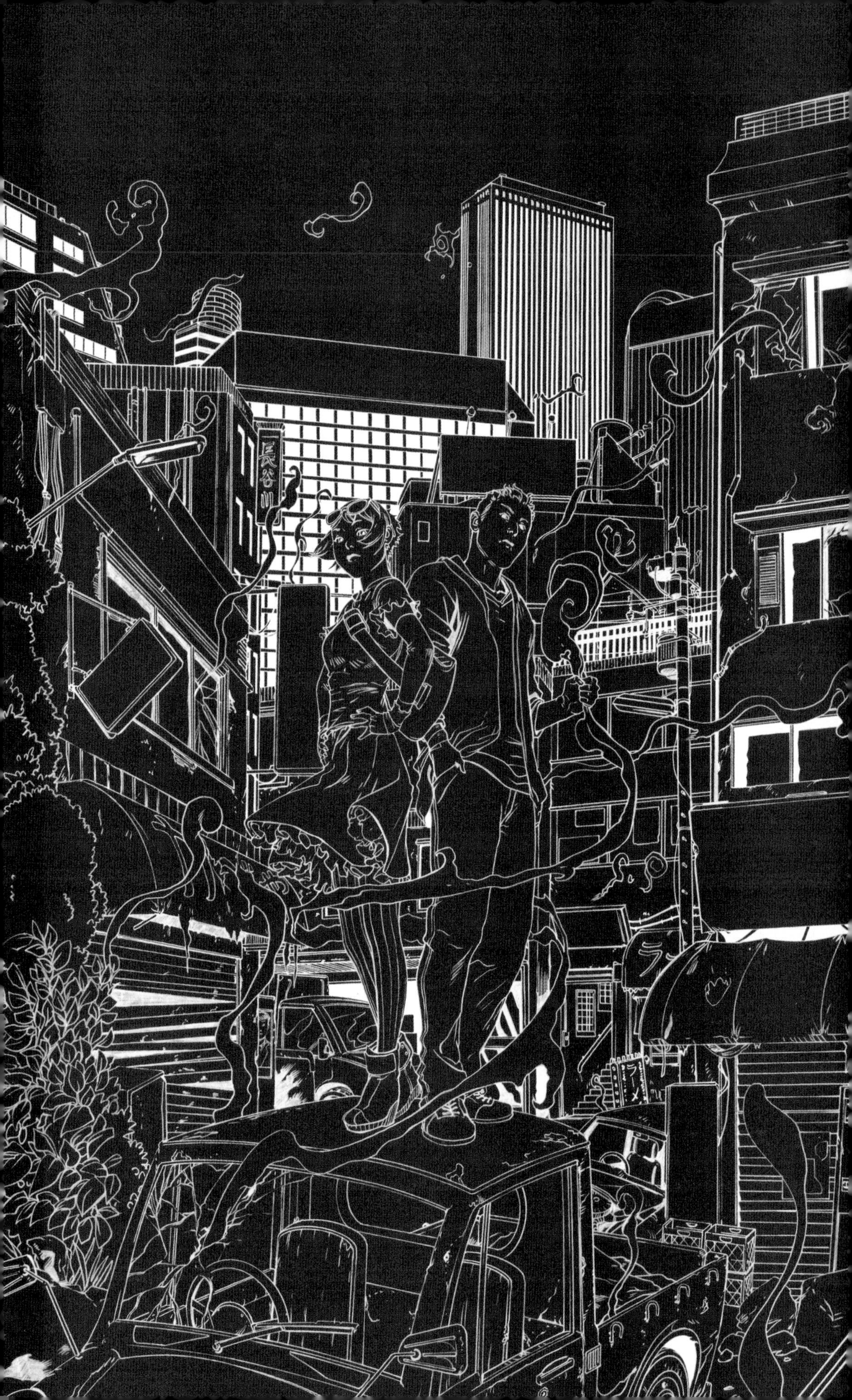
長谷川

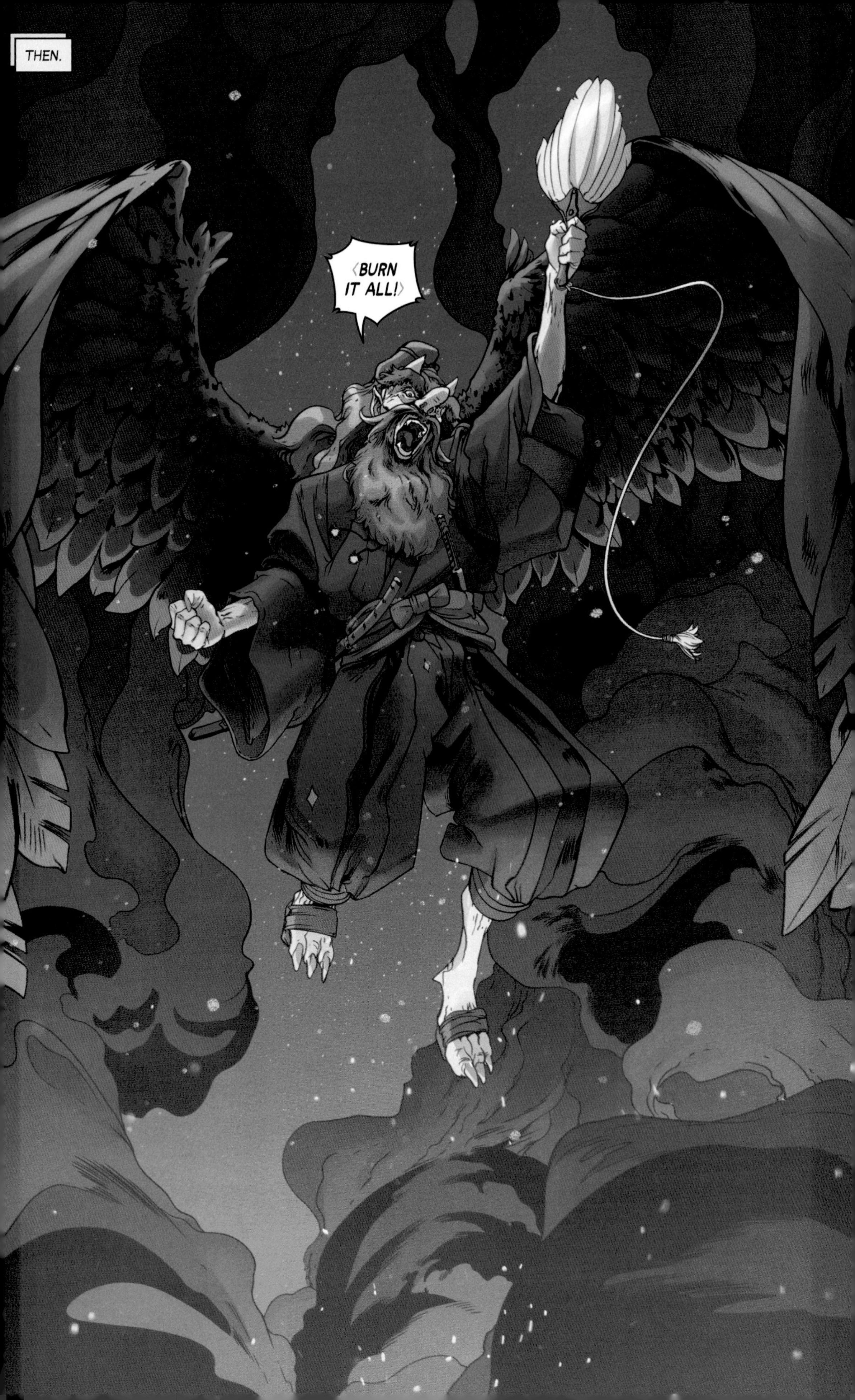
THEN.
⟨BURN IT ALL!⟩

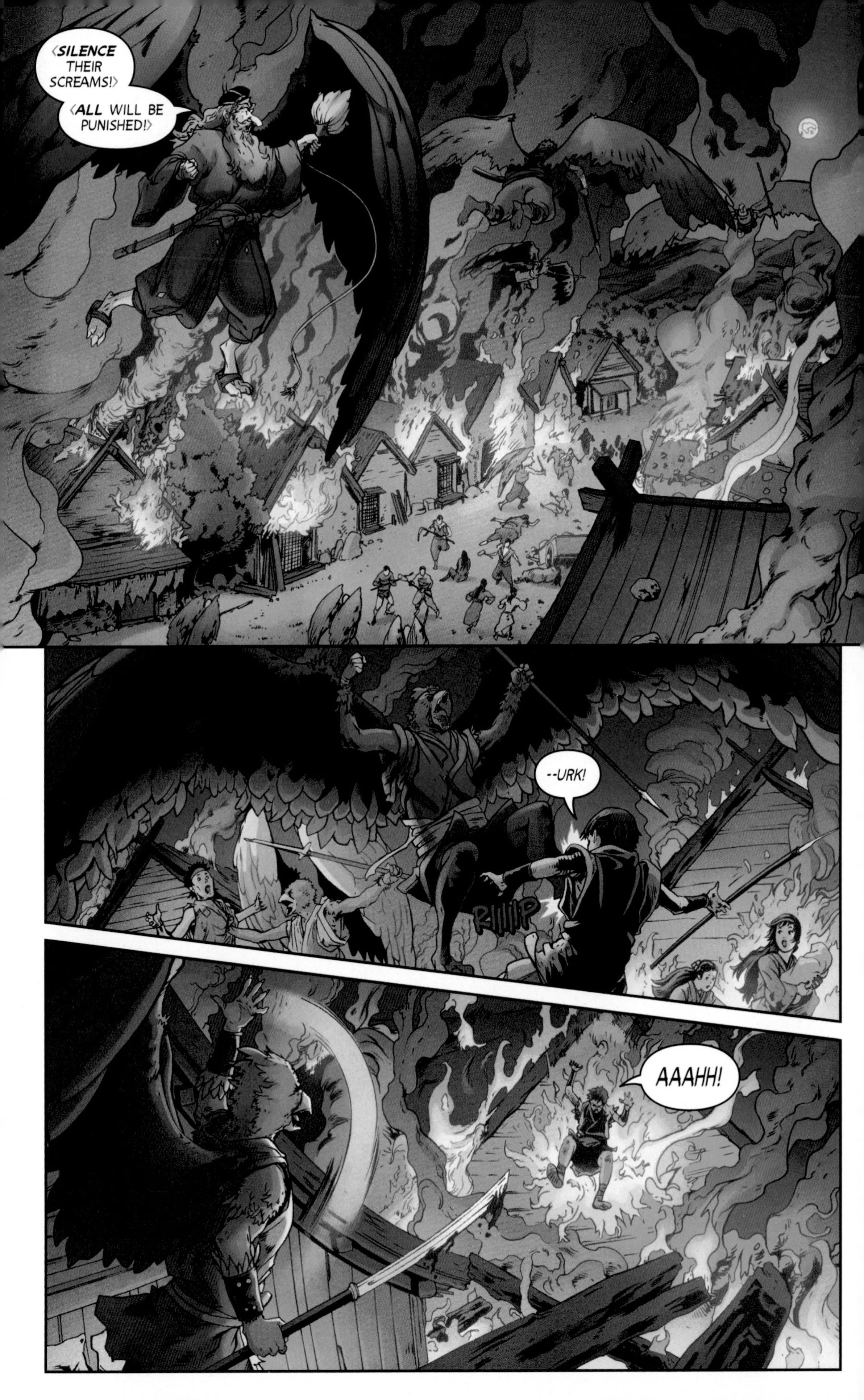
‹SILENCE THEIR SCREAMS!›
‹ALL WILL BE PUNISHED!›
--URK!
RIIIIIP
AAAHH!

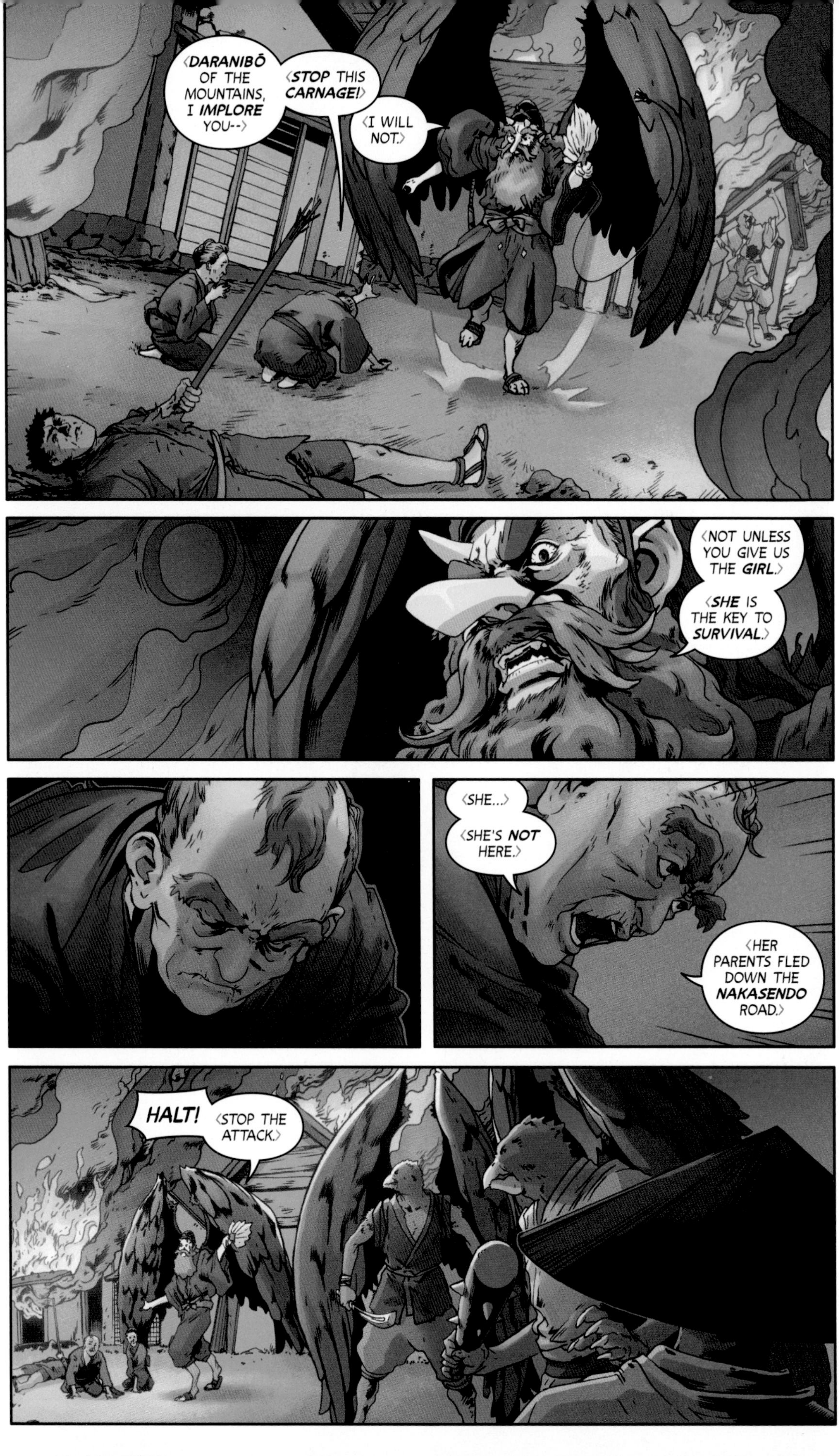
⟨DARANIBŌ OF THE MOUNTAINS, I IMPLORE YOU--⟩
⟨STOP THIS CARNAGE!⟩
⟨I WILL NOT.⟩
⟨NOT UNLESS YOU GIVE US THE GIRL.⟩
⟨SHE IS THE KEY TO SURVIVAL.⟩
⟨SHE...⟩
⟨SHE'S NOT HERE.⟩
⟨HER PARENTS FLED DOWN THE NAKASENDO ROAD.⟩
HALT!
⟨STOP THE ATTACK.⟩

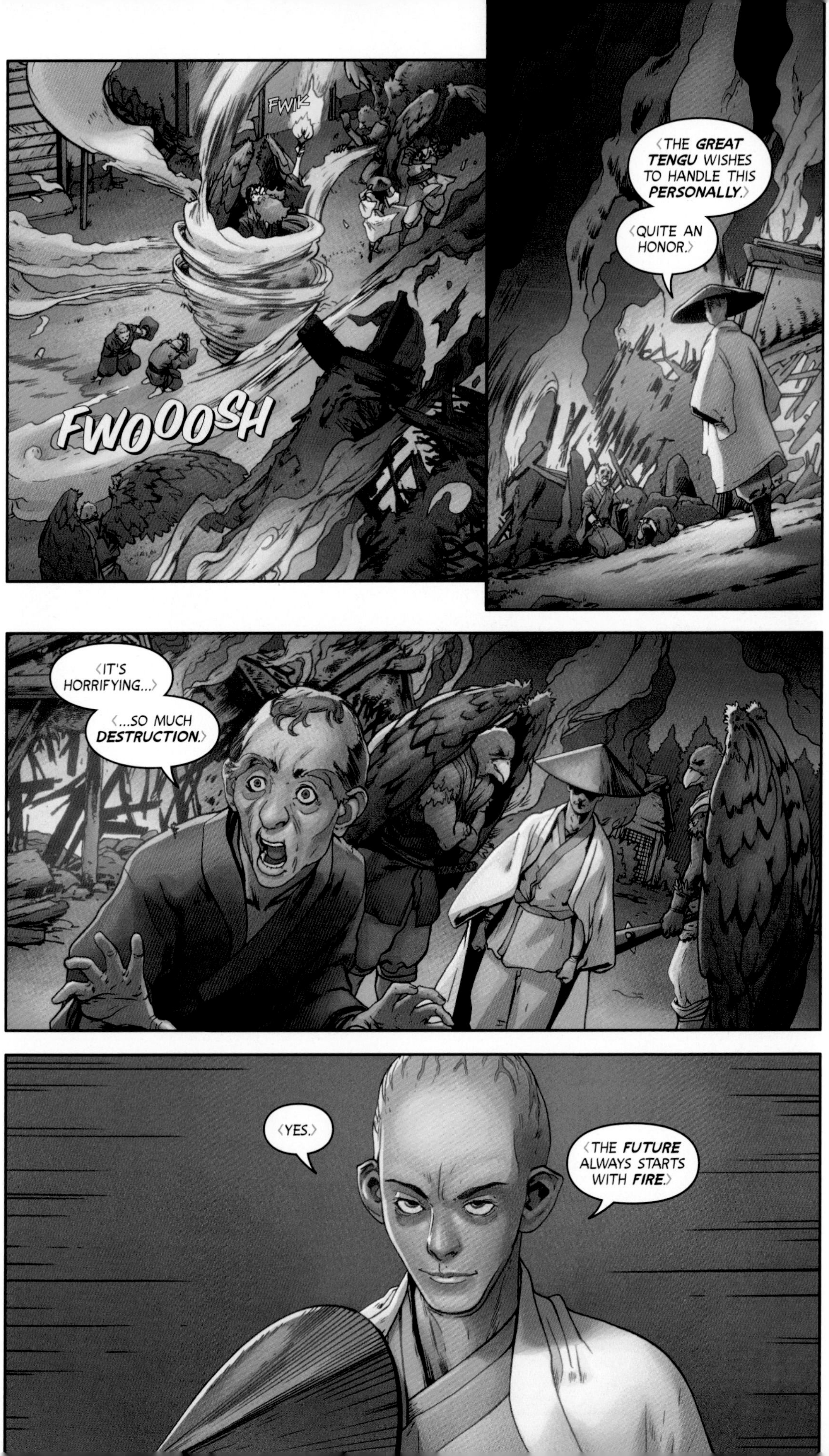
FWIK
FWOOOSH
〈THE GREAT TENGU WISHES TO HANDLE THIS PERSONALLY.〉
〈QUITE AN HONOR.〉
〈IT'S HORRIFYING...〉
〈...SO MUCH DESTRUCTION.〉
〈YES.〉
〈THE FUTURE ALWAYS STARTS WITH FIRE.〉

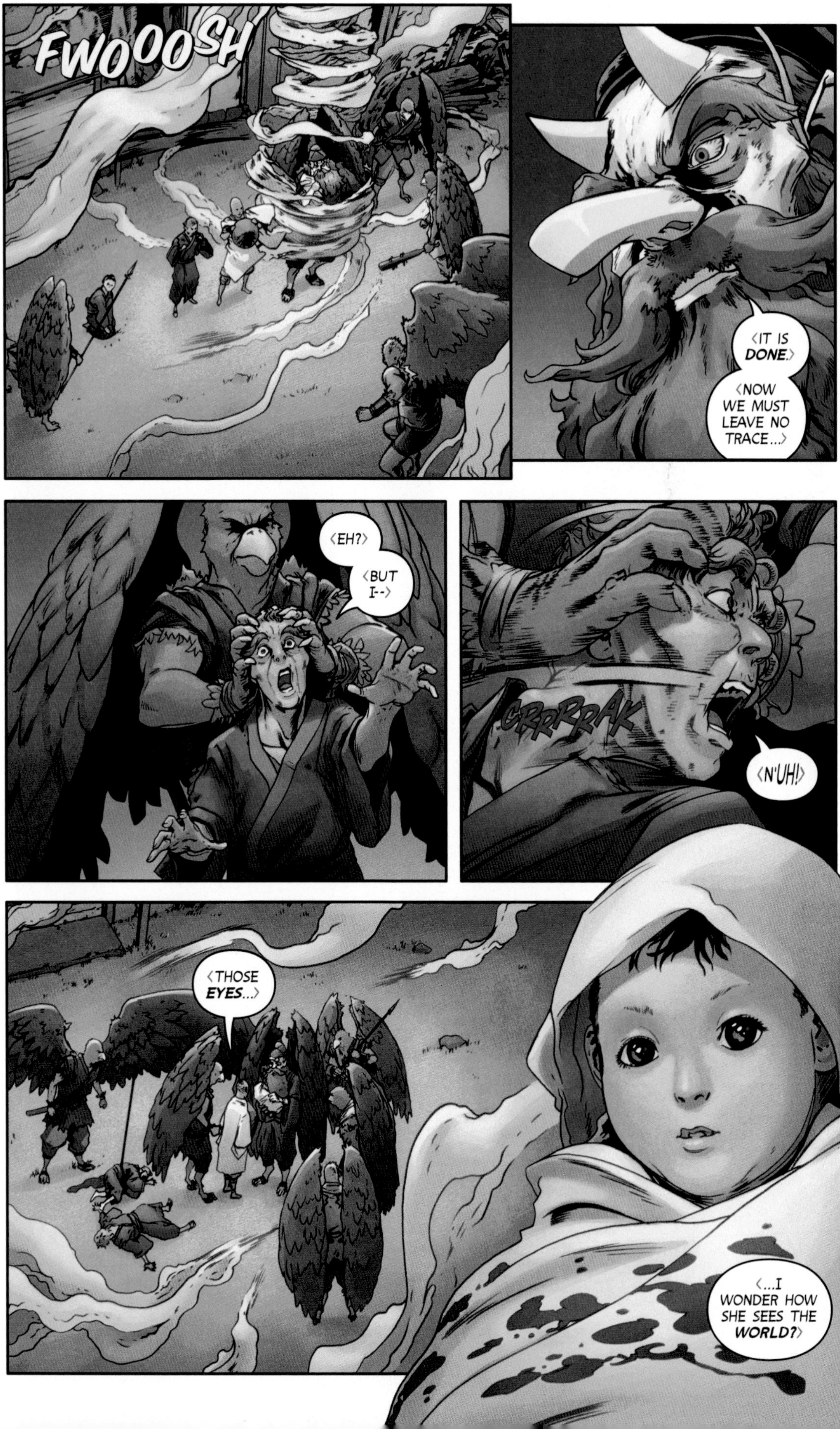
FWOOOSH
‹IT IS DONE.›
‹NOW WE MUST LEAVE NO TRACE...›
‹EH?›
‹BUT I--›
CRRRRAK
‹N'UH!›
‹THOSE EYES...›
‹...I WONDER HOW SHE SEES THE WORLD?›

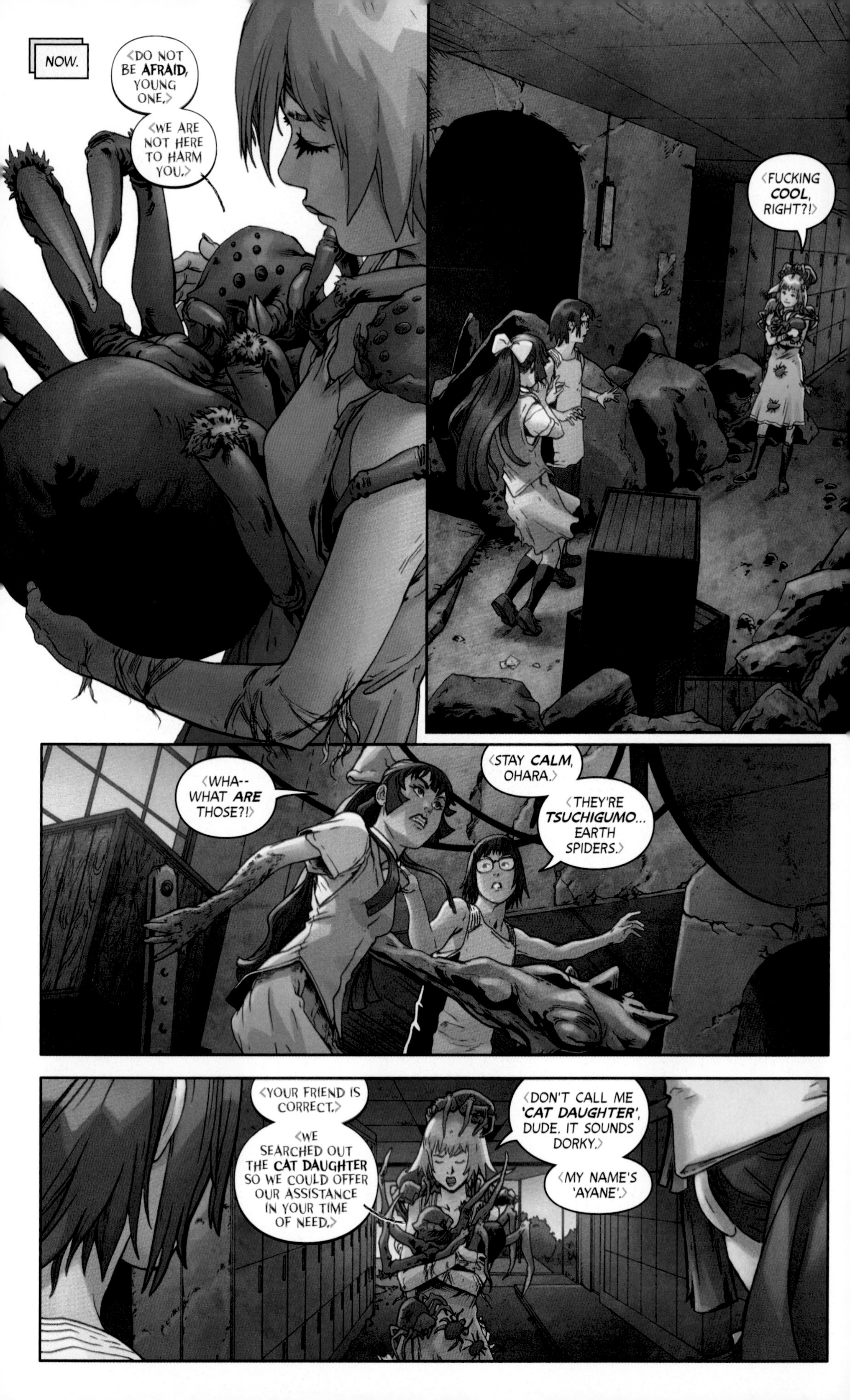
NOW.
<DO NOT BE AFRAID, YOUNG ONE.>
<WE ARE NOT HERE TO HARM YOU.>
<FUCKING COOL, RIGHT?!>
<WHA-- WHAT ARE THOSE?!>
<STAY CALM, OHARA.>
<THEY'RE TSUCHIGUMO... EARTH SPIDERS.>
<YOUR FRIEND IS CORRECT.>
<WE SEARCHED OUT THE CAT DAUGHTER SO WE COULD OFFER OUR ASSISTANCE IN YOUR TIME OF NEED.>
<DON'T CALL ME 'CAT DAUGHTER', DUDE. IT SOUNDS DORKY.>
<MY NAME'S 'AYANE'.>

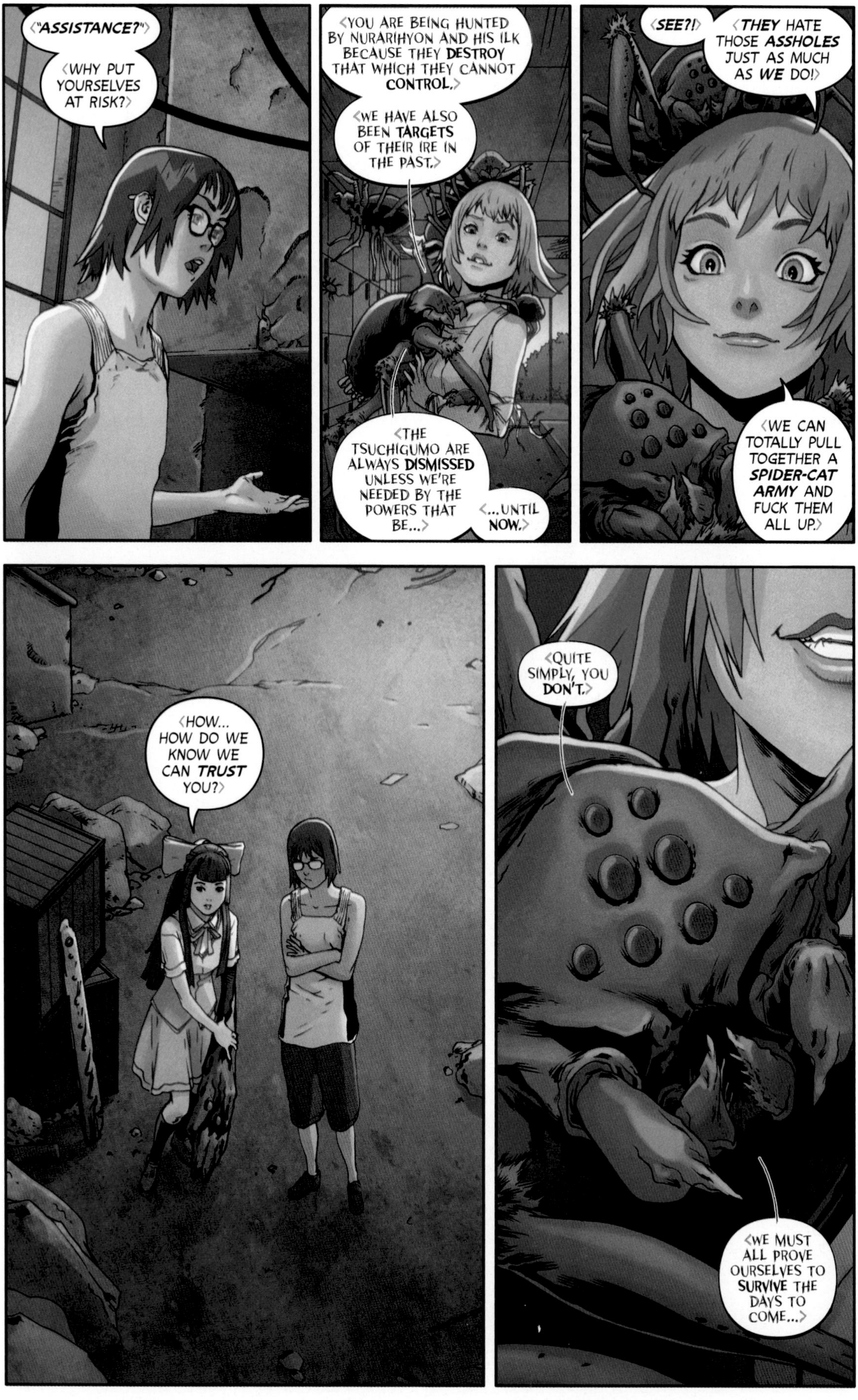
<"ASSISTANCE?">
<WHY PUT YOURSELVES AT RISK?>
<YOU ARE BEING HUNTED BY NURARIHYON AND HIS ILK BECAUSE THEY DESTROY THAT WHICH THEY CANNOT CONTROL.>
<WE HAVE ALSO BEEN TARGETS OF THEIR IRE IN THE PAST.>
<THE TSUCHIGUMO ARE ALWAYS DISMISSED UNLESS WE'RE NEEDED BY THE POWERS THAT BE...>
<...UNTIL NOW.>
<SEE?!>
<THEY HATE THOSE ASSHOLES JUST AS MUCH AS WE DO!>
<WE CAN TOTALLY PULL TOGETHER A SPIDER-CAT ARMY AND FUCK THEM ALL UP.>
<HOW... HOW DO WE KNOW WE CAN TRUST YOU?>
<QUITE SIMPLY, YOU DON'T.>
<WE MUST ALL PROVE OURSELVES TO SURVIVE THE DAYS TO COME...>

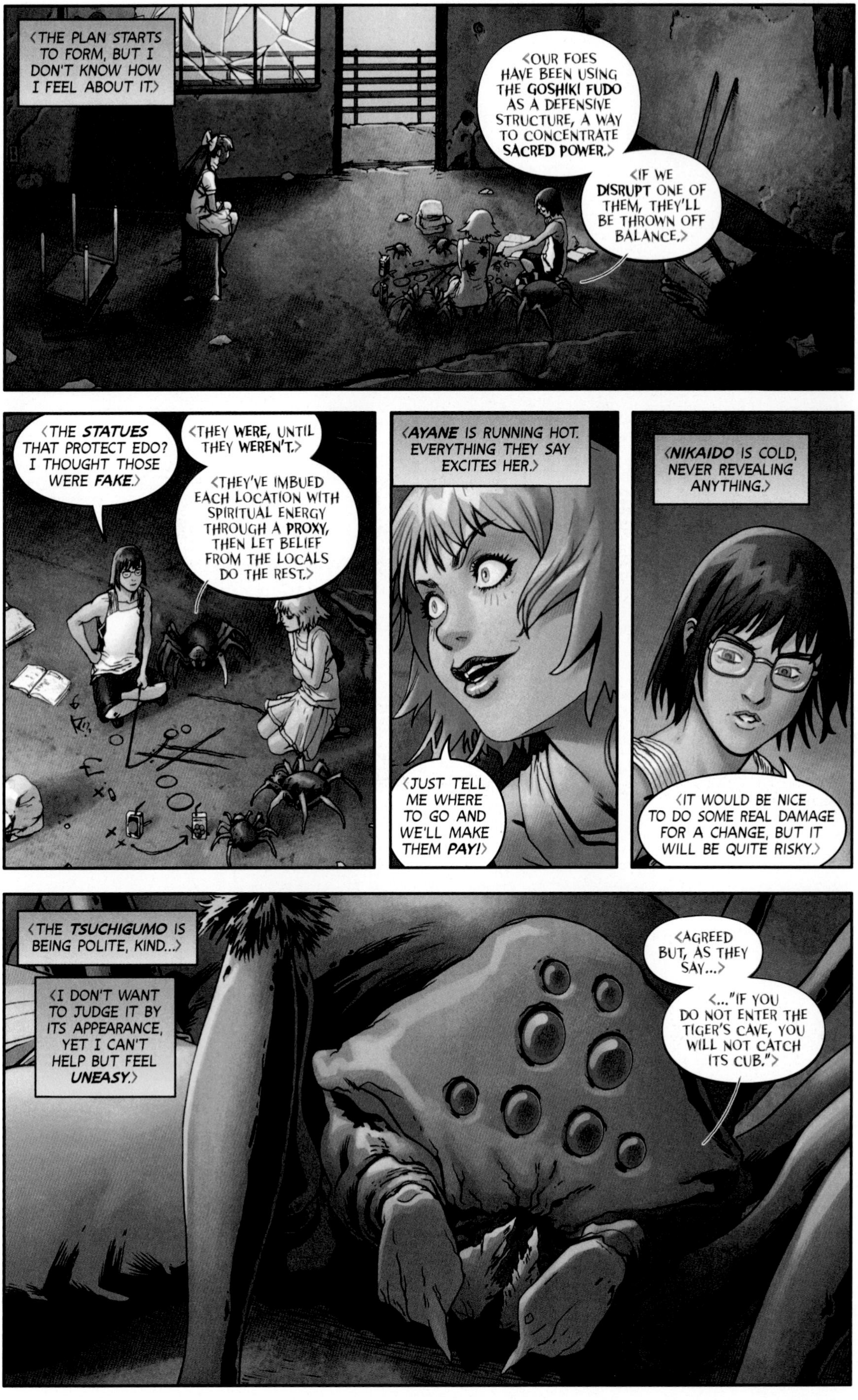

⟨THE PLAN STARTS TO FORM, BUT I DON'T KNOW HOW I FEEL ABOUT IT.⟩
⟨OUR FOES HAVE BEEN USING THE GOSHIKI FUDO AS A DEFENSIVE STRUCTURE, A WAY TO CONCENTRATE SACRED POWER.⟩
⟨IF WE DISRUPT ONE OF THEM, THEY'LL BE THROWN OFF BALANCE.⟩
⟨THE STATUES THAT PROTECT EDO? I THOUGHT THOSE WERE FAKE.⟩
⟨THEY WERE, UNTIL THEY WEREN'T.⟩
⟨THEY'VE IMBUED EACH LOCATION WITH SPIRITUAL ENERGY THROUGH A PROXY, THEN LET BELIEF FROM THE LOCALS DO THE REST.⟩
⟨AYANE IS RUNNING HOT. EVERYTHING THEY SAY EXCITES HER.⟩
⟨JUST TELL ME WHERE TO GO AND WE'LL MAKE THEM PAY!⟩
⟨NIKAIDO IS COLD, NEVER REVEALING ANYTHING.⟩
⟨IT WOULD BE NICE TO DO SOME REAL DAMAGE FOR A CHANGE, BUT IT WILL BE QUITE RISKY.⟩
⟨THE TSUCHIGUMO IS BEING POLITE, KIND...⟩
⟨I DON'T WANT TO JUDGE IT BY ITS APPEARANCE, YET I CAN'T HELP BUT FEEL UNEASY.⟩
⟨AGREED BUT, AS THEY SAY...⟩
⟨..."IF YOU DO NOT ENTER THE TIGER'S CAVE, YOU WILL NOT CATCH ITS CUB."⟩

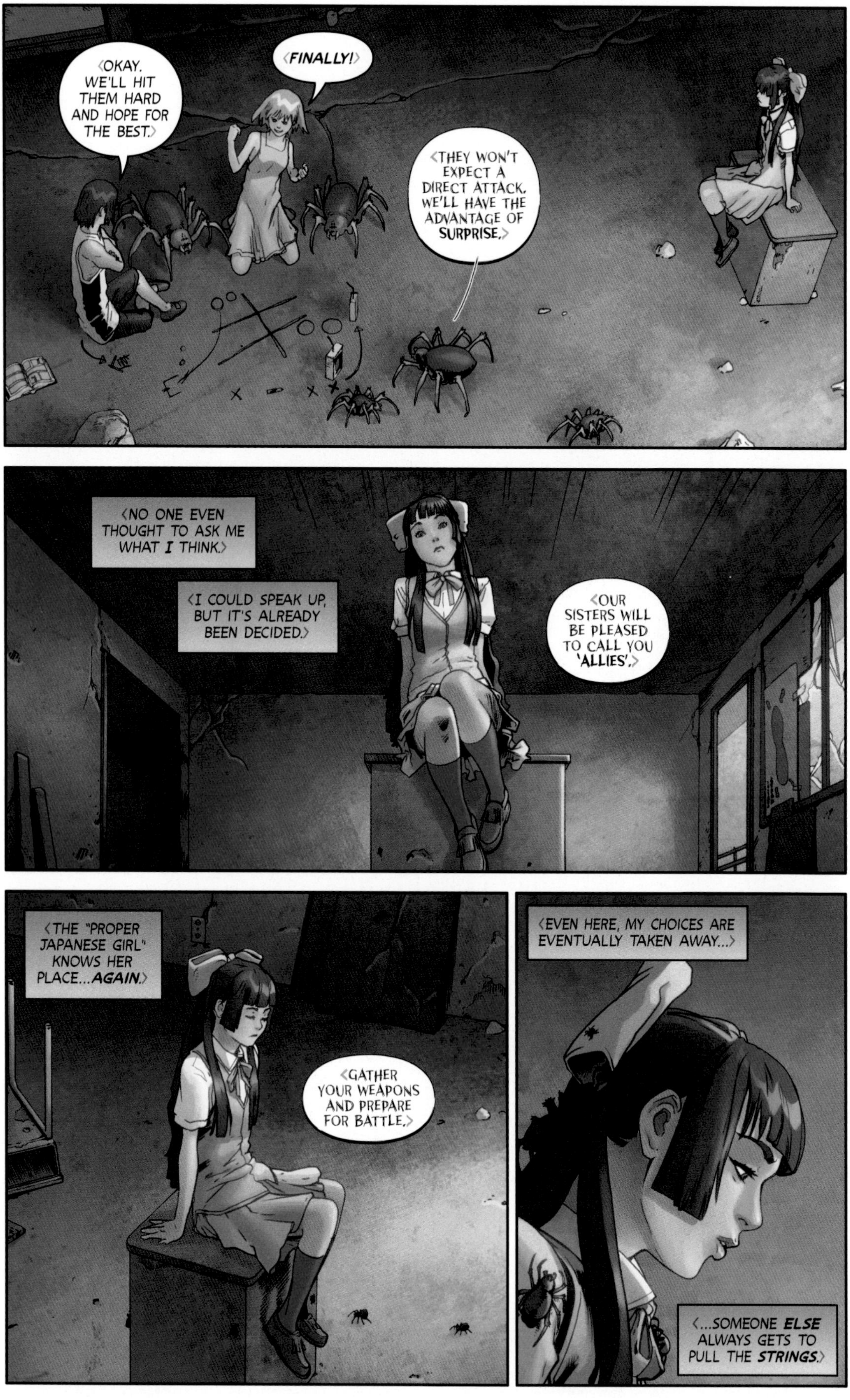

‹OKAY. WE'LL HIT THEM HARD AND HOPE FOR THE BEST.›
‹FINALLY!›
‹THEY WON'T EXPECT A DIRECT ATTACK. WE'LL HAVE THE ADVANTAGE OF SURPRISE.›
‹NO ONE EVEN THOUGHT TO ASK ME WHAT I THINK.›
‹I COULD SPEAK UP, BUT IT'S ALREADY BEEN DECIDED.›
‹OUR SISTERS WILL BE PLEASED TO CALL YOU 'ALLIES'.›
‹THE "PROPER JAPANESE GIRL" KNOWS HER PLACE...AGAIN.›
‹GATHER YOUR WEAPONS AND PREPARE FOR BATTLE.›
‹EVEN HERE, MY CHOICES ARE EVENTUALLY TAKEN AWAY...›
‹...SOMEONE ELSE ALWAYS GETS TO PULL THE STRINGS.›

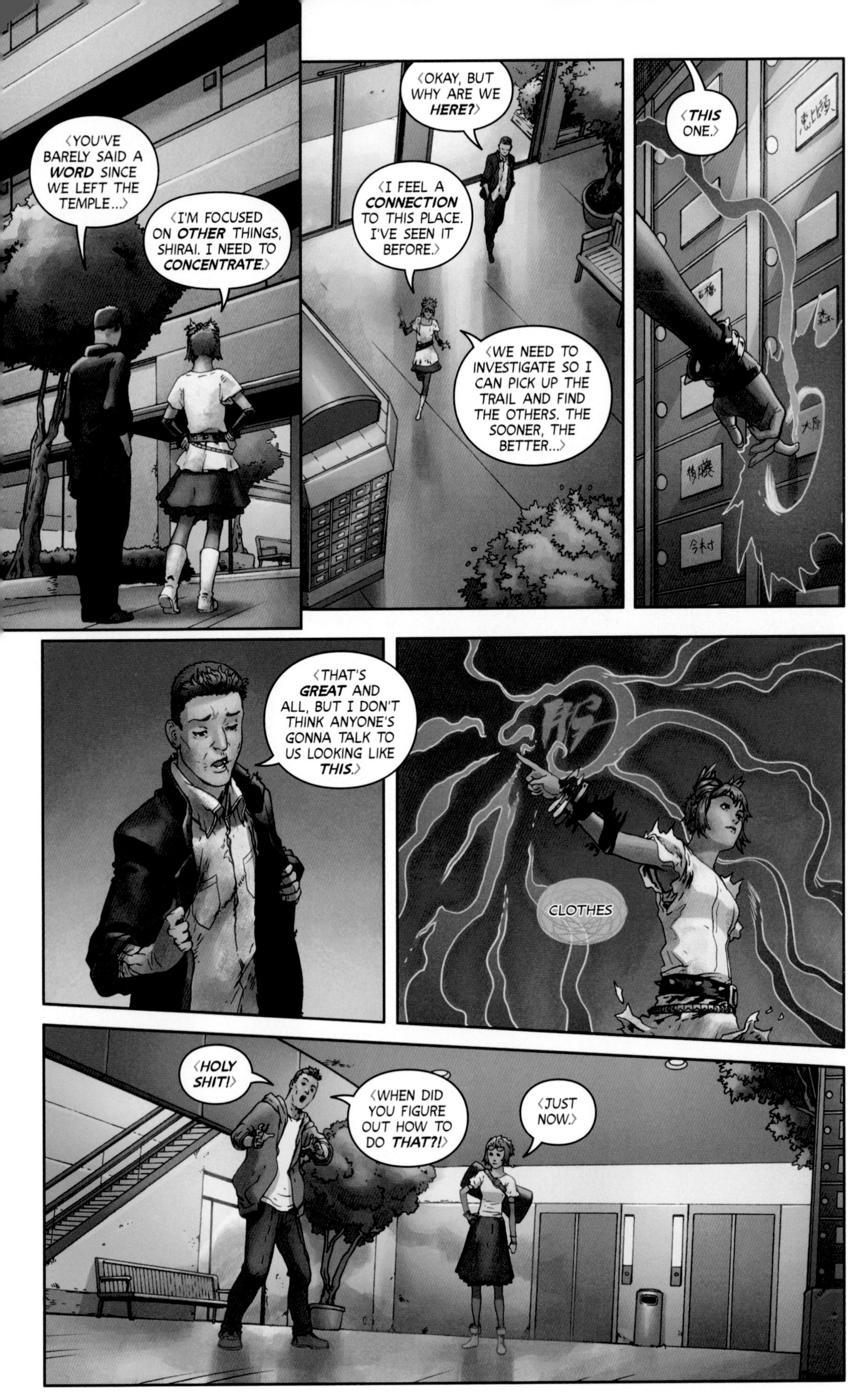

〈YOU'VE BARELY SAID A WORD SINCE WE LEFT THE TEMPLE...〉
〈I'M FOCUSED ON OTHER THINGS, SHIRAI. I NEED TO CONCENTRATE.〉
〈OKAY, BUT WHY ARE WE HERE?〉
〈I FEEL A CONNECTION TO THIS PLACE. I'VE SEEN IT BEFORE.〉
〈WE NEED TO INVESTIGATE SO I CAN PICK UP THE TRAIL AND FIND THE OTHERS. THE SOONER, THE BETTER...〉
〈THIS ONE.〉
〈THAT'S GREAT AND ALL, BUT I DON'T THINK ANYONE'S GONNA TALK TO US LOOKING LIKE THIS.〉
CLOTHES
〈HOLY SHIT!〉
〈WHEN DID YOU FIGURE OUT HOW TO DO THAT?!〉
〈JUST NOW.〉

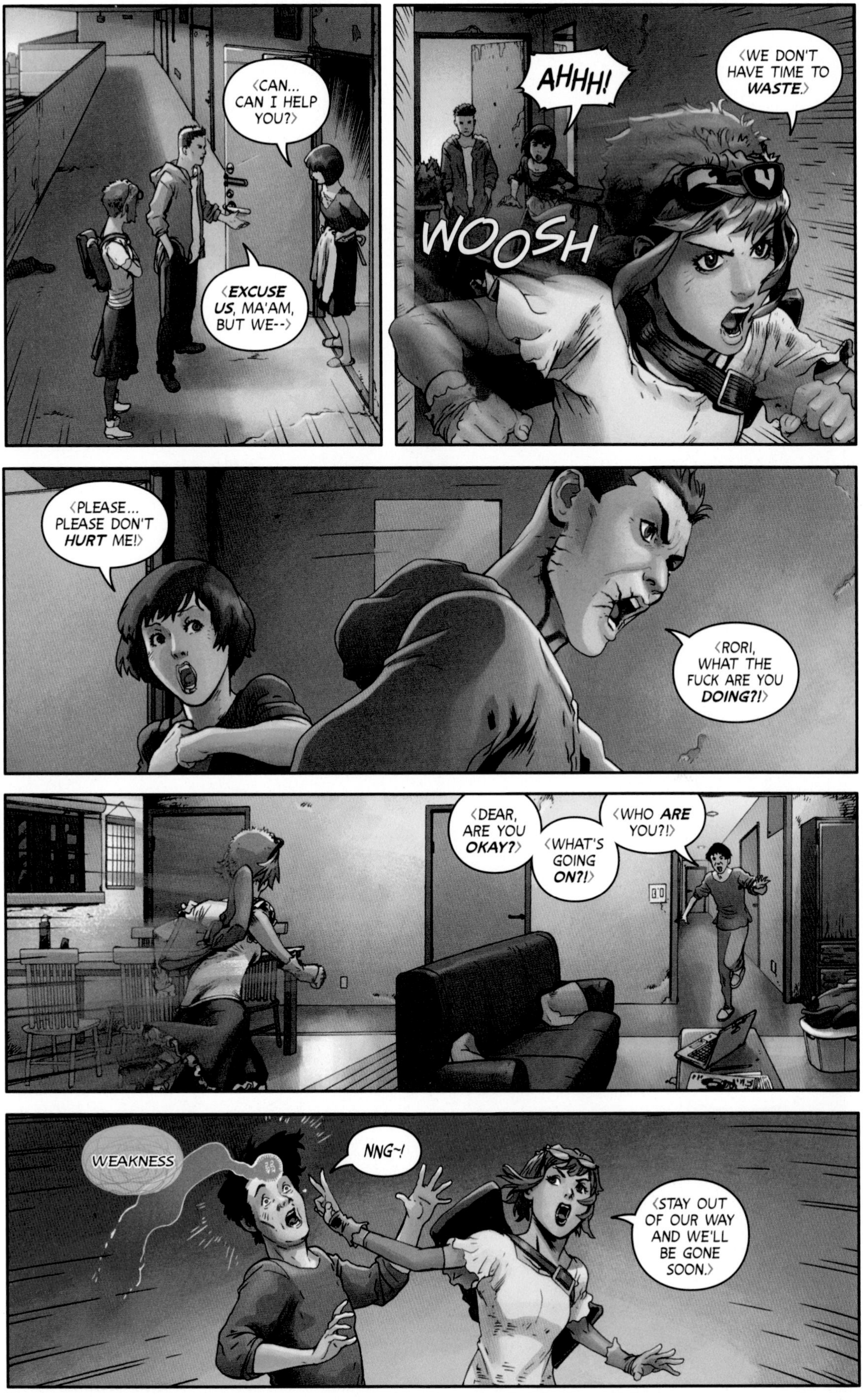
‹CAN... CAN I HELP YOU?›
‹EXCUSE US, MA'AM, BUT WE--›
AHHH!
‹WE DON'T HAVE TIME TO WASTE.›
WOOSH
‹PLEASE... PLEASE DON'T HURT ME!›
‹RORI, WHAT THE FUCK ARE YOU DOING?!›
‹DEAR, ARE YOU OKAY?›
‹WHAT'S GOING ON?!›
‹WHO ARE YOU?!›
WEAKNESS
NNG~!
‹STAY OUT OF OUR WAY AND WE'LL BE GONE SOON.›

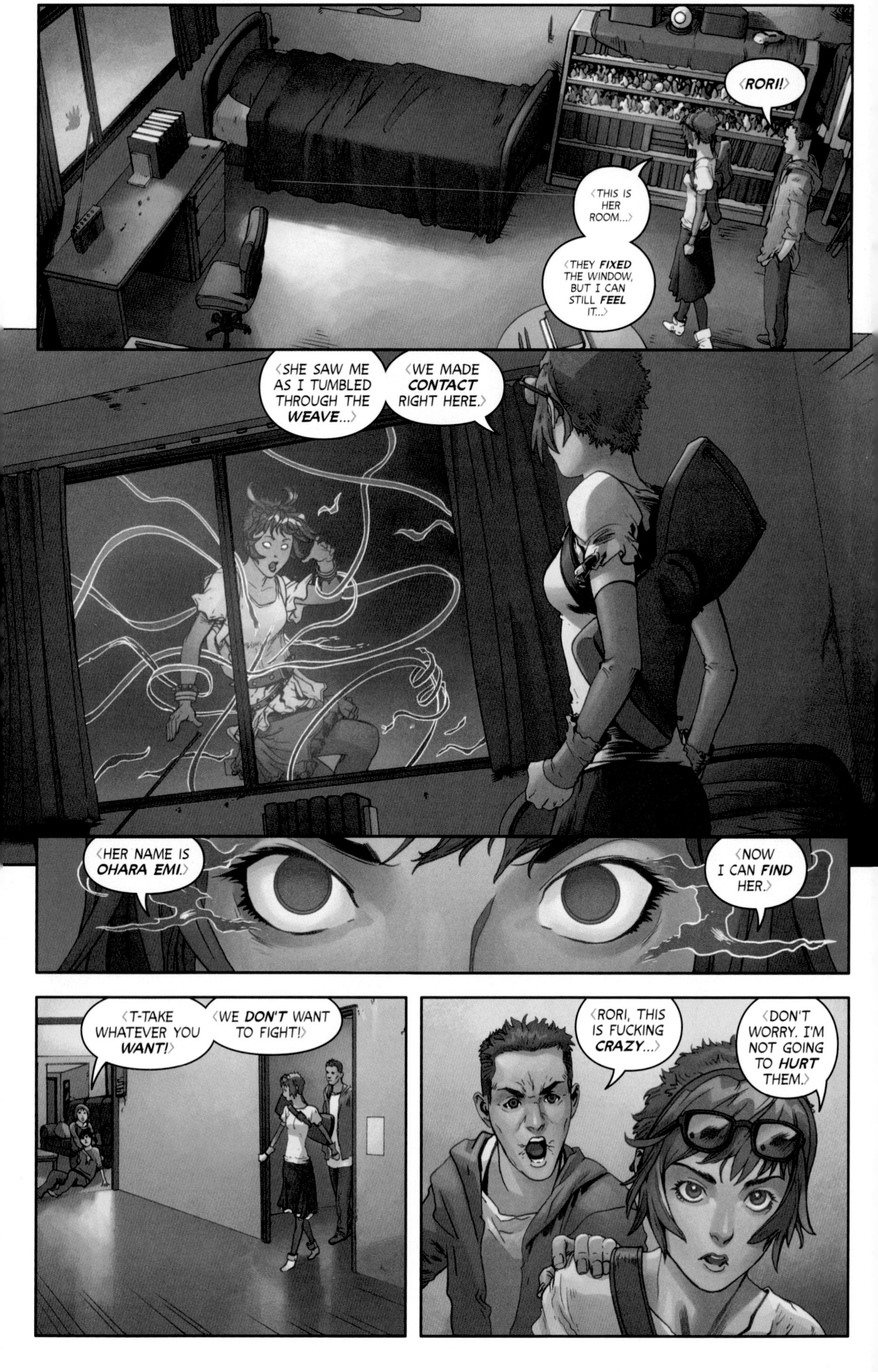

‹RORI!›
‹THIS IS HER ROOM...›
‹THEY FIXED THE WINDOW, BUT I CAN STILL FEEL IT...›
‹SHE SAW ME AS I TUMBLED THROUGH THE WEAVE...›
‹WE MADE CONTACT RIGHT HERE.›
‹HER NAME IS OHARA EMI.›
‹NOW I CAN FIND HER.›
‹T-TAKE WHATEVER YOU WANT!›
‹WE DON'T WANT TO FIGHT!›
‹RORI, THIS IS FUCKING CRAZY...›
‹DON'T WORRY. I'M NOT GOING TO HURT THEM.›

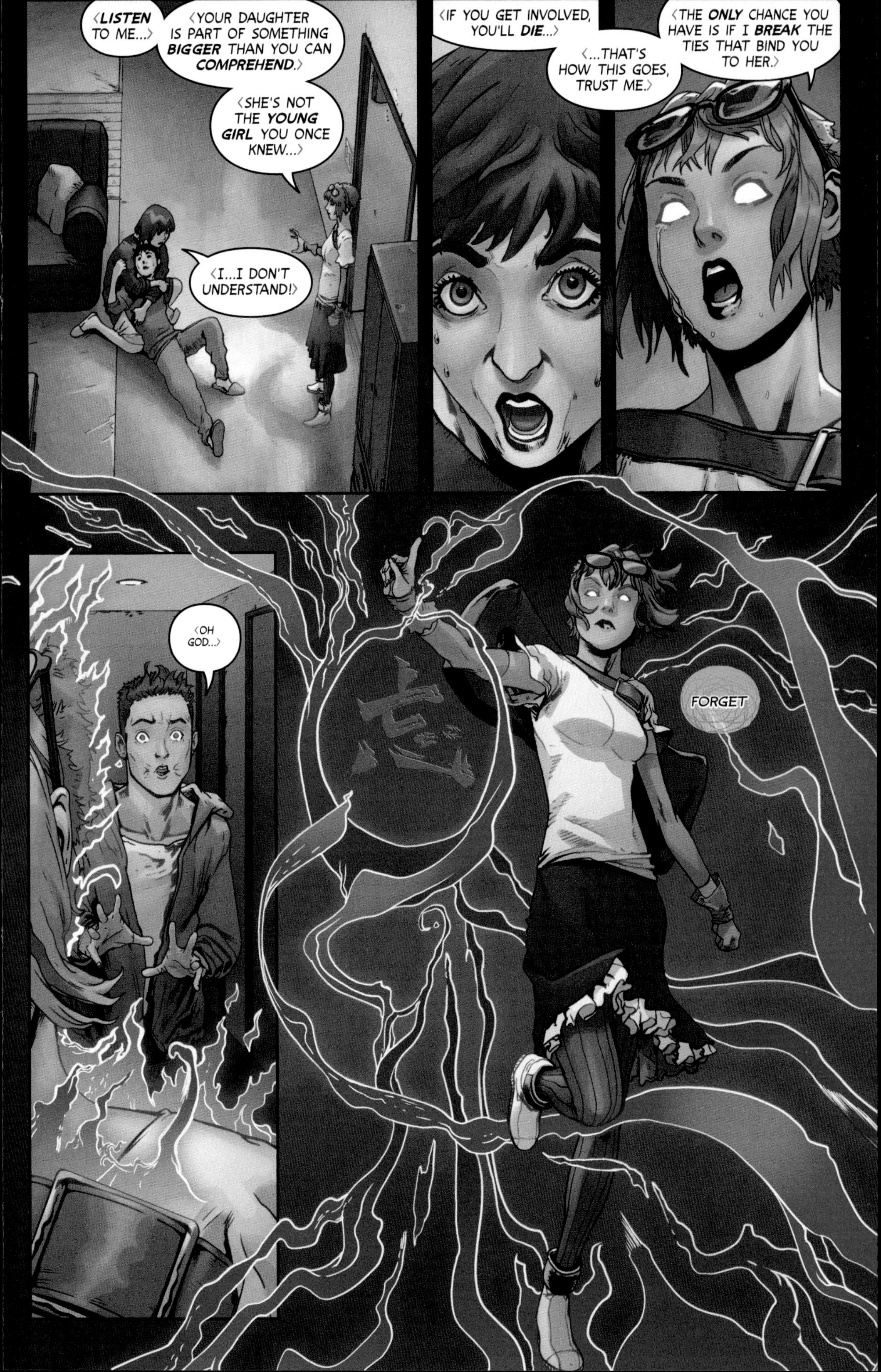

<LISTEN TO ME...>
<YOUR DAUGHTER IS PART OF SOMETHING BIGGER THAN YOU CAN COMPREHEND.>
<SHE'S NOT THE YOUNG GIRL YOU ONCE KNEW...>
<I...I DON'T UNDERSTAND!>
<IF YOU GET INVOLVED, YOU'LL DIE...>
<...THAT'S HOW THIS GOES, TRUST ME.>
<THE ONLY CHANCE YOU HAVE IS IF I BREAK THE TIES THAT BIND YOU TO HER.>
<OH GOD...>
FORGET

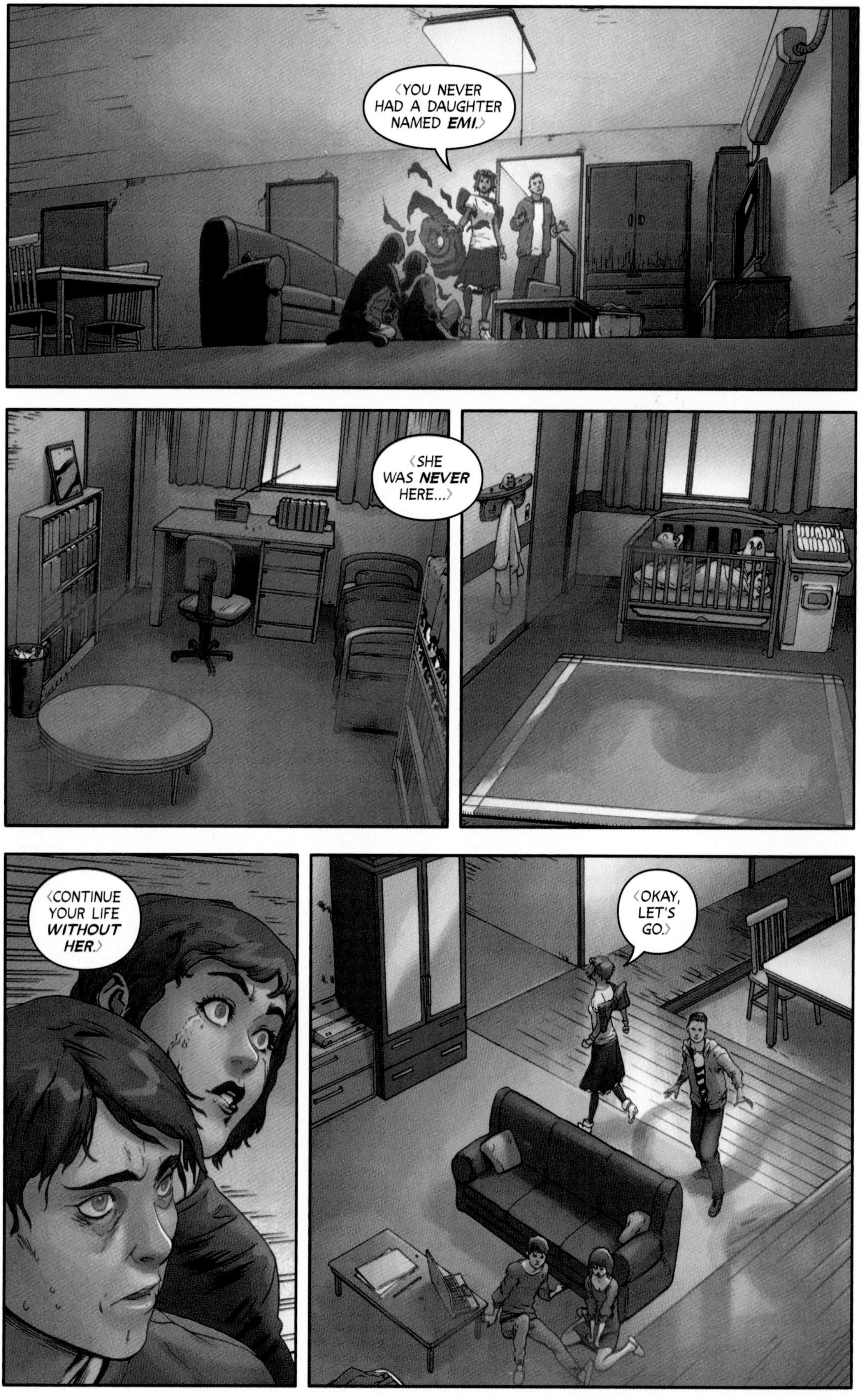

‹YOU NEVER HAD A DAUGHTER NAMED **EMI**.›
‹SHE WAS **NEVER** HERE...›
‹CONTINUE YOUR LIFE **WITHOUT** HER.›
‹OKAY, LET'S GO.›

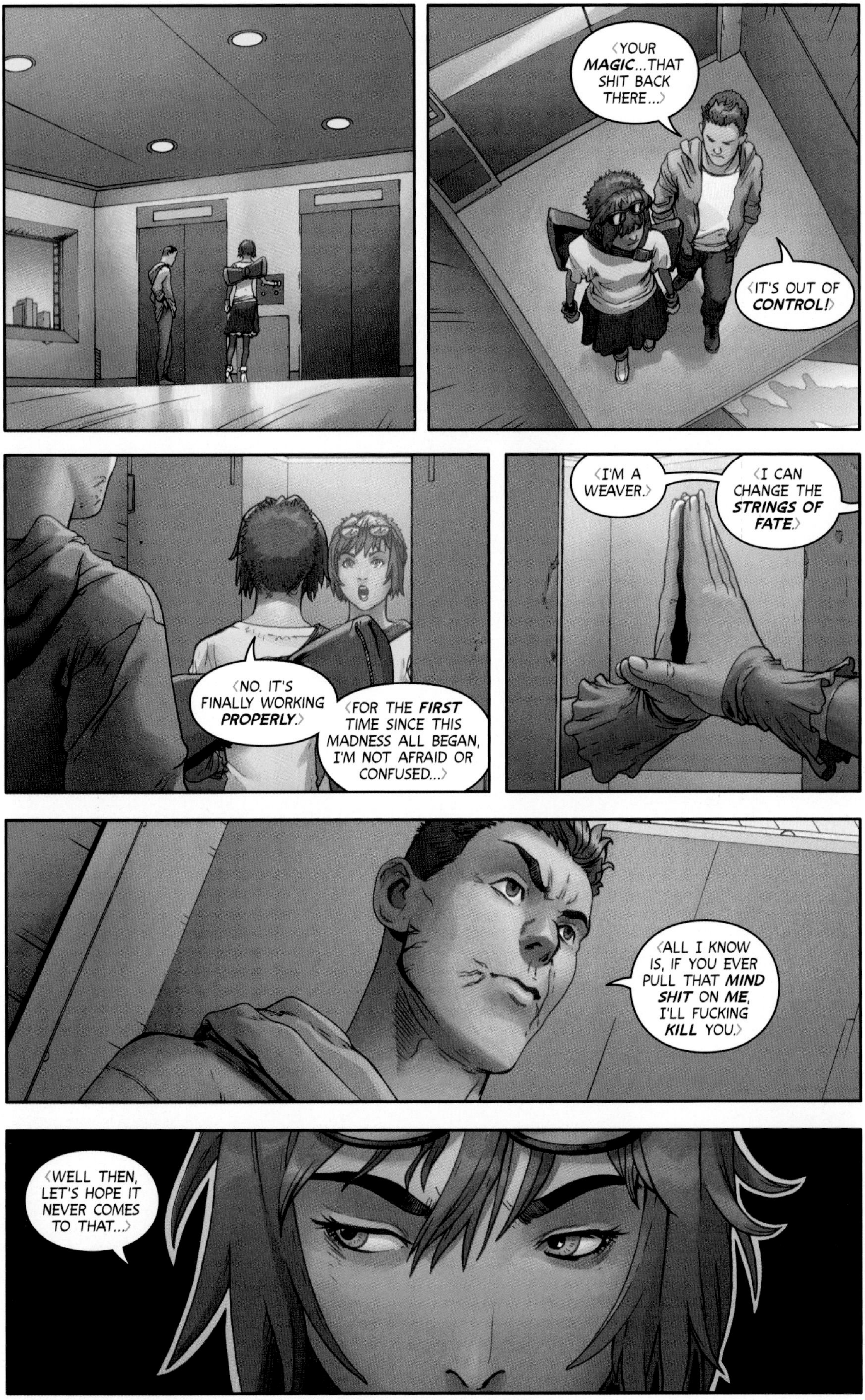
⟨YOUR MAGIC...THAT SHIT BACK THERE...⟩
⟨IT'S OUT OF CONTROL!⟩
⟨NO. IT'S FINALLY WORKING PROPERLY.⟩
⟨FOR THE FIRST TIME SINCE THIS MADNESS ALL BEGAN, I'M NOT AFRAID OR CONFUSED...⟩
⟨I'M A WEAVER.⟩
⟨I CAN CHANGE THE STRINGS OF FATE.⟩
⟨ALL I KNOW IS, IF YOU EVER PULL THAT MIND SHIT ON ME, I'LL FUCKING KILL YOU.⟩
⟨WELL THEN, LET'S HOPE IT NEVER COMES TO THAT...⟩

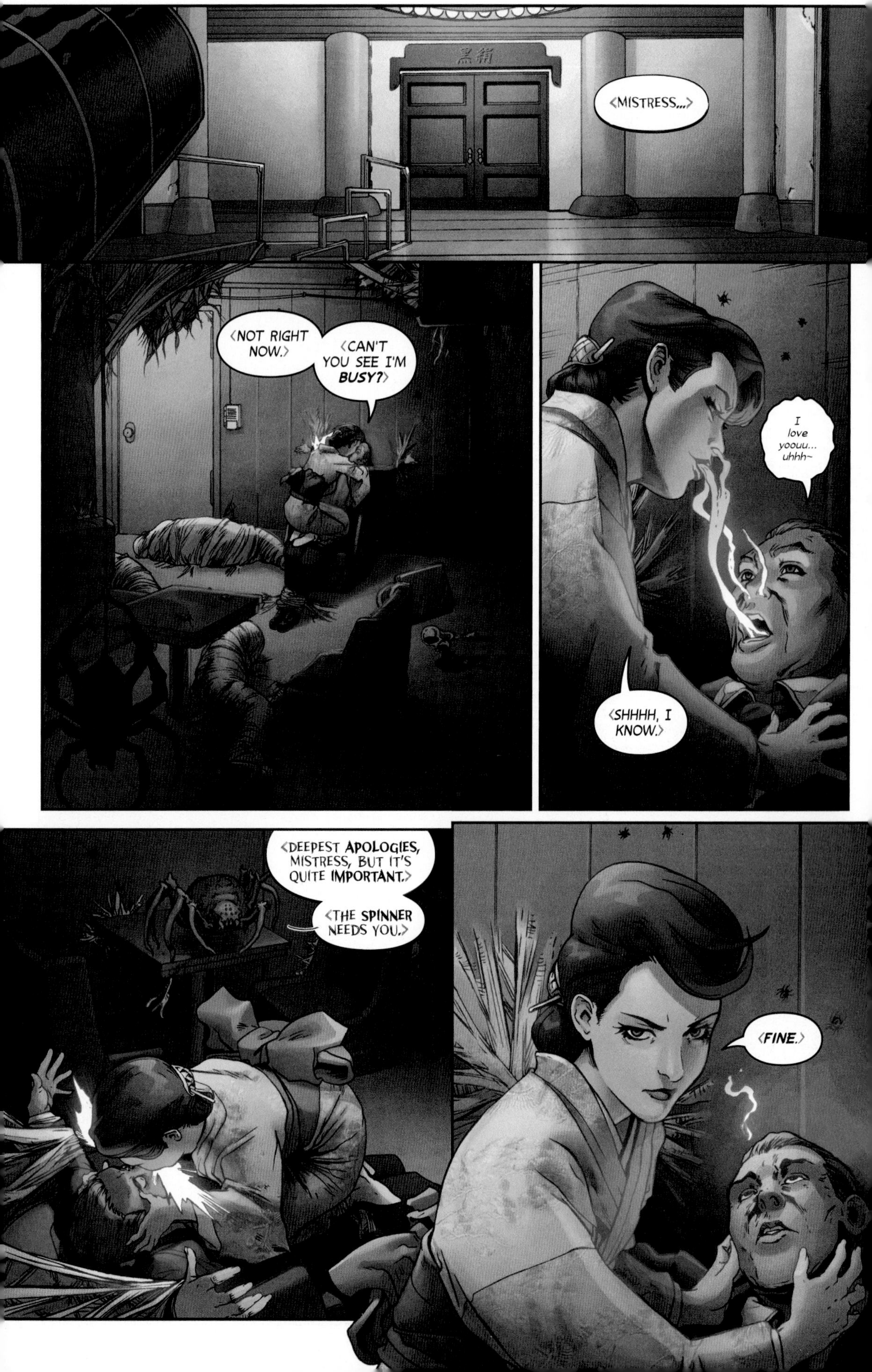
‹MISTRESS...›
‹NOT RIGHT NOW.›
‹CAN'T YOU SEE I'M **BUSY?**›
I love yoouu... uhhh~
‹SHHHH, I KNOW.›
‹DEEPEST **APOLOGIES**, MISTRESS, BUT IT'S QUITE **IMPORTANT**.›
‹THE **SPINNER** NEEDS YOU.›
‹**FINE.**›

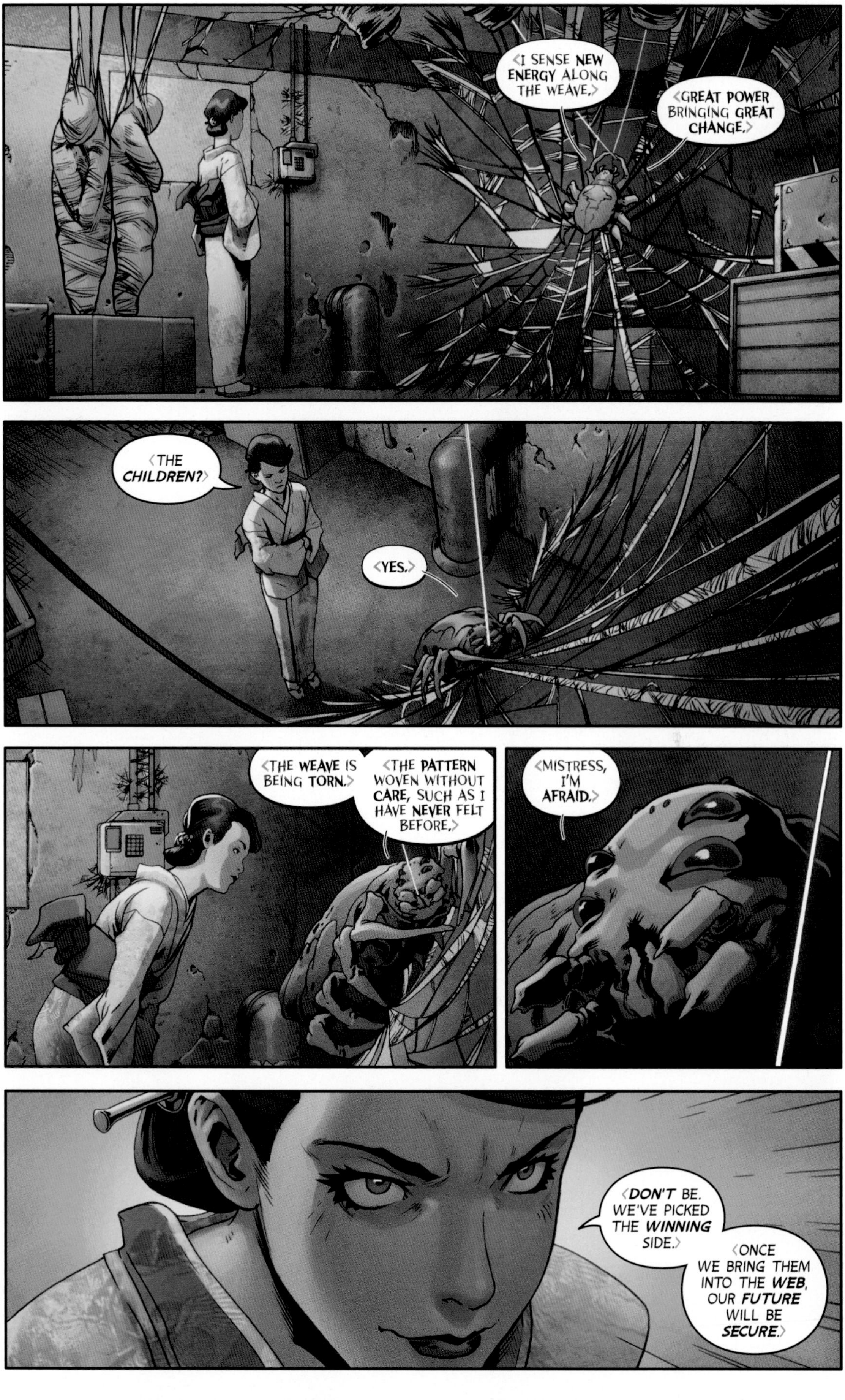
<I SENSE NEW ENERGY ALONG THE WEAVE.>
<GREAT POWER BRINGING GREAT CHANGE.>
<THE CHILDREN?>
<YES.>
<THE WEAVE IS BEING TORN.>
<THE PATTERN WOVEN WITHOUT CARE, SUCH AS I HAVE NEVER FELT BEFORE.>
<MISTRESS, I'M AFRAID.>
<DON'T BE. WE'VE PICKED THE WINNING SIDE.>
<ONCE WE BRING THEM INTO THE WEB, OUR FUTURE WILL BE SECURE.>

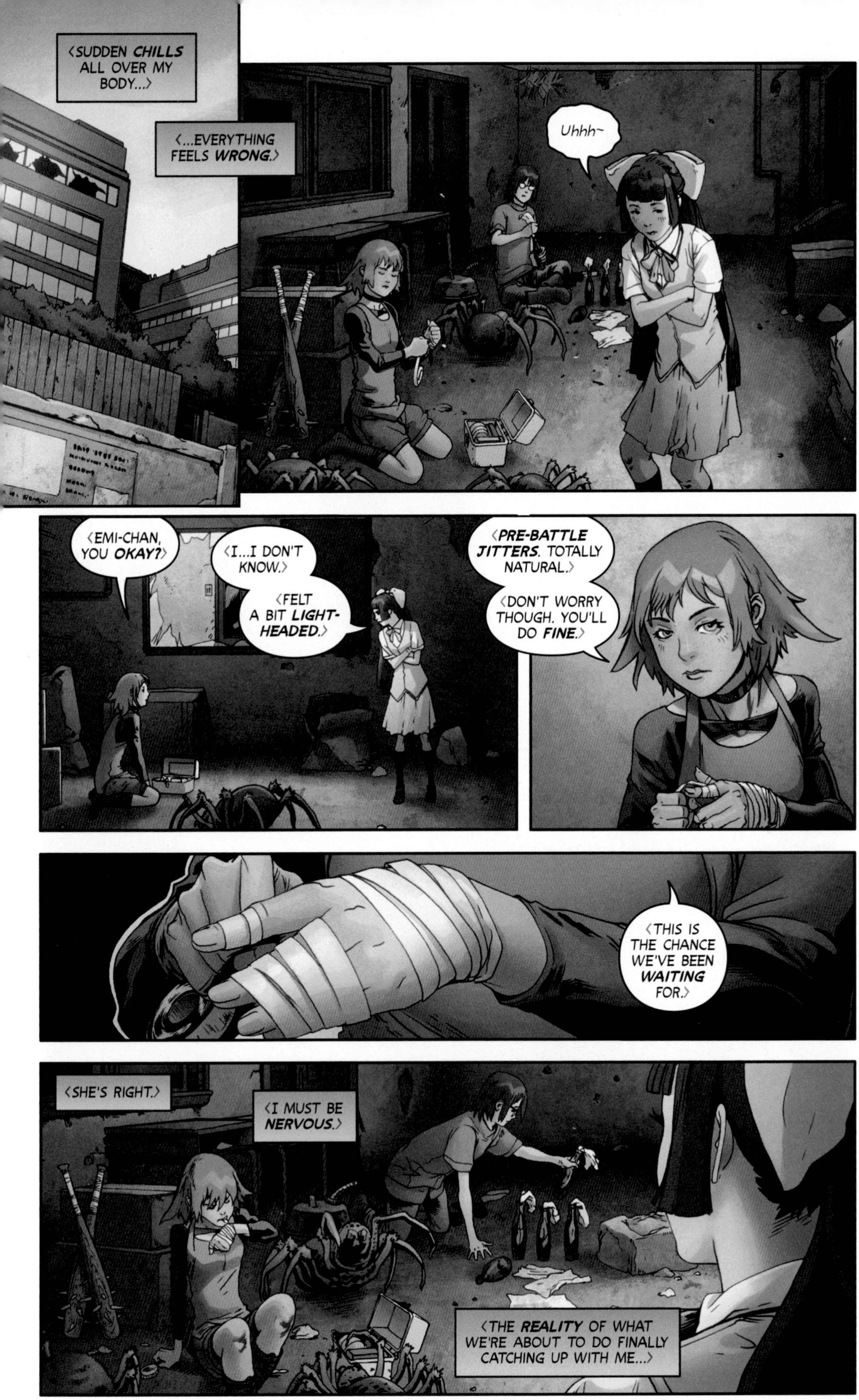

‹SUDDEN **CHILLS** ALL OVER MY BODY...›
‹...EVERYTHING FEELS **WRONG.**›
Uhhh~
‹EMI-CHAN, YOU **OKAY?**›
‹I...I DON'T KNOW.›
‹FELT A BIT **LIGHT-HEADED.**›
‹**PRE-BATTLE JITTERS.** TOTALLY NATURAL.›
‹DON'T WORRY THOUGH. YOU'LL DO **FINE.**›
‹THIS IS THE CHANCE WE'VE BEEN **WAITING** FOR.›
‹SHE'S RIGHT.›
‹I MUST BE **NERVOUS.**›
‹THE **REALITY** OF WHAT WE'RE ABOUT TO DO FINALLY CATCHING UP WITH ME...›

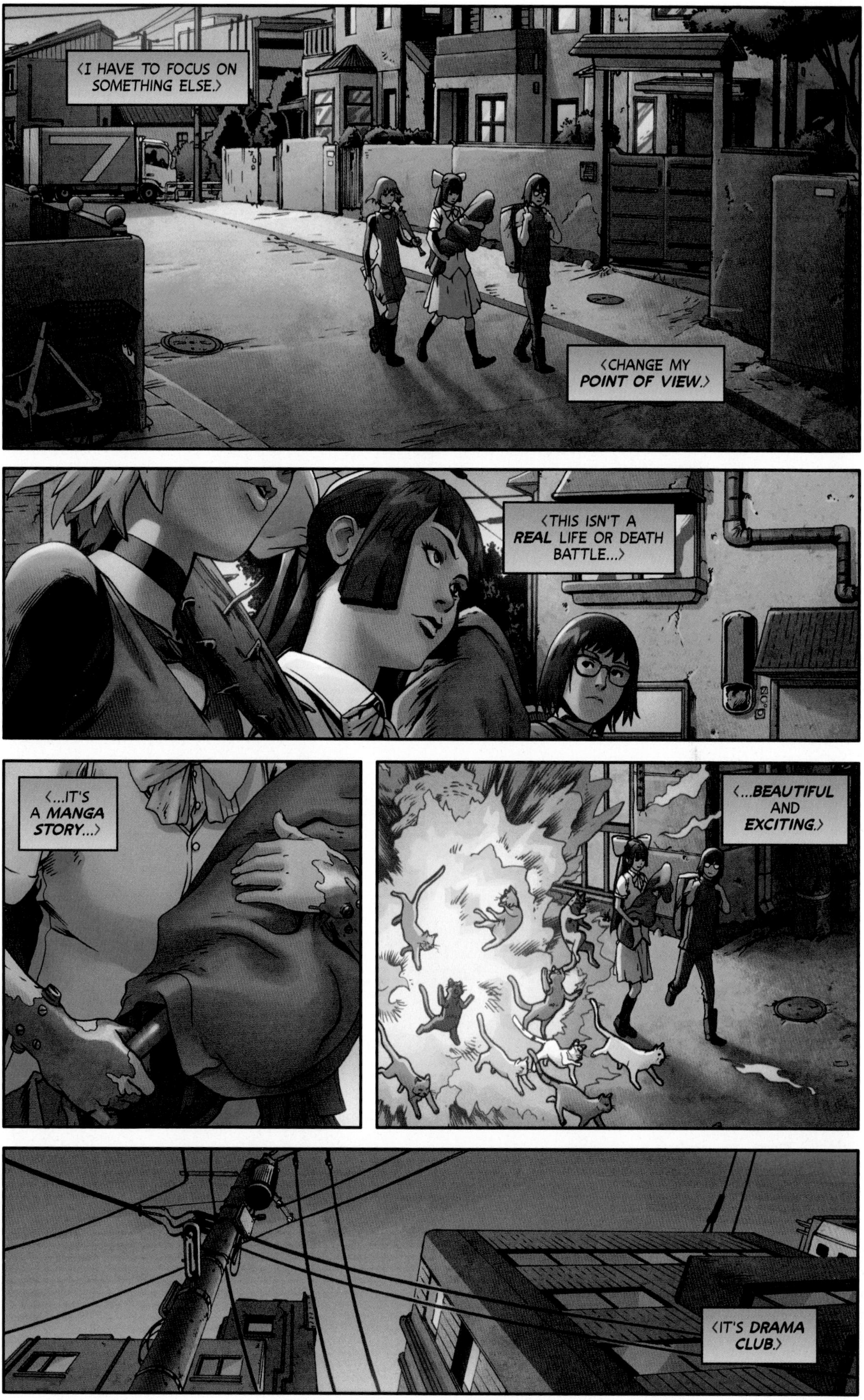

‹I HAVE TO FOCUS ON SOMETHING ELSE.›
‹CHANGE MY POINT OF VIEW.›
‹THIS ISN'T A REAL LIFE OR DEATH BATTLE...›
‹...IT'S A MANGA STORY...›
‹...BEAUTIFUL AND EXCITING.›
‹IT'S DRAMA CLUB.›

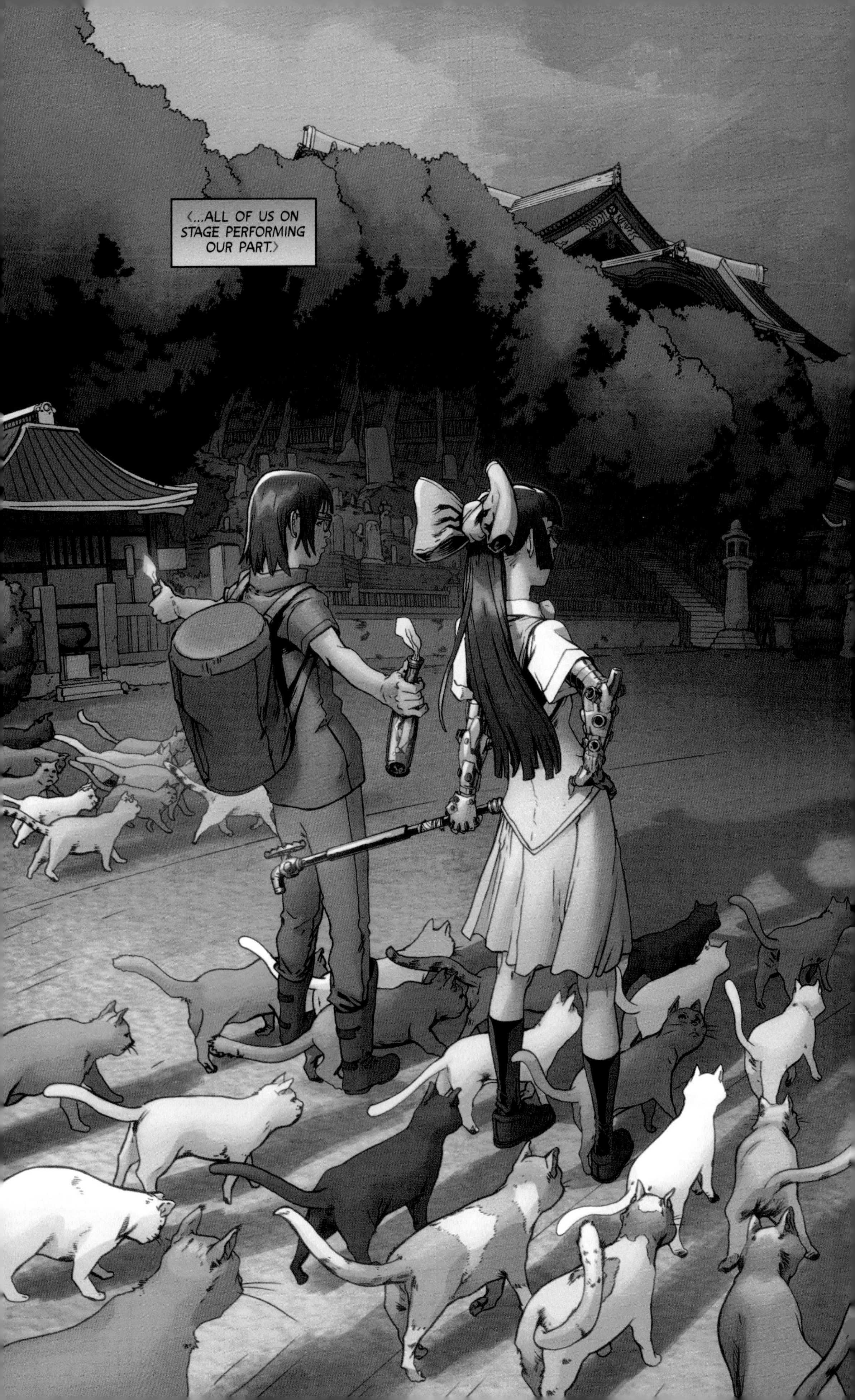
‹...ALL OF US ON STAGE PERFORMING OUR PART.›

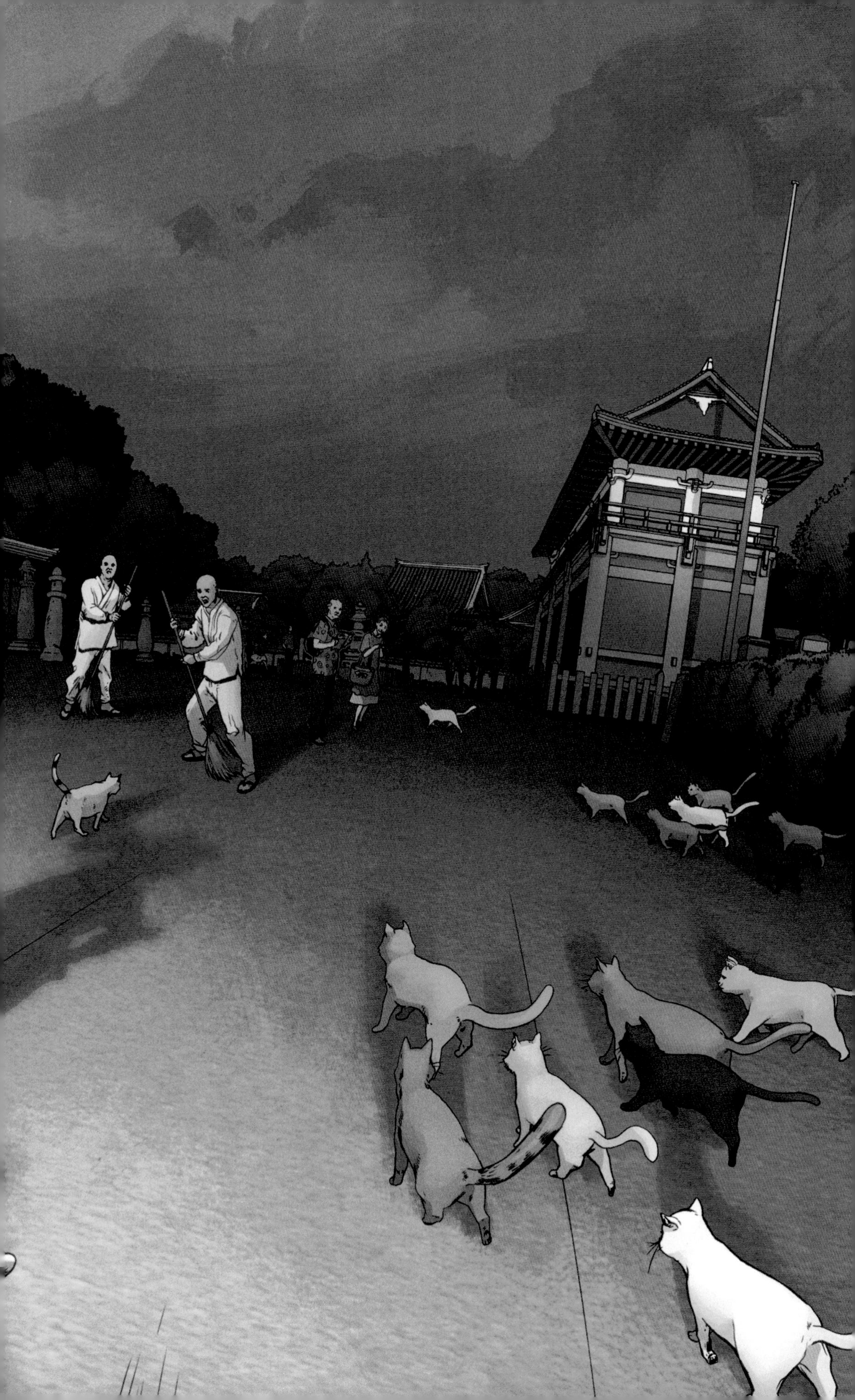

Chapter Ten

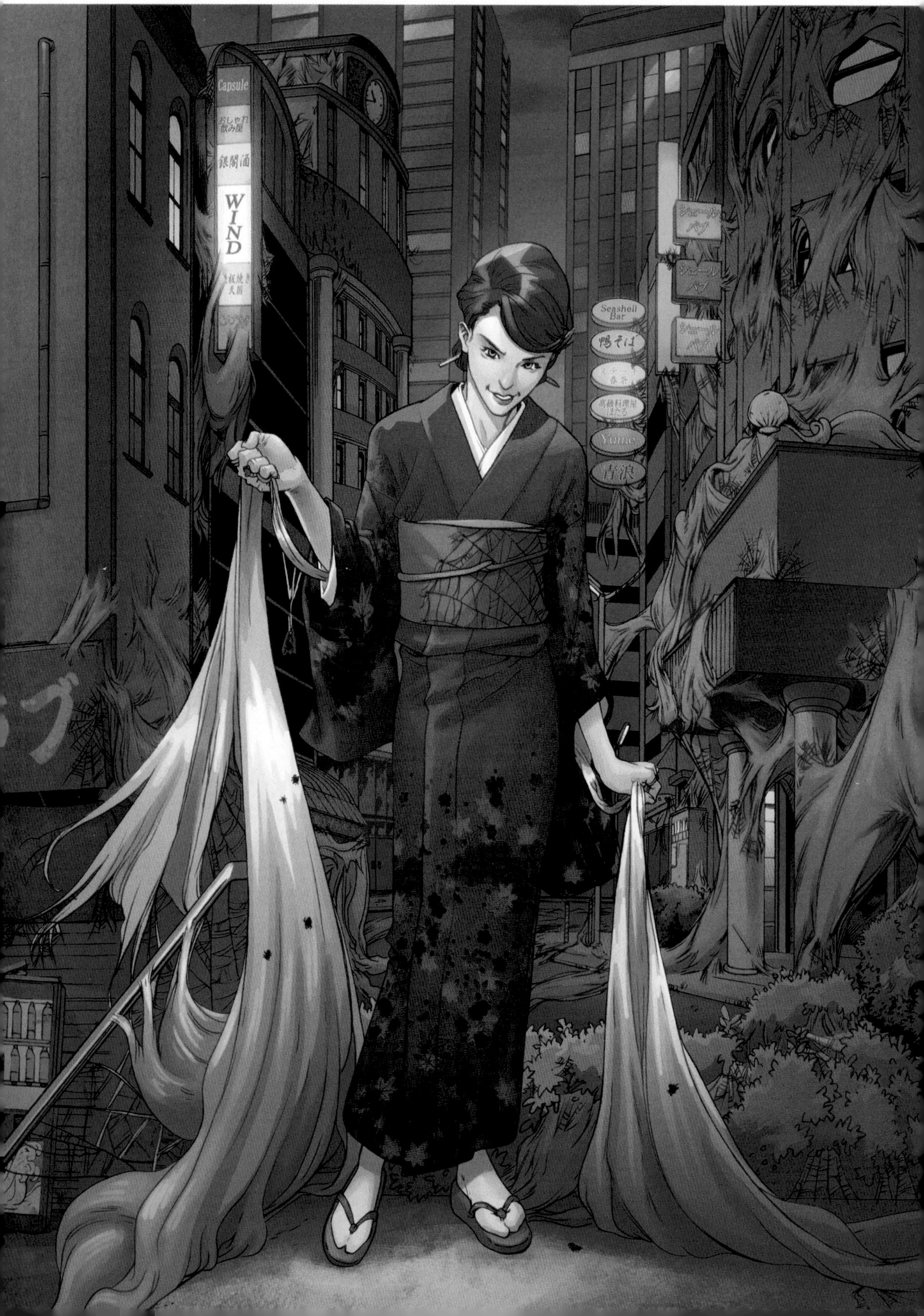
Capsule
おしゃれ飲み屋
銀閣酒
WIND
Seashell Bar
鴨そば
Yume
青浪

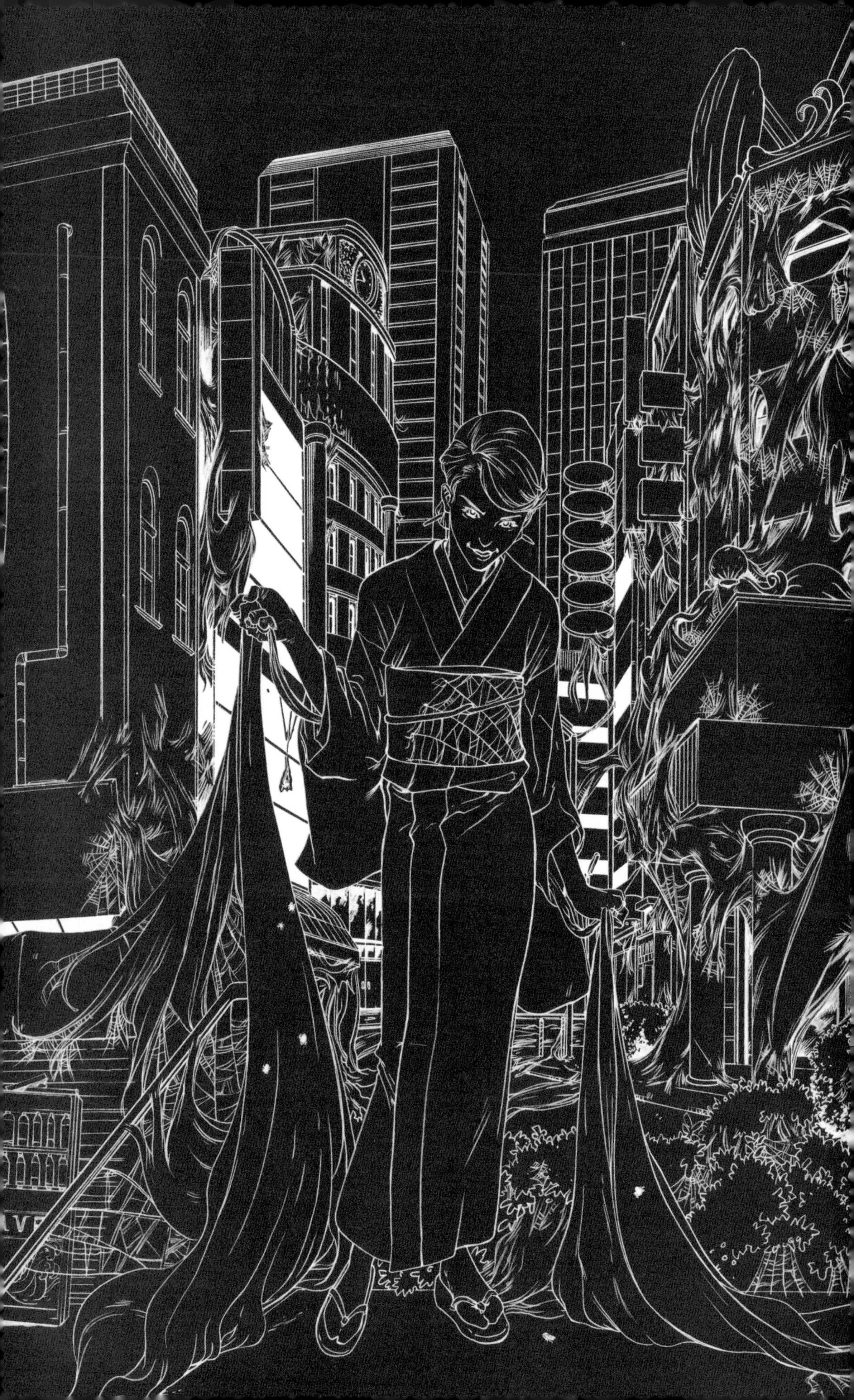

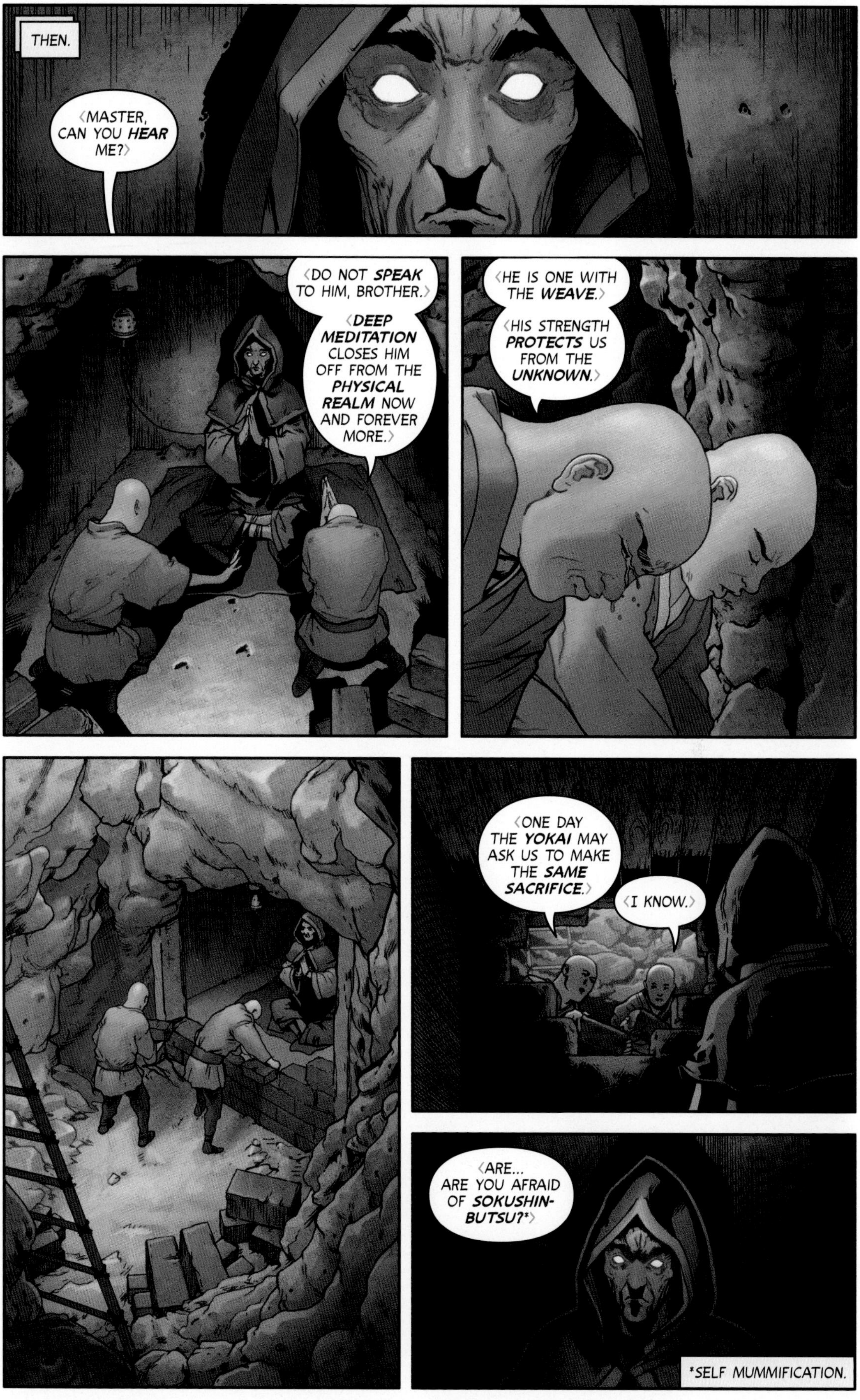
THEN.
⟨MASTER, CAN YOU HEAR ME?⟩
⟨DO NOT SPEAK TO HIM, BROTHER.⟩
⟨DEEP MEDITATION CLOSES HIM OFF FROM THE PHYSICAL REALM NOW AND FOREVER MORE.⟩
⟨HE IS ONE WITH THE WEAVE.⟩
⟨HIS STRENGTH PROTECTS US FROM THE UNKNOWN.⟩
⟨ONE DAY THE YOKAI MAY ASK US TO MAKE THE SAME SACRIFICE.⟩
⟨I KNOW.⟩
⟨ARE... ARE YOU AFRAID OF SOKUSHIN-BUTSU?*⟩
*SELF MUMMIFICATION.

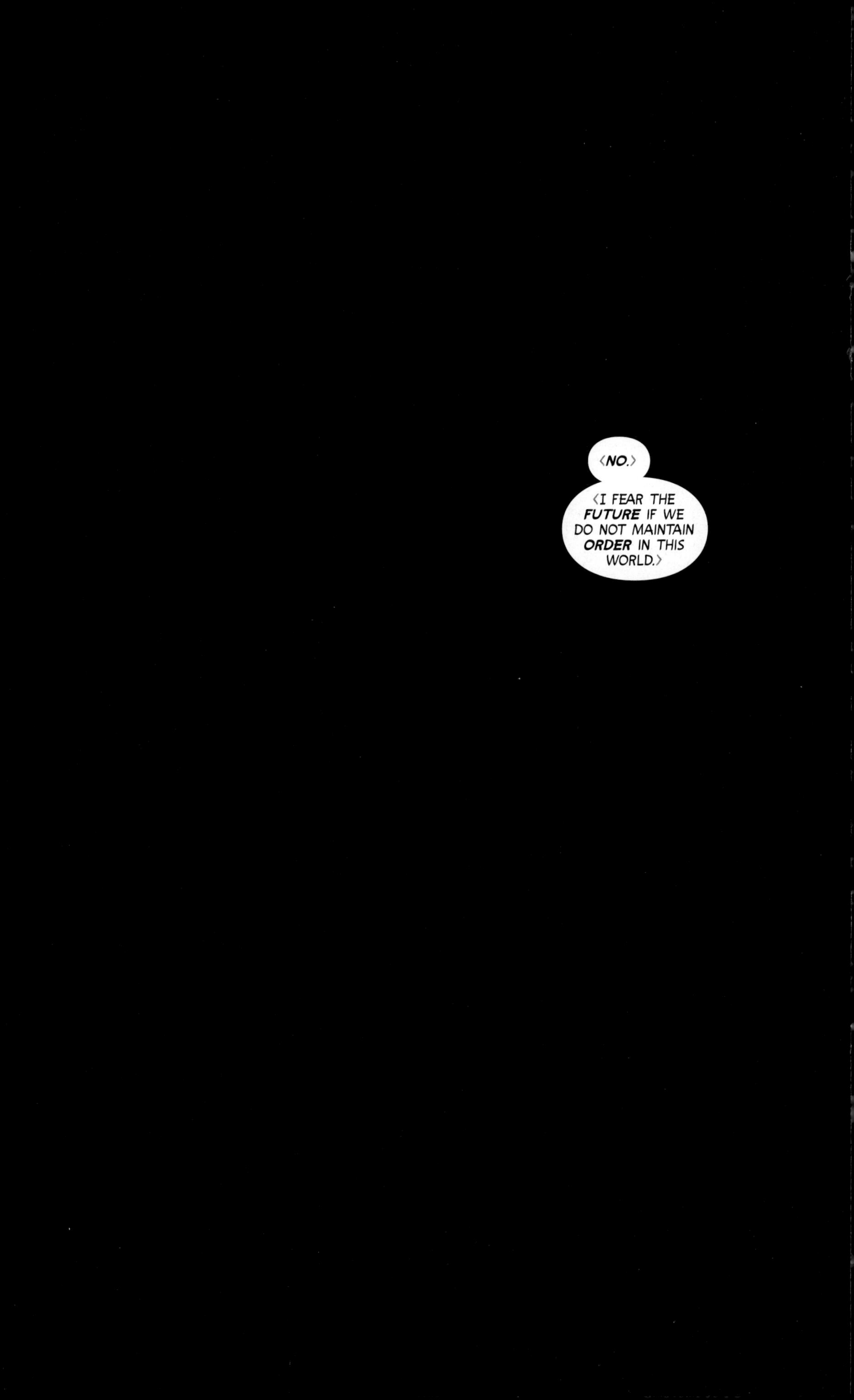
⟨**NO.**⟩
⟨I FEAR THE **FUTURE** IF WE DO NOT MAINTAIN **ORDER** IN THIS WORLD.⟩

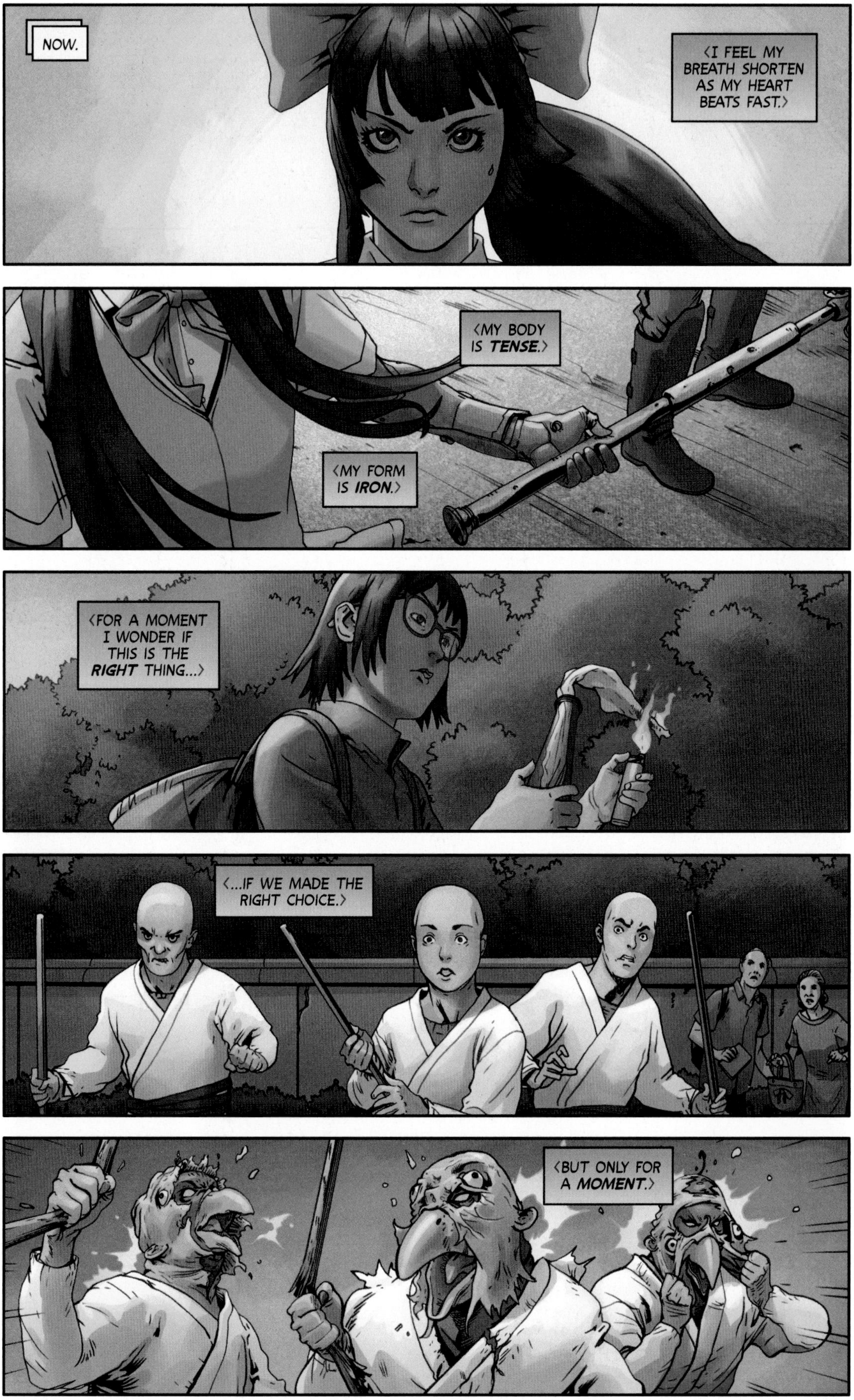
NOW.
⟨I FEEL MY BREATH SHORTEN AS MY HEART BEATS FAST.⟩
⟨MY BODY IS TENSE.⟩
⟨MY FORM IS IRON.⟩
⟨FOR A MOMENT I WONDER IF THIS IS THE RIGHT THING...⟩
⟨...IF WE MADE THE RIGHT CHOICE.⟩
⟨BUT ONLY FOR A MOMENT.⟩

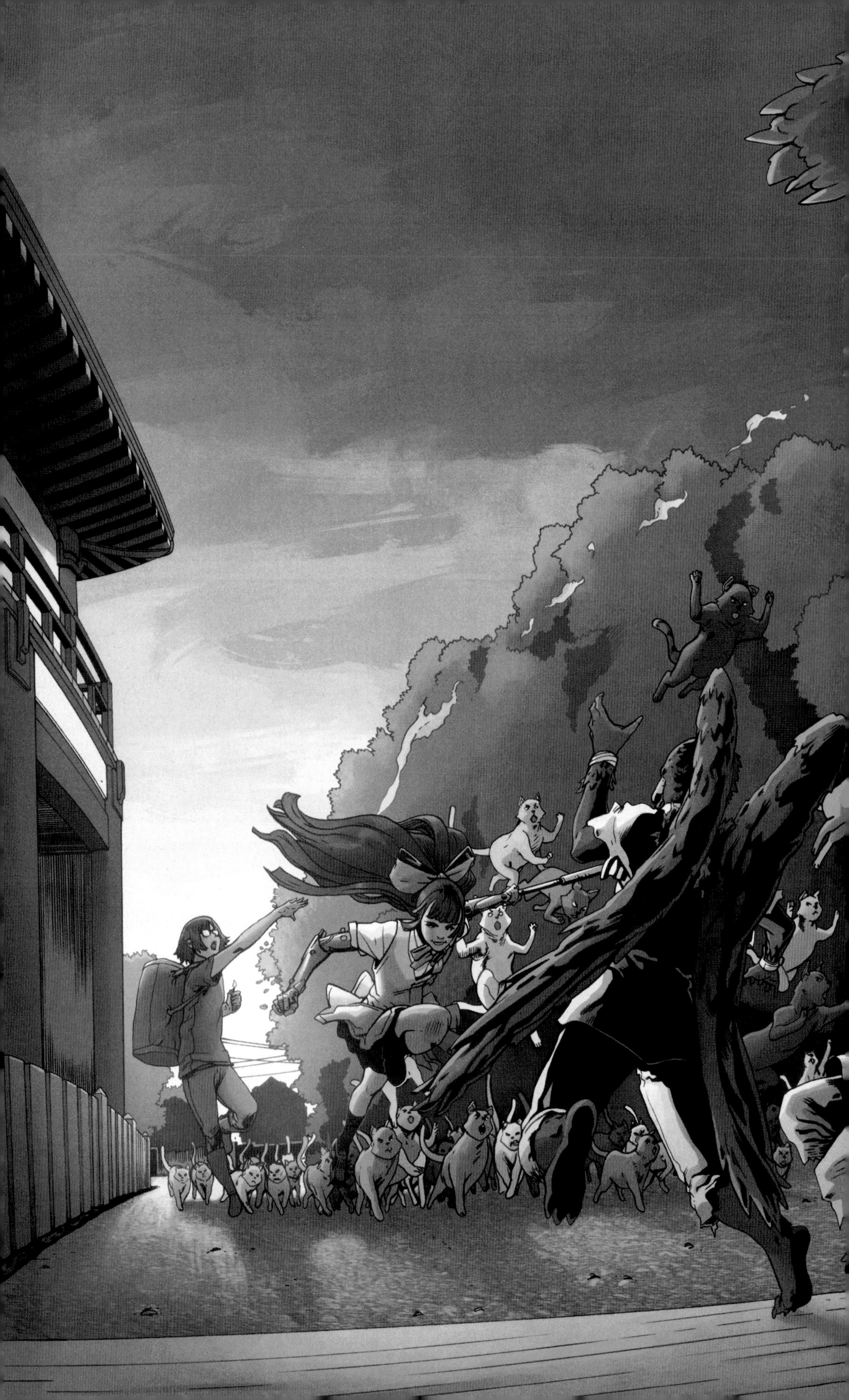

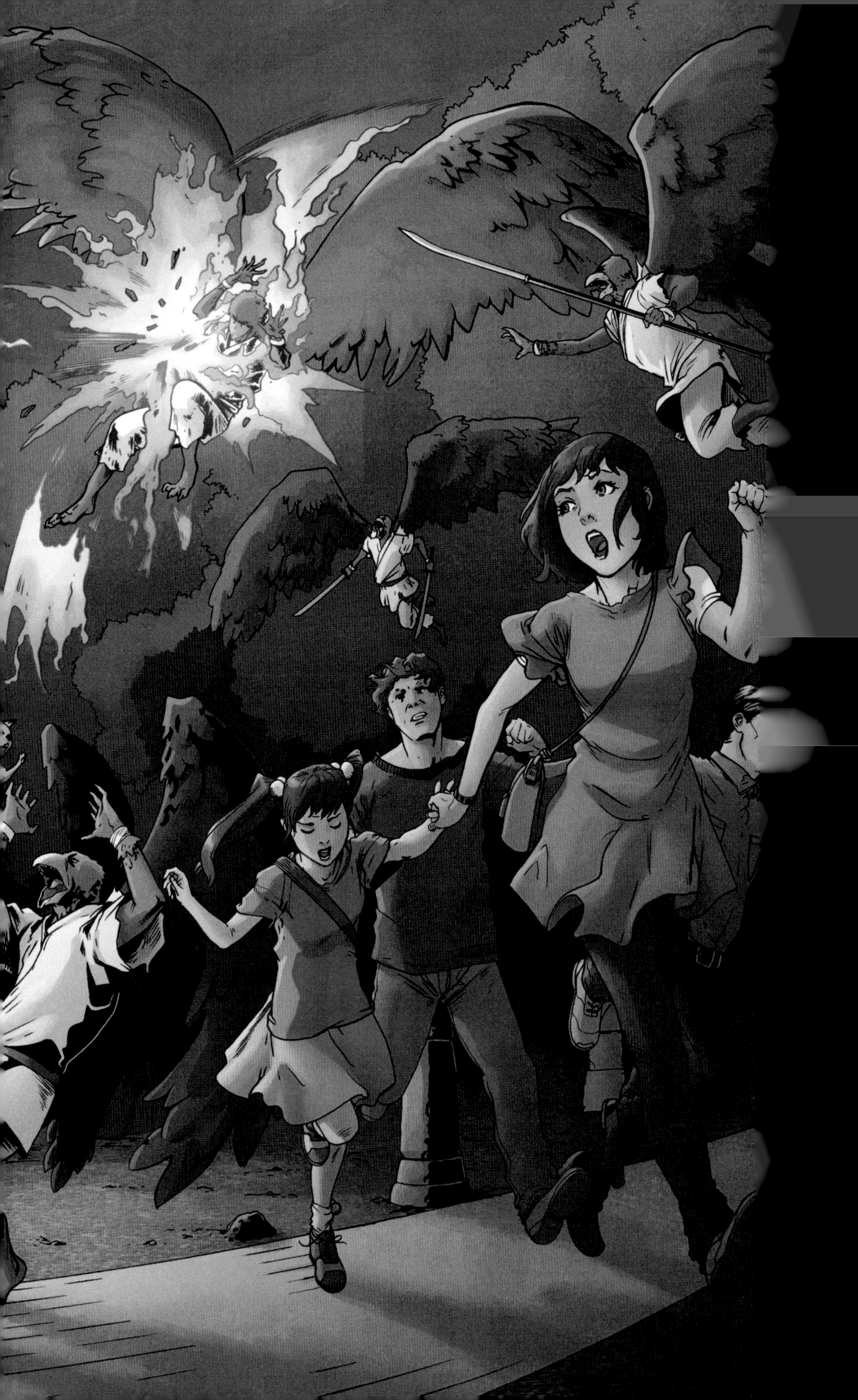

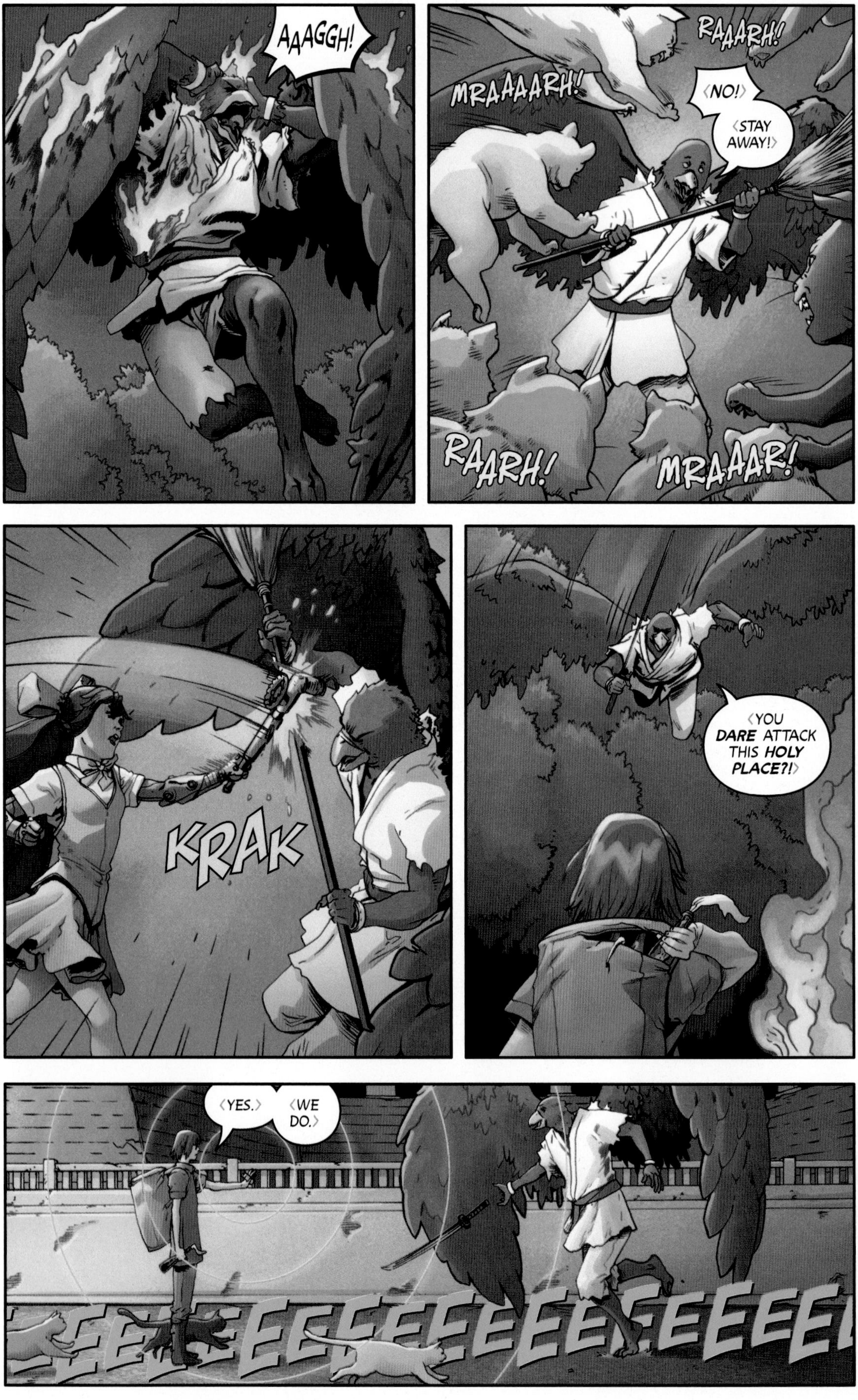
AAAGGH!
MRAAAARH!
RAAARH!
⟨NO!⟩
⟨STAY AWAY!⟩
RAARH!
MRAAAR!
KRAK
⟨YOU DARE ATTACK THIS HOLY PLACE?!⟩
⟨YES.⟩
⟨WE DO.⟩
EEEEEEEEEEEEEEEEE

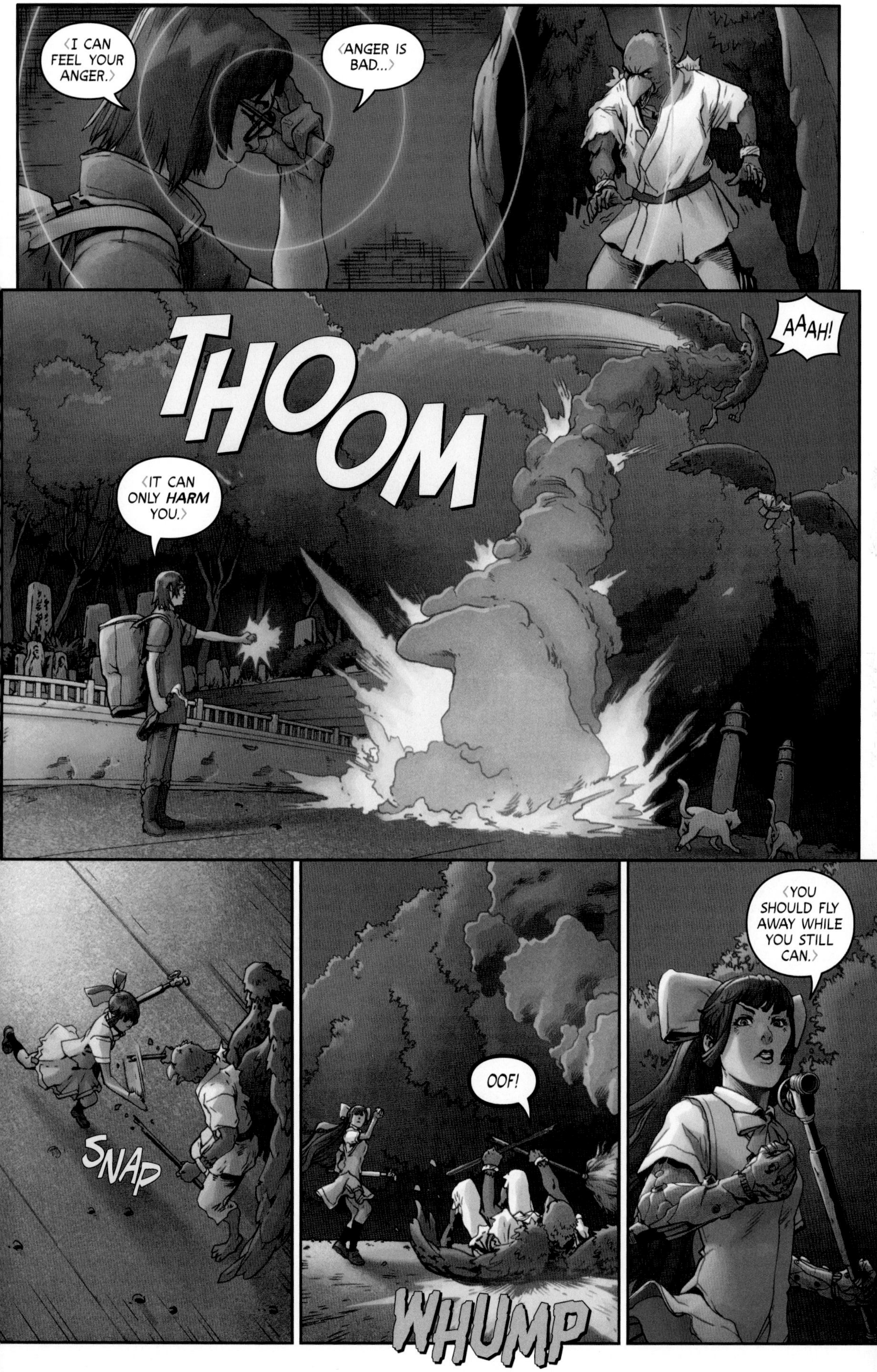

〈I CAN FEEL YOUR ANGER.〉
〈ANGER IS BAD...〉
THOOM
AAAH!
〈IT CAN ONLY HARM YOU.〉
SNAP
OOF!
WHUMP
〈YOU SHOULD FLY AWAY WHILE YOU STILL CAN.〉

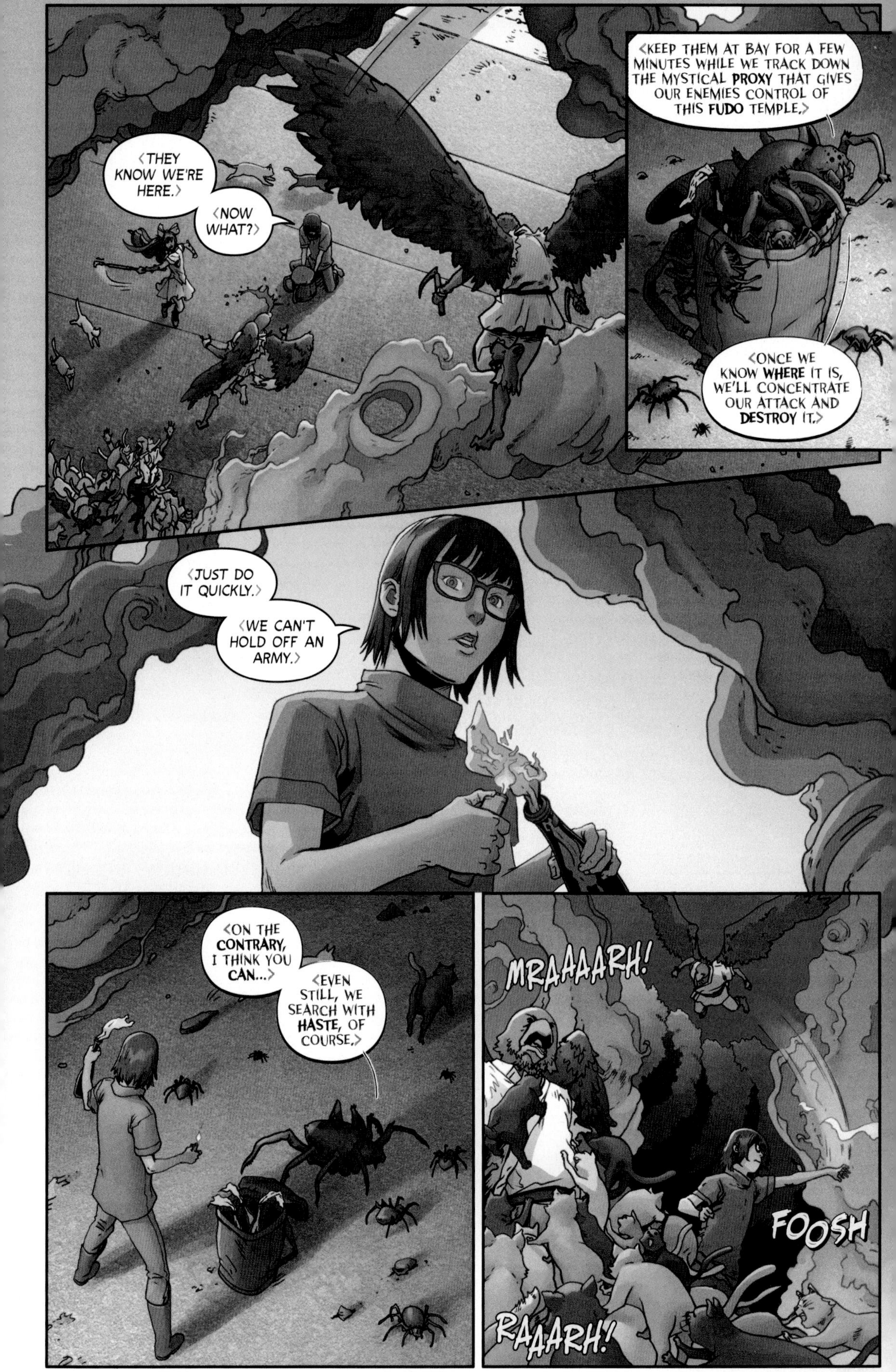
<THEY KNOW WE'RE HERE.>
<NOW WHAT?>
<KEEP THEM AT BAY FOR A FEW MINUTES WHILE WE TRACK DOWN THE MYSTICAL PROXY THAT GIVES OUR ENEMIES CONTROL OF THIS FUDO TEMPLE.>
<ONCE WE KNOW WHERE IT IS, WE'LL CONCENTRATE OUR ATTACK AND DESTROY IT.>
<JUST DO IT QUICKLY.>
<WE CAN'T HOLD OFF AN ARMY.>
<ON THE CONTRARY, I THINK YOU CAN...>
<EVEN STILL, WE SEARCH WITH HASTE, OF COURSE.>
MRAAAARH!
FOOSH
RAAARH!

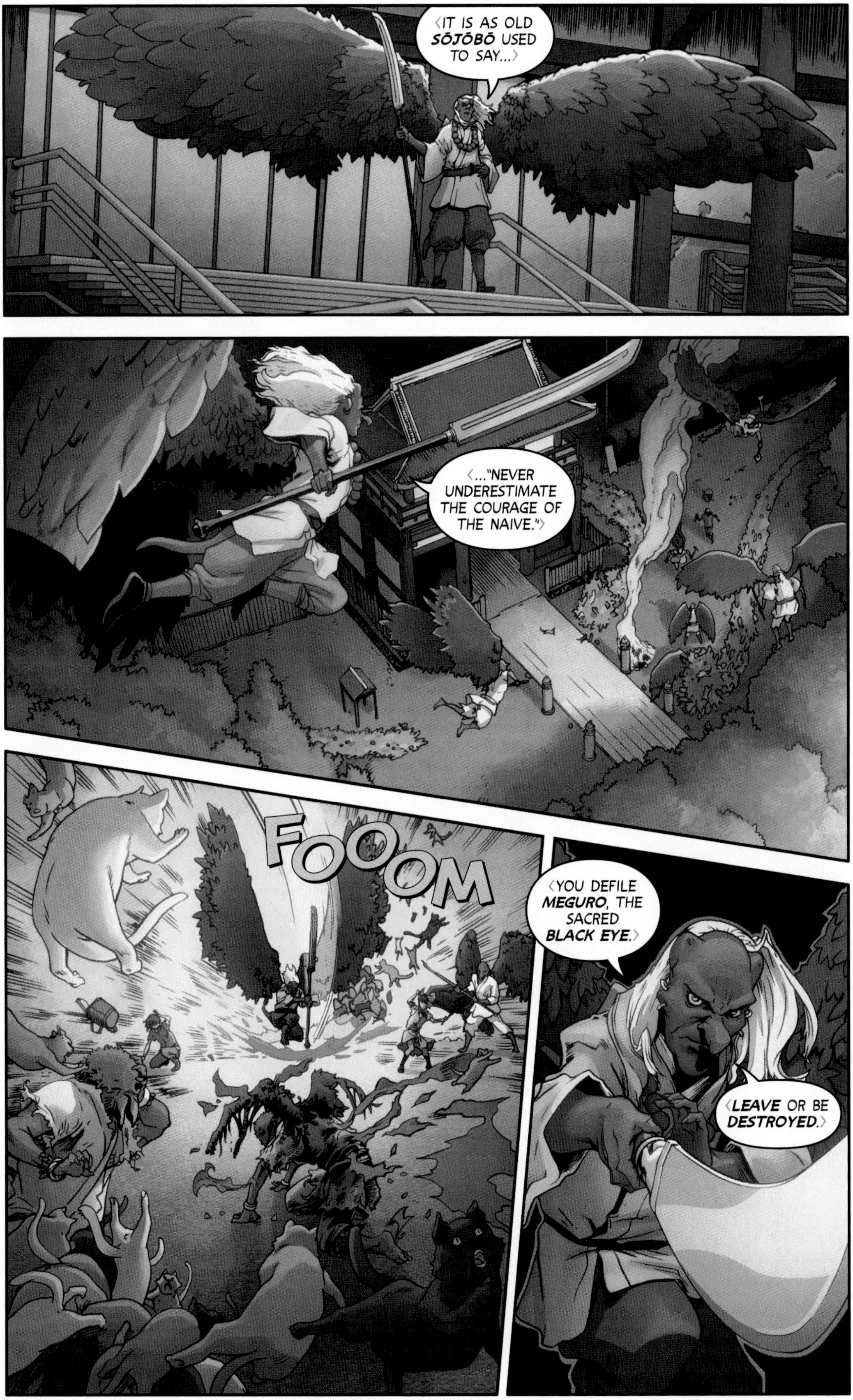
‹IT IS AS OLD SŌJŌBŌ USED TO SAY...›
‹..."NEVER UNDERESTIMATE THE COURAGE OF THE NAIVE."›
FOOOM
‹YOU DEFILE MEGURO, THE SACRED BLACK EYE.›
‹LEAVE OR BE DESTROYED.›

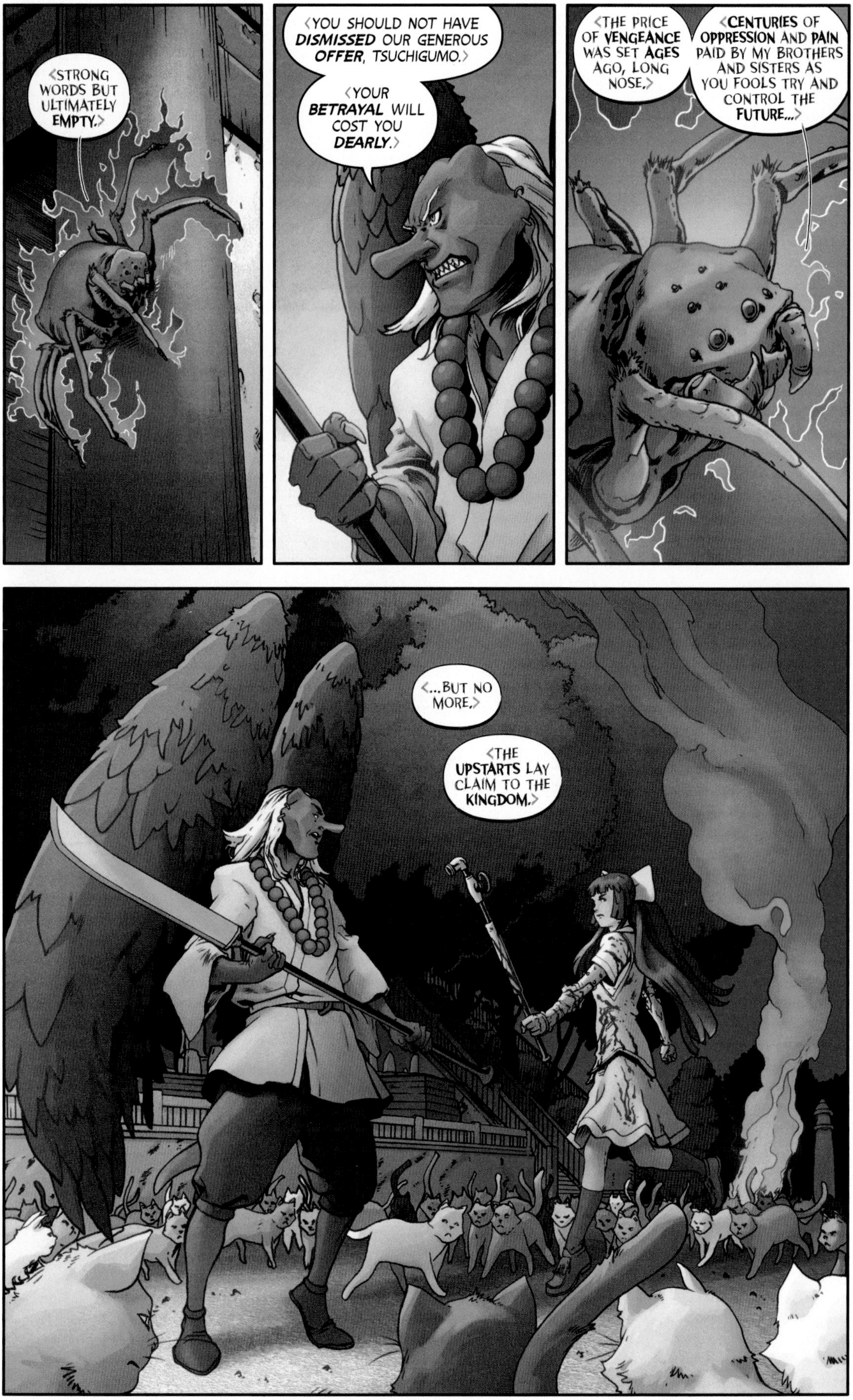
<STRONG WORDS BUT ULTIMATELY EMPTY.>
<YOU SHOULD NOT HAVE DISMISSED OUR GENEROUS OFFER, TSUCHIGUMO.>
<YOUR BETRAYAL WILL COST YOU DEARLY.>
<THE PRICE OF VENGEANCE WAS SET AGES AGO, LONG NOSE.>
<CENTURIES OF OPPRESSION AND PAIN PAID BY MY BROTHERS AND SISTERS AS YOU FOOLS TRY AND CONTROL THE FUTURE...>
<...BUT NO MORE.>
<THE UPSTARTS LAY CLAIM TO THE KINGDOM.>

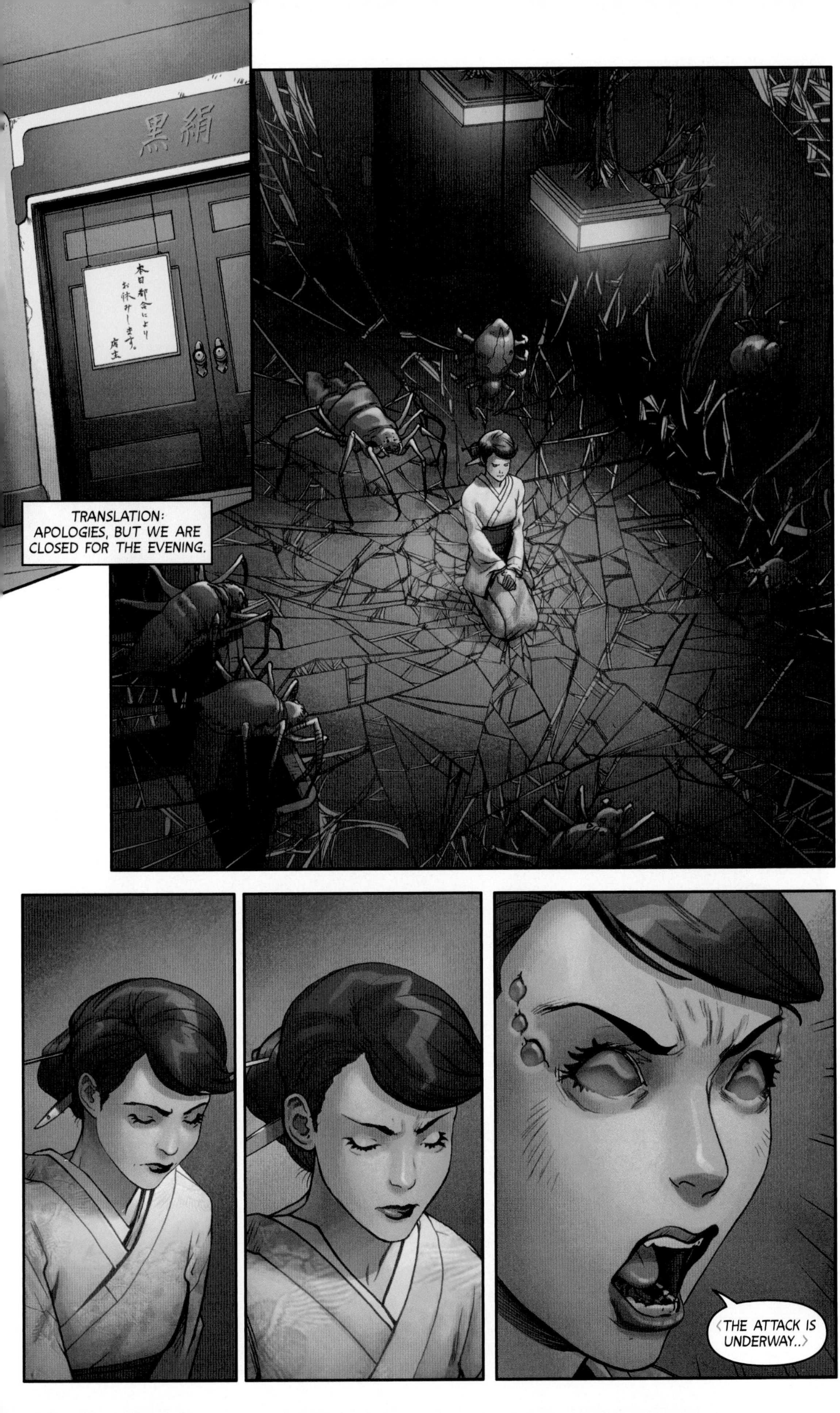
黒絹
本日都合により
お休みします。
店主
TRANSLATION: APOLOGIES, BUT WE ARE CLOSED FOR THE EVENING.
‹THE ATTACK IS UNDERWAY..›

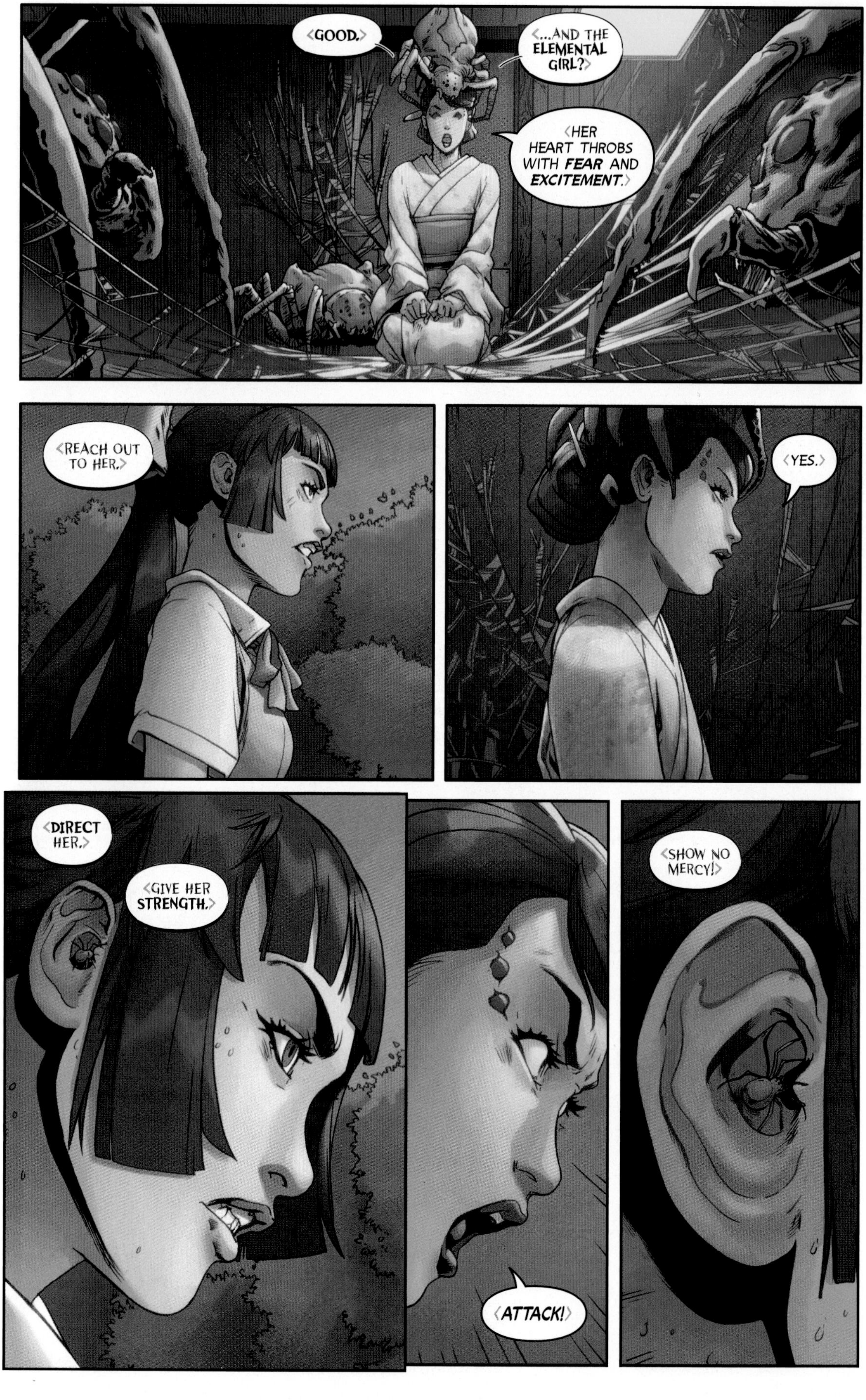

<GOOD.>
<...AND THE ELEMENTAL GIRL?>
<HER HEART THROBS WITH FEAR AND EXCITEMENT.>
<REACH OUT TO HER.>
<YES.>
<DIRECT HER.>
<GIVE HER STRENGTH.>
<ATTACK!>
<SHOW NO MERCY!>

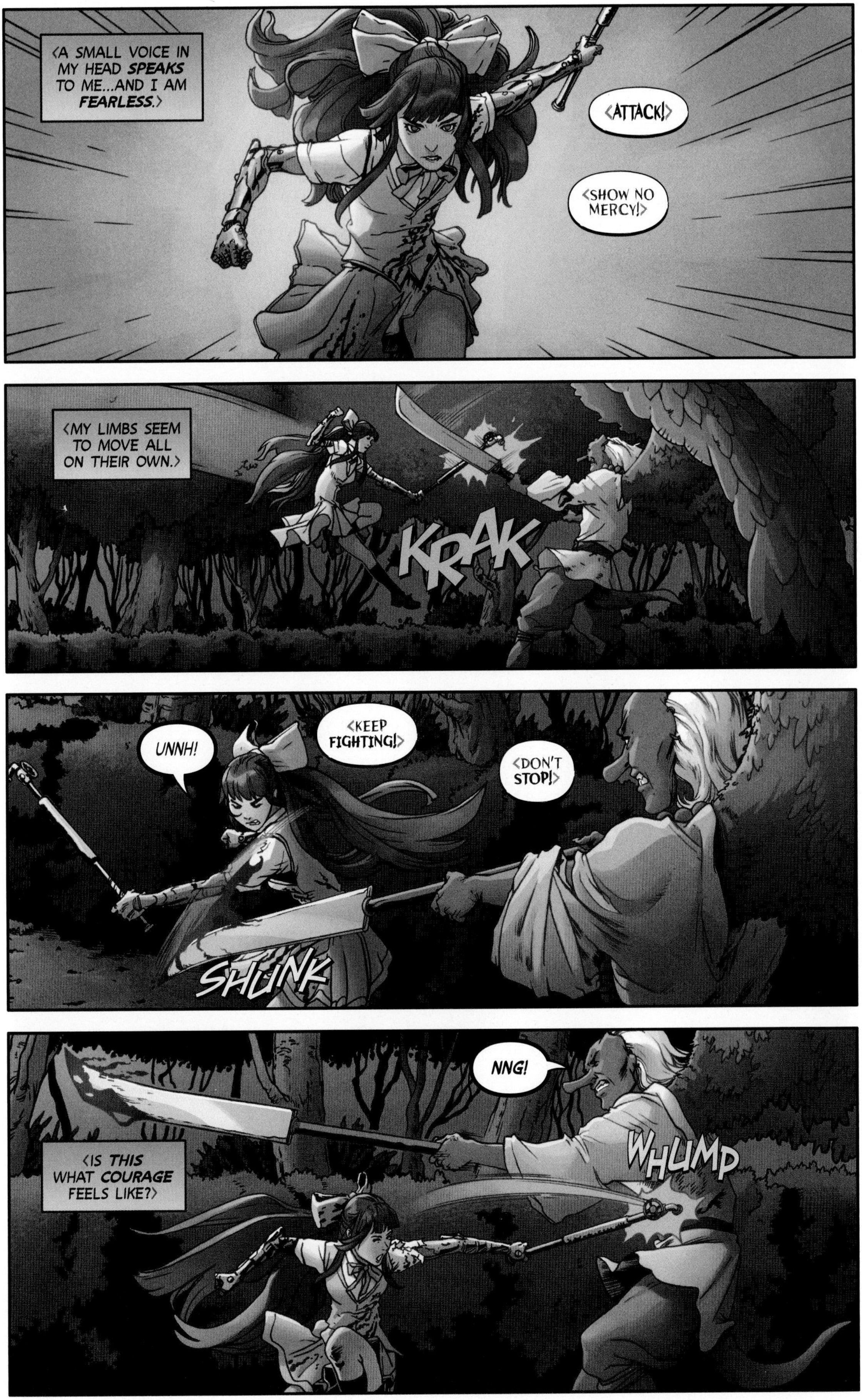
<A SMALL VOICE IN MY HEAD SPEAKS TO ME...AND I AM FEARLESS.>
<ATTACK!>
<SHOW NO MERCY!>
<MY LIMBS SEEM TO MOVE ALL ON THEIR OWN.>
KRAK
UNNH!
<KEEP FIGHTING!>
<DON'T STOP!>
SHUNK
NNG!
<IS THIS WHAT COURAGE FEELS LIKE?>
WHUMP

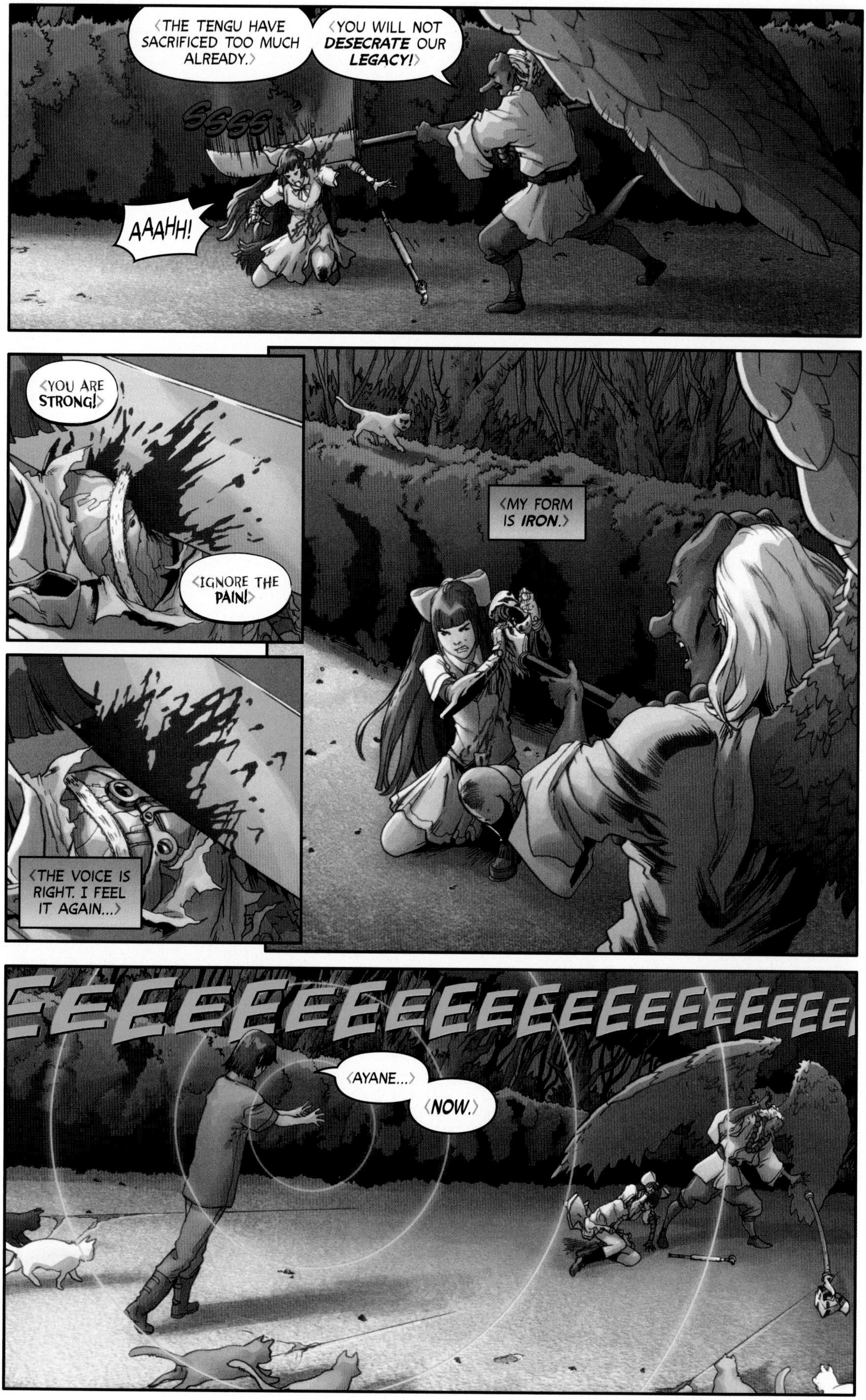

⟨THE TENGU HAVE SACRIFICED TOO MUCH ALREADY.⟩
⟨YOU WILL NOT DESECRATE OUR LEGACY!⟩
SSSS
AAAHH!
⟨YOU ARE STRONG!⟩
⟨IGNORE THE PAIN!⟩
⟨MY FORM IS IRON.⟩
⟨THE VOICE IS RIGHT. I FEEL IT AGAIN...⟩
EEEEEEEEEEEEEEEEEEEE
⟨AYANE...⟩
⟨NOW.⟩

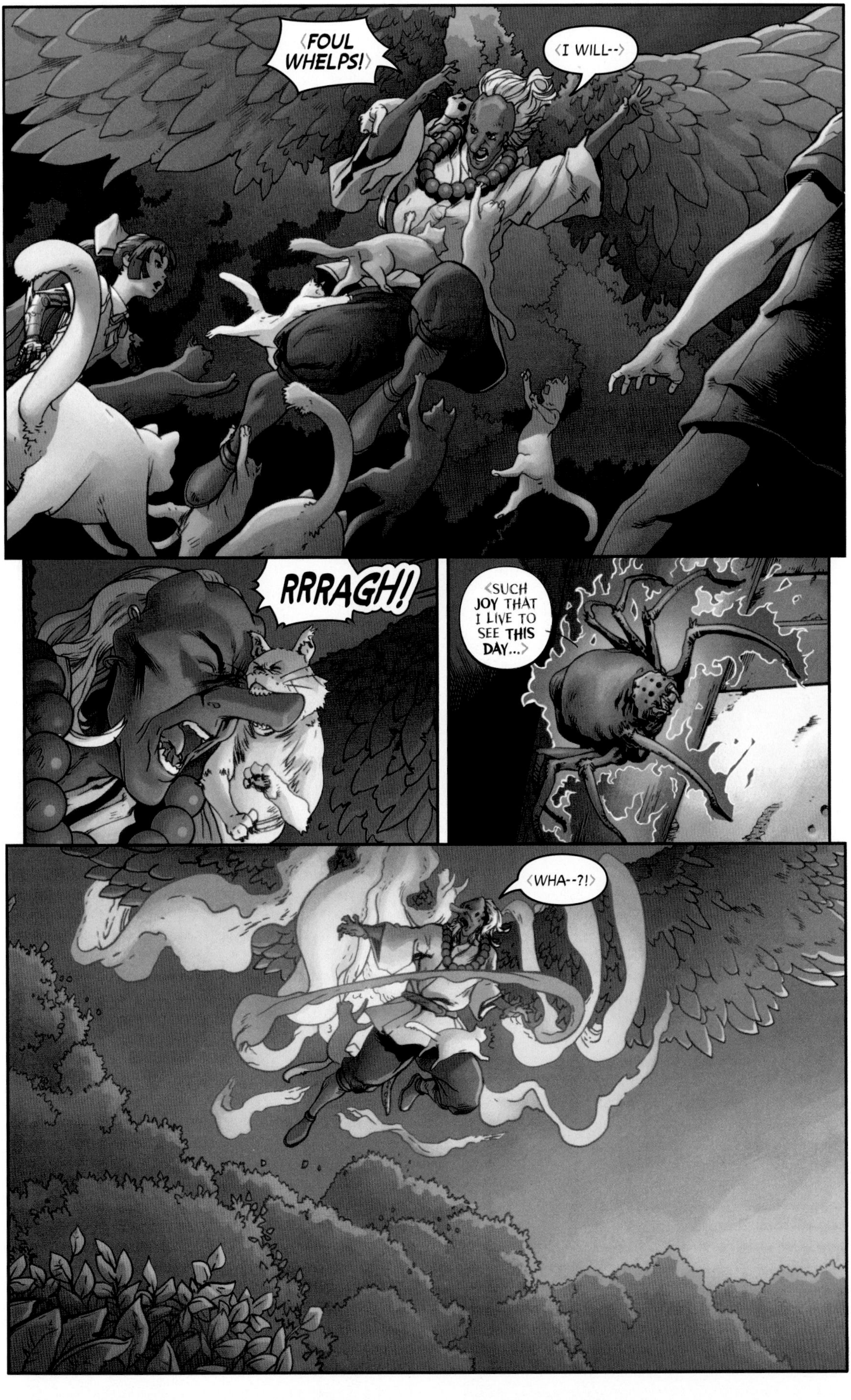

⟨FOUL WHELPS!⟩
⟨I WILL--⟩
RRRAGH!
⟨SUCH JOY THAT I LIVE TO SEE THIS DAY...⟩
⟨WHA--?!⟩

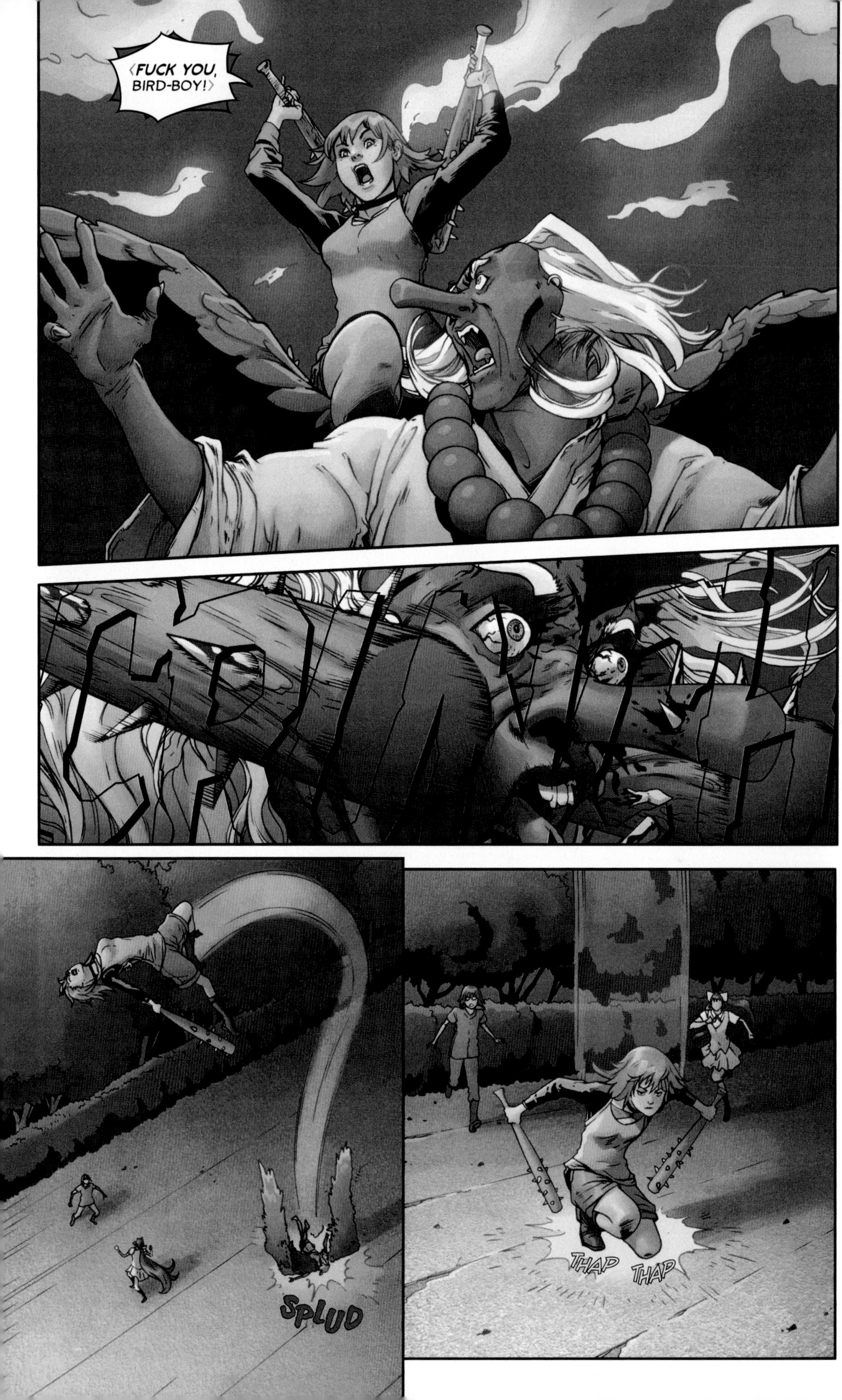
<FUCK YOU, BIRD-BOY!>
SPLUD
THAP THAP

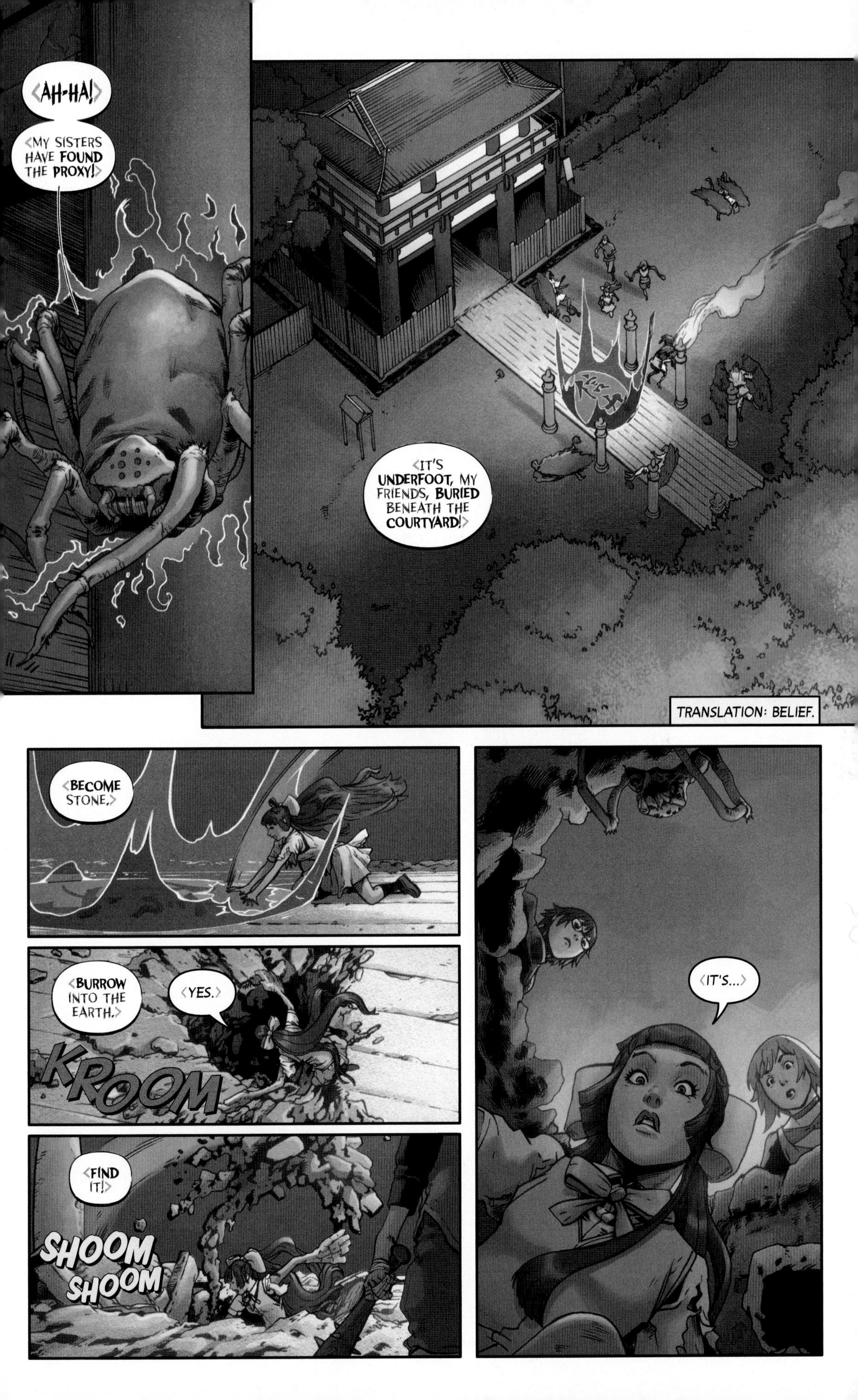

<AH-HA!>
<MY SISTERS HAVE FOUND THE PROXY!>
<IT'S UNDERFOOT, MY FRIENDS, BURIED BENEATH THE COURTYARD!>
TRANSLATION: BELIEF.
<BECOME STONE.>
<BURROW INTO THE EARTH.>
<YES.>
KROOM
<FIND IT!>
SHOOM
SHOOM
<IT'S...>

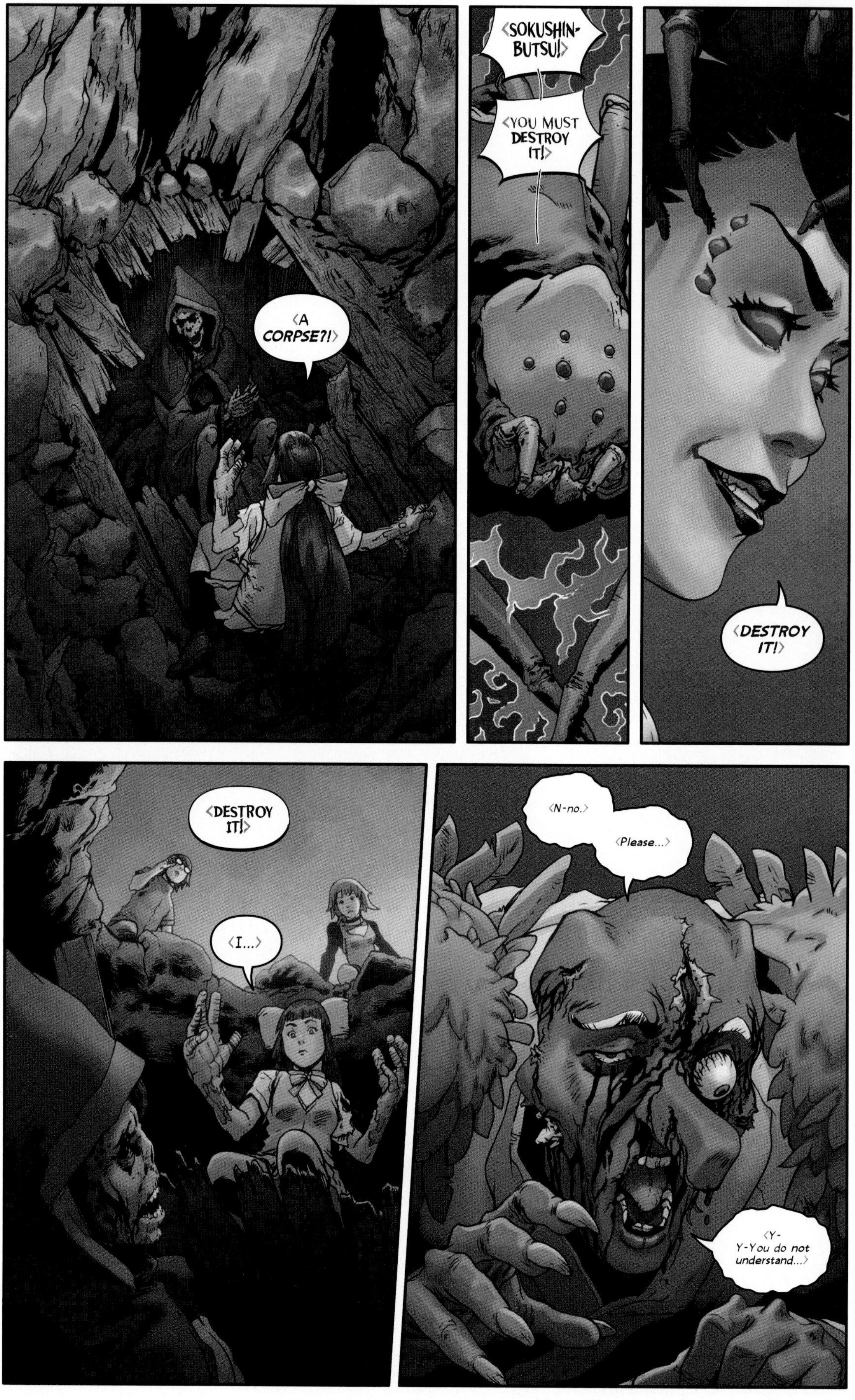

〈A CORPSE?!〉
〈SOKUSHIN-BUTSU!〉
〈YOU MUST DESTROY IT!〉
〈DESTROY IT!〉
〈DESTROY IT!〉
〈I...〉
〈N-no.〉
〈Please...〉
〈Y- Y-You do not understand...〉

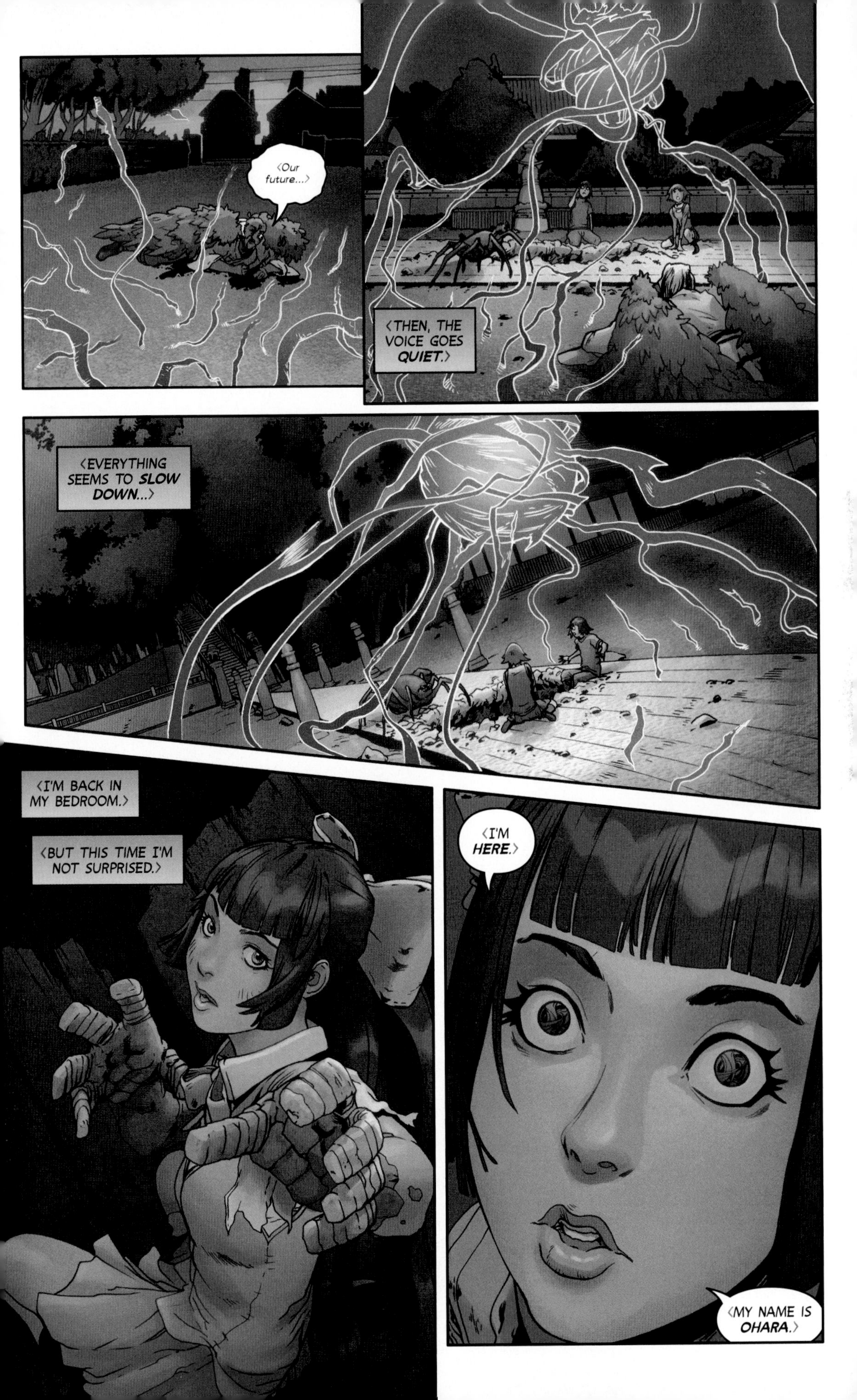

〈Our future...〉
〈THEN, THE VOICE GOES QUIET.〉
〈EVERYTHING SEEMS TO SLOW DOWN...〉
〈I'M BACK IN MY BEDROOM.〉
〈BUT THIS TIME I'M NOT SURPRISED.〉
〈I'M HERE.〉
〈MY NAME IS OHARA.〉

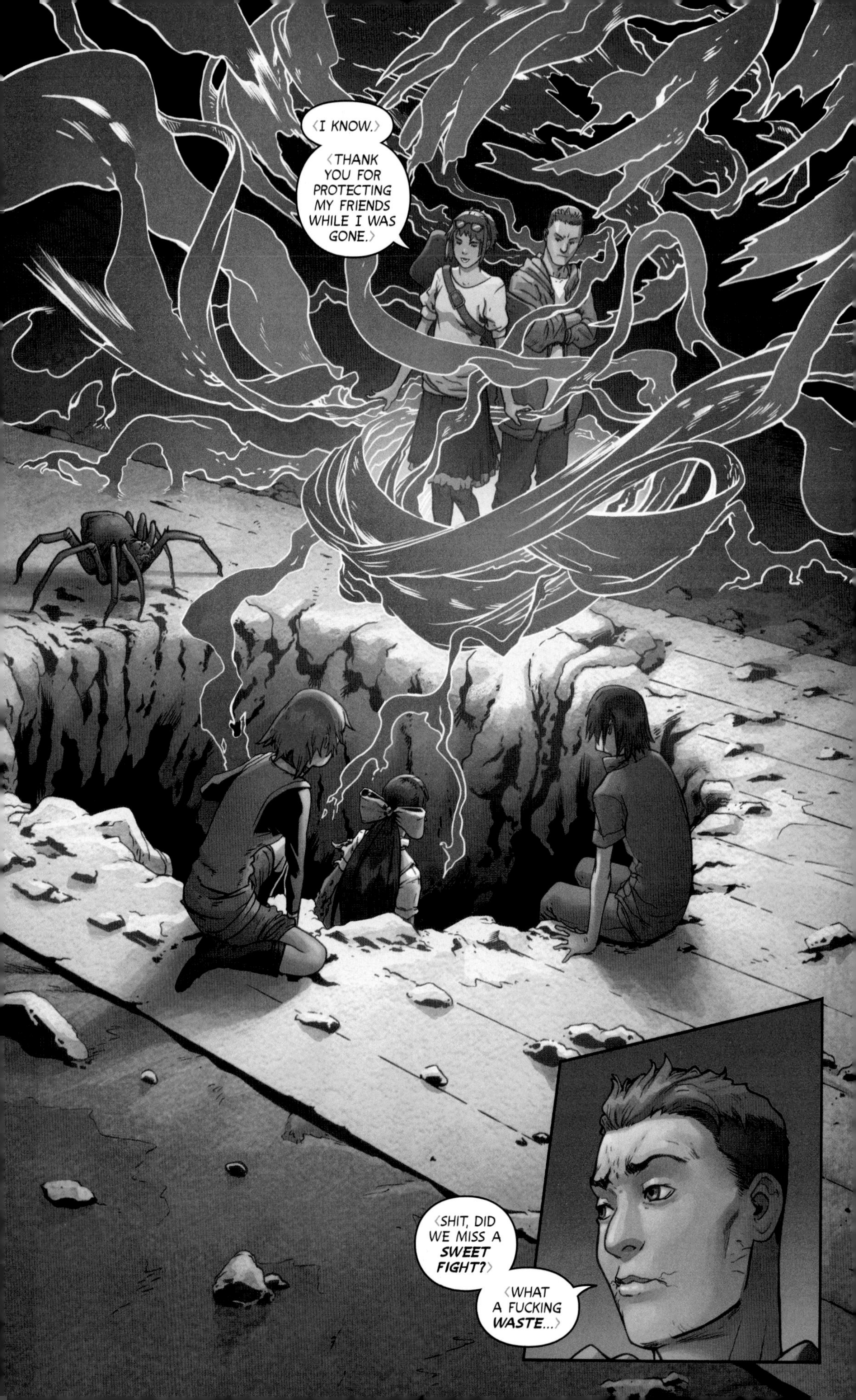
⟨I KNOW.⟩
⟨THANK YOU FOR PROTECTING MY FRIENDS WHILE I WAS GONE.⟩
⟨SHIT, DID WE MISS A **SWEET FIGHT?**⟩
⟨WHAT A FUCKING **WASTE**...⟩

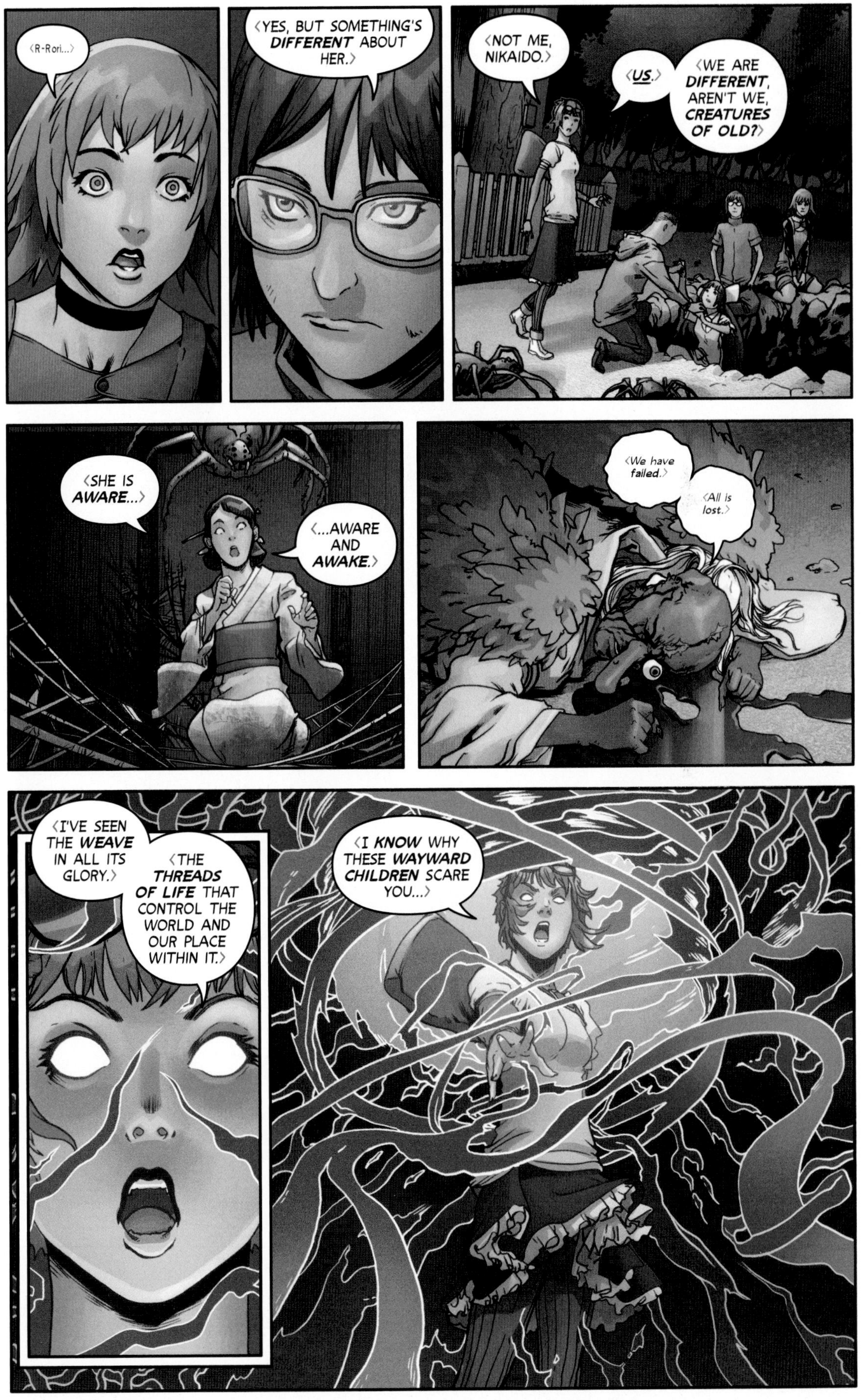
‹R-Rori...›
‹YES, BUT SOMETHING'S DIFFERENT ABOUT HER.›
‹NOT ME, NIKAIDO.›
‹US.›
‹WE ARE DIFFERENT, AREN'T WE, CREATURES OF OLD?›
‹SHE IS AWARE...›
‹...AWARE AND AWAKE.›
‹We have failed.›
‹All is lost.›
‹I'VE SEEN THE WEAVE IN ALL ITS GLORY.›
‹THE THREADS OF LIFE THAT CONTROL THE WORLD AND OUR PLACE WITHIN IT.›
‹I KNOW WHY THESE WAYWARD CHILDREN SCARE YOU...›

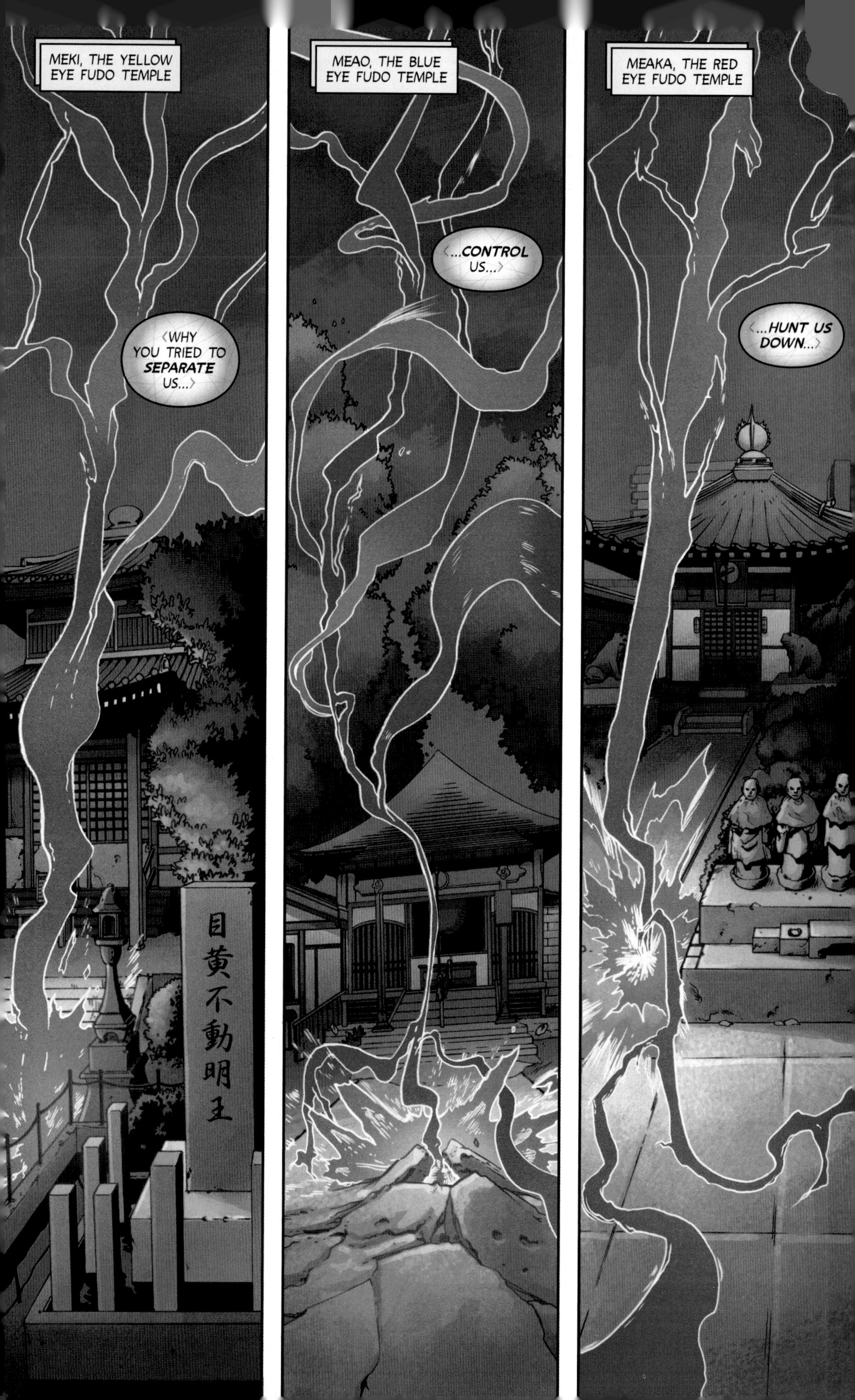
MEKI, THE YELLOW EYE FUDO TEMPLE
⟨WHY YOU TRIED TO SEPARATE US...⟩
目黄不動明王
MEAO, THE BLUE EYE FUDO TEMPLE
⟨...CONTROL US...⟩
MEAKA, THE RED EYE FUDO TEMPLE
⟨...HUNT US DOWN...⟩

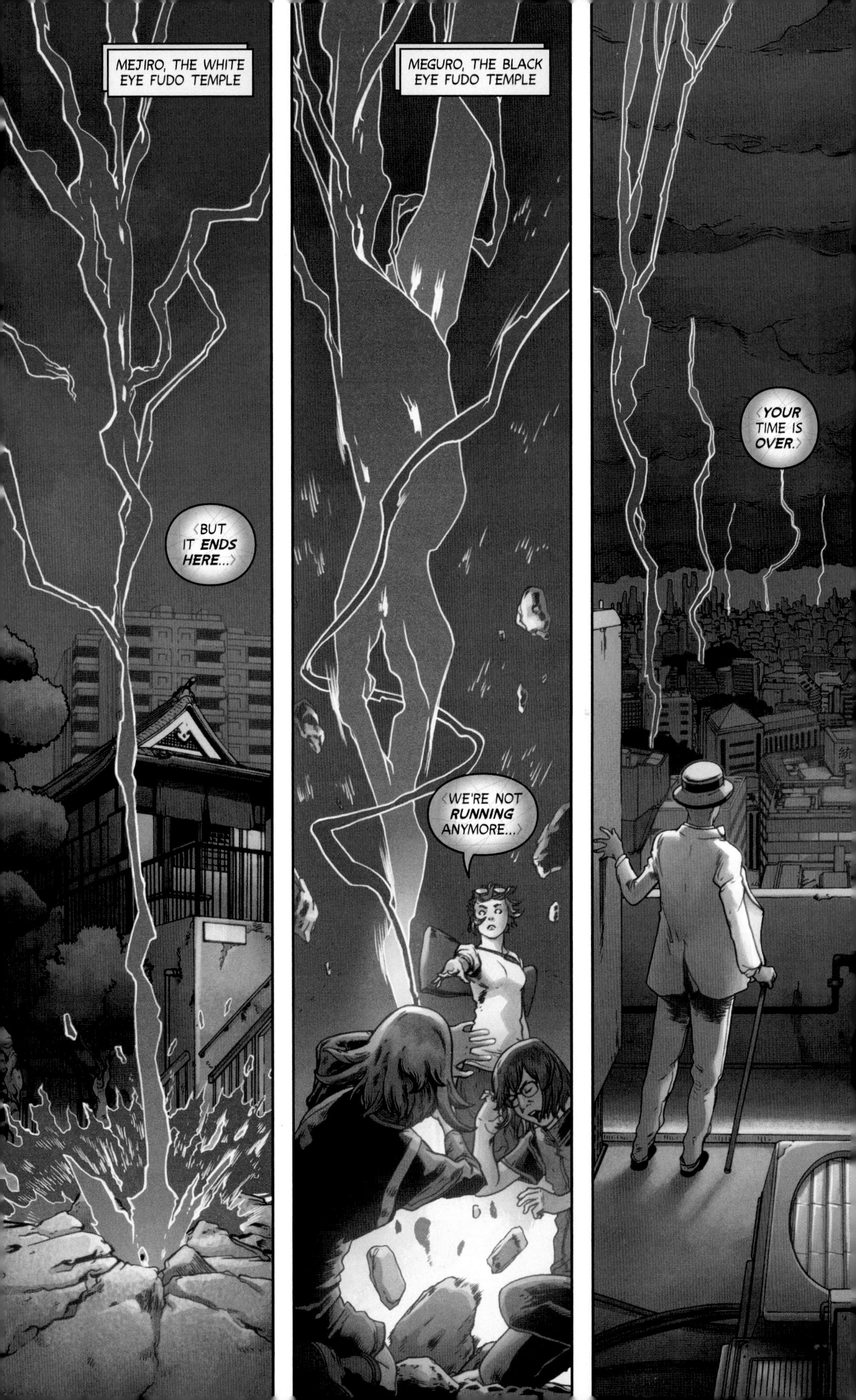
MEJIRO, THE WHITE EYE FUDO TEMPLE
‹BUT IT ENDS HERE...›
MEGURO, THE BLACK EYE FUDO TEMPLE
‹WE'RE NOT RUNNING ANYMORE...›
‹YOUR TIME IS OVER.›

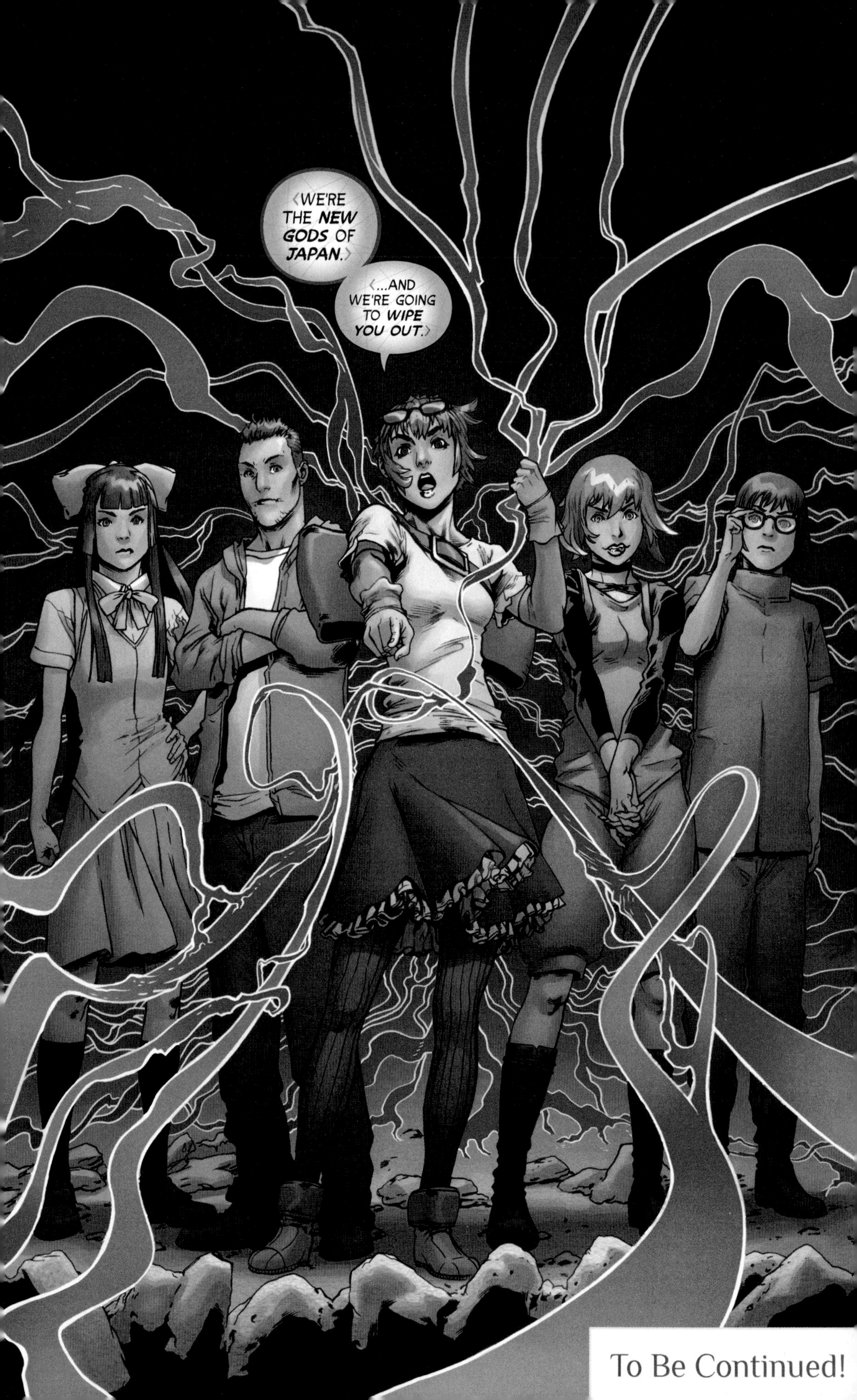
‹WE'RE THE NEW GODS OF JAPAN.›
‹...AND WE'RE GOING TO WIPE YOU OUT.›
To Be Continued!

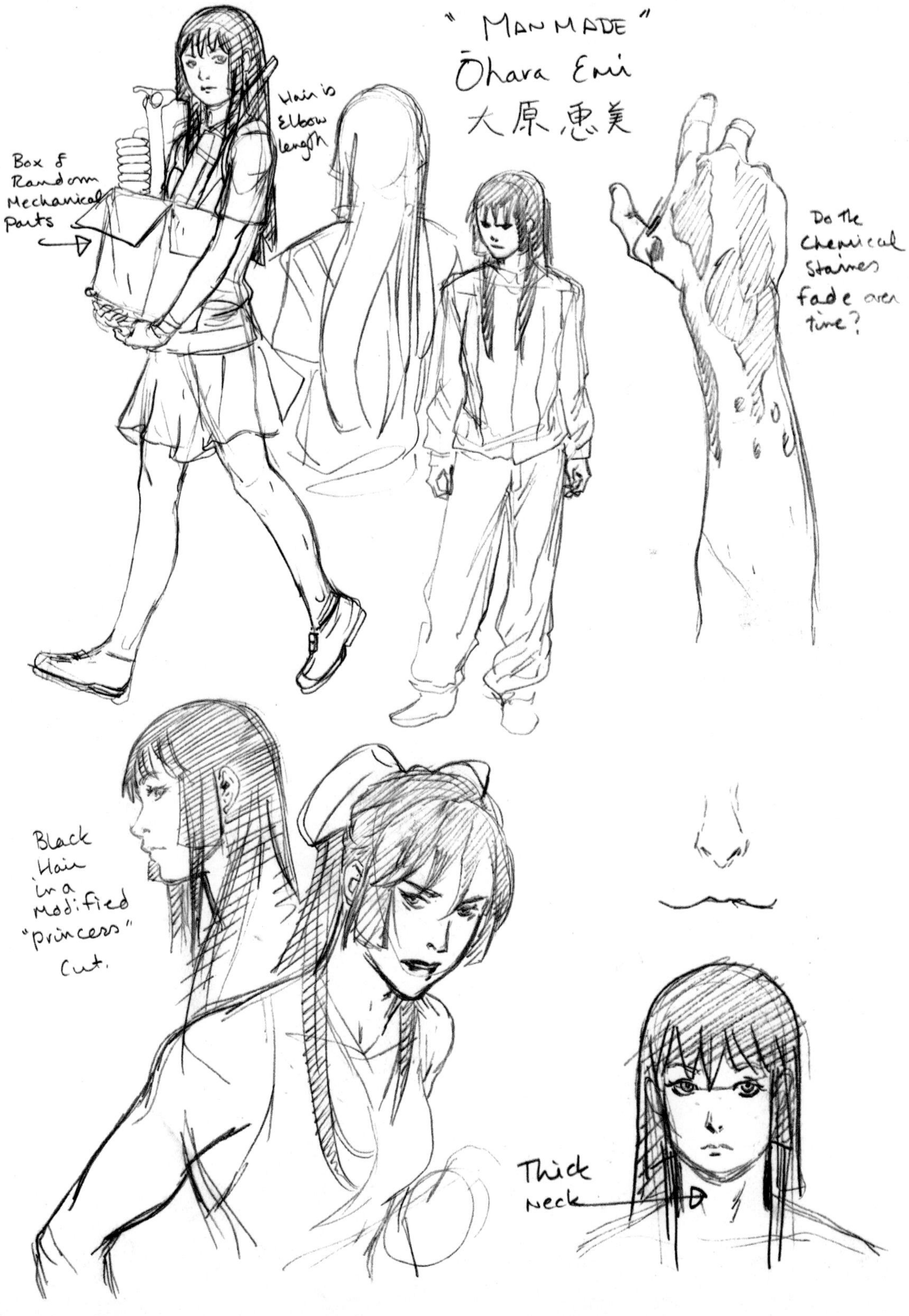
"MANMADE"
Ōhara Emi
大原恵美
Hair is Elbow length
Box of Random Mechanical Parts
Do the Chemical Staines fade over time?
Black Hair in a Modified "princess" Cut.
Thick neck

The legend goes that in the early 17th century, shogun Tokugawa Ieyasu commissioned the abbot Tenkai to generate a mystical power field surrounding Edo, the new capital of Japan. Tenkai drew a 5-pointed star around the city—the symbol of the onmyōji sorcerers. He consecrated each point of the star with a temple. Inside each temple stood a statue of the god of Fudo, each with a different eye color, facing a different direction.

• **Me-guro** (目黒: Black Eye: North; Water)
  Ryosen-ji (Spring Waterfall Temple)
• **Me-jiro** (目白: White Eye: West; Wind)
  Kornjyo-in (Parliament of the Power of Money)
• **Me-aka** (目赤: Red Eye: South; Fire)
  Nankoku-ji (South Valley Temple)
• **Me-ao** (目青: Blue Eye: East; Wood)
  Saisho-ji (Great Victory Temple)
• **Me-ki** (目黄: Yellow Eye: Center; Earth)
  Eikyu-ji (Eternity Temple)
• **Me-ki** (目黄: Yellow Eye: Center; Earth)
  Saisho-ji (Great Victory Temple)

And then there is Fudo himself. His name translates literally as "unmovable," and he looks like an oni with his fierce visage, proudly upheld sword, seated on his flaming throne. Powerful and terrifying, if you are going to pick a deity to defend your city, Fudo is a good god to gamble on.

The statues bind the power of the five sacred colors with the five elements and five directions to form a *goshiki* (五色)—a circle of protection that ensures the city's prosperity and safety. The Goshiki Fudo—the Five Fudo Temples—protect Tokyo to this day.

Or so the legend goes ...

If you look at a map, the story unravels. The temples don't make a pentagram, except in the most imaginative sense. There aren't even five. On top of that, the Goshiki Fudo are conveniently located along the central Yamanote train line that circles Tokyo.

That's right; the Goshiki Fudo are a tourist trap, with little historical basis.

The oldest known mentions of the Goshiki Fudo supposedly comes from a mystery novel popular in the Meiji period (1868-1912). The novel used the idea of the five-temple circle of protection as a plot device. It was a popular book, and the idea of a magical circle around Edo captured the imagination. Readers assumed the locations were real and went in search of them. The Black Eye and White Eye were easy enough to find. They were probably where the writer got his idea. But the other ones were a bit harder—due to the fact that they didn't exist.

With all those tourist dollars up for grabs, it didn't take long for enterprising priests to turn these fictional locations into reality. They painted the eyes of existing statues to match the legends and declared themselves the home of the missing three Fudo. Multiple temples vied for authenticity. Finally, these settled into the six temples known today, with two still claiming to be the authentic "Yellow Eye." In reality, with the exception of the Black and White Eyes, the Goshiki Fudo can be traced to around the 1800s.

Me-guro (Black Eye) is the oldest, dating from 808 CE. Next comes Me-jiro (White Eye) from 1594, although it was actually named for a type of bird called the Japanese white-eye. Me-aka (Red Eye) dates from 1616. Its Fudo statue suddenly changed eye color in 1788 when it declared itself the authentic Red-Eyed Fudo. The statue and temple were burned to the ground in WWII, then reconstructed in 1985. The temple was relocated in 2011 with the old grounds converted into a parking lot. Me-ao (Blue Eye) is a youngster dating from 1882. It was built over the top of a previously ruined temple, and the blue-eyed Fudo statue was installed as part of construction. Of the two Me-ki (Yellow Eye), Eikyu-ji dates from 1880 with the yellow-eyed Fudo newly installed. The book *Kanto no Fudosan to Shinko* identifies this as the true Me-ki. The rival Me-ki Saisho-ji shares a name with Me-ao but is unrelated. Dating to 860, it was moved to Hirai district in 1912. The exact date of its association with the Goshiki Fudo unknown.

When researching the Goshiki Fudo for *Wayward*, the truth was disappointing. I prefer the magical and mystical. It's more fun. However, the tourist trap truth of the Goshiki Fudo was inescapable. But then I wondered if that even mattered. After all, belief often creates reality, not the other way around. In Japan, the fact that it was originally a tourist trap doesn't stop people from embracing the power of the Goshiki Fudo. The story trumps history. As it does in many cases.

Thousands visit Kinkaku-ji (*Temple of the Golden Pavilion*) in Kyoto every year, even though it was only built in 1955 and finished in 1987. They pay homage to the graves of the 47 Ronin, even though the story owes more to kabuki than history. These sites serve as a focus of belief and cultural heritage–a way to reinforce what it means to be "Japanese"—more than some factual record.

It is no different from Christians going on pilgrimages to see holy icons. They aren't "real." Any amount of research reveals that they were tourist traps too, from the Shroud of Turin to pieces of the True Cross. Or for that matter American pilgrims going to see the Liberty Bell. The fact that it could not possibly have been rung on July 4th, 1776 (as the legend goes) does not mean that the story isn't good, or prevent it from being a powerful symbol of the country. In Scotland, the Wallace Sword on display was mostly likely never held by William Wallace.

I've been to all of these sites, and felt their power. When I was in London, I went to 221b Baker Street to see the home of Sherlock Holmes and swung by Platform 9 ¾ to catch the train to Hogwarts. I knew it was pure fiction, but that didn't dampen the feeling that I was standing in the home of the Great Detective. It was magic.

Every country has similar venerated forgeries. But that doesn't affect the honest emotions they summon up for believers and non-believers alike.

After all, as a wise man once said "When the legend becomes the fact, print the legend."

Sometimes a yōkai tells you almost everything you need to know about it in its name. That's the case with hyakume, the 100-eyed yōkai. It's a blobby fellow with a body covered in a hundred eyes. However, hyakume does hold a rare place in the yōkai pantheon by being one of the first to debut on the modern medium of television.

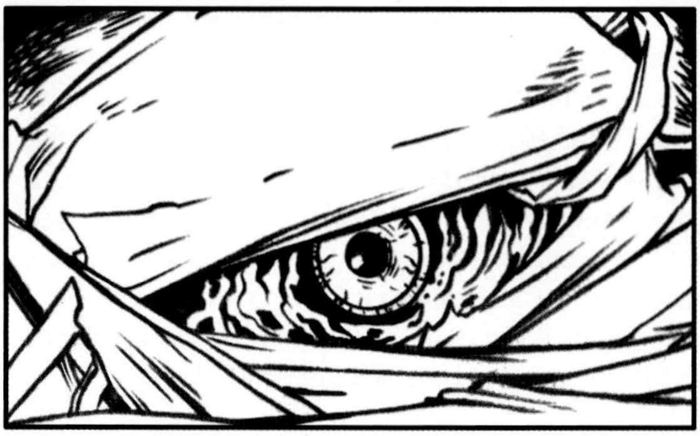

From 1966-67, yōkai grand master Shigeru Mizuki had his first TV hit with a tokusatsu (special effects) adaptation of his comic *Akuma-kun* (*Devil boy*). Tokusatsu shows like *Ultraman* and the various *Sentai Rangers* series (known in English as *Power Rangers*) thrive on weekly oddities and monsters that can be thrown at their heroes. For *Akuma-kun*, Mizuki created a host of weird creatures, including the all-seeing beast hyakume.

Some note that hyakume bears a resemblance to an illustration in Carl Jung's *Symbole der Wandlung* (*Symbols of Transformation*). Well-read and deeply interested in philosophy and symbols, this is most likely the source of Mizuki's design. There is also an Edo period illustration of a hyakubyakume oni (百々眼鬼; *hundreds and hundreds-eyed oni*) that may have been an influence.

As a yōkai, hyakume's strength is also its weakness. They often set up as guards, their all-seeing eyes able to spot thieves in the thickest of darkness. Their eyes can even detach and stick to infiltrators. But their sensitive eyes cannot tolerate sunlight—nor has the sunglasses been made yet that can shield all hundred eyes.

Mizuki liked hyakume. He later pitted him against his other famous creation *Kitaro*, and even added hyakume to his yōkai encyclopedias that form the foundation of supernatural knowledge for Japan. It wasn't long until hyakume was absorbed into Japan's monster lore, the monster's television origins forgotten.

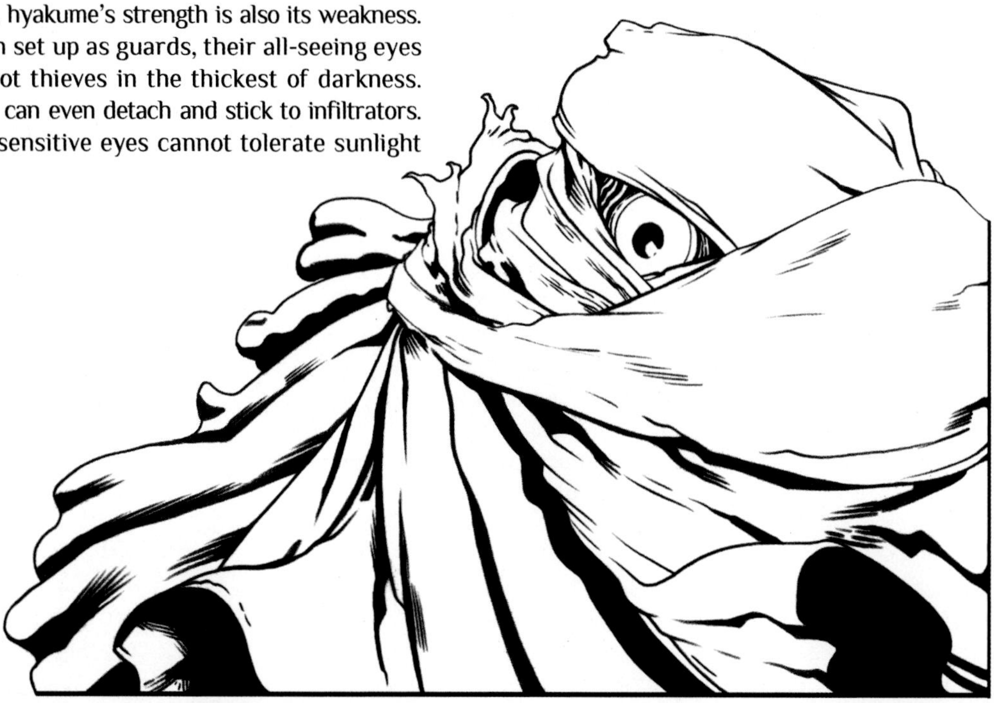

Jorōgumo

女郎蜘蛛 (Lit: Whore Spider)

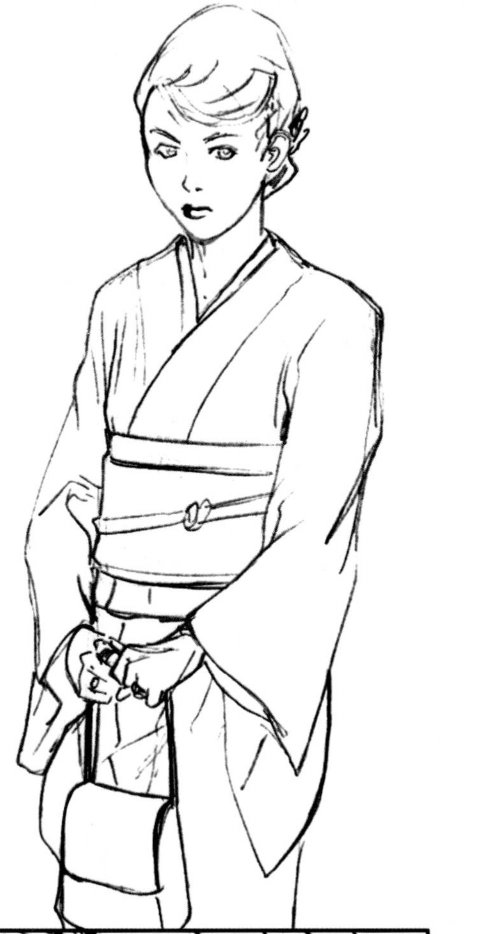

When Tokugawa Ieyasu seized control of Japan as shogun in 1603, he established peace by absolute control. Unable to ban people's desire for pleasure and indulgence, he attempted to contain it. Tokugawa established three great walled pleasure quarters (*yakuko*), in Kyoto, Edo, and Osaka. These pleasure quarters were like Disneyland and Las Vegas combined. Cloaked in fantasy, it was only a short time before urban legends and mythologies arose about their denizens. Many of the prostitutes of the yakuko were rumored to be yōkai—bakeneko or kitsune or other transformed animals. But none were more dangerous than *jorōgumo*—whore spiders.

As you can see by their name, jorōgumo were predatory yōkai prostitutes disguised as beautiful women. They are said to be proficient in biwa music, and strummed their instruments to lure in customers. Once inside, customers would be wrapped in spider silk and slowly consumed by the evil yōkai.

There are several known nests of jorōgumo throughout Japan, such as the Jōren Falls in Shizuoka or Kashikobuch in Sendai. Most of these are near water, relating to legends of hapless lumberjacks who were almost pulled in by the jorōgumo's webs. The lumberjacks managed to survive by fixing her silk to a nearby tree stump. Belief persists in jorōgumo in these locations, and shrines have been created attempting to transform the monsters into guardian spirits who protects people from drowning.

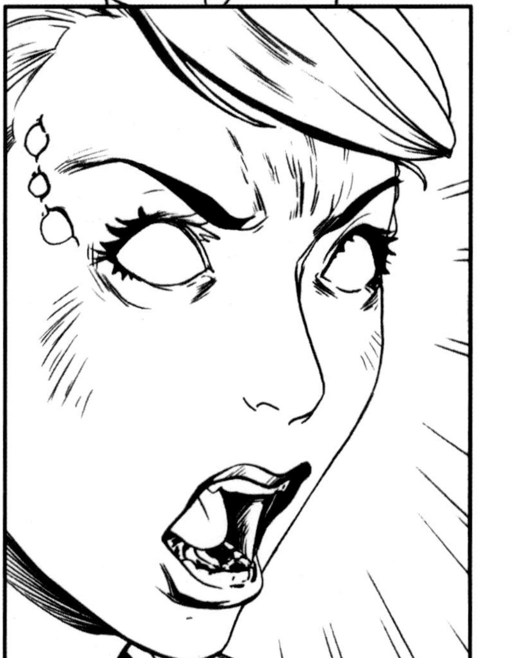

Jorōgumo were included by Toriyama Sekien in his first yōkai encyclopedia, *Gazu Hyakki Yagyō* (*The Illustrated Night Parade of a Hundred Demons*). Their inclusion in this first volume marks her as a legitimate folkloric creature, instead of one of Sekien's own creations. However he wrote nothing more about them than their name.

Neko Musume

猫娘 (Lit: Cat Daughter)

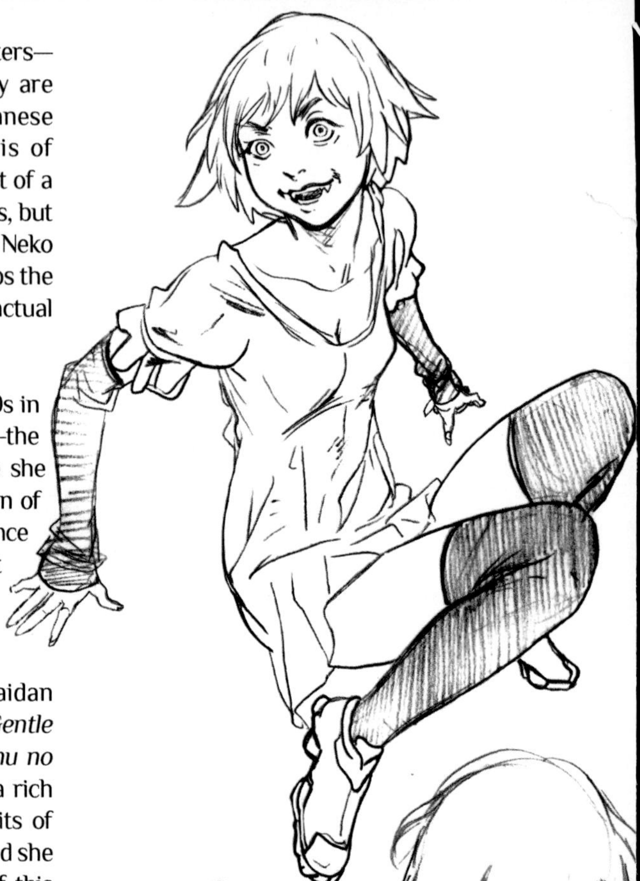

Half-cat. Half-human. Neko musume—cat daughters—have a unique place in Japan's yōkai lore. They are some of the few *hanyōkai* (half-yōkai) in Japanese folklore, although the cat/human blending is of essence not blood. Neko musume are the result of a curse or magic. There are human/yōkai marriages, but the children are almost always 100% human. Neko musume are something else. They are also perhaps the only yōkai who can be traced back to a single, actual person.

The first neko musume was exhibited in the 1760s in Asakusa, Edo as part of a Misemono Show—the equivalent of 19th century Freak Shows—where she claimed to be a cat/human hybrid. Little is known of this original cat daughter, other than her appearance was startling and that she looked exactly like what she claimed to be. When the Misemono Shows faded, the neko musume disappeared.

She emerged again in 1800 as a story in the kaidan collection *Ehon Sayoshigure* (*Picture Book of a Gentle Rain on a Late Autumn Evening*). The story *Ashu no Kijo* (*Strange Woman of Ashu*) told the tale of a rich merchant whose daughter had the strange habits of licking things. Her tongue was rough like a cats, and she was nicknamed the neko musume. Variations of this story appeared in later kaidan collections, and by the 1850 *Ansei Zakki* she was a full-fledged yōkai, able to scurry along hedges and rented out by her mother as a rat catcher.

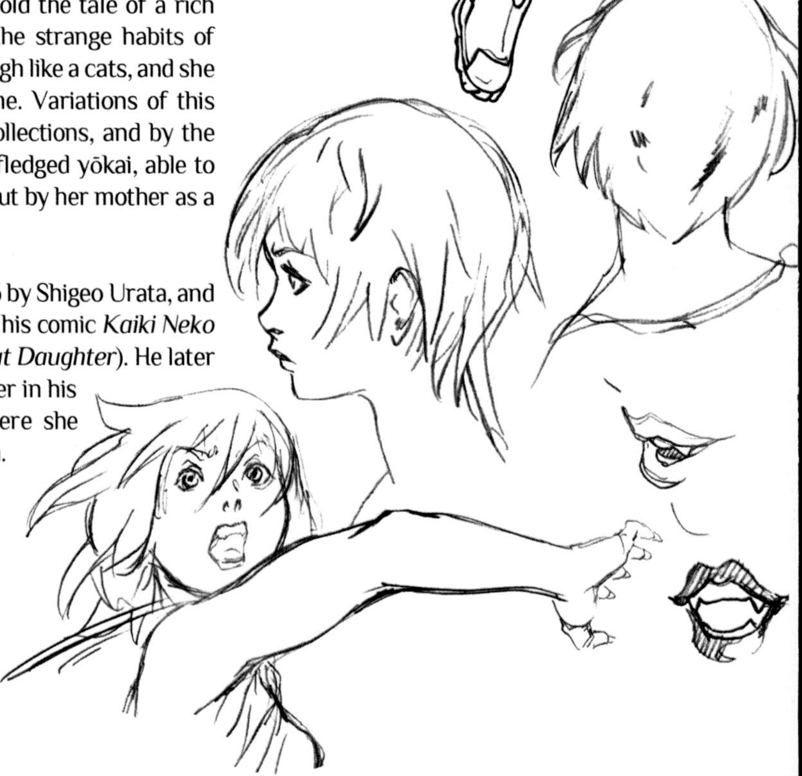

Neko musume was revived in 1936 by Shigeo Urata, and later by Shigeru Mizuki in 1958 in his comic *Kaiki Neko Musume* (*Bizarre Tales of the Cat Daughter*). He later included her as a regular character in his popular yōkai comic *Kitaro*, where she became known across all of Japan.

Few yōkai straddle the sacred and the profane like tengu. Perhaps only the demonic oni and the elusive kitsune are as immersed in the triple worlds of Buddhism, Shinto, and folklore superstitions. Disruptors and bringers of war. Impious anti-Buddhas who lead people into temptation and ruin. Mighty warriors who taught the secrets of martial arts to the famed Minamoto no Yoshitsune. Deities and spiritual focus of the mountain ascetics known as Shugendō. Tengu have played many roles over the centuries.

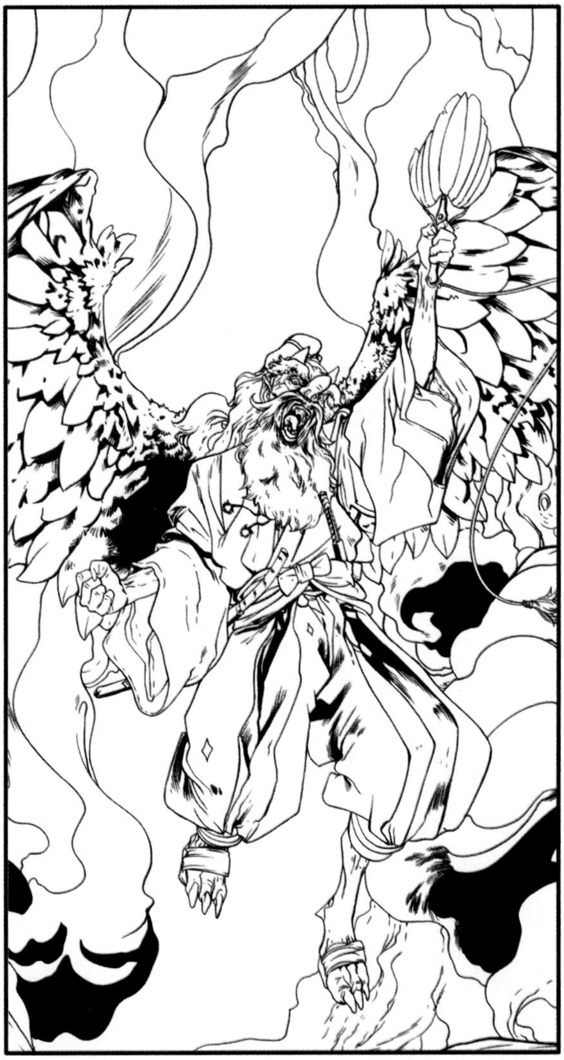

Tengu are one of Japan's most ancient yōkai, first appearing in the 720 CE book *Nihon Shoki* (*Chronicles of Japan*). They are thought to take their name from the Chinese *tiāngou*, a dog-shaped meteor that heralds war and misfortune. Name aside, Japan's tengu have always been more bird-like than dog-like; the earliest depictions are of a kite-like bird person dressed in the sacred garb of a Buddhist priest. There is speculation this appearance comes from the Hindu eagle-beings called *garuda*, identified as one of the major non-human races in early Buddhist scripture. Tengu later became associated with the long-nosed Shinto deity Sarutahiko, altering their appearance into the red-faced, long-nosed, winged goblins you see today.

Accounts of tengu are too numerous to list. The 11th century *Konjaku Monogatari* shows tengu as powerful beings able to carry off dragons under their arms. The 14th century *Genpei Jōsuiki* describes the tengu road, a third path that lies between the roads to Heaven and Hell. Edo period books such as Inoue Enryo's *Tenguron* list and rank tengu in the same way as medieval demonology books ranked demons in Hell.

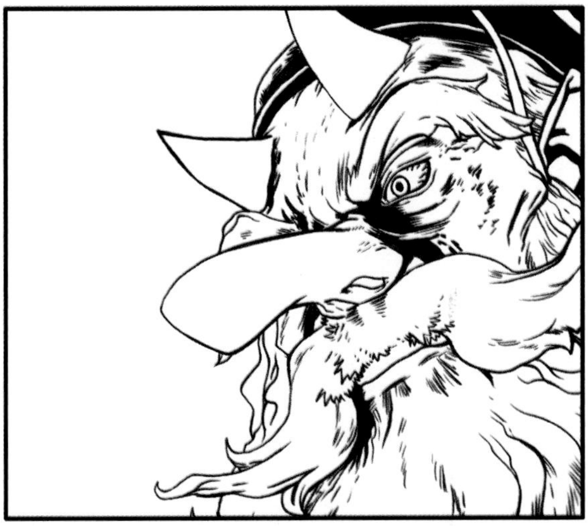

A further legend tells of the evil emperor Sutoku, who resurrected as the Ō-Tengu, the Great Tengu and Lord of Evil. Along with the nine-tailed kitsune Tamamo-no-Mae and the oni lord Shuten-dōji, Sutoku is one of the Three Great Yōkai of Japan.

The Secret History of the Dirt Spiders

The history of the *tsuchigumo*—the dirt spiders—is the history of Japan itself. But it is a secret history. A shameful history. One known by few in the modern era, due to ancient propaganda that buried the truth deep under the earth where the spiders still hide today.

This secret is that the people living in Japan today—the people known as Japanese—are actually invaders. Once there were several distinct tribes native to the islands: To the north, the Ainu, remnants of whom still survive on snowy Hokkaido. On the island of Kyushu were the Kumaso, the bear people, now long extinct. To the south were the Ryukuan people, known today as the ethnic Okinawans. And on the mainland, were the Tsuchigomori, known only as "those who hide in the ground."

The history is sketchy, written by the victors and with archeological evidence still tampered with and tainted to this day. Facts and legends can be pieced together and sifted through as best possible to achieve a general picture. Sometime during the Yayoi period (300 BCE to 300 CE), invaders sailed across the Sea of Japan from China and the Korean peninsula. Landing on populated islands, they started a pattern as old as humanity itself—the technically superior invaders displaced the aboriginal populations, driving them off the mainland and onto the less hospitable islands of the north and south. These invaders took ground and established their own kingdom, identified in 8th century Chinese literature as the Wajin—the People of Wa. They called themselves the Yamato.

Along with technology and civilization, the Yamato wielded the weapon of religion in their battle against the native tribes. They raised their own emperor and declared him divine. In order to cement their divine Right of Rule, they commissioned the books *Kojiki* (*Record of Ancient Matters*) and *Nihon Shiki* (*Chronicles of Japan*) showing how their emperor was a direct descendent of the sun goddess Amaterasu. Along with raising up themselves, they also used the *Kojiki* and the *Nihon Shiki* to demonize their enemy, portraying them as less than human. It should be no surprise that these books contain the first mention of the tsuchigomori.

The reason for the name is unknown. There is speculation that it is literal, that the tsuchigomori were underground dwellers who dug their houses under the earth instead of building them upwards. The word-switch from descriptive (tsuchigomori, 土隠; those who hide in the ground) to the derogatory (tsuchigumo, 土蜘蛛; earth spider or dirt spider) was a short leap. However, more strange is the description of these people. Instead of the multi-limbed spider-people you might imagine, they

were described as having long glowing tails which they used to push around rocks.

This odd appearance makes a little more sense when you realize that Japan has no native species of tarantula or other large spiders. Referring to their enemies as filthy ground-digging spiders may sound good, but didn't bring up a particularly fierce image. They had to come up with something scarier—apparently stone-shoving glowing tails fit the bill.

Use of the term tsuchigumo spread from these indigenous people to other enemies of the empire. Eventually all who refused to bow down to Yamato authority were branded as tsuchigumo, and dehumanized as monsters. There are several descriptions of the emperor attempting to tame these rogue people. In the *Hizen no Kuni Fudoki*, it states that the Emperor Keiko captured the tsuchigumo Oomimi and Taremimi on a state visit to Shiki Island. Other legends tell of five great tsuchigumo gathering forces in the Katsuragi Mountains to oppose the emperor.

So how did they become spiders? That transformation would not happen until the 14th century.

By the 14th century the Yamato were firmly established as the dominant people. The 12th century Genpei War had been the last serious challenge to their authority, and they were no longer worried about random tribespeople. Commerce with China had brought new and wonderful things, including fabulous animals like the Chinese bird spider, a large, tiger-striped tarantula that burrows into the ground to build its nest.

The monster was almost too perfect; Japan had its true dirt spider at last. The 14th century scroll *Tsuchigumo Soushi* reinvented the historical tsuchigumo as a tribe of monstrous yōkai that invade the capital. The heroic commander Minamoto no Yorimitsu repelled the invasion. Following the trail of skulls, he was led to a cave in the Rendai field, in a mountain north of Kyoto. There he hacked his way through an army of yōkai, fighting through the night until dawn arose.

With the welcoming rays of the sun, a beautiful woman emerged from the cave. Claiming to be held prisoner. Yorimitsu was no fool, and he drew his katana and slashed her. She left a trail of white blood as she fled into the cave. Following her, Yorimitsu confronted her true form, a gigantic spider with the striped body of a tiger. He battled the tsuchigumo for hours, finally cutting off her head. The heads of 1,990 dead people came pouring from her stomach, while countless small spiders—her babies—came flying from her body to seed the country with more tsuchigumo.

The *Tsuchigumo Soushi* was extremely popular, inspiring further legends of Minamoto no Yorimitsu and battles with tsuchigumo. In one story, Yorimitsu fell ill, and only recovered when he followed a dubious monk into the forest where he found he was under the spell of a giant tsuchigumo. Yorimitsu pierced it with an iron spike, that later became the sword *Kumo-kiri* (*Spider Cutter*). For yōkai, the tsuchigumo were unusually crafty and vengeful. They formed alliances with oni, and attacked the Minamoto family including Yorimitsu's father.

In modern Japan, the giant spider legends are all that remain of the aboriginal people who once fought against an invading army and defied their emperor. The Yamato clan was almost successful in striking the tsuchigumo from the record books, leaving them only as half-whispered legends. But still they persist.

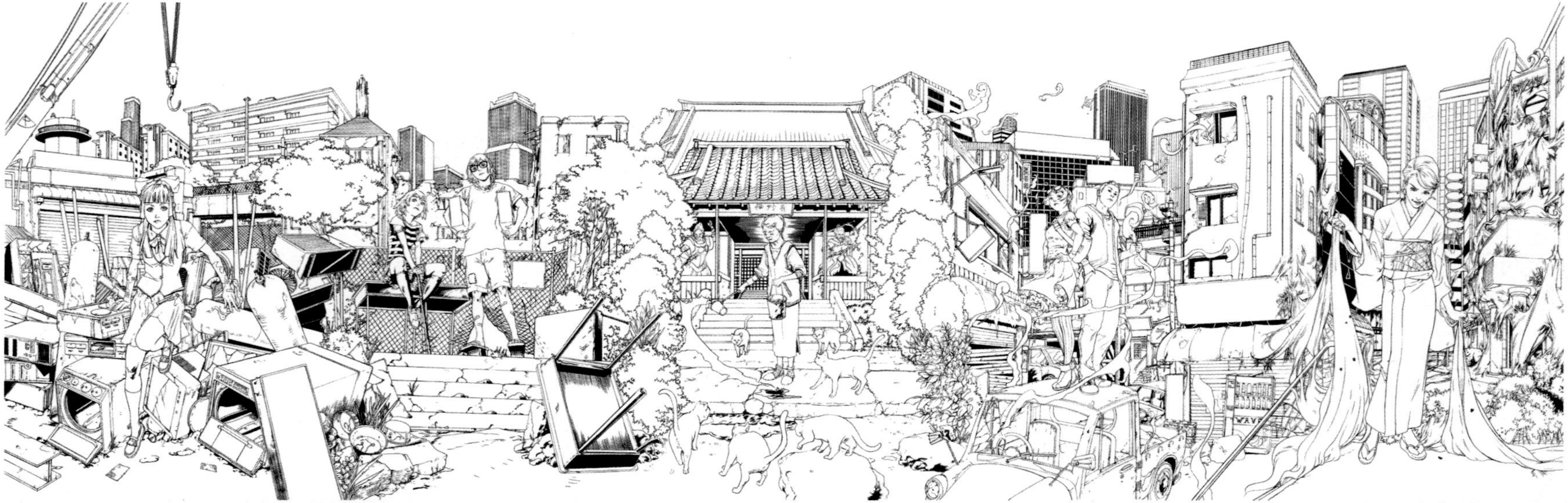

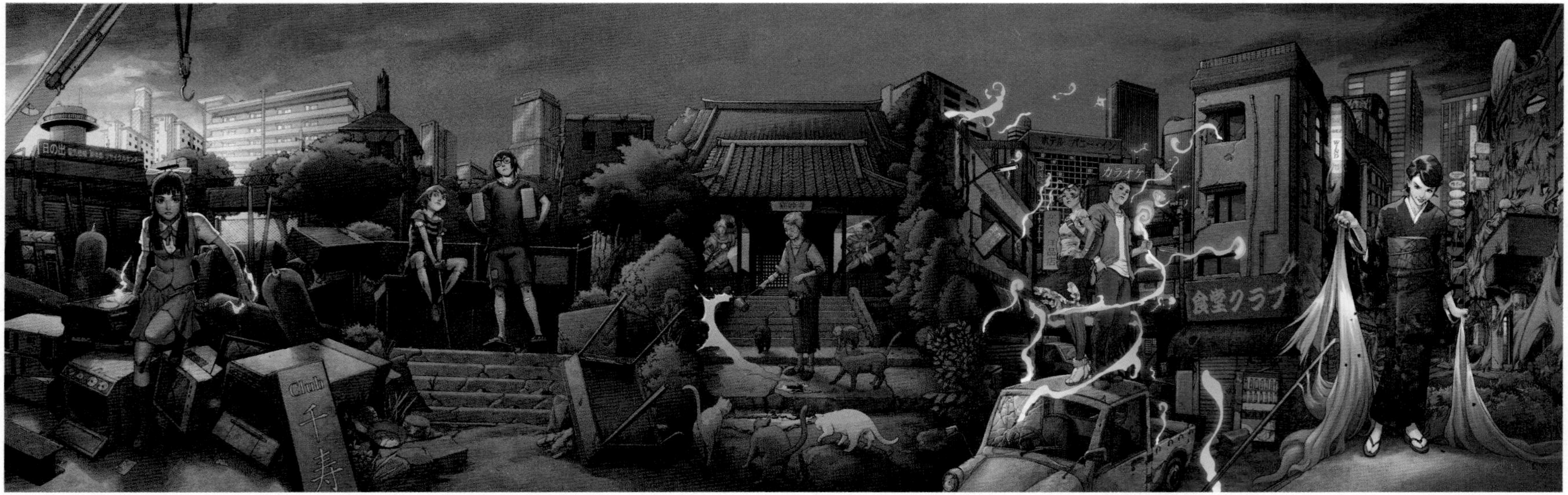
日の出
Club
千寿
カラオケ
食堂クラブ